FROM THE ASHES OF A SCORCHED LAND,
A RAGING DESIRE FOR POWER . . .
AND PASSION

ALANA—A proud, raven-haired beauty, she'd survived a devastating war only to be caught between one man's obsession and another's greed, between her marriage vows and a woman's deepest need.

RAFE—A rival's treachery had made him prisoner of war. He rode into the ruins of the South seeking vengeance—and the woman he was forbidden to love.

JASON—He returned from battle unable to fulfill the woman he'd promised to marry, unable to let her go even if he destroyed them both with his twisted demands.

LEDOQUE—Charming and sensual, he schemed to control an empire. He'd stolen one fortune; now he planned to take command of all that was Alana's: her estate, her freedom—her future.

Other historical romances by Monica Barrie:

Queen of Knights
Gentle Fury
Turquoise Sky
Silver Moon

Alana

Monica Barrie

A Dell Book

Published by
Dell Publishing Co., Inc.
1 Dag Hammarskjold Plaza
New York, New York 10017

Dell ® TM 681510, Dell Publishing Co., Inc.

ISBN: 0-440-10092-5

Printed in the United States of America

November 1986

10 9 8 7 6 5 4 3 2 1

WFH

For Devon Leah Wind

ACKNOWLEDGMENT
Leslie O'gwin Rivers, for her invaluable research
assistance in South African diamond and
gold mining.

Book
I

Charleston, South Carolina—
Riverbend Plantation
September 1865

1

Thunderheads, in all their mighty force, gathered in the east to hang over Charleston like a dark blanket, and the heavy scent of magnolia clung to the humid breeze. It was obvious that the roiling mass was moving westward, toward the large plantation called Riverbend. However, the thick, restless sky was not unwelcome, for a storm might bring some relief from the unbreathable air that suffocated the river country.

Alana Belfores sat on an old wooden bench on the veranda gazing out at the murky horizon. Mosquitoes whined in the air, yet she paid them no heed. Her raven hair was aglow in the slanting light of the late September afternoon; the expression in her dark blue eyes seemed distant—although her mind was anything but idle.

Inner turmoil festered, bringing Alana's attention back to the plantation. She wondered if it would still be standing in another year. The war was over and most of the men had returned, but not Jason. Tall, strong Jason Landow, who had sworn his love to her and had then ridden off to fight the Yankees; handsome, gallant Jason, who with his unselfish giving had saved Alana and the plantation from disaster time and again after Alana's father had died and she had been left to run Riverbend alone.

She shook her head as if to deny her thoughts and then lifted the plantation's account book from her lap. She glanced at it once more before closing it with an angry slam. The thunder rumbling in the distance seemed to echo her thoughts. She shut her eyes, but the figures she'd just read would not leave her sight.

Along the packed dirt of the drive, a solitary rider walked his horse. From beneath brows dark as midnight, his deep green eyes looked everywhere. As he rounded the bend in the drive and came within full view of Riverbend, the rider pulled back the reins and momentarily stopped his mount.

Before him, in mighty splendor, stood what once had been a tall and elegant plantation home. It was clear that the war years had taken their toll; the house was chipped and stained and worn. Yet it still held a fierce pride, a denial of any force that might try to claim or destroy it.

In the distance the rider heard the sound of workers in the fields going about their jobs as if the world were unchanged and everything in it peaceful.

As he drew closer to the open veranda of the house, the rider's gaze fastened on the woman who sat there, unaware of his presence. Without taking his eyes from her, he reined in his horse and dismounted, then started toward the house and the slender, seated woman. As he came closer to her, his breath halted and his heart raced. Long raven hair spilled along her back; her tanned face was a study in beauty. Silently he stopped to marvel at her profile; the soft sweep of her cheekbones, her elegantly straight nose, a mouth shaped like a drawn bow. Moisture glinted on her soft peach lips, and the sweeping, graceful lines of her neck were visible to him as he watched her silently staring outward. Her long fingers gripped a ledger.

She was even more beautiful than he had envisioned her for two long years. He had dreamed of her, thought of her, and used her image, taken from a photograph, to remind him that there was more to life than the barbed wire of the prison camp.

But she had always been an elusive dream, a woman of fantasy and delirium; a photograph to be looked at, a hope to believe in, but never a woman of flesh and blood.

He had come here because he knew he must. Now he was uncertain if he should stay. He almost turned back to his horse, but he did not. As his thoughts grew strained, his muscles tensed, and the woman opened her eyes.

He froze, then realized she had not yet seen him; rather, she was looking up at the malevolent sky drawing closer to the plantation.

So beautiful, he thought.

"Alana," he whispered, and started toward his destiny.

Sighing, Alana drew her attention from the gathering storm clouds and looked back at the account ledger. Before she could open it, she sensed eyes upon her. Turning her head slightly, she saw a man standing at the foot of the veranda's steps.

Her breath caught, and her mind reeled. The man started toward her.

He was tall and moved with catlike grace. Through Alana's befogged thoughts, he seemed to grow out of all proportion. His chest, confined within an ill-fitting cotton shirt, pressed against the material in such a way that she could see the play of the powerful muscles beneath it.

His presence was powerful. His hair, black as midnight, was lightly sprinkled with silver and glinted in the last rays of the setting sun. His face was thin, as if he'd not eaten well for a long time, but in that face she saw strength. His chin was square-set and showed the iron will of determination. His mouth was a straight, firm line, yet she imagined, strangely, a certain subtlety, and how his lips might be shaped to a smile. The strongly angular face was unlined except for the crow's feet of an outdoorsman that crinkled from the corners of his now-sparkling emerald eyes.

Her breath, which had suddenly bated, returned. Just as suddenly, a giant hand grasped her heart and squeezed it tightly. Her stomach fluttered as the man came to a stop not two feet from her. His sudden arrival and her unwarranted reaction to him made her feel as if she must be dreaming. But when he spoke, this illusion was shattered.

"Miss Belfores," he began, his voice deeply resonant, his lips sensual and wide, "my name is Rafe—Rafael Montgomery."

Before she realized what he was doing, he took one of her hands within his. Her fingers relaxed against her will as he brought the back of her hand to his mouth. His lips whispered across her tanned skin, and her heart pounded.

Alana's hand was numb, her mind sluggish in a way she'd never before experienced. A wavering thread of the unknown wove through her when she discovered she could not find the strength to pull her hand from his grasp nor tear her gaze from the endless green depths of his eyes. She felt as though she were being pulled within twin whirlpools.

When at last he released her hand, she saw him straighten, and she saw, too, an invisible barrier fall across his eyes. Alana's breathing was still forced, and her head seemed to grow lighter. Concentrating, she took a calming breath and did her best to control the unexpected feelings that were rising within her.

"Mr. Montgomery, you have me at a loss." After another silent second, she asked, "Who are you?"

"A friend of Jason's," he replied. A low rumble of thunder accented his words.

Alana's mind spun; her thoughts froze. His words bounced relentlessly within her mind; her ability to speak had momentarily deserted her. That he would come alone to bring her news of Jason could only mean one thing.

After several long seconds, the shock of his words eased, and she recovered her aplomb. "You have news of Jason?" she asked tentatively.

"He is almost here."

Again Alana was at a loss. "Then—"

"Why am I here?" Rafe asked, his eyes locked to hers.

Alana nodded, unable to speak.

Rafe Montgomery spoke in a low voice, barely louder than a whisper, but his eyes were steady and unblinking. "He asked me to prepare you for his arrival," he said, his manner overly formal.

"Prepare me?" A chill raced along her spine. "Prepare me for what?" Her hand went to her throat and grasped the small golden locket that rested there as a sinking sensation tried to capture her.

When Rafe broke the intensity of their gaze and drew his shoulders back further, Alana was again aware of the straining muscles of his chest.

"You knew he was a prisoner of war, did you not?"

Alana nodded mutely.

"Did you know he was wounded?"

Alana stared at him for a moment before slowly shaking her head from side to side. "No," she whispered.

She saw that Rafe was watching her closely, studying the angles of her face while he spoke. "It was in Virginia. His cavalry unit had been cut off from the main body of troops. He had rallied his men together, and they'd charged at the Federal position. It was the only way to get through. Jason's horse was shot out from under him. Before he could regain his feet, a rocket exploded nearby. He took several pieces of shrapnel in his back."

Rafael Montgomery paused as he gazed into the moist blueness of Alana's eyes. "I'm sorry, Miss Belfores, but a piece of shrapnel lodged in Jason's spine. There was little that could be done. He no longer has the use of his legs."

Alana squeezed her eyes shut, the horror of the words striking deeply into her. She had prepared herself for Jason's death, but never for his being maimed. She was aghast at the idea—not for her own sake, but for Jason's. Her hand tightened around the locket, pulling it so harshly that the chain dug into her neck. The pain from the golden links reached her, breaking through her onslaught of grief and heartache. Stiffening, Alana drew in a deep breath and then opened her eyes.

"He'll be here shortly," Rafe said softly, as if reading her mind. "Miss Belfores, I am truly sorry."

The veranda grew silent. Alana gathered her wits about her and rebuilt her shattered thoughts. She lifted her head, and the ghost of a smile was etched on her lips. "And I am sorry for failing to give you a warmer welcome to Riverbend."

"Jason will be glad to see that Riverbend has survived the scourge," Rafe said. Alana had the distinct impression that he was speaking softly to aid her at this terrible moment.

"His own home did not," she stated sadly.

"He knows that already."

A dark curtain of misery fell across Alana's eyes. After so much time, her hopes had been devastated. Yet Alana's years of standing against all odds helped her now, and she knew she would not allow herself to give in to pain and grief.

Instead, she fastened onto the one anchor that was in her world at this instant: Rafe Montgomery. Slowly, she shook her head. "Again, my apologies. You've had a long ride, and I've been thinking only of myself. Would you like a drink? Something to eat?" She rose and gestured toward the large mahogany doors of the house.

Rafe shook his head quickly.

"Did you serve with Jason?" Alana asked suddenly.

A bitter laugh escaped his lips. "Unless you consider the time in prison. No, the first time I met Jason was in prison camp, two years ago."

"Are you from these parts?"

"California."

"So far away," Alana whispered as she looked into his face. Rafe was so vital and strong. Her eyes misted as she thought of Jason Landow, wondering how he had withstood both pain and imprisonment.

Be strong! she commanded herself. Resolutely, Alana cleared the mists shrouding her eyes. She drew her shoulders straighter and looked at Rafe Montgomery. "I am indebted to you, Mr. Montgomery, for bringing me this news."

With her words, she saw a flicker of change cross his face, but it vanished as quickly as it had come. "No, it is I who must thank you."

"Thank me?" she asked, confused by the strangeness of his statement.

"Yes." He said the one word only, and Alana intuitively knew there would be no others at this time.

In the ensuing silence Alana looked about and saw Rafe's untethered horse grazing upon the short grass near the veranda's steps. "When will Jason arrive?"

"Two hours at most," Rafe replied.

"Lorelei!" Alana called loudly. There was no time for tears and hardly any time to prepare for Jason's arrival. As she had always done during times of adversity, Alana turned away from her grief and sought relief in action. She knew that preparations must be made immediately.

Turning back to Rafe, she looked up into his handsome, taut face. "I—" she began, but paused to organize her thoughts.

"Try to be calm," Rafe advised. "To relax will be difficult but not impossible."

Her eyes locked with those deep green pools of his, and she

almost let herself be calmed by what she saw within them—almost. Then she delved within her own reservoir of strength.

At that moment a black woman, wearing a white bonnet, appeared on the veranda. "Miss Alana?" she asked.

Alana turned to Lorelei, the housekeeper. Lorelei had been at Riverbend when Alana was born, had been Alana's nurse from infancy, and was the only constant person in Alana's life. Shaking away the grip of sadness, Alana said simply, "Master Jason is coming home."

"De Lord be praised," cried Lorelei, a wide smile breaking across her countenance.

Alana didn't smile in return, and a second later, Lorelei saw that something was wrong. She stood still, her smile fading.

"He's been wounded, Lorelei, very badly. He cannot walk, so we must prepare a room for him on the ground floor. Have Ben and Gabriel bring a bed down." Sensing Lorelei's confusion and fear, Alana spoke swiftly in an effort to make the older woman react. "And see that Mr. Montgomery's horse is attended to."

When Lorelei disappeared into the house, she turned to Rafe. "You will stay the night?" she asked. For some reason that she could not yet fathom, Alana believed that it was important for Rafe Montgomery to stay with Jason and herself at Riverbend.

"Thank you, I will," Rafe said. His eyes were unreadable. Alana tried not to think about what they might be saying behind their barrier.

With her hands clasped together before her, Alana said softly, "Tell me everything. Tell me the worst," she added, her voice breaking on the last word.

Alana stood at the foot of the stairs, her account book still gripped in one hand, watching until Rafe's broad back disappeared above. Her mind was mired in a darkness that she fought but could not completely defeat. *Jason is coming home,* she told herself. *Dear God, he's crippled,* she added.

She did not know how long she stood there, but when she heard Lorelei's orders echoing through the hall, she forced herself to go to the study.

Entering the study, she put the ledger on the desk. As she stared at the wood-paneled walls, she summoned from within her the deep-rooted determination that had helped her to survive the war and the last two grim years.

Twenty thousand of the twenty-five thousand acres that constituted Riverbend's lands had lain bare in the final stages of the war. Only enough food to keep Riverbend's workers alive had been grown, and these staples had had to be cultivated far from the eyes of any passing people. Rice had been harvested regularly, and enough had been hidden from the Federal troops to feed the people of Riverbend.

When the war had finally ended, Alana had realized that her troubles were not yet over. Riverbend was still in danger. A migration of monied people had flowed into Charleston at the conclusion of the war, protected by the Federal troops who remained to control the state. These unscrupulous and avaricious businessmen bought every business that was available and every acre of land they could lay their hands on at prices that were but a joke.

A half dozen times, Alana had refused to sell Riverbend to these northern businessmen. Six times she had held fast. But with every passing day, Riverbend and its mistress went further into debt.

She had been forced to sell half her jewelry, jewelry that had been in the Shockley family for over seventy years. Sadly, her gems had gone for but a fraction of their true worth in order to keep Riverbend alive for Jason's return.

Shaking her head at the thought of Jason, Alana squared her shoulders and left the study. She paused in the main hallway and, from years of habit, glanced around.

The main hall of Riverbend was a magnificent room. A full thirty feet deep and twenty-five feet wide, it still retained its air of grandeur. Twin staircases radiated upward, their mahogany banisters gleaming in the low light. The floor's wood planking was now dull with age, and because of the war, oil was almost impossible to find. Alana missed the grand oriental carpet that had protected the floor, yet even without it the room still held an ageless splendor—a reminder of what Riverbend had been like in its prime.

That the plantation had survived the war intact was a miracle. Whether Alana would be able to keep her home after she had come so far was yet to be determined.

Suddenly the walls of the house seemed to close in on her. Turning, Alana quickly went out onto the rear veranda and stood at the top of the steps. She looked at the dark clouds that stretched toward Riverbend from Charleston, some seventeen miles east, then saw a thin black man hurrying in from the fields. The overseer, Ben, had received Lorelei's message. As she watched him, she could not stop the lump building in her throat, for Ben had been the mainstay of Alana's and Riverbend's survival these past years.

Alana had given the slaves of Riverbend their freedom shortly after the war had begun. Ben, along with two-thirds of the others, had remained. Alana had not deceived herself that most had stayed out of loyalty; they had not—except for Ben, Lorelei, and a few others. For most of them, there had simply been no other place to go. If they had left Riverbend, they would have ended up in one of the two armies. And from the stories of those who had made it to the North, there was no good news there. Starvation often overtook those seeking to be free of slavery and the South.

The workers who had stayed had been accepted by Alana without question, and she had taken on the responsibility of keeping them fed and clothed, just as her family had done since 1789, when Alana's ancestor, William Shockley, had come to South Carolina from England. She had kept meticulous records throughout the war years, detailing all the wages due the former slaves. And when Riverbend was alive again, they would be paid. After their shared years of hell, the workers knew she would keep her word.

Looking down at her hands, Alana realized they were trembling uncontrollably. Clenching her fingers to stop their shaking, Alana started off toward the garden. Behind her, the smoke from the outside kitchen wafted skyward, looking as if it were trying to join the coming storm clouds.

In the distance, she could hear the sounds of the fieldworkers. Their voices were tired but resolute as they went about their duties. Pausing at the entrance to the garden, Alana looked back at the once-magnificent plantation house. Her eyes swept across the facade; her heart grew heavy. How poor a homecoming this would be for Jason.

The main house badly needed a coat of paint to prepare for

the approaching change of season. Two weeks ago, she had
gone to Charleston to buy the paint. She had been unable to
find any. The storekeeper had assured her that he would do his
best to get her what she needed, but Alana knew it was futile.
The northern businessmen who had bought so much of the
countryside had also taken all the supplies for themselves.

When Alana entered the garden, she glanced eastward at the
thunderheads. A breeze was rising, blowing with it the smell of
the storm. Alana recognized the scent for what it was—a scent
of danger and change.

A few moments later, Alana reached her destination, a special flower bed that held four rosebushes. The flower bed was
separated from the azaleas and camellias by a double row of
white stones. These rosebushes held a special meaning for
Alana. Slowly she knelt down before them, her fingers automatically seeking out the weeds that were trying to choke the rosebushes' roots.

Only here, of all the places at Riverbend, could Alana feel
peaceful and secure. But not even that solace was granted her
today, for her mind was spinning.

With her head held upright, she studied the rosebushes' gentle green leaves. For four long years, no flower had blossomed.
The heady, sweet smell of buds had not come; it was as if the
bushes themselves had felt those first horrid shots fired on Sumter. When war had been declared, the bushes had seemed to
turn to hibernation to escape the torment of the land.

Now the war was over, peace was supposed to reign. Alana
had hoped that when Jason returned she would be able to find
some of that peace, but now even that small hope was shattered.

Alana gazed at the first bush, set at the fore of the garden. It
had been planted by her mother on the day after her marriage
to Alana's father. The second bush had been planted at Alana's
birth; the third and fourth at the births of her two brothers. But
although the rosebushes survived, only she was still alive to
tend them. Her mother had died when Alana was twelve. Her
two brothers had died years before, in the same month, of
swamp fever. The older had been four; the younger, two.

"Why?" she asked the rosebush that had been planted in her
honor. Her mother had been a beautiful, gentle woman who

had given to everyone unselfishly. Her brothers had hardly known life at all when it had been taken from them.

How well Alana remembered the promise she had made her mother ten years before, on the day Rachel Shockley Belfores had taken her last breath. Alana had been sitting on her mother's bed, holding her hand and trying not to think of what was happening. "So young, Alana. You are so young, and you will be asked to do so much," her mother had said.

Alana had turned her teary eyes to her mother, but she had been unable to speak.

"You must look after your father for me. He will need you when I'm gone."

"No, Mama, you can't go," Alana had pleaded.

Rachel had smiled gently through her pain. "I cannot stay, Alana. But you will. Be gentle with him. He is not a strong man, but he is a good man. And, Alana," Rachel had said after taking a deep, rattling breath that tore through Alana's heart, "no matter what happens, you must see to Riverbend. Riverbend *must* survive. Promise me!" On her last words, Rachel had tried to sit, her hand tightening desperately around Alana's.

Through her pain, Alana had nodded. Her words had been hoarse with grief. "I promise."

Alana, although only twelve, had grown up that day. Both she and her father had survived, yet her father's life had really ended the day her mother had been buried. That special spark that had always glinted in his eyes had dulled, and the once tall and proud man had seemed to shrink before her eyes. When the final words had been said over Rachel Belfores's grave, her father had turned and walked away. Hours later, Alana found him in his study, passed out from drink.

She had remembered her promise to her mother and with Lorelei had taken her father to his room and put him to bed. Almost every day after that, her father had drowned himself in spirits, forcing Alana to grow up and face the world alone.

With the help of the household slaves, Alana tended her father and Riverbend. At first her anger clouded every minute of the day, but as the weeks passed, Alana's anger at the loss of her mother and at the helplessness of her father had abated. Soon she was again loving her father completely, instinctively knowing that through his weaknesses he loved her but could not show it.

From sunrise to sunset, Alana did her best to act as mistress of Riverbend. Her days of playing with friends and learning the ways of adolescence disappeared. Her education under the tutors continued, but instead of learning how to play the piano and charm a man, Alana had learned how to work with figures and run a plantation.

The hardest lesson had been learning to accept what her father had become. Alana knew that he had survived the deaths of his sons only because her mother had helped him; the death of his wife had broken him. Because Alana had known how much he loved her mother, she understood, even at her young age, what had driven him to drink, and she pitied him. But she could not forgive him for giving up on life and for forgetting that he still had her and Riverbend. She felt abandoned, and tried not to hate the father she once had idolized.

On rare and wonderful occasions her father would come out of his depression and look at Alana with sparkling, loving eyes that gave her hope that he would again become the man he had been.

"You are your mother," he had told her one night when she was halfway through her thirteenth year, "beautiful, strong, and valiant. You are life itself Alana; never, never forget that."

When she had turned fourteen, Thomas Belfores had suddenly stopped drinking. For months he'd remained sober. While he did, he taught Alana as much as he could, but what he taught her was pitifully little in comparison to what he knew.

Then came the day she had found him standing in the cemetery, looking down at her mother's grave. Tears stained his cheeks. Sobs rent the air. When he turned, he'd seen Alana staring at him.

"I'm sorry, child. I tried. I really did." An hour later he had gone to Charleston, to their townhouse. He did not return for several weeks. When he did, she saw that he had resumed drinking, and she sensed that he would never come out of it again.

By fourteen Alana's body had fully matured. She did not have the round, soft shape that was so much in vogue; rather, her body was willowy, lean, and strong. She had a narrow waist, long, slender legs, and full breasts, which the seamstress was barely able to hide.

With the ripening of her body had also come the maturing of her mind and spirit. With her father too besotted to function, Alana ran the plantation as though she were years older.

Alana had been sixteen when her father had finally succumbed to the combination of grief and drink. As the only surviving child, and to the shock of her neighbors, she had inherited Riverbend.

For four generations, Shockleys had ruled Riverbend, growing cotton and rice and breeding the finest horses in the Carolinas. But the Shockley dynasty had come to an end with William Shockley the fourth had produced only one child, a daughter—Alana's mother. When Rachel Shockley had married the aristocratic Thomas Belfores, a noble but penniless gentleman, Riverbend had gained a good, knowledgeable master. The Shockley dynasty lost its name, but Riverbend retained its grandeur.

By the time Alana inherited the great plantation, however, it was on the verge of bankruptcy and in disrepair. The Shockley fortune had been eroded; Alana acquired both Riverbend and a great, unpayable debt.

Yet during the time of Alana's greatest need, fate had been kind. In four years the debts had been paid, the plantation had been rebuilt, and the land had turned profitable once again, all because of the goodness of one person—Jason Landow, Alana's neighbor and friend, with whom she had grown up.

Jason was eight years Alana's senior, and it had been his steady hands and thoughtful, unselfish giving that had saved her home.

"This will be your home!" she had stated to him in a hoarse voice, willing the mists to unveil her eyes. "And I will love you."

Love . . . the word echoed within her mind. Alana knew that she was different from most women her age. She believed she always had been. She'd accepted the early responsibilities forced upon her that had robbed her of her childhood, but she had no complaints.

At the occasional socials she'd attended before and at the onset of the war, she had always felt out of place. Her mind forever dwelt on her duties at Riverbend, from which she was never free, while the other girls of her age danced and made endlessly inane conversation with their beaus.

Not once had any boy or man lit a spark of need or desire within her heart. Alana had never cared, for she saw how much energy was wasted in those senseless pursuits. She had devoted herself instead to gaining knowledge and learning how to run a plantation and make it profitable.

She was also very aware that she had created a scandal along the river and in Charleston itself. Never before had a plantation been left to be run by a sixteen-year-old female child. Cries of outrage from every quarter had resounded, but Alana had won out even in that.

The Landows—Jason, his brother Robert, and their mother Esther—had come forward to claim guardianship until Alana reached her maturity. Their act helped to keep Riverbend under her control and to stifle the scandal that her father's death had brought about.

Although Alana believed herself to be in love with Jason, she understood that it was not a love of great passion but a love of loyalty, gratitude, and hope for the future. Jason had done so much for her—how could she not love him? When he had asked her to marry him, just before the outbreak of the war, she had accepted without qualm, knowing that she would never find a kinder man, nor one who better understood her needs. She knew that Jason would make a good master for Riverbend.

She had kept her hopes high throughout the war, never once surrendering to self-pity. She had kept Riverbend alive. She had salvaged much from what might have been lost and had lived every day hoping for the war's end. But when the end came, it had not brought Jason back to her as she had prayed.

Now, five months after the war's end, her waiting was finally over. Her life would begin again.

Rising slowly, Alana again drew upon her deep well of determination. It was time to return to the house and ready herself to meet Jason. Come what may, she knew she would stand by her promise to Jason, and their wedding would take place as soon as possible.

But when she took the first step toward the house, her legs

froze and her heart lurched. Within her mind's eye, Rafe Montgomery's face appeared. She stared at the image for a full two seconds before realizing what she was doing. Then, forcefully, she banished the handsome face from her mind.

2

Rafe Montgomery stood bare-chested, staring out the window of the guest bedroom. Behind him, spread out on the bed, were the few items he could call his own.

The servant who had taken him to this room, a young former slave named Kitty, had unpacked his traveling bag and had taken his one change of clothes to press out the wrinkles. Five minutes later, she had returned with a basin of hot water.

After washing the grit of the road from his hands and face, Rafe walked to the window and tried to sort out his thoughts, which were running rampant.

He had known better than to come here. He had known not to accompany Jason but to return home and avenge those who had been so treacherous to him.

But for two years, he had been Jason Landow's cell mate. In those two years, strong feelings had grown between the men. They did not have a conventional friendship, but there was a strong bond between them nonetheless. It had been Rafe who had cared for the injured Jason. He had nursed him after his operation and had done whatever he could to make Jason's life comfortable. They had shared a common life—and shared, too, the same dreams.

When they had been freed, they had been given clothing and enough money to return home. Jason had been given one other item: a wheeled chair.

Upon their release, Jason had asked Rafe to accompany him

home. The comradeship they had forged had kept Jason alive,
for Rafe had not let Jason die, as Jason had wanted. It would be
a difficult but not impossible task for Jason to go home and face
the rest of his life as a cripple. He needed help, and Rafe had
been unable to refuse him this.

Besides, Rafe had realized, California was a long time away,
and after two years a few days' delay would mean nothing.

Secretly Rafe knew he'd had another reason for agreeing to
return home with Jason. The reason was raven hair, blue eyes,
and the face of the angel that had allowed him to keep his
sanity.

Although he thought he had prepared himself for meeting
Alana, he had not in fact been ready for what he had found. He
had known of Alana for two long years, from having listened to
Jason's unending talk of her. She was the only reason Jason
could find for living. Rafe knew everything about her, from the
moment she had been born to the start of the war. He thought
he knew her as well as any other man in the world.

But when he'd stood before Alana, he had realized he had
been wrong. Her large, almond-shaped eyes had looked questioningly at him. Her long, dark hair had glistened wherever the
sun caught its waves. Her tanned face was absolutely elegant.
Yet her beauty radiated not from her skin but from within her
very person.

Above all else, Rafe had been struck by the strength that
Alana Belfores possessed. When he had told her his news of
Jason, he'd watched her close her eyes, had seen her gather
herself proudly. It had been in that instant that he knew she
was different from any other. He hadn't wanted it to happen,
but the moment he'd set eyes on Alana, he knew that no other
woman would ever satisfy him again.

Rafe knew, too, that the intensity of his conviction was not
simply because of his years of being deprived of the company of
women; rather, it was because Alana Belfores had become a
part of his life.

He recalled the stricken look on her face when he had told
her of Jason's injury. The image tore at his heart. He had
wanted to take her in his arms and hold her close, but that was
impossible.

Rafe was being torn apart by his life and his desires. Even if there were no Jason Landow to stop him from loving Alana, there were many miles he must yet cover and debts that must be repaid. Not a debt of money, but of revenge.

But what now? he asked himself. To leave seemed the only sane response, but he knew he could not do that. He'd known from the first moment he'd seen Alana that he could not leave. Whatever thoughts had driven him during his years as a prisoner, whatever desires and dreams he'd had, all came rushing back to him in that instant. Until that moment, he could have gone away, he could have been free—but once his eyes had met hers, he could not turn away.

I am in love with her, he told himself. *I can't be,* he remembered.

An hour and a half after Rafe Montgomery had appeared, Alana was again sitting on the veranda, waiting for her first sight of the carriage and of Jason Landow. Her nerves were taut. All her hopes, her dreams, and all the plans she had made during the long years of war had been destroyed, to be replaced by . . . what?

Doing her utmost to compose herself for Jason's homecoming, she tried to understand what was happening to her life. She refused to yield to tears. Instead, she replayed her conversation with Rafe over and over again, trying to imagine what her future might hold.

Can this be happening? she asked herself sadly. Alana made herself think of how fortunate she was. Jason could have been killed; he might never have returned. Was this not better?

Alana grasped the locket on her neck. She took the necklace off and stared at the golden scrolled surface. As thunder resounded in the distance, Alana opened the locket with trembling fingers. As she had done almost daily for the past few years, she gazed at the small photograph within. Jason's visage —his fine-spun light hair, his intelligent, querying eyes, and the firm set of his mouth—looked back at her.

The picture had been taken the day before Jason had ridden off to the war. It was taken from a larger photograph that Alana had cut to fit the locket. The picture did not show Jason's strong and muscular body, his broad, powerful shoulders, or his long, tapering legs that had lent themselves to the lines of his uniform. But Alana, whenever she had looked at the picture, had seen not just Jason's face but all of him.

Alana shivered. Just as she would never desert Riverbend, she would never desert Jason. No matter what fate had befallen Jason, she would stand by him, just as he had done for her before the war. She would marry him and be his wife. Together, they would run Riverbend; for without Jason Landow, Riverbend would have been lost long before the war.

A memory of years ago flashed in her mind. She had been seventeen and had been obliged to attend the wedding of a neighbor.

She had been in the salon, sitting with three young women of her own age. They were talking about the men in their lives—their desires and their needs. Marietta Handly had turned to Alana.

"Isn't this exciting?" she'd asked girlishly.

Alana had shrugged her shoulders but remained silent.

"Oh—you have such airs," Marietta had declared, fanning herself elegantly while she smiled snootily at the other two girls.

Alana had ignored the remark, but she had not been able to ignore what followed as Marietta started talking about her beau, Clayton Drysdale.

"Whenever he kisses me, I swear I almost swoon. I—" Marietta paused to raise her fan and cover her face, leaving only her eyes for the others to see. "When he kisses me, I get so . . . warm inside. Sometimes I think I'll give in to him right then and there. It's so hard to wait. I do love him so, and I *want* him!" Her last words had been spoken with such conviction that Alana had been taken aback.

"Want him?" she had asked without realizing she'd spoken aloud.

Marietta looked slyly at her. The other two girls smiled. "Don't you want Jason? Don't you just burn with desire?" she'd asked.

Alana had become embarrassed, partially because of the vulgar talk but also because she had never experienced any such desires. Then her face flushed, she had stood and glared at Marietta. "I don't know what you're talking about," she'd stated. Without another word, she had left the room, but not before she'd heard the girls giggling at her.

Outside, she'd leaned against the closed door, but the wood was a thin barrier to the acid of their words. "Can you believe her?" a voice had said. "She puts on those virginal airs! But we all know that she's been living alone with no one watching over her, don't we? And we know how she trapped Jason Landow, don't we?"

Alana had fled then from their false accusations—and from her own inability to understand why she couldn't truly desire Jason and be in love with him.

Alana had thought a great deal about that exchange and had often wondered why she had never felt the passions that Marietta had spoken of. It had bothered her for a long time, and she had tried to understand that unknown part of herself. She had let Jason kiss her ardently. She had felt his excitement and passion. But try as she would, she could feel nothing in herself.

She believed that her own coolness toward Jason existed because she had put all her passions into Riverbend. She accepted this as best she could, understanding what her duties were to her home and land.

And now Jason is coming home, she told herself, and she would be his, with or without the passions that husband and wife are supposed to have.

She closed the locket. After replacing the golden chain about her neck, she shut her eyes for a brief moment. When she did, another picture blossomed fully, startling her with its power. It was the same image that had come to her in the garden—it was Rafe Montgomery.

Alana shivered, remembering her reaction to him. Again she felt the burning touch of his lips on her hand, and her stomach knotted as it had in the garden.

Forcefully, she opened her eyes and willed his image away. Alana turned her head and saw that the sun had set and that the horizon was painted with a hundred varying hues.

She could smell the jasmine in the air, and the scent of rain grew stronger. Only a few insects welcomed the coming of the night, and Alana, waiting to greet the man she had not seen in over four long years, did her best not to think of anything else.

* * *

Dusk settled over the river country; Alana watched the shadowy form of a carriage pull up the drive. Her nerves tightened, and her legs threatened to give way.

Refusing to show any weakness, Alana started toward the steps of the veranda. A feeling of dread overcame her and she grasped the railing, taking a deep, preparatory breath. Suddenly a warm, strong hand was holding her arm. Support and strength flowed from it to her.

"He'll be in a lot of pain from the ride. He may not even be conscious. He takes a great deal of laudanum for the pain, especially when traveling."

Alana glanced up at Rafe. His face was partly obscured in the shadows of the day's end. In the drive some of the household staff and fieldworkers awaited Jason Landow's arrival. Ben and Gabriel stood at the forefront, ready to carry Jason inside.

The carriage was halfway to the house when Alana set her foot upon the first step. A jagged streak of lightning illuminated the sky; thunder followed closely on its heels. "Courage," she whispered to herself, not realizing she spoke aloud.

"You have that and more," Rafe said, releasing her arm.

Alana whirled to stare at him. Her nerves were ragged, her hands shook, and her mind seemed numb. She was unable to take her eyes from him. She wanted to say something but was afraid that if she spoke, she would lose her courage. Silently she turned and went down the steps and to the front of the waiting group. Her heart raced nervously. *Be calm,* she sternly ordered herself. *I must show no weakness.*

When the carriage came to a halt, Alana stepped forward. In the same instant, the thunderstorm erupted. But the violence of the storm was nothing in comparison to the violence of Alana's emotions.

The storm's fury roared about her, but Alana ignored the torrents of rain. She walked proudly to the carriage and gazed up at Jason Landow for the first time in over four years.

Not in her walk, nor in her face, nor in her eyes did she allow the least sign of weakness to show. No matter what hurt was being visited upon her, her prayers had been answered, and Jason had been returned to her.

A lancing ache shot through her heart when she looked at

Jason's face. His cheeks were sunken, his face gaunt and filled with pain. His eyes were the worst. They were dull, lifeless, and unseeing.

She stared up at him and waited, unsure of what to do. Then she felt, more than saw, Rafe Montgomery step into the carriage, and the driver followed suit. Between them, they lifted Jason. Ben and Gabriel waited for the two men to maneuver Jason from the carriage and into their waiting arms.

Still ignoring the torrents of rain, Alana reached out and grasped Jason's hand, bringing it to her breasts as she stared into his eyes. Tears fell from her eyes and mixed with the rain that had already soaked her skin and clothing as she raised his hand and pressed it to her cheek.

Her eyes held his for several more seconds before she spoke. "Welcome home, Jason," she whispered, unable to say more lest her voice break and the fear behind her mask of welcome show through.

Jason stared at her but did not speak.

She released his hand and stood aside so that Ben and Gabriel could carry him into the house.

When she started up the steps after Jason, she felt a strong hand grasp her arm and help her. Turning, she again looked into Rafe's face.

"You must give him time," he cautioned.

"I know," Alana replied. Then Alana remembered her other duties. She called out to the driver, who was unlashing Jason's wheeled chair from the back of the carriage, "Will you stay the night?"

"I can't, ma'am. De boss, he wants dis rig back by mornin'."

"At least have something warm while you wait out the storm." Alana called for Lorelei, and an instant later the housekeeper appeared. "Fix a warm drink for the driver, and some food, too."

Lorelei, already soaked to the skin, skittered past Alana and Rafe and went to the driver. A moment later the carriage started off toward the rear of the house.

Inside, Alana let the water drip from her. "Dinner will be served at eight," she told Rafe. "There's time for a bath and a change of clothing."

Rafe didn't speak. He simply nodded his head, looking at her.

Alana almost shrank back from the intensity of his gaze. She drew her eyes away, searching for something. Kitty appeared just then, and with relief she asked her to prepare Rafe's bath.

When he was gone, she hugged herself, shivering slightly. Then she walked over to the library, which had been converted to Jason's quarters, and looked in. Jason, still under the influence of his drug, was being undressed by Ben. Suddenly, it was too much for Alana to watch.

She closed the doors and went upstairs to her room, where she undressed and was drying herself when Lorelei appeared with two house servants, bringing enough hot water for a bath.

"You'll catch a death of a col' less you take dis bath," Lorelei warned her, and Alana did not argue.

Once she got into the tub, she closed her eyes and tried to blot out the reality of Jason's homecoming. But she was unsuccessful, and when she was finished with her bath and began to dress she was still thinking of the changed man she had seen.

A few minutes later, Alana stared at herself in the mirror. The storm could still be heard in the distance, sounding like war cannons in Alana's tired ears.

In the glow of candlelight, Alana took several breaths to clear her mind. After years of waiting, her fiancé had returned. But he was no longer the man she remembered.

But he will be again, she vowed silently. *I will bring back the Jason I knew!*

She looked at her dress. Five years ago she would have worn a fine gown, accented by jewels. Tonight she wore a simple off-white dress, an old one that had been an informal dress for nights spent without company. It was one of the few dresses that had survived the war. Most of her clothing had been procured, first by the Confederacy and then by Federal troops, for bandages.

Her hands went to her hair, which was still damp from the storm, and she checked to make sure it was secured in its bun. As she lowered her hands, a low knock sounded on her door, and Lorelei stepped into the bedroom.

"Everything be ready, Miss Alana," the housekeeper informed her.

"Thank you, Lorelei," Alana responded, keeping her voice firmly under control.

"Let me help," Lorelei said as she stepped close to Alana. Without another word, she adjusted the dress and fastened the three eye hooks at the back. When she stepped back, she appraised Alana with a critical eye before nodding.

"It be a long time since I see you dressed like dis. You looks very beautiful."

Alana closed her eyes for a second. "Thank you, Lorelei," she whispered. "How is Jason?"

"He sho don't seem to be de same man who left."

"But he will be, Lorelei. We have to help him become that man again."

She saw the doubt in Lorelei's eyes but dismissed it. She squared her shoulders. "He is in the library?"

"Yes'm."

Suddenly realizing how much Lorelei had done in the last few hours, Alana took her housekeeper's hand and squeezed it warmly. But she did not trust herself to speak.

When Alana left her room, she paused in the center hall to listen to the sounds coming from the guest room at the other end. For the first time in over four years, there was life in the house. She could picture Rafe Montgomery in his quarters, preparing himself for dinner as so many guests had done in the past.

Enjoying this uplifting thought, Alana descended the curved staircase. When she reached the main floor, she turned and went to the closed doors of the library.

She raised her hand to knock on the door, but her nerves betrayed her in that moment, and she could not. Suddenly she was being attacked by terrible thoughts, and as hard as she tried to fight them off, they would not retreat. Her face flamed scarlet with her shame.

Turning, she rested her back against the mahogany door. After ten years of running Riverbend and devoting her life to it, did she really want to relinquish control to another? And could she possibly love the man who had come home to her?

She had seen Jason's dull, uncaring look. It was not the first time she'd seen eyes like that. Her father's, after her mother's death, had been exactly the same.

Was Jason now what her father had been then? *No!* she told herself, *Jason will not be like that. He is not weak.*

With that thought, Alana knocked gently on the door and waited. When no answer came, she called Jason's name. Finally, she opened the door and went inside.

3

Jason was sitting in his wheeled chair. The rough cream-colored cotton of his shirt contrasted with his pale white skin. Alana gazed at him, taking in the haggard, pinched features, and sadness spread through her like a wave. Firming her resolve, she walked toward him. In that moment, Jason opened his eyes.

"Pretty sight, aren't I?" he asked, his voice bitter, his words slurred from laudanum.

Alana willed herself not to see him as he was but as he had once been. "You are home. You've come back to me, and that makes any sight of you a pretty sight."

"Alana—" he began, but she cut him off quickly.

"Are you tired from the trip? Do you want to join us for dinner?"

"I'm tired from life," he whispered.

Tears blurred her sight. She knelt slowly by Jason. Taking his hands in hers, she looked deeply into his haunted eyes. "So much has happened to you. You must rest, give yourself a chance, and things will improve. You are a strong man, Jason. We will survive!"

"Will we?" he asked. "Not one day passed that I didn't think of you. I thought of what it would have been like to be with you, to ride our land together, and live out our lives happily . . . if this hadn't happened to me." Jason grimaced as a jolt of pain lanced along his back. He closed his eyes against it, and after several deep breaths he opened them again.

"But whenever I thought of ending my life, freeing myself from this prison of a body, I saw your face before me, and I could not do it."

"We will ride our land Jason, in time we will," Alana promised, her heart aching with his sadness.

"No, we won't." For a few moments after he uttered those words, his eyes were vacant.

Alana did not speak; rather, she waited until he saw her again.

"Did Rafe tell you everything?" he asked in a low voice.

Hesitantly, Alana nodded. "It doesn't matter to me, Jason."

"It will," Jason stated. Pulling one hand free from hers, he wiped the tears that spilled from her eyes. His fingers were gentle, his eyes momentarily the same as they used to be. "It will, in time."

Then Jason glared at her, his eyes turning into dark, burning coals. "This!" he shouted, slapping his thigh. *"This* is what's important. Without legs, I am nothing!"

"You are Jason Landow."

"I am only half a man!"

"You are Jason Landow, my fiancé, and soon to be my husband," Alana said in a serenely calm voice.

Jason stared at her, his eyes slightly less glazed, his head cocked at an odd angle. Then he shook his head. "No, Alana, I can never be a husband to you."

"I will not accept that," Alana stated, ignoring the tears that welled afresh in her eyes. Her loyalty to Jason, and her deep need to repay him for all the kindness he had ever given her, helped to shore up her inner strength.

She stared directly into his eyes and then grasped his hands and raised them to her lips. She kissed each one in turn without taking her eyes from his. "You are no less a man for your injuries. We are no less betrothed now than we were at the onset of the war. And fathering children is but one small part of marriage."

Jason tried to pull his hands from hers, but she would not let them go. Her strength grew in proportion to her determination, fueled by the guilty denial of the thoughts she had had outside the library door. "Listen to me, Jason. I have not waited all these years only to be pushed aside. We will be married. We will be husband and wife. We will make a life together here at River-bend."

"In name only!" he snapped, his anger heavy in the air.

"In the most important way: because we choose to."

"Alana," he said in a low voice, "I will not allow you to become my nursemaid."

"I intend to be your wife, not your nursemaid. Jason, we have a plantation to salvage, and your shipping business must return to Charleston. We have much to do, and I cannot do it alone. I need you, Jason, I need you beside me." No matter what her thoughts had been before this moment, Alana fully believed her words to be true, for those were the very words that she had been repeating to herself through the years of his absence.

"Alana, I am dooming you to a terrible life."

"No, Jason, it is a life of my choosing, and one that we will not allow to be terrible. Please, Jason, do not forsake me."

Alana's hands tightened on his. She saw the doubt in his eyes and could almost feel the pain that wracked his body. He started to shake his head, but stopped. Then she felt an answering pressure on her hands.

"Dear, sweet Alana," he whispered, "I know you are doing this out of obligation. But we have known each other too long for that. There is no obligation between us. I release you from your promise." Jason paused, his breathing loud in the silent room. His face was set in harsh, serious lines.

"Take your freedom, Alana. Dear God, take it while I still have the will to give it!"

Alana ignored his impassioned pleas. She saw something else behind his pale blue eyes, something that said the opposite of the words he had spoken aloud. "Do you think I would marry you out of obligation?" she asked, forcing her voice to stay level.

Again silence descended in the room. Their eyes were locked, and Alana's heart beat too fast.

"Yes," he answered.

Forcing away the truth of his words, and knowing that she owed him more than she could ever repay, she slowly shook her head. "I will be your wife, Jason, because I want to be. Now," she said as she released his hands, "it's time for dinner."

Alana smiled, although she did not feel any happiness within her; then she bent and covered his mouth with hers. The kiss was gentle and lasted only a second, but when she straightened, she saw that Jason's eyes were shut.

Stepping back, she said, "When you're ready to join us in the dining room, call for Ben. He's waiting to take you there."

Jason opened his eyes and nodded slowly. Before Alana could leave, he spoke in a husky whisper. "I am not the same man who rode off to war with a dream in his heart. I hold no promise sacred. Free yourself, Alana."

"I *am* free, Jason, free to be your wife." With that, Alana left. When she closed the library doors, she turned and started toward the dining room.

"It's not what you expected, is it?" came a deep voice from beside her.

Alana whirled, her hand going automatically to her throat. Tension swirled thickly in the air as she found herself once again staring at Rafe Montgomery. Just his nearness seemed to rob her of her voice.

"Is it true?" Rafe asked.

"Is what true?"

"That you're marrying him from obligation?"

Alana stiffened, and her mouth grew into a tight line. "You were eavesdropping!" she charged.

"No," he said truthfully, "I was on my way downstairs and heard the two of you talking."

Alana didn't respond; instead, she turned from him. Before she could take another step, his hand was on her bare shoulder. Heat scorched her skin. Spinning to face him, she dislodged his hand. Before she could speak, he did.

"You haven't answered me."

"Nor do I intend to. The matter is between Jason and myself."

"My apologies, Miss Belfores," Rafe said with a slight bow.

Alana, her body stiff, inclined her head to him and again started toward the dining room. Upon entering it, she glanced around. The large chandelier was missing, as were the paintings, but the long oak table still glowed with years of oiling, and the china looked as new as it had fifty years before when her grandmother had brought it to the house.

A large candelabra lit the table, and on each wall of the room several candles burned in sconces. The table was set for three, with Jason's place at the head, hers at the far end, and Rafe Montgomery's in the center of the right-hand side.

A decanter of burgundy sat on the table; the reflection of candlelight upon its surface was like a dark flame. Rafe stood unmoving behind her. She heard footsteps and turned to see Ben pushing Jason in his wheeled chair.

A few moments later they were seated around the table in silence. Alana forced herself to speak. Instead of addressing Jason, she turned to their guest.

"I must thank you for helping Jason to return home."

Rafe's gaze went from Alana to Jason. "No thanks are necessary." His face was an unreadable mask.

Jason laughed, and Alana heard the sorrow within it. Then he looked at Alana. "Rafe had been offered transport to California. He refused it, didn't you, Rafe?"

Rafe sat silently, wondering what senseless game Jason was now playing.

"He refused it because I asked him to come with me. I was afraid of coming home. Afraid of facing you. Afraid of what I would see on your face when you learned I am but half a man."

Alana, gripping her crystal goblet in her hand, tried to remain calm, but every word he spoke was like a gunshot. The stem of the wineglass snapped suddenly, and a spray of red liquid spilled outward.

Even as the sound of breaking glass echoed in the dining room, Rafe had left his seat and was at Alana's side, examining her hand to see if she had been hurt.

"Only a scratch," she said lightly. Pulling her hand free from his, she staunched the light flow of blood with her napkin. But try as she might, she could not take her eyes from Rafe's, nor ignore the lingering feeling of the way his hand had moved on hers while he had checked the cut.

When Rafe returned to his seat, his face was stiff, and his eyes were hard as he looked at Jason. "Are you finished playing the martyr yet?" His voice was harsh, but after two years of dealing with Jason's black moods, he knew how to get through to the man.

Jason suddenly smiled. "For now. Alana," he called. His voice was soft, almost gentle. "Forgive me, I am truly sorry."

Alana nodded slowly and tried to understand Jason's sudden shifts of mood. But Lorelei's entrance with the meal saved her from having to speak. Tense silence soon returned to the room.

Halfway through the meal, the silence grew torturous to Alana. Glancing at Rafe, she saw that he was intently studying his plate.

"Which division of the army did you serve in, Mr. Montgomery, before your capture?"

"Rafe," he said as he put down his fork and looked at her. His chest grew tight, his emotions heavy.

"Rafe," she agreed.

"Treachery and misfortune were my army."

Alana sensed a dark undertone to his words and gazed at him while she tried to puzzle out his meaning.

"It took me a long time to understand, but in the end I did." Rafe looked absently at a sconce on the wall across from him. When his gaze settled back on Alana, she saw that his eyes were angry and haunted.

"I was a supplier during the war. It was my misfortune to be captured by the Confederate army as I was en route to deliver supplies to the Federal army."

"You—you're a Yankee? A profiteer?" she asked, shocked by this revelation.

Rafe's eyes hardened. "I'm neither a Yankee nor a profiteer. I am, like Jason, the owner of a shipping company." Rafe paused for a moment to look at Jason, whose eyes were once again vacant.

"Unlike Jason's, my ships plied the Oriental trade routes. With the coming of the war, I had agreed to supply the Federal troops. My fees included no profit, but covered only my costs of goods and shipping. I did not believe in this war at all, but I didn't believe in slavery, either."

"What happened?" Alana asked, drawn more fully into the story than she had realized. As she stared into Rafe's eyes, the beating of her heart accelerated.

"Usually I didn't travel with any of my ships, but I received a special request from the minister of procurement for me to come to Virginia with the ship. He had urgent matters to discuss with me, of 'the utmost importance to the war effort.'

"Because of the way the letter was worded, I had no chance to refuse. We were to meet a Federal transport ship and transfer the supplies off the coast. Somehow, the Confederate navy learned of the rendezvous. When we arrived and were waiting for the Federal ship to take on the supplies, we were attacked. I was taken prisoner and sentenced to be hanged as a spy."

"A spy?" Alana gasped. "But that's not possible."

"I found out more before I was sentenced." Rafe's voice turned dark; his eyes clouded for a moment.

"The date for my execution was set, but the night before, I managed to knock out my guard, steal a Confederate officer's uniform, and begin my escape. However," he said, shaking his head and smiling sardonically, "the camp was attacked by Federal troops just as I was escaping. In the ensuing bedlam, I was taken to be a Confederate officer. No matter how I tried to explain what had happened, the Federal soldiers refused to listen to me. I was sent to the Rockville prisoner of war camp."

"But for two years? They never once learned the truth?"

"Two years, three months," Rafe stated calmly. "When I finally convinced one of the officers in charge of the prison to check my name with the war department—especially with the minister of procurement—he came back to me, laughing. 'I sent an inquiry as you asked, and I received a reply today. James Branch unequivocally states that he has proof of the death of Rafael Montgomery. The man you are impersonating was hanged as a spy by your own army!'

"It was then that I had to face the truth. I had been betrayed," Rafe stated, his eyes never leaving Alana's. "James Branch had been the man who had signed my original contracts to supply the army. He could not have learned of my execution, for it had never happened. I realized he must have had advance knowledge of my fate. Obviously some kind of advance arrangement had been made. That was when I accepted the fact that someone had arranged for my capture and death."

"But why?" Alana asked.

"That is what I have to learn," Rafe said.

Alana shivered when she saw the determination within his

eyes. "When will you leave for California?" For some reason, she was afraid to hear the answer to her question.

"Ironic, isn't it?" Jason asked before Rafe could answer her.

Both Alana and Rafe looked at him and saw that he had returned from wherever his mind had wandered.

"That I should be befriended by a Yankee sympathizer," he explained.

"I would call that luck, not irony," Alana whispered.

Jason shrugged his shoulders eloquently but said nothing more.

Once again, silence reigned. Alana watched both Rafe and Jason savor their food. Although it wasn't a large meal, it was a good one, and she could tell by their faces that it had been too long since they'd eaten properly.

"Coffee and brandy are set in the salon," Lorelei announced after the meal had ended.

The moment Lorelei said it, Alana realized the mistake. "Have it brought in here," she said.

Then she gazed at Jason. "Are you comfortable?" she asked.

He didn't answer immediately. Instead, he continued to gaze at her, his face immobile. "As comfortable as I'll ever be." A dark cloud seemed to spread across Jason's face. A nerve twitched at the corner of his mouth, and he turned away for a moment.

"Jason . . ." she began, but faltered.

"Rafe," Jason said suddenly, ignoring Alana's call, "tell her she's about to make a terrible mistake."

Angry, Alana stood, her hands grasping the edge of the table for support. "Damn you, Jason Landow, I'm not sixteen anymore! I have a mind of my own, and I know how to use it. I will not listen to any more of your self-pitying words. We will be married, and soon! And this is not Mr. Montgomery's problem, it's our own. Don't drag him into it."

"He already has been!" Jason spat. He stared at her for several moments before saying calmly, "I love you, Alana. I have for many years. Because I do, I have offered you your release. Think about having to care for a helpless man, unable to walk with you in the gardens, unable to share—"

Alana fiercely cut off his words. "And who was it who cared

for me when I was helpless, when I was about to lose everything? No, you won't chase me away."

Jason exhaled slowly. "As you wish, Alana, but remember: *You will regret this.*"

"I will regret nothing!" Alana knew that it was true. She might have many regrets in her life, but marrying Jason would not be one of them.

"Tell me that tomorrow."

"My answer will still be the same. Tomorrow I will send word to Reverend Latham that we would like him to marry us as soon as possible."

She turned to Rafe, who had been sitting silently, and found his face unreadable. With a sudden insight, Alana intuitively knew that she needed Rafe Montgomery to be nearby, to be a buffer between them, until she was wed to Jason. She realized that there was danger in this, but she accepted the fact that she needed the strength that Rafe exuded with every breath he took.

"You will stay for the wedding?"

Rafe drank in the subtle lines of her face as if he were savoring a rare wine. Desire rose within him, and he made himself wait before he answered. He looked at Alana and then at Jason.

Concealing his thoughts, Rafe forced his voice to remain emotionless. "I must return to California."

Jason stiffened; his eyes turned wild. "Stay with me until the wedding. You are my friend, and I would have you stand up for me."

Rafe slowly shook his head, but Alana would not let him speak. She had watched him and had seen the brief slippage of his mask.

His face was a study of smooth lines and determined angles. It was a face she did not want to be gone in the morning. "Please, Rafael," she whispered, using his full name for the first time, "do this for Jason."

Rafe looked at her. The need burning in his chest threatened to tear him apart. Slowly, carefully, he moistened his lips. He knew he had to refuse. He must leave in the morning and never look back. But the plaintive look on Alana's face and the moist blue depths of her eyes cut through his protests. In that instant

Rafe knew that he would never be able to refuse her anything she asked.

"All right," he said in a low voice, looking at Jason, not Alana.

Lorelei entered the dining room with a tray and started toward the table. Before she reached it, Jason, wincing, shook his head. "I must take my medication."

Alana started to rise, but Rafe waved her back. "I will see to it." Going to Jason's chair, he pulled Jason away from the table. "I'll be back shortly," he promised as his eyes locked with hers.

As he wheeled Jason from the dining room, he heard Alana tell Lorelei to return the coffee and brandy to the salon.

It took Rafe ten minutes to get Jason settled in bed and to measure out the laudanum. While he worked, he explained everything he was doing to Gabriel, who would be acting as Jason's personal manservant. When he was finished, he stepped away from the bed and turned to Gabriel. "That will be all, thank you."

Gabriel silently left the library and Rafe fixed Jason with a probing stare. "Why?"

"Why what?" Jason asked sourly, his features pinched from pain.

"Don't play games with me. Why are you acting like a self-pitying jackass? Why are you trying to hurt her?"

"Perhaps I enjoy the part," Jason replied sarcastically. Then his eyes changed. "Or perhaps after four years of waiting, I'm scared to death of the future."

"It will be whatever you make it. Jason, you still have your wealth—something that few southern gentlemen have. You have a beautiful woman who has been faithful to you and has waited for your return. You have land, and years of life ahead of you."

"You speak so eloquently, Rafe. I wonder if you could do the same without legs?"

"We'll never know, will we?" Rafe shot back, angry not at the question but at the inability of the man to see the good parts of life that awaited him.

"Rafe," Jason said, the lines of tension in his face easing as the laudanum took effect, "I don't want to force her into having a cripple for a husband."

"You're not forcing her into this. She's a grown woman with her own mind. It's her choice to make—don't try to make it for her. She's a strong woman, Jason."

"I know," Jason replied, his voice faltering, his eyes closing.

Rafe stayed at his side until he heard the familiar rhythm of Jason's drug-induced sleep. Before he left the room, he placed his hand over Jason's. "You are a fortunate man, for she is a special woman."

Turning, Rafe started from the room, knowing that he must speak with Alana and make her understand that he could not stay for the wedding. He could not watch the woman he loved go into a life of caring for a man who cared not for himself.

4

Alana sat on the salon's faded brocade settee, her back to the large window that faced the Ashley River. A silver tray sat on the serving table; the aroma of coffee floated in the air. However, Alana did not notice the rising rich scent, nor did she see anything else in the room, for she was waging a battle with her confused thoughts.

Ever since Rafe Montgomery had appeared, the world had seemed to be speeding by and her life careening madly along with it. The man she had known all her life had returned from the war a stranger, filled with bitterness and self-loathing. And the stranger she had met today seemed like someone she had known all her life.

Although she had met Rafe Montgomery a bare four hours before, she instinctively accepted his strength. There was something special about Rafe that called out to her and drew her to him in a way she had never imagined possible. The very intensity of her emotions frightened her in a way that nothing had ever been able to do before.

When he looked at her, she grew weak. When he touched her, her skin blossomed with new and exciting sensations. His voice sent a resonance through her, and whenever his eyes lingered on her face, it was like all the caresses she had never felt. It was exquisite, but it was alarming.

For many years, Alana had been in total control of her life. She'd had to learn how to push aside her own emotional needs in order to do the things that were necessary. From the age of twelve, Alana had known she had a destiny to fulfill, a destiny that included Riverbend and, in time, Jason Landow. This destiny precluded Rafe Montgomery. There was no room in her life for anything other than Riverbend and the duties she had accepted—and especially no room for a weakness for a man.

Alana bent her head, absently massaging her forehead with her fingers. But she could not erase the image of Rafe, with his powerful body, his handsome face, and those endlessly deep green eyes, from her mind. Tendrils of heat spread through her body, a heat she had never experienced in all her twenty-two years of life, a slow burn that she was helpless to control.

Rafe stood absolutely still within the doorway of the salon, watching Alana. While he had this chance to watch her unobserved, he took it greedily.

He retraced the path of her form. Her raven hair was pulled back in a severe bun that, on anyone else, might have detracted but that on Alana only served to emphasize the regal beauty of her face. He saw a vein beating slowly beneath the tanned surface of her graceful neck. His eyes followed the skin of her shoulders until it disappeared under the puffed sleeves of her dress.

Then he retraced his path until his eyes rested on the swelling tops of her breasts, which were barely contained by the dress's bodice. He knew she wore no pretentious hoops and only a minimum of petticoats beneath the dress. That there was no corset he was positive, for he had been able to see the smallness of her waist without the telltale lines of braces.

Her hips flared enticingly, and without being able to see her legs, he knew they would be slender, yet strong.

Rafe stepped back from the doorway until his iron control over his thoughts and emotions was firmly in place. Only then did he move toward Alana. As he did, Alana lifted her head, and their eyes met.

Rafe stopped five feet from her.

Slowly Alana rose. Her mouth was dry, the palms of her hands suddenly moist. The tip of her tongue traced her lips and, in the candlelight, moisture glinted invitingly.

"Thank you," she said at last, "for helping with Jason."

"I'm used to it," Rafe replied, stepping closer to her. "Alana," he whispered, his voice deep and husky.

Alana stared at him, unable to break the spell. But as he whispered her name again and his hand lifted toward her, she could no longer trust herself to look at him. Turning, she faced the window, her arms crossed beneath her breasts.

Rafe accurately read her conflict and held himself back when she turned away. He studied the set of her shoulders and the soft curving lines of her body until his desire became a relentlessly crushing force.

Then he stepped close to her, and as he did, he smelled the heady perfume of her own scent, mixed with the lingering fragrance of her rain-washed hair.

His hands went to her shoulders and, as he grasped her skin lightly, he breathed deeply of the woman.

"I can't stay, Alana, and we both know why."

Alana heard his words, but they came from a thousand miles away. Her skin was afire where his hands rested. Everything she had ever believed herself to be was falling apart, and a new reality was fast overcoming her.

Turning slowly to face him, she looked beseechingly into his eyes. "You can't leave me—us now," she pleaded.

A muscle trembled in his jaw. "I have to. God in heaven, Alana, I can't stay near you."

Her eyes widened as she lost herself within his burning gaze.

"Damn you," he whispered, pulling her to him. His mouth covered hers, his lips fitting perfectly over hers. His arms went around her, one hand high on her back, the other low.

Fire exploded inside Alana with the kiss. Her lips parted, and his tongue gained entry to dance with her own. Sparks of fire sped through her blood. And then her arms went around him, her fingers digging into his broad back and powerful muscles. Her breath exploded with a cry, and the heat she had been fighting broke free to ravage her body with need and desire, desire she had not known herself capable of. Her entire length was pressed to him, and she luxuriated in the feel of his hard, lean body.

Her hips pressed instinctively to him, and deep within her throat a low moan was born, rising upward with an abandon that shook her to her very core. Her head grew dizzy, and she thought she would fall if not for the support of his arms.

Yet even as she surrendered to Rafe, her mind fought to reassert control. Shame flooded her senses, and as suddenly as her passion had been freed, her shame turned it cold again. She pulled from Rafe's embrace and, backstepping, held her hands protectively before her.

"No more," she pleaded, her voice shaking as she spoke. "This is wrong."

Rafe, his chest rising and falling with the passions that he fought to contain, finally said, "I must go."

Senseless terror gripped Alana. "You can't! I need you!" she cried.

"Can we be together and deny what we feel?"

Alana's eyes raced across his face. Her confusion was insurmountable, yet her strength was undeniable. "You can't leave Jason."

"Damn it, Alana, I can and will. You know what's happening to us. You can't close your eyes to it." His words were forceful, yet as he spoke again, his voice was low. "I made a mistake in coming here."

"No," Alana whispered, shaking her head in denial. "Jason needed you to bring him home."

"Jason needed me?" Rafe asked, his voice self-mocking. "No, Alana, I needed to see you! I had to see in the flesh the woman I've dreamed of for two years. Now that I have, I can't stay here and watch you throw your life away by marrying a man out of the mistaken belief that you owe him yourself."

"I do," Alana stated, knowing that she spoke both the truth and a lie at the same time. "He saved—"

"Riverbend. He loaned you the money to pay your debts. He taught you how to run the plantation and to be its mistress. But that was years ago. It was a different world then, and you were both different people."

"I gave him my word!" Alana stated defiantly, refusing to accept what Rafe said as the truth.

"Your word? Will your word keep you warm on cold nights? Will your word fill your womb and give you children? Will your word satisfy your desires?" Rafe's voice was coarse, his tone unyielding, but his eyes were filled with longing.

"I will do what I must," Alana said in a tight voice.

"What you must?" he echoed sarcastically. His voice turned sharp and cutting. "Must you be his caretaker, as you were to your father?"

Alana's gasp was loud in the room. She stared at him, shocked by his words. "How——?"

"I know you, Alana. I know everything about you. For two years you were all that Jason spoke of." Rafe paused, determined to find a thread of self-control. As he challenged her with his stare, the muscle in his jaw began to jump again.

Turning away from Alana, he looked at the empty fireplace. He was silent for a long moment, his eyes tracing the joining of stone and marble until he had composed himself. This time, when he spoke, his voice was so low, Alana had to force herself to hear him.

"When we were released, Jason invited me to come home with him. I think I was already half in love with you then. The stories he told about you, the descriptions of you and of what you have done with your life. . . . At night, before I fell asleep, I would stare out the window, look at the stars, and picture you above me, smiling down. It was almost an obsession, but it was an obsession I willingly embraced. I was fascinated by you, but I was also afraid to meet you."

"Afraid?" Alana asked. Unconsciously, she reached out toward him. When she realized what she was doing, she recoiled.

"Because I can't fall in love with you. You belong to someone else."

"I belong to myself," she stated, her words louder than she'd intended. But Rafe went on as if he hadn't heard.

"And I have people to find—the people who put me in that prison. It's a debt I must repay before I can rebuild my life. I can't be in love with you, Alana."

Alana closed her eyes to block the vision of this wonderful man who was the first to spark her desire—a man who, under other circumstances, she would have given herself to willingly.

"Please, Rafe, you can't leave, not yet," she whispered.

Rafe turned suddenly. His eyes locked with hers; his mouth was a tightly drawn line. "If I remain, I will not be able to stay away from you."

Alana shuddered at his words but refused to heed his warn-

ing. "Then we must deal with that when the time comes. I need
you here. I need your strength."

Rafe gazed deeply at her. "You're asking for too much."

"I know that, Rafe. But I also know that I will be married
soon, and I will never see you again." Her voice caught as she
spoke, and the truth of her words was like a death knell ringing
in her mind. Sadness washed through her, and the loss of something she was never to have. She closed her eyes to ward off the
sensation, but its heaviness stayed with her.

"God help us, Rafe, I don't know what's going to happen. I
only know that I can't let you leave yet."

Rafe closed the distance between them. Alana's eyes opened,
and their blue depths caressed him. Once again he was lost to
her.

"I love you, Alana, and because I do, you must let me go."

Slowly Alana raised her hand. She cupped his cheek gently
and then traced his face with her fingers, impressing onto them
every line of his face. It was as if she were trying to capture him
for all eternity.

A single tear spilled from the corner of one sparkling eye, and
her throat seemed to be closing. Her fingers trembled as they
explored his face, and her heart was breaking.

When her trembling fingers left his face, she slowly backed
away. Stopping at the doorway, she stared at him. The terrible
realization of what she must do broke through.

"I've never known a man like you, Rafael Montgomery. You
bring out things within me that I never knew existed. I don't
know what's happening to me: I only know that I must marry
Jason. Please, Rafe," she whispered, "don't leave me yet."

And then she was gone.

Rafe stared at the empty doorway. Slowly he turned and
went to the serving table and filled a snifter with brandy. Lifting
the glass, he drained half its contents. As the fiery liquid burned
at the back of his throat and traced a scorching path to his
stomach, he released his breath.

Turning, he walked out of the salon and went to the library.
He opened the door quietly and stepped inside. Moonlight
filtered through the window, and he saw Jason sleeping peacefully. He walked over to him and covered the man's hand with
his.

"Good-bye, old friend."

He looked at Jason Landow for several minutes. Two years of memories lay before him, and the bond that those memories had created resurfaced.

Jason owed his life to Rafe, but Rafe knew he owed Jason a great deal as well. Even as he had nursed Jason back to health, it had given him something to do besides rail at fate. It had also given him a way to hold back his anger and rage before they could drive him insane.

"Good-bye," he whispered again.

As quietly as he had entered, Rafe left, closing the door behind him. Five minutes later he was in the guest bedroom, his possessions already packed.

He went to the window and looked out. The sky was clear, as if the storm that had recently battered them all had never happened. Stars dotted the sky in a profusion of diamondlike sparkles. The three-quarter moon shone silver in the night. A traveling moon, Rafe thought, a good moon to ride beneath.

Turning back to the bed, Rafe crossed the room and picked up his bag. Just as he started for the door, there was a soft knock.

Pausing, he stared at the door, wondering if it was Alana coming to stop him from leaving.

"Come in," he called.

Lorelei had been watching Rafe and Alana all evening. She had seen the way Alana and Rafe had looked at each other, and she sensed that changes were happening at Riverbend. The tension in the air was unbearable. Master Jason's injury was a terrible blow, but something else seemed to have been born this day: the heady scent of desire that she felt surrounding both Alana and the tall, handsome stranger who had brought Master Jason home. It was a presence she had never expected to feel again in this house.

Lorelei had seen, too, whenever Alana had looked at Rafe, the glow that suffused her and gave a special sparkle to her large blue eyes. It was a look that Lorelei had always wished to see on Alana but never had until tonight.

Lorelei had been eighteen years old when Alana was born, and she had reared Alana from infancy. At times, although the notion was unthinkable, she had almost felt that Alana was her own flesh and blood—the daughter she could never have. Throughout her life, Lorelei had cared for Alana and loved her deeply. She had suffered through all of Alana's losses and had been near whenever Alana needed her. And she knew that just as she loved Alana, so did her mistress love her.

Tonight Lorelei's heart had grown heavy, for she understood what was happening to Alana and Rafe. For years Lorelei had prayed that Alana would find a man she could truly love, a man who would capture her heart and free the loving woman hidden within the shell that Alana always wore.

Lorelei had known both the pleasures and the pain of love. As a slave, there was little time for love; she had learned early in life to take every moment when it was offered and to use those fleeting moments of happiness to ward off the painful times.

Seeing the unmistakable signs of love that Rafe offered Alana, Lorelei knew that Alana should reach out and accept them. Without this brief chance at love, Alana would never become whole.

Lorelei recognized that loyalty motivated Alana's actions. Alana's obligation to Jason would not allow her to do anything other than marry Jason. And this, Lorelei understood, would make Alana no less a slave than Lorelei herself had been all her life. This short time before her marriage would be the only chance Alana would have to experience love.

At the door to the guest bedroom, Lorelei willed her trembling hand to knock. She was terrified at what she was about to do, but her love for Alana made her strong. When she opened the door, she saw Rafe dressed, his bag in hand.

"Mr. Montgomery, I be sorry to bother ya'll—"

"What is it, Lorelei?" Rafe asked, surprised.

"I needs to talk wit you."

Rafe shook his head slowly. "I have to go."

"Ya'll cain't," she stated, her voice stronger than she felt.

Rafe's eyebrows shot up in response to her unexpected declaration. "Lorelei, Jason will be fine. I've shown Gabriel everything he needs to know."

"It ain't dat. I knows how to take care of Master Jason. Many's de slave who los' his legs. It ain't dat."

"What is it, then?"

"It be Miss Alana. You cain't leave her now." As soon as she said the words, a ripple of fear slashed through her, but she stood her ground.

"Did Alana send you?" he asked suddenly.

"Nossir, I comes myself. Master Rafe—"

"Don't ever call me that. I am no person's master," he stated sharply.

Lorelei was taken aback by this, but she continued, "She need your love. De rest of her life be empty. Don' make her face dat without her knowing what love ken be. She need de memory to survive, Mister Rafe. She surely do."

Rafe stared at the former slave and saw the love she bore for her mistress. Her words hammered at his heart, but he knew he could not listen to them.

"And what about *my* future, Lorelei? What about me?"

Lorelei blinked and shook her head. "You be a strong man. You be a good man, I ken tell. But you gots to have your memories, too, Mister Rafe, you sure gots ta have dem, too."

Rafe stared at her. He knew he was trapped as neatly as he had been that long-ago night when the Confederates had boarded his ship. But, he wondered, what would happen this time?

With a deep sigh, Rafe tossed his bag onto the bed and nodded his head.

5

The aromas of liquor, tobacco, and salt air permeated the second-floor room above the largest warehouse in Charleston. Three oil lanterns burned, giving just enough light for the two men sitting across from each other to see by. Even so, the air in the office was charged with an aura of darkness and corruption that no amount of light could lessen.

One man, sitting in a leather wing chair and smoking a cigar, projected wealth, power, and importance in equal proportions. He had a full head of white hair and thick, gray eyebrows that hovered above dark eyes. He had the pasty complexion of an indoorsman and the jowly face of one whose exercise comes from too many social occasions.

Yet the forces emanating from him left no doubt regarding his strength. This man was James Allison, the head of Allison Shipping Company, the largest shipping company in America.

Across from him, his face shaded, was another man, from whom vast power also emanated.

Several sheets of paper, discarded moments before, lay on the table between them. Allison, drawing on his cigar, nodded at them.

"Very good," Allison stated. "Very good indeed."

"I'm glad you're satisfied with our progress."

Allison leaned back in the chair, his head resting on its soft cushion of leather while he looked at the other man through half-closed eyelids. He drew again on the cigar and, after exhaling a cloud of bluish smoke, spoke again.

"I will only be satisfied when we control *all* southern ports and *all* the shipping from them, as we do in the East and the West." Allison's voice was hard, his eyes penetrating. "I had expected our operations to be concluded by now. Apparently I must remind you of our timetable."

"They will be," the man said, his words forceful.

"I hope so, for your sake, and for that of the consortium. What is the problem?"

"The Haversham Company is ready to accept our terms. It seems they had a bit of misfortune with their last two shipments. Much of the goods had spoiled on the voyage—vermin, I understand. We'll have their contracts within the week."

"But the other?" Allison asked.

"That one has been operating out of Bermuda since the onset of the war."

"So?" Allison said, impatiently. Little details were not for him.

"I've been negotiating with the agent, but he can't speak for the owner, who was an officer with the rebels."

"We've used other methods before," Allison said, the reprimand unmistakable.

"This isn't like that company in San Francisco," the man said with a dismissing wave of his hand. "And I've already accepted the responsibility for deciding against that sort of action. The Montpelier contract is the single richest shipping contract in the South. By itself, it has made and kept the Landows wealthy. And the contracts are family tied. If I had used any of our *other* methods, it might have endangered our chances to get this important contract. Besides, the Landow ships are excellent and would make a good addition to any of the consortium's shipping companies. Taking all of this into consideration, I thought it best to wait for him to return from the war and then approach him directly.

"My people have just informed me that the owner returned home this very week. I have dug into his history. He has always run the shipping company through an agent. It was his grandfather who formed it."

"What makes you think he will sell the company now?"

The man smiled greedily, his eyes suddenly cold and calculating. "He returned home a cripple. He cannot defy me. One way or another, we will control it!"

"Then get on with it! We don't want any more delays."

They were silent for several minutes while Allison smoked his cigar. When he spoke again, his voice was far away. "Do you remember when we formed the consortium? Eighteen fifty-nine," he answered himself. "It was something I had always dreamed of, and when I was certain that war would become a reality, I was certain, too, that my dream would come to life."

"And it has!"

"Almost. Oh yes, we control the majority of shipping for America, and we own most of the warehouses. But there is more to come." Pausing, Allison took another draw on his cigar.

"Within the next two years, those independent shipping companies who survived the war will fold. We've seen to that by adjusting our rates or denying them warehouse space. Those who remain will live on the leftovers with which we cannot be bothered. We have no need of further shipping acquisitions, save this one company that still eludes us. But we must start to expand again. South Africa is our next target."

"South Africa?"

Allison's smile was predatory. "I have reports on my desk in New York indicating that South Africa may become one of the major countries of the world. Spotty reports of gold, but the geologists say that it is but surface findings—the frosting on the cake, so to speak."

"The consortium plans to diversify into mining?" the man asked, hiding his surprise.

"There have been isolated discoveries of quality diamonds unlike any others. My sources believe that within the next five years, South Africa will become one of the richest countries in the world. Because of this information, I have just gotten several valuable shipping contracts with the largest exporter in Cape Town. I am also in the process of negotiating with a mining company.

"In two more years, your share of the consortium will make you one of the richest men in the world. You, I, and the others will control not only the economy of the nation, but the politics and the people themselves! We will be in control of our world. We will be the economic rulers, far above those who seek to manipulate others merely through politics. We shall control the economy of America, and therefore the country itself: I from the East, you ruling over the South from Virginia to Louisiana, and those bumbling fools, Murdock and Caruthers, will help us control the West."

The man smiled conspiratorially at Allison. He noted the fanatical glint in James Allison's eyes and—not for the first time since he had joined the consortium—realized the shipping magnate was insane. Yet this did not bother him, for he too had plans, and the consortium was a major part of them. To humor Allison—who could, after all, have him killed at any moment— the man added, "I will have everything under control, I guarantee you. Tell that to the others."

"I already have," Allison said ominously.

Seventeen miles from where James Allison and his companion sat, Alana stood on Riverbend's small dock, beneath the full moon, staring at the calm surface of the Ashley River. A week had passed since Jason and Rafe had arrived at Riverbend, and her emotions had become more confused than ever.

Above her, the stars were spread in a jeweled canopy, an umbrella of shimmering lights that should have made her feel at peace with herself, but they did not. An owl hooted from deep in the woods across the river. Crickets called to their mates, and the sounds of small animals echoed in the woods. Yet these familiar sounds gave her no comfort.

The lazy creaking of the old wooden dock was a lullaby she'd heard all her life, but tonight it grated in her ears. A fish jumped toward the heavens, but she did not see its iridescent beauty; all she saw was a disruption of the smoothness of the Ashley's surface.

Alana closed her eyes, but the instant she did, memories rocketed through her mind. For the past week, her sleep had been troubled by a single, constantly repeated dream, a dream best not thought of. But the more she tried to ignore it, the more persistent it became.

Not once before in her life had she ever dreamed of a man, much less dreamed of sharing her body with him and relishing every moment of it. Yet in this dream she had given herself to Rafe Montgomery, and she had been glad.

Standing in the cool night air, Alana felt her body reacting to the dream. The tips of her breasts grew rigid and rasped against the fabric of her bodice. A feeling deep within her, part ache, part need, called out to her. Subconsciously, she clamped her thighs together, doing her best to ease the ache spreading through her.

The last seven days had been the longest of her life. She'd felt as though she were walking on eggshells, afraid of giving in to her emotions, and afraid of not giving in. The thought of spending the rest of her life caring for Jason was not one she wanted to dwell on, yet neither was the thought that Rafe would soon be gone from her life.

After her confrontation with Rafe, Alana had scarcely slept. She had replayed their encounter again and again in her mind, and in the morning her first thought had been of whether he had left as he had said he would, or if he'd remained. Alana did not know of Lorelei's intervention, and she had gone downstairs with a heavy heart.

When she had found Rafe below, drinking coffee as the sun rose, a wave of love-laced sadness had washed through her. Her heart had swelled at his presence, even as her mind spun in confusion. She had wondered how she could feel the way she did about Rafe when the man she was to marry was not twenty feet away.

When they'd faced each other that day, she'd realized how dangerous their situation was. From that moment on, she'd done her best to avoid being alone with Rafe. And although his presence seemed to throw her into confusion, the knowledge that he was nearby also aided her ability to cope with Jason. Rafe treated her quite formally, and never spoke of what had happened that first night.

The afternoon of Jason's first day home, Alana had sat with him and planned their wedding. No matter what she'd suggested, he had agreed—and had constantly declared that he would not hold Alana to this wedding.

Each time he'd offered her escape, the conviction behind his words had dwindled until she knew that he was but mouthing

them. No, Alana could not leave him in his time of need, as he
had not left her.

But after a week of being near Rafe, there was no doubt in
Alana's mind that she had found the man she loved and had
given him her heart, although she could not tell him so.

During the endlessly long hours of each day, she and Rafe
had been players in a tense game. When he was near, she was
conscious of the way her hands trembled as she fought not to
touch him. When they walked side by side in the garden, she
never once let her hand accidentally brush his, although she
could feel the heat of his body near hers.

Whenever she dropped her guard and raised her eyes to look
at him, her head grew light and her body heavy with desire—
desire that directed even her dreaming thoughts in a way that
shocked her, embarrassed her, and made her half insane with an
impossible longing for him. She would wake in the morning, her
breasts swollen, her stomach knotted, and her loins aching. At
those times, Alana made herself think of Jason, lying helpless in
the library, and vowed that she would be a proper wife to him—
although they could never be lovers.

Facing the truth boldly, Alana accepted the fact that once she
had wed Jason, her body would never know another's. Jason
would never father children, and her womb would never fill
with life. Her breasts would never know the hungry mouth of a
child.

"Dear God, make me strong," she pleaded as her eyes
searched the heavens. No tears spilled onto her cheeks, and
none had fallen since she'd fled the salon after pleading with
Rafe to stay. She would not allow any weakness to overcome
her and take her from the path she must walk.

Rafe paced the confines of the study, the glass of whiskey in
his hand forgotten as he tried to calm his thoughts. He had
hoped to be gone by the end of the week, but the pastor had
sent word that it would be at least two weeks before he would
be able to hold the wedding service.

Two weeks, he thought grimly, two weeks of torture and denial. But then he shook his head. It would be two weeks of
being with Alana, fourteen days that would have to last a lifetime.

Rafe stopped walking and shook his head in amazement. Rafe Montgomery, the most eligible bachelor in San Francisco, the man who had always had his pick of women, and the man who had always left them behind, was in love with the one woman he could never have.

Putting his glass down, he left the study and stepped outside onto the terrace, which faced the river. The restless energy that had constantly dogged him would not subside. Leaving the terrace, he walked along the path that led to the river.

When he stood on the center of the wooden overpass that bridged the series of rice fields, he paused. The light of the full moon lit the land around him, and he saw, not thirty feet ahead on the old receiving dock, Alana's silhouette.

Go back, he cautioned himself even as he started to cross the distance that separated them. When he reached the dock, he stopped. His eyes roamed Alana's form, coming to rest upon her profile. She was looking up at the stars, and he could not bring himself to speak.

Her skin glowed almost silver in the moonlight. He saw lines of tension near her eyes, and his heart went out to her.

And illuminated by the silvery light, Rafe suddenly realized the duality that was Alana. Just beneath the surface, there was another Alana, a woman waiting to be set free from the bonds that held her back.

Then he knew why she was different from other women and, not for the first time, Rafe wondered why Alana could not see herself as others saw her.

So Rafe marveled at her beauty for her, because he knew she did not see it herself. Perhaps her naïveté even enhanced her beauty. Rafe knew that Alana was one of those rare women who possessed the ability to make men not only desire her but push themselves to any length to satisfy their desire.

When he could stay still no longer, he stepped onto the dock and called her name. He saw her stiffen, then saw her hands release the wood railing.

Alana turned to face Rafe, her heart racing. She saw the strain on his features and smiled sadly. "It is hard for you," she whispered, longing to touch his face but unwilling to risk it for fear she would lose her resolve.

"I will survive," he said dryly but not without emotion.

"I know you will. We both will."

Rafe walked past her and leaned on the railing. He looked across the river at the dark shadows of the trees. "Tell me how you managed to keep Riverbend whole during the war."

"It was something I had to do," she said simply.

Rafe turned on her, his eyes narrow and piercing. "Like marrying Jason?"

Alana held her ground, her tone flat. "Yes, like marrying Jason."

Rafe stepped close to her, his eyes never leaving her face. His arms went around her and drew her to him. He could feel the heat of her breasts branding him. When Alana did not pull away, he lowered his mouth to her warm lips.

This kiss, unlike their first, was soft and gentle. When it ended and Rafe drew back, he saw passion flooding Alana's eyes.

Before he could kiss her again, Alana pulled free. "No more," she pleaded. "I cannot think when you do that. I cannot stop myself from giving in to you."

"And you want me to prevent that for you?" he asked in a tightly controlled voice.

"You must," she said.

"When I'm with you, it takes all my willpower not to touch you, not to pull you to me and make love to you. And knowing that you want me, how can you ask me not to take you?"

"Because you're strong, Rafe, stronger than I."

"You love me Alana, even though you won't speak the words; I can see it on your face and in your eyes."

Alana felt as if she were trapped. She wanted to shout her love to the heavens, but she could not. Instead, she asked, "How could I carry that shame into my marriage?"

"How can you live knowing that you did not take happiness when it was offered?" he challenged in return. "Alana, I have stayed because of you. I am living every day as if it were my last. I find it impossible not to hold you next to me, not to feel the softness of your breasts upon me. You ask a lot of one man."

"Only because I know that man and know what he is capable of doing," she said. Her hand, no longer obeying her mind, rose to his face. She traced the deeply etched grooves that framed his full mouth and then let her fingertips brush across his lips.

"Because I love you and would see you until I no longer may. You have my heart, Rafe—is that not enough?"

"It will never be enough! Only having you at my side, in my bed, waking when I do, laughing with me, living with me, and raising our children together will be enough—and perhaps not even that will be enough," he whispered truthfully.

Alana's fingers shook. She clasped her hands together before her and looked across the water. When she spoke, her voice faltered, but she didn't care.

"Until a—a week ago, I did not know what—love could really mean." She stopped then, her mouth dry, her throat trying to prevent the words that needed to be said. "I—Rafe, I must be satisfied with that knowledge only, for anything else would be a betrayal."

Rafe studied Alana's face, then reached out and grasped her hands. She lifted her eyes to him.

"You forget how much I know about you, Alana. There were too many nights in prison that Jason and I spent talking of you —or should I say that Jason talked and I listened."

Rafe took a deep breath. "All your life has been spent fulfilling obligations put upon you. The first was to your mother, to protect Riverbend. Then you had to care for your father until he walked out on you. When Jason asked you to marry him, you accepted because of your obligation to him and to Riverbend. Didn't you, Alana?"

"Still," Alana said, freeing her hands, pulling her shoulders straight and arching her neck proudly in the face of Rafe's truths, "I will marry him."

"What about *you*, Alana? What about your obligation to yourself? Is your entire life to be lived for others? You're not some old woman who has no other purpose in life but to play nursemaid. You're young, alive, and the most vital woman, the most beautiful woman I have ever known. You have passions within you that will destroy you if they aren't released. You have needs, Alana, strong needs. If you didn't, you would not have asked me to stay."

Rafe stared into the pools of her eyes. Her mouth was set in a tight line, and a vein in her neck throbbed visibly in the moonlight.

"You don't know everything, Rafael Montgomery; if you did,

you would know that I cannot change what must be, nor can I betray the man who has given me so much in my times of need."

"You talk of betrayal, Alana, and you are right. It doesn't take the powers of a god to see into your heart, it takes the power of a lover. And I can see, even if you won't, that no matter what you do, you will betray someone. And that someone might be you. Think about it, my love." Rafe released her, then stepped around her to disappear into the blackness of the night.

6

As her wedding day drew near, Alana found herself busier than she had ever been before. She had delegated all responsibility for the wedding banquet to Lorelei, who she knew was more than capable of handling it.

To Ben she issued instructions for constructing and setting up the tables and seats for the guests. She had also told Ben to open the guest wing of Riverbend, which had long been closed, for those people who would be arriving from Charleston the day before the wedding.

The wedding itself and the celebration after would be held on the north lawn, adjacent to the gardens. And although the expenses were high, and Alana knew she would have to sell the remainder of her jewelry, she did not mind, for she believed that a large social gathering might help Jason recover some of his lost spirit.

While the field hands worked in the north lawn, every morning for three days Alana had stood impatiently while the seamstress refitted her mother's wedding gown to her. After that she had spent another hour sitting with Jason to discuss the plantation and his shipping business.

At first, Jason had resisted her efforts to get him involved again and had refused to advise her on business matters. Patiently, she had been able to draw him, albeit reluctantly, into the problems they faced under the harsh economic changes that now ruled the South. The moment she was finished, however, he would retreat into the drug-induced stupor that Alana had come to know so well.

After the fittings, her meetings with Jason, and whatever else happened to interfere with her regular routine, she, Jason, and Rafe would sit down for lunch.

By that time, Alana could no longer stay in the house. She would change into her work clothes—a pair of men's riding pants and a white cotton shirt—and would ride across the plantation, checking on everything and breathing the scents of freedom and life.

Today, like the days before it, Alana rode through the fields, forcing herself to do whatever was necessary to keep her mind free from thoughts of Rafe and of the life she would never have with him. Yearning for Rafe filled her heart, making it swell with love whenever she looked at him, but she could not allow herself to give in to her desires.

"Better to not know his touch than to feel it once and never again," she said again to herself. But she knew that when night fell and the heavy perfume of fall flowers bathed the air, her body would again tremble with unfulfilled desire, and her passions, so long dormant, would rise up to taunt her mercilessly.

"Three more days," she whispered to the air.

Reining in her horse, Alana looked about. She was at the southern edge of Riverbend, which was the joining of her land and Jason Landow's. In the distance, she saw the burned-out shell of his old plantation house, and again she felt the deep loss within her soul.

Alana knew that in time she and Jason would reclaim the lands, long gone to weed, and cultivate them as they had been cultivated for over a hundred years.

Sighing, Alana started toward the ruins.

"I think you look rather elegant," Rafe said as he studied Jason in the gray uniform of an infantry officer.

Jason glared at him, his eyes not as glazed as usual. "The war is over; this army no longer exists," he said tersely, flicking his fingers across the brass buttons of the jacket.

"Does that make you any less an officer who served bravely for his cause?" Rafe asked sharply, refusing to listen to any more of Jason's ill-tempered remarks.

Rafe's nerves were badly frayed, and each day found him more raw-edged than ever. His one vain hope was that Jason would begin to return to life instead of running away from it—for if he did, Rafe could leave with the knowledge that Alana's life would not be completely ruined.

Silence fell between the two men. The seamstress removed the jacket, being careful not to prick Jason with any of the needles. Then she went over to Rafe and put on the jacket she had made for him to wear for the ceremony.

As she worked, Rafe studied Jason. There were many things he wanted to say but none that he could until they were alone. When the seamstress finished and withdrew from the library, Rafe stepped close to the man in the wheeled chair. He spoke in a low voice, but the power behind his words cut through Jason's barriers.

"Don't throw away what Alana is giving you, Jason. Accept it and live with it. Make something of your life together."

Jason stared at Rafe, his eyes open and clear. "I have nothing to use to make a life."

"Then let her go!" he snapped angrily.

"She won't let me—as you wouldn't let me do what I wanted to do."

A cloud of anger swept across Rafe's face. "If you wanted death so badly, Jason, nothing I have ever said would have stopped you. What you want, my friend, is pity!"

Unexpectedly, Jason smiled. "How often did you say those words to me when we were in prison? Too often," he answered for himself. "Perhaps you are right, perhaps what I want is pity. But damn it, man, I earned that pity when the rocket fragment destroyed my future."

"You unfeeling son of a bitch!" Rafe swore angrily. "That fragment has injured your spine, but not your mind. You're destroying your future yourself!"

Again Jason smiled, and Rafe's anger lessened.

"Some pair we make, eh? I've lost my home and half my body, and you don't even know what has happened to everything that was once yours. We both have our crosses to bear, Rafe, and we must do it in our own ways."

"Is your way to inflict pain on another?"

Jason stiffened, and the friendly lines that had softened his features disappeared. "If you were anyone else, I would challenge you, wheeled chair or no. But we two have survived hell together, and that surmounts anything we might say. I will forget you spoke those words. What Alana and I do is between us, and only us!"

"Is it?" Rafe asked.

Jason winced, and a low groan of pain escaped his lips. *Damn him,* Rafe thought, *for hiding behind his injury.* But then his anger abated, and the very pity that he had tried never to feel for Jason finally came out.

Shaking his head, he went to Jason. "This is no time for arguing, old friend," he said.

Jason looked up and slowly nodded his head. "I need you to do something for me."

"What?"

"I learned today that Alana has been selling her jewels to pay the creditors. It will be awhile before my business funds are accessible. The bills are mounting here, and Alana has no money left." Jason paused to take a deep breath.

Rafe watched him, knowing that the laudanum had worn off and that Jason was in a great deal of pain. He started toward the bed table, but Jason stopped him.

"Gabriel can do that. I need you to go to my old home. I took precautions before I left for the war. Behind the stable is a well. Two feet beneath the lip, you will find a series of irregular bricks. Behind the bricks is a strongbox of gold. Bring it to Alana for me."

Carefully, Alana approached the burned-out husk of the house on foot. When she was twenty feet from it, she stopped. The scent of rot and decay reached her.

A horse's whinny echoed, and Alana whirled. Quietly circling the burnt timbers, she came upon the horse tied to a sapling that grew near the ransacked stable—and breathed a sigh of relief when she recognized it as Rafe's.

Hearing a scraping sound, she walked toward it. She stopped when she saw Rafe bent over the well, his upper torso hidden within it. She walked to where he was, sat on the rim of the well, and spoke. "What are you doing here?"

Rafe pulled himself up and turned to Alana. His gaze washed across her face and a smile curved his lips. "Doing an errand."

"I think we have enough water at Riverbend," she stated.

"Water, yes—but gold?" he asked.

Alana's eyes narrowed. "What gold?"

"Jason's." With that, he returned to his task, leaving Alana to her thoughts. Five minutes later, and after several loud splashes from falling bricks, Rafe straightened up, his cheeks smudged with dirt. Silently, he handed Alana the strongbox.

Alana took the box and carefully opened it. When the lid was raised, a gasp escaped her lips. Sunlight glinted from a pile of shiny golden coins. Just this morning she had been trying not to panic over Riverbend's lack of money—and suddenly here was hope. She looked back at Rafe. "Thank you," she whispered.

"Don't thank me. Thank Jason."

Alana nodded and put the strongbox on the ground. "Rafe, I —I know this has been hard on you, and I just want to thank you again for being my friend."

Rafe tensed, then shook his head. When he spoke, his words were not what she expected. "Don't delude yourself, Alana. I am not your friend. At least, not the kind of friend you mean."

Confused, Alana tried to explain herself, but Rafe would not let her. "If you can't tell me the truth, at least do me the kindness of not deceiving yourself."

"Truth?" she asked, her voice bitter for the first time as her emotions, long held in check, now erupted. "You want truth, Rafe? All right, then truth you shall have!

"You walked into my life eleven days ago. You turned everything in my world upside down. You awakened a need in me, a desire that should never have been born." She stared at him defiantly, unable to stop the flow of words she had unleashed. "You touched me, and my heart became yours. You looked at me, and I melted under your gaze. Until I met you, I had never wanted anyone. Now all I can do is think of you and of what I will never have. I *hate* you for doing this to me, Rafe Montgomery, I hate you almost as much as I love you!"

And then the tears at last broke through, cascading along her cheeks. Alana, her eyes fixed on Rafe, uttered no sound.

As he had wanted to do ever since he had first laid eyes on

Alana, Rafe reached for her and pulled her to him. Gently he stroked her mane of long raven hair.

Alana buried her face in his chest and let her tears continue to flow. She leaned on him to gather strength from his rocklike stability, but even as she did she realized that her own weakness was once again claiming her.

Suddenly she lifted her arms and curled her hands into fists. She pummeled his chest and shoulders, striking him harder and harder as she finally cried out her frustration. Yet his hands never loosened on her, not did he try to stop her from what she did.

And then she jerked herself free and fled back to where she'd left her horse. Untying him, she jumped onto the gelding's back and kicked his flanks cruelly in an effort to escape from herself as well as Rafe.

Behind her, Rafe remained motionless until she was gone. Only then did he retrieve the strongbox and start back to Riverbend.

Sitting at her dressing table in her nightgown, Alana brushed her hair. The sun had long since set, but her mind had not yet calmed from her confrontation with Rafe.

There was a low knock at the door and Lorelei, carrying a tray, came in.

"I thought you mights be hungry," Lorelei said when she put the tray on the dresser.

"I'm not hungry, Lorelei, but thank you," Alana said in a listless voice.

Lorelei looked at her, her heart going out to Alana. "We's got to talk, Alana chile'." Only when they were alone did Lorelei call Alana by her name instead of Miss Alana. It was something they had always done, from the time Alana was crawling.

Alana sighed and shook her head. "I'm all talked out, Lorelei."

"Nonsense," Lorelei stated as she stared at Alana, her hands on her hips. "De only time a body be all talked out is when de body be under de ground. And chile', it be a long time afor dat be happenin' to you."

Alana smiled hesitantly. "Why did you stay, Lorelei? Why didn't you go North when you had the chance?"

"I swear, chile', sometime you act like you doesn't have any sense a'tall. You is my family, Alana, I couldn't no mo' leave you den you could leave Riverbend."

"We are family, aren't we?" Alana asked in a whisper.

"Dat is just what we be," Lorelei stated. Then she went close to Alana and gazed deeply into her eyes. "Talk to me, Alana chile'. Tell ol' Lorelei what be botherin' you. You be scared of de marriage?"

Alana shook her head. "I'm scared of myself."

Lorelei nodded her head knowingly. "You be speaking of Mister Rafe."

Alana stiffened at Lorelei's words. Her eyes widened as she looked at the woman who had raised her. "You know?" she whispered.

"Honey, for twenty-two years you and me been together. Dere ain't nothin' I don't knows if'n it be concernin' you. 'Specially when I sees dat you be in love."

"Oh, Lorelei," Alana cried, "what am I going to do?"

Lorelei smiled. "I cain't answer dat for you. But I knows dat no matter what you does, it won't be no mistake."

"Won't it?" Alana asked.

"Only if'n you want it to be. Only if'n you thinks you be doin' wrong. And ain't nobody to tell you what be right or wrong 'ceptin' you, Alana."

"How can I love one man and wed another?" she asked quietly.

Wisely, Lorelei stayed silent.

"He'll be gone soon," she whispered after a moment.

Alana took a deep breath and stood. "I love you, Lorelei."

"I knows dat, chile'," Lorelei said, her voice breaking. Opening her arms, Lorelei took Alana to her large bosom and held her there for several long moments. When she released Alana, she stepped back. "I brung you a fine dinner, chile'. I thinks it be time you eat it."

"I thinks you be right!" Alana said, mimicking Lorelei's dialect as she used to do when she was a little girl.

"Hush now!" Lorelei ordered, but her words were softened by the smile on her face as she left the room.

Alana nibbled at the food on the tray, but she was still not hungry. When she finished all she could, she rose and went to the window that overlooked the garden, staring at the starry sky for a long time.

A crescent moon hung in the heavens, and though its light was faint, it reflected on the whitewashed roof of the gazebo. The longer Alana looked out at the clear and quiet night, the more she wanted to walk outside in the softly-scented air. She listened intently for sounds in the rest of the house, but all was silent. By now Lorelei and the others would be asleep.

Feeling suddenly trapped within her room, Alana decided to try to calm her troubled thoughts by taking a short walk. It was impulsive, she knew, but if she went to the gazebo she was certain no one would see her.

Rafe sat on the veranda smoking a cheroot. He was a fool, on a fool's errand, he told himself as he blew a stream of smoke skyward. From the moment he had left the prison camp with Jason, the course of his life had changed.

Jason. Rafe was worried about his friend. In the beginning, all he had worried about was keeping Jason alive. Now that Jason was as healthy as he would ever be, Rafe was concerned about how the man would live the rest of his life. At his worst, he was a demanding, self-pitying person filled with hatred that struck out in random directions. At rare times the bright, articulate man who Jason had once been escaped from the barriers he had erected. The problem was that those times were becoming less and less frequent.

What will happen when they marry? Rafe asked himself pointlessly. He knew there was no answer, not for him, for Alana, or even for Jason. Only time held the answer—and Rafe's time with Alana was almost at an end.

The thought of losing her was unbearable. Standing swiftly, Rafe tossed the cigar away and walked to the steps leading from the veranda.

He paused only when he reached the start of the garden path, then he walked aimlessly forward, letting his feet choose the direction he would follow.

As it happened, he took the far left path, the one that circled the entire garden. While he walked, he did his best to let the night sounds soothe his nerves. He refused to think of Alana and instead thought about San Francisco and what awaited his return.

When he had embarked on his ill-fated voyage, he had left his sister in charge of the shipping company. At the time, Elizabeth —a bright, intelligent woman who had learned the shipping business at the same time as he—had been twenty-three.

Rafe knew that the family business was in competent hands, but a gnawing worry had always interfered with that thought. None of the letters that he wrote while in prison had ever been answered. He had figured that the mails hardly ever got through—if the prison guards had allowed the letters out in the first place, which they always assured him they did.

Who was behind his arrest? Rafe wondered for the ten-thousandth time. Who had arranged for his death, and why? What had happened after he "died"?

Stop! he ordered himself. His circular thinking was futile. Nothing would be settled until he arrived in San Francisco and went to his offices.

Rafe paused in his stroll to look up at the moon. Only a few clouds rode the sky, shining silver-white as they passed beneath the glowing crescent. He gazed at the stars for a moment, then started off again, following the pathway without caring where it led. He did not realize he had reached the white-roofed gazebo until he almost walked into it.

When the awareness of where he was filtered into his brain, he saw a ghostly white shape sitting within the lattice walls, illuminated by the rays of the moon.

"Alana," he whispered.

Alana lost herself to the night, concentrating on the sounds of nature that filled the sweetly scented air. Gone were her thoughts of the future and of the years ahead that she would spend with Jason. Vanished too were thoughts of the wanton desire that Rafe brought out in her.

Memories of better times helped to ease her torment, but she could not bear to linger upon them. Shifting on the divan, Alana smiled as she remembered those early summer nights when, as a child, she had begged and cajoled Lorelei to let her sleep on this very divan instead of in her bedroom. Lorelei had slept on a feather comforter near her.

She had loved to spend those peaceful minutes before sleep looking up at the sky through the circular opening in the center of the gazebo. And for a few moments, Alana was able to escape the present in happy memory.

But then she heard a sound that was not part of the night. She froze for an instant, lifting her head and looking at the entrance to the gazebo.

Her breath caught. Her heart thudded so loudly, she thought it would explode as Rafe stepped into the gazebo.

Even in the shadows, the smooth, handsome lines of his face stood out. The aura of his masculinity surrounded her and tantalized her with its musk. And although it was night and no lanterns glowed, Alana could see Rafe's massive chest and the tense muscles that played beneath his partially open shirt. When he spoke, his voice was soft but determined.

"I didn't follow you, Alana, but neither will I leave now that I'm here."

Alana's head was light; everything solid around her was falling away. Her breathing deepened, and heat was spreading through her body.

"Please, I want you to leave," she pleaded. But as she spoke, she heard the falseness of her own words.

"Stand up, Alana. Come to me."

Her body and heart overrode her mind's intentions. She suddenly knew what must happen, for her future was to be made out of the memories of the past.

Her arms were outstretched as she rose; her heart thudded, and she feared that in her dreamlike state the muscles in her legs would collapse.

But he too was moving, and although time itself had seemed to stop, Rafe reached her and drew her into his arms. Their mouths met; their arms went around each other. They took the first step into a new world which only they could enter.

Fire lanced through Alana's body; her hips pressed to his with wanton urgency. Her mouth opened; fire and ice flowed simultaneously through her veins. Little explosions of desire burst within her breasts as they were crushed upon his chest.

She felt him swell against her; the heat of his manhood was a burning brand separated from her only by their clothing. And then she was being lifted, and her mouth was torn from his. Her eyes opened to stare into the endless green depths that mirrored her own need.

The crazy spinning of the world steadied as Rafe lowered her to the cushioned divan in the center of the gazebo beneath the circular opening of the roof.

Rafe's lips returned to hers, and their fiery taste was a nectar she had never imagined. Her hands moved freely, racing along his back until they reached upward and wove into the thickness of his hair. Her fingers caught his jet and silver hair and pulled it harshly, forcing his mouth harder upon hers.

Their tongues danced together as Alana's passions rose. Her blood raced madly, and her desires dictated her every move. When Rafe drew away, Alana cried in despair and looked pleadingly up at him.

"Don't rush, my love," he said gently. "Our time is too short for that. We must learn each other while we may." As he spoke, his hands went to the bodice of her dress, and for the first time since they had come together that night she felt an icy tentacle of fear.

When her eyes clouded, Rafe smiled softly. "There is nothing to fear in love," he promised while his fingers unlaced the bodice and separated the material.

With the first whisper of air on her breasts, Alana closed her eyes and lay back. She cried out an instant later when his heated lips took one already-rigid nipple.

Rafe tasted the sweet satin of her breast and ran his tongue along the velvet tip of her nipple. Blood rushed to his head, making him swim within the sea of his desire. His hands caressed her full breasts.

A raging fire burned within the breast that Rafe lavished with his mouth, and Alana's body arched closer to him.

And then his mouth was gone, but the flames roared on. Opening her eyes, Alana saw him gazing at her. The moonlight filtering through the opening above cast an iridescence on his features that took her breath away. Love and desire blazed from his handsome face. She saw the promise of a love that would be eternal, a giving of himself that would never leave her as long as she lived.

"Rafe," she whispered, her voice made low and throaty by the forces driving her, "I love you."

Rafe's chest rose and fell powerfully. Muscles bunched in his neck; his breath exploded outward with her words. "As you are mine, I am yours," he promised.

Alana reached up to him, cupping his face within her palms to draw him to her. She knew he could taste her tears within her mouth, but it did not matter, for they were tears of joy and love.

After a slow and loving kiss that overflowed with tenderness, Rafe pulled free and stood. Without taking his eyes from Alana, he slid her nightdress from her. His hands were gentle as they worked the material free.

In the silence of the gazebo, hearing only the magnified night sounds, Alana bathed within the warmth of Rafe's unguarded inspection and glowed from the wordless praise she read on his face.

Even as he gloried in her nakedness, Alana herself drank in the tall masculine beauty that towered above her. Passion and need stirred powerfully inside her, and tendrils of burning burrowed deep within her. Her stomach was tight with want, her thighs tense, her entire body singing with expectation.

When his shirt was gone, she let her eyes roam across his chest, taking in the dark curled hair that spread in wild profusion. The two dark, perfect circles of his nipples were hard and peaked, yet beneath the denseness of his hair she could see the finely etched lines of his muscles. Alana's gaze trailed downward while Rafe's hands worked at the waistband of his pants.

There, where the mat of hair thinned, she saw the lines of muscles coalescing into the narrowness of his hips. And then her eyes trailed further downward as he kicked off his pants.

Her gasp echoed in the night when she saw the ramrod straightness of his manhood standing proudly before him—an arrow of desire that she knew would soon be hers. She tried, but could not tear her eyes away from its largeness; Alana felt both a chill of excitement and a flash of fear.

Then she wrenched her eyes from the awesome sight and once again met his look as he came toward her. The fear she had felt was pushed away by the gentle strength of his face. And then he was with her, lying next to her on the divan. The heat from his body reached hers, stoking the flames higher and higher beneath her skin. She luxuriated in the hardness of his body; the subtle play of his tight muscles was but another caress that sent her mind soaring on the dizzying heights of welcome passion.

Quickly, Alana's world shrank until it contained only herself and Rafe. Surrounding them was a symphony of sound, a concerto played for their ears only. The owl called out in the night, and the insects accompanied him with a whispering chorus in the background. Just outside the gazebo, a nightingale sang its sweetly sad song, and the melody raced through Alana's mind and heart.

Yet too soon, those sounds disappeared as her ears shut out everything except the sound of their breathing and the beating of their hearts.

His mouth scorched hers, his hands roamed and caressed—lightly at first, more passionately when their kisses deepened. Her body vibrated when his fingers strummed its length, and when he again caressed her breasts, a low moan built within her throat.

Her hands too were moving, roving over the broadness of his back, tracing the lines of his muscles, racing butterfly-quick along his sides while exploring and learning about the man she loved.

When his mouth left hers, she felt loss. When his lips pressed upon the throbbing vein in her neck, she discovered joy. Then his lips explored her chest, tracing a path to one breast, going across it to gently nip at her nipple and then fleeing, only to reach the other breast and take its hard tip within the warm comfort of his mouth.

This time when Rafe slowly withdrew from her breast, he looked into her eyes. "You are perfection, my love. You have the scent of love on your skin, a scent that arouses all within me."

Alana reeled with his words, her head light, her heart singing his praise. "Love me, Rafe. Teach me so that I may never forget. I—I must have you, all of you," she whispered.

"You have, my sweet love, since the day I arrived." He bent close to her and let his lips and tongue caress her flat stomach. His fingers slid along her length, caressing and teasing her silken thighs while his mouth journeyed through the triangular line of downy soft hair.

His fingers lulled her even as they excited her. Sparks of

lightning raced along her legs; her muscles trembled with every glancing touch. When his fingers grazed the portal of her womanhood, she gasped in astonishment. A probing finger caressed the moist entrance for only a moment before slipping deliciously within. Her hips arched and her thighs closed involuntarily on his hand. All movement ceased, but a heartbeat later, Alana willed her muscles to relax when a gentle warmth emanated from where his fingers rested.

She cried out when he explored deeper. Sharp lances of pleasure grew from his touch until he drew back his hand and shifted his body. Alana looked at him, then raised her hand to trace her fingers through the hair on his chest. When she touched his nipple and felt its stiff peak, she could not stop herself from lavishing it with moist kisses.

His hands went into her hair, grasping it tightly as she kissed him, and when he loosened his hold, her intake of breath was long and shuddering.

And then he was laying her down again, kissing her, and moving above her. Without Alana's realizing what was happening, her body led where her thoughts feared to go. When Rafe settled himself above her, his eyes caressing and loving her, her legs opened and she instinctively raised her knees on each side of him.

Their eyes were locked together, the intensity of their emotions a solid force between them. Before Alana could fully prepare herself, the burning tip of his manhood entered her.

With its first branding touch, Alana's back arched; her head was tossed back and her eyes were wide open, and as she saw the crescent moon fill the opening of the roof, a sharp pain shattered the pleasures of her passion.

Her fingers curled and her nails dug into the skin of his back, commanding him to stop but not to withdraw. Heat rose from their joining as the hot velvet rod that was within her throbbed but did not move.

"Slowly, my love," Rafe whispered. "First there is pain, and then there is joy."

Even as he spoke, the waves of pain were leaving, and a warm wetness came from deep within her to flood the inner recesses of her body and to cover the thrusting hardness that was Rafe.

Suddenly her hips moved in an ageless pattern that she could

not control. Upward and down they moved, slowly rotating in
an effort to draw him deeper within her sweet confines. Yet she
was aware that Rafe himself did not move. His muscles trembled against her, while he held himself up with his arms, waiting for her to acclimate herself to him.

Then the movements of her hips became faster. Her back
arched again when his length filled her completely. Her fingers
pressed into his back as a rain of pleasure assaulted her. He
lowered himself completely onto her, crushing her breasts to his
chest as his hands went around her.

She felt the strength of his hands when one raised her molded
roundness, lifting her and pushing her harder against him while
the other hand went to the small of her back, supporting her,
making it easier to accept his largeness. And then she could no
longer think as her passion released itself totally, and her body
shuddered uncontrollably with pleasure.

Her eyes snapped open, and she saw her passion reflected
within his—a passion that she knew instinctively would never
dim. But all too soon another force gripped her with its fierce-
ness, an energy so powerful that it turned her breath into loud,
groaning gasps.

"Oh, Rafe!" she cried. "I—Help me, Rafe, help me!" And
then she was swimming in a tornado that sent her spinning
upward into the star-filled heavens while her legs locked around
his narrow hips and her nails raked the flesh that covered his
muscles. "I love you, Rafe. Dear God, how I love you!" she
cried.

As she spun within the mists created by love and passion, the
anchor of reality that was Rafe pulled her back. While the
spasms of her love rippled through her body, she felt him grow
harder, hotter, and larger within her. Suddenly, when she could
stand no more, she felt his explosion, felt his body being rocked
by the passions that he shot forth into her. As the burning
liquid of his love poured within her, and his body eased and
rested upon hers, the darkness of the night stole into her mind.

But that darkness could not withstand the truths she had
found this night, and as Rafe's hand gently stroked her cheek,
Alana looked at him.

"Sweet Alana, you are the treasure of my life," he told her.
She could still feel his length within her and felt gentle satis-

faction that although their passion had abated, they were still one.

"I—" she tried to speak, but the heaviness of her breathing blocked the words.

Rafe waited, his hand on her neck, softly caressing her skin. He shifted, and Alana unlocked her legs to reluctantly let him free. He drew slowly from within her, but when he moved from atop of her, he did not rise up; instead, he turned them both on their sides, her arms still around him, his hand still on her cheek.

"I have never thought myself capable of such feelings," she admitted before burying her face in the joining of his neck and shoulder so he would not see her tears.

"Until tonight you were but the mistress of Riverbend. Now you are a woman first and mistress of your lands second. And Alana," Rafe said, using his hand to force her to face him, drinking in the pure essence of the radiant beauty that had been unleashed this very night, "I have never known a woman such as you, nor will I ever again."

She tried to pull away but could not summon the willpower to leave the comfort of his arms. "What have we done?" she whispered.

"What we were destined to do. I could not live without having known you, no matter what the cost."

Alana's fingers traced along Rafe's back. His words reverberated within her mind until she too realized that they were but an echo of her own heart's desire.

"I will carry both shame and love into my marriage," she said sadly, "but I shall also carry the knowledge that I have loved as few have ever done."

Hesitantly, sweetly, she kissed him, and when they parted and Rafe opened his mouth to speak, Alana's fingers closed his lips. She spoke then, her words accented by a bittersweet tone. "No more, Rafael. Just love me again."

The eastern horizon was slowly coming alive with purple and pink bands heralding the dawn. Above Riverbend, the crescent moon had long since said good night. A few random stars winked in the sky. The sounds of the night had ended, not yet replaced by the birds that would sing the song of day. Awak-

ened by the silence, Alana lay still, her eyes closed as she wondered if the night had been a dream. But when she opened her
eyes, Rafe was lying next to her. She bathed in the warmth of
his body and the security of his arms, which had allowed her to
sleep so peacefully.

Her body too told her that she was no longer the same person
who had walked the garden last night. There had been a change
within her, a feeling of fulfillment that far surpassed the low
ache of the soreness, which reminded her of their passions.

Sighing, Alana moistened her lips with her tongue and gently
kissed Rafe's forehead while slipping from between his arms. In
the light of early dawn she could see his eyes were open and
looking at her.

"Wait," Rafe commanded, his voice low but strong. "Let me
look upon you again."

Alana stood proudly before him, naked and unashamed. Rafe
feasted upon this vision and took his fill. But when she saw a
curtain of sorrow descend across his eyes, Alana knew that
their one night together was at its end.

"You are a beautiful woman, Alana, strong and proud. The
pain of my leaving you will never equal the joy I have known
with you this night."

Conflicting forces rose within Alana and threatened to tear
her apart. She started to reach toward him, but even as she did,
she felt herself drawing away. Her hands fell helplessly to her
sides. Before she could weaken further, she turned from him
and bent to retrieve her nightdress.

A moment later she was dressed. Unable to look back at him
for fear she would die the instant their eyes met, Alana left the
gazebo and the man she loved and walked toward the house
and to the future that awaited her there.

Rafe did not move for several minutes. But when Alana's
ghostly white silhouette was gone, he sat up.

Refusing to give in to the feelings that bombarded him, Rafe
dressed and stepped outside. Rather than return to the house,
he took the garden path leading to the Ashley and, once there,
sat on the dock and gazed vacantly into the depths of the river.

Although Alana had wanted the day to stop with the dawn, it
had not. From the moment she had returned to her room to

reluctantly cleanse herself of her night of love, the sun had begun to shine through her windows and the real day had started.

With time running out, the minutes sped by like shooting stars, and before she had a chance to stop and breathe the air of the warm fall day, she was half through it.

As the noon sun warmed the earth, Alana watched the field hands scythe the grass of the north lawn so that it would resemble a luxurious carpet.

At the far side of the lawn, Ben, supervising the other workers, walked along the line of tables and benches that were being refinished or built anew.

Watching the work, Alana realized that in two days from now, at this time of day she would have been wed almost two hours. *Think of something else!* she commanded herself. A picture of Rafe grew within her mind. Crystal clear she saw him above her; the moon crowning his jet hair, the force of his manly power within her.

What am I going to do? she asked herself. Nothing! Nothing could be changed. Her one night with Rafe would be a memory saved, to be carefully brought out and cherished in the times ahead when she needed that comfort.

But not now! The thought was forceful enough to shake away his image and return her senses to her. Behind her, smoke rose skyward from the brick chimney of the large kitchen, which was the outbuilding closest to the main house.

Turning, Alana walked to where the women scurried back and forth between the kitchen and the food storage building. The aroma of baking pastry teased her senses, an odor she had not smelled in many years.

The scents made her think of the past, when social events had happened all the time, and when parties were the rule rather than the exception. Perhaps that was why so many people were attending her wedding—it was a link to the prewar days. And of course everyone wanted to see the woman they had all talked about for years become a wife.

This morning, when she'd eaten breakfast with Jason—Rafe had been thankfully absent, and she was sure it was because he understood that she could not sit with both of them so soon after last night—she had seemed to look at him with eyes that were suddenly open.

She had sensed that Jason would never be a true master of the land again, that his will to live had been taken from him along with his legs. Yet his injury would not stop her from trying to make him rise above his misfortune. Alana would never give up on Jason, just as he had never given up on her before the war.

Again the aroma of sweet pastry filled her nostrils, reminding her of where she was. Pushing aside her thoughts, Alana watched the kitchen workers prepare for the banquet. She watched Madera, the cook, working on three separate pots, while two other women tended the pastries in the brick oven.

And as she stood framed in the doorway, the cook turned and saw her. Madera smiled, and her deep black face was wreathed with the lines that her wide smile produced.

"You gots to have one o' dese, Missy Alana," she said, picking up a small puffed pastry and handing it to her.

Alana took it and popped it into her mouth the way she used to do when she was five. She let the feel of it grace her tongue, and as she tasted the sugar and cinnamon, a smile formed on her mouth. "Oh, Madera, you are wonderful!"

"No, ma'am," Madera stated with an emphatic shake of her head. "Dat weren't notin' compared to whats I's a'fixen for de day afta tomora!" With that, the cook retreated proudly into her kitchen and began shouting orders to the other women.

Alana stepped back just as Lorelei came out of the storeroom. She was gently scolding one of the younger house servants as they walked toward the guest wing. Alana's heart lifted, not for the coming wedding, but because until today she had never expected Riverbend to be so alive again.

"Miss Alana! Miss Alana!"

Alana looked toward the small boy running toward her. It was Jeremy, Ben and Kitty's son. His face was bright, and he was waving his arms wildly. When he reached her side, he had to pause to catch his breath.

"What on earth's so important?" Alana asked him, bestowing him with one of her dazzling smiles.

"De supply boat be here," Jeremy stated. "Captain Bowers, he want to talk wit' you afore dey unload."

"Of course," Alana said in a whisper. When she had sent in her order for the wedding supplies, she had known they would not extend any more credit to her, and she'd written that the supplies would be paid for when they arrived. At the time, she hadn't known how she would do that, but Jason's strongbox had solved that problem.

"Tell them I'll be at the dock immediately," she ordered Jeremy as she walked to the house. Inside, she went to the study and the safe that her grandfather had installed within the book-lined wall.

Opening it, she took out seven gold coins, more than enough to pay for the supplies and cover her past bills. But when she started to close the safe, she caught a reflection of gold and paused.

She reached toward the object that had caught her attention and picked up the wedding band that had been her mother's. She looked at it wistfully and, not knowing why, clasped it in her hand while she locked the safe.

Stopping at the desk, Alana opened a small drawer on the left side and put the ring into it. When that was done, she took a deep breath and started out of the house and toward the receiving dock, where she could see the riverboat and its captain waiting for her.

"Thank you, Miss Belfores," said the captain as she stepped toward his craft. "I just want you to know that it wasn't my doing—about collecting for the supplies. Especially since it's for your wedding. But Mr. Cochran insisted." The old riverman's leathery face was solemn. "And I do want to wish you the best on your forthcoming vows," he added in the same earnest tones.

"Thank you, Captain Bowers," Alana replied. She had known Tim Bowers all her life. Everyone along the Ashley did. He was as much a fixture of the river as the plantations to which he carried supplies. He was called Captain out of respect and friendship, although it was not a title for a riverboat man.

As the white-haired man stepped back, he paused again. "Almost forgot," he said, reaching into the leather satchel that hung from his shoulder. "I have a letter here for you."

Alana took the envelope from him and watched Tim Bowers

return to the deck of his boat and start issuing orders to the hands. For the next hour or so she forgot about the letter as she supervised the unloading of her supplies.

When the riverboat pulled away from the dock, Alana looked at the envelope. It was of a fancy printed linen, and in dark, almost glittering letters, it proclaimed that it came from one Charles Ledoque, of Bay Street, Charleston.

Her fingers absently went to the seal but stopped when she realized that the envelope was addressed to Jason, not to her. Shaking her head, she reminded herself that from now on, not every letter that arrived at Riverbend would be for her.

8

"To the last dinner alone that we three shall share," Jason toasted. As he held the goblet of wine aloft, he looked at Rafe and then at Alana.

Willing her tense nerves not to betray the delicate balance she strove to maintain, she looked questioningly at Jason.

"Tomorrow night we will be overrun by our guests. The day after, we will be married and Rafe will be gone. So in truth," Jason explained, "tonight is the last quiet meal we will enjoy together."

"That sounds so final," Alana said in a low voice. She quickly turned her eyes to Rafe. In that instant, her heart threatened to stop, but she willed her iron control to hold firm. When she spoke, her voice was level and showed nothing of her emotions.

"Will you not wait for one of Jason's ships to take you to California?" she asked Rafe, referring to an offer Jason had made earlier in the day.

Rafe shook his head. "I appreciate the offer, but no one knows when the ships will arrive. I must be on my way; I cannot wait any longer."

As he spoke, his eyes told her the true meaning that his words could not contain, and Alana had no choice but to accept.

Sighing, she addressed her next words to Jason. "We have done all we could to keep him with us, Jason. All we can ask is that he return again one day."

Jason lifted his glass again in a silent toast to accent her words. After he sipped the wine, he placed the glass neatly on the table, wincing as he did.

"Are you all right?" Alana asked immediately.

"For now," Jason stated. "The medication does not seem to last as long as it used to. The pain comes more frequently."

"Perhaps when Dr. Lawrence arrives tomorrow, he will be able to help with the pain?" Alana offered.

Jason's laugh was bitter and filled with irony. "Only if he has a stronger medicine than laudanum. But even if he does, I will not use it, except at night, until after we are wed."

"But the pain—" Alana protested.

"Will be with me all my life. No, Alana, I shall not let all the river country as well as all Charleston know that I spend my days in a senseless stupor. Until everyone is gone, I will suffer the increased pain."

"Is that the only reason?" Alana suddenly challenged. "To show our neighbors that you still have your fine aristocratic wit about you?"

He ignored her question, as he now always did when Alana questioned him about issues he did not want to discuss. Jason turned his attention to Rafe. "How do you plan to travel to California?"

Rafe bit back his anger at Jason's affront to Alana and, taking a deep breath, he answered, "I'm sure I'll find a ship bound for New Orleans that will hire me on. From there I'll cut cross country, unless I'm fortunate enough to find a ship going to California—but who knows what shipping lanes are being plied since the war's end?"

It was then that Alana belatedly realized Rafe could not possibly have much, if any, money after being released from prison. She also knew that he would not accept any money they offered.

Seeing her pained look, he spoke softly to her. "It's not so terrible a hardship as others I've faced," Rafe responded, his words proper, his eyes not quite so.

Alana shivered under the impact of his gaze but forced herself to look away. In that moment, Lorelei entered with their meal, and all conversation was thankfully ended.

Halfway through the meal, Jason spoke again. "Rafe, before the war, had you ever heard of a Charles Ledoque?"

Rafe thought about it for a moment, thinking of the many shipping contacts he had known. "Who is he?"

"I received a letter from him today. He writes that he has moved his shipping fleet to Charleston to help rebuild it as a seaport. He also says that he was recently made aware of my own vessels and is offering his services for the docking of my ships and the warehousing of their cargo. It seems he's taken over the warehouse and docking locations of the people I did business with before the war."

"He doesn't waste much time, does he?" Rafe asked. "Seeing that you've been back barely two weeks."

Jason shrugged. "I'm sure he learned that I've always run the business through agents and is applying for that job. Besides, for Landow Shipping, one agent can be no worse than another."

"But we agreed to run it ourselves," Alana cut in. "We can't let others control our assets."

"*You* agreed," he stated roughly. "That, my dear, is the Belfores's philosophy of business, not that of the Landows. And we both know what Thomas Belfores did to you and to River-bend!"

"Jason," Alana pleaded, not wanting to have an argument in front of Rafe, "no decision has to be made yet. Besides, you don't know the man. Please wait until we meet him."

Jason seemed about to argue but held himself back. Instead, he simply nodded his head and turned his attention to the food.

When they finished eating, Alana noticed that Jason's face was taut with pain, and again she felt the burden of that pain.

"Will you have coffee, Jason?" she asked, her voice soft and gentle.

Jason shook his head. "My bed is what I need. Good night, Alana, Rafe," he said. Before he could call out to Gabriel, the tall black man appeared and took him from the room, leaving Alana and Rafe alone for the first time that day.

"You've been gone all day," Alana whispered after the doors of the dining room clicked shut.

"This is beautiful country. I spent the day walking along the river bank."

"I was afraid of sitting down for dinner tonight," she admitted in a low voice. "I didn't know if I could face Jason with you sitting near me." Alana's hand was on the table and, as she spoke, she reached toward him. Before she could touch his fingers, Rafe spoke.

"No."

Alana's hand trembled, but she did not let her fingers touch his. Instead, she drew her hand back and closed her eyes against the hurt his single word produced.

When she spoke, her eyes remained closed and her words were barely audible. "I am not ashamed of what happened between us. I will never be!" Slowly she opened her eyes and looked at him. "I—I just wanted you to know that."

Rafe did not speak. He didn't have to. Alana saw the answer written on the planes of his face and in the deeply-etched grooves that radiated from his eyes.

"I love you, Rafe," she said. Then she stood and started from the room. Before she reached the doors, Rafe was out of his seat and at her side. His hand captured her arm, and he spun her to face him.

He stared at her, his eyes probing as if he were trying to see into her very soul. His hand on her arm was tight; the heat radiating from it pulsed through her body.

"Let me go, Rafe."

"I can't," he said in a husky voice.

"We have no choice."

"No choice? Are you a slave then, with a master holding a whip over you? No, Alana," he said, swift, "there is always a choice. Do not make yourself a slave to Jason."

As the warmth of his breath washed across her cheeks, she fought against his closeness and battled the overpowering desire that flared within her at his touch.

Once again, she tried to escape from his grasp, but he would not let her go. "Can we really give up what we've found?" he asked. Then he pulled her to him and covered her lips with his.

Against her will, passions burst within her as she surrendered to the warmth of his mouth. Her arms stole about him, her breasts pressed against his chest, and as her mouth opened and welcomed him, she realized what was happening.

"No!" she gasped, pulling back from him. She wrenched her arm free and backstepped. "Please, Rafe, no more."

"You can't throw away your life because you pity him!" Rafe

stated harshly, knowing it was his last chance to claim Alana as his own.

"It's not pity. Rafe, you must understand. I have a duty to fulfill," she said in as level a voice as she could.

Rafe stared at her, his blood pounding at his temples. "Come to me tonight, Alana," he whispered.

Her heart soared at his words, but her mind trembled with her heart's traitorous joy. Not trusting herself to answer, she shook her head mutely, then walked out of the dining room and up the stairs to her bedroom.

Rafe watched her until she reached the top landing, and although his blood still ran hot, he held himself back from following her. Instead, he went into the salon, where Lorelei had already set out the coffee service and a decanter of brandy.

Rafe splashed the amber fluid into a snifter and downed it in one gulp. While the fiery liquid worked its way into his stomach, he refilled the glass and drained that as well.

Two hours and five more brandies later, Rafe realized that he was not going to get drunk tonight and that no amount of brandy would grant him escape from his thoughts. Throughout the long day, he had tried to banish Alana from his mind, but all he could think of was the perfection of her moonlit form, the exquisite touch of her body on his own, and the taste and essence of her skin.

With every step he'd taken today, every passion-filled moment of their time together had replayed within his mind. When he'd returned to change for dinner, he'd wondered if he would be able to sit near her without taking her in his arms. But he had been able to control himself. Sighing deeply, Rafe left the salon.

When he reached his room, he realized that although the brandy had not deadened his ache, it had helped to make him tired. The light gauze curtains stirred restlessly in the breeze as he undressed and lay down on the large, four-poster bed. He stared up at the canopy above him and let his mind race free with thoughts of the beautiful woman who could never be his.

After returning to her room, Alana sat silently on the side of her bed, doing her best to calm her troubled thoughts. After a few moments she realized that she could not sit still, and she pulled the cord that went to the servants' room. Three minutes later Kitty opened her door. "Ma'am?" she asked.

"Would you see if there's any hot water left in the kitchen? If there is, I would like a bath."

"Yes'm, Miss Alana, I knows dere be plenty of water," Kitty said as she turned and left the room, closing the door behind her.

Alone again, Alana refused to yield to the sorrow that reached out to her. Deliberately she turned her thoughts to the letter Jason had received from Ledoque. "I will not let his business be run by another!" she promised aloud. "Never!"

Too often, Alana had seen her neighbors go marching into bankruptcy, guided along the path by men who manipulated their fortunes without any care for the people themselves. She would not let this happen to Landow Shipping.

Kitty returned, bringing the tub with her. When it was in the center of the room, she left again to bring the water. Alana undressed and readied herself for the bath while Kitty poured the steaming water into the tub. After the fourth bucket of boiling water, the servant added two buckets of cold water, knowing the exact temperature that Alana preferred.

"Thank you, Kitty," she said.

"Yes'm. If'n you needs anything else, I be downstairs."

With one foot in the tub, Alana paused to look at Kitty. "Jeremy's growing into a fine young man," she said.

"Yes'm," Kitty replied, a bright smile on her face.

"Are there any other servants in the house tonight?"

"Aside fo' myself, dere jes be Gabriel. He be listenin' fo' Master Jason."

A picture of her and Rafe blending together within the gazebo rose before her. "I won't need you anymore tonight, Kitty. Spend the night with Ben and Jeremy."

"But de tub?" Kitty protested.

"In the morning. Go, Kitty; be with your husband tonight."

"Tank you, Miss Alana, tank you!" With a happy smile, Kitty left.

Once in the tub, Alana rested her head against the metal rim and closed her eyes. For the first time since leaving Rafe that morning, she allowed the full memory of their loving to surface

and felt within her body an answering response from where he
had filled her with himself.

She soaked in the tub for an hour until the water turned
tepid. After drying herself and putting on a simple nightdress,
she went to stand at her window. As it had last night, a crescent
moon rode the heavens, and with its light she was able to see
the roof of the gazebo.

She remembered the taste of Rafe's lips on hers in the dining
room, and his words roared within her mind, intensified by the
very silence of the large house.

In the morning, she realized, the first of the guests would be
arriving. There would never again be a chance for her and Rafe
to be alone. With that knowledge, a devastating revelation
struck her. She knew that, for as long as she could, she would
go to him as he had asked.

Turning from the window, Alana walked to her dressing table, where a candle burned. She lifted the brass candle holder
and went to the door. Once there, she found herself unable to
continue.

Alana closed her eyes again and finally allowed her heart to
break free. Hesitantly, she opened the door and stepped into the
dark hallway.

She paused to listen for sounds but heard none. Taking a
deep breath, Alana crossed the hallway and went to Rafe's
door. Her heart was beating much too fast, and her stomach
was knotting tighter and tighter with each step.

By the time she was at his door, her nerves were taut. The
desire to feel his hands on her, his lips on her, and hear his
gentle voice in her ear was the force that made her push his
door open without knocking.

After closing the door behind her, she turned and froze. He
was lying in the center of the bed, his naked body aglow in the
candle's faint light. She took it all in, every inch of his sleeping
might, until she could no longer hold herself back.

"Rafe," she called in a soft, tremulous voice. When he did
not respond, she walked to the bed. Placing the candle on the
dressing table, she bent over him.

She could smell the brandy that he'd drunk earlier, but overpowering that scent was the fragrance that was Rafe's own essence. As it struck her, a flashing memory of last night's love-

making riveted her to the spot, and as it did, her love for him erupted within her.

Lowering her mouth to his, she kissed him softly, her lips whispering across his in a brief touch. When she raised her head, she saw his eyes were open.

Rafe gazed at the vision of his love that had awakened him, and his mind spun with the knowledge that she had come to him as he'd asked.

He reached up to her, his fingers stroking her cheeks as he watched the play of candlelight on her face. Emotions rolled across him like the swells of a stormy sea. In the moistness within her blue eyes and in the tight corners of her mouth was the story of the battle she was fighting with herself.

But the scent of her reached him, and with the sweet perfume that was her femininity, Rafe gave himself up to her even as she had done to him last night.

He started to speak, but she would not let him. He sensed that it was because she feared that any word spoken might destroy her willingness to be with him tonight.

So instead of speaking, Rafe drew her to him and accepted the subtle warmth and softness of her mouth on his. The kiss lasted for a long time, and when it ended, their eyes again locked, and the desire and passion that was within them was plain to see.

As Alana slipped from the bed and started toward the candle, Rafe called out, "Leave it. Let me see all your beauty."

Turning, Alana looked at the man she loved and started toward the bed. Standing beside it she undid the lace of the nightdress and let it slide from her shoulders.

The whisper of fabric upon skin was loud in the room, and when the dress was gone, she heard Rafe's sharp intake of breath.

Still silent, Rafe ravished Alana with his eyes as he gazed unashamed at the perfection of her body—a perfection that was already imprinted within his mind.

Then Alana went to the bed, and as Rafe started to sit up, she placed her hands on the tight skin of his shoulders and pushed him back.

Rafe started to protest, but when he saw the bold gleam in her eyes, he let himself fall back onto the mattress. His skin was alive, and when her fingers released his shoulders, he felt low sparks tingle from where they had been.

He watched as she drew herself closer to him, her torso above him, her eyes locked with his. She bent and covered his lips with hers, and the already-hardened tips of her breasts pushed into his chest.

Her tongue entered his mouth to weave with his, the heated tip maddening as it danced within the warm cavern. Then his arms rose to capture her, but even as they did, she pulled her mouth from his and slipped away.

Then her lips were pressing warmly on his neck, her tongue flicking across it in a random, seeking way that forced him to accept the pleasure she was bestowing upon him.

His hands rested lightly on her back, caressing without holding, exploring without stopping her.

Alana's lips were molten against his skin, tracing a blistering path downward from his neck to his chest. Her fingers toyed with his nipples, tracing circles with her nails even as her lips replaced them and her teeth nipped at the hard, small tips. Soon Rafe was lost within the passion that Alana was unleashing.

Her mouth flowed downward, her lips and tongue making a damp outline of his finely etched muscles. Explosions of fire burst within him, but he willed himself to stay still and not to hold her back. While her hands caressed every inch of skin, his body responded to the love she lavished upon him.

A muscle trembled in his inner thigh when her fingers stroked it ever so gently. His hardness grew, and he felt it press against the leanness of her abdomen. The heated points that were her nipples seemed to burn holes into his skin, and her hands threatened to chase the last vestiges of sanity from his mind.

Alana was caught within the magic of Rafe's body, the taste and feel of which drove her on. She was lost to time as the exciting reality of his flesh became hers.

Her lips traced paths everywhere, crossing beneath his stomach as she teased and bit at the fine hair that covered his torso, relishing the taste of his skin and the hair that tickled her nose.

Her hands stroked his thighs gently, but soon they were pressing harder against him as she tried to grasp her fill of him. Lower yet, her hands wandered, and as she traced the outlines of his calves, her breasts rubbed across the hardened staff of his manhood.

It was like a burning rod laid against the sensitive skin of her breasts, and Alana had to bite her lip for an instant to stifle her surprised cry.

Then slowly she retraced her path, and when her hands reached the top of his thighs, she paused to look down at him.

Her breath, already forced, seemed to become even more ragged. The flickering light made his manhood glow as it arched proudly before her. Gently, she grasped it with one hand and felt the silky smoothness of his throbbing member. Bending her head, she tasted the tight skin just below his navel.

She felt his body arch beneath her, while her hand stroked him, rising along his length, then returning back until it rested in the bed of curled hair that was its base.

Rafe accepted the pleasure she bestowed upon him, even as his hands went into her thick raven mane and tried to bring her back to him, but Alana would not respond to his urging.

When he eased his grip on her hair, Alana moved closer to the pulsing staff she held trapped in her hand. Even as she caressed its hardness, her lips met the joining of skin and hair, and an explosion of fire spread through Rafe.

Her lips moved upward, bestowing glancing, moist kisses upon him, while her other hand found the heavy sack between his legs and caressed that with the most gentle and fleeting of touches.

Alana shuddered at the pleasure she felt Rafe accepting, and within her even more love began to come forth. There was no part of him that she was afraid to touch, afraid to kiss, afraid to love. She was being driven by a need that pushed aside any hesitation, any doubt, and that made her and her love the most powerful force in the world.

But then Alana stopped what she was doing and raised her head to look at him. She saw Rafe's eyes locked on hers, and she felt the flood of love that came from him.

Moving through the fog that was both desire and love, she released her hold upon him and went into his arms. She stayed above him, pressing her entire length upon him, as he had done with her last night.

Alana felt the powerful hardness pressing against her lower

abdomen, felt heat radiating from its velvet smoothness even as a matching moistness began to flow from within her.

Her mouth went to Rafe's, hungrily seeking his lips. Passion exploded when their mouths joined, and his hands suddenly grasped her about the waist and lifted her upward.

Moving without thinking, Alana's hips rose and her legs went to either side of Rafe. With his hands guiding her, she lowered herself onto him, gasping aloud when his length slid quickly into her, impaling her upon a rod of fire.

Alana's head dropped. Her hair cascaded across Rafe's chest. Her breathing was loud as she held herself stiffly. But her body soon adjusted to the heated spear that rested within her, and again her hips began to move with the ageless pattern of love.

She flicked her head back, and her hair whipped behind her head. She stared directly into Rafe's eyes and drew upon the love she found there. Then his hands left her hips and went to her breasts, to fondle and caress them, while their bodies moved together in perfect harmony.

Alana rode Rafe, her eyes never leaving his. She abandoned herself to the full glory of their lovemaking and found security within the warm caresses of his hands on her breasts.

But as strong as her passion was, she did not let it rule her. She held herself back, moving on him slowly, as he moved within her. Then she felt a change. She saw his eyes begin to glow within the candlelight and felt his hands leave her breasts.

Suddenly his hands were on her hips again, and he was pulling himself up. An instant later their faces were only inches apart. Rafe guided her legs around him, adjusting them both to this new position, and then he pulled her against him, his mouth covering hers in a passionate kiss that burst her thin threads of control.

He filled her completely, and as her ankles locked behind his back, she rocked on him, guided by his own body's movement. A moment later she cried out when his mouth left hers; but his lips returned quickly to the hollow of her neck, and when they did, her back arched and her eyes closed. She could feel her hair brushing the small of her back as his mouth went lower to capture a rigid nipple.

Suddenly there was nothing except the catapulting sensations of leaving her body even as Rafe held her close. She felt him grow within her and felt her own muscles contracting around him, squeezing him as if she would keep him within her forever.

And then it happened as it had the first time. Her senses spun, her body arched within his grip, and when she felt him burst forth moltenly within her, she reached that same dizzying universe she had visited last night.

Her hands held on to his back, her head whipped forward. To stop herself from giving voice to the scream that was building within her throat, she buried her face into his shoulder and only then allowed the sounds of her unending release to go forth.

Waves of pleasure flowed through her. Her body shuddered and trembled upon his, and her arms and hands held him more and more tightly to her. She was afraid to release him, and afraid not to at the same time.

But Rafe was not trying to move. He held her clasped tightly to his chest, and as the aftereffect of their love washed across them, he stroked her head gently.

Only when their breathing eased and they were able to look at each other did Alana unlock her limbs from around him. When she did, Rafe helped her, his hands strong and sure. Finally, Alana found herself cradled within the crook of Rafe's arm, breathing deeply of their now-mingled scents.

Against her will, tears formed and fell from Alana's eyes. Rafe caught them with his fingers, and Alana's heart skipped when he carried his tearstained fingers to his own lips. When he did it again, she stopped him, kissing the tears from his fingers.

She pulled away from him and sat up. She looked at him, and as her words poured forth, she remained unaware of her nakedness. "I love you, Rafe. I love you with every part of me: with my heart, my soul, and my very life's blood. I would give myself over to you; I would give my life itself for you, so strong is my love."

"Then no more need be said," Rafe began as he sat up and reached for her. But Alana shook her head and held off his arms.

"There will never be another man who will fully have my heart. But yes, my darling, there is more to be said." With that, she reached out and took his hand within both of hers and brought it against her breasts.

"Jason needs me. You are a man, whole and complete. Your

strength is only a small part of you. You are a man who can
survive in the world. And more, Rafael my love, you are a man
who will bend the world to your own bidding.

"Jason cannot," Alana stated without bitterness. "I could no
more leave him now than I could deny my love for you."

Rafe's throat was dry, his voice rough-edged. "Alana, I cannot leave you behind."

Alana smiled through the tears that fell from her face. "And
you shall not. I will be with you always," she whispered. Releasing his hands, she bent toward him and pressed her lips to
his chest. She could almost taste the beating of his heart as her
lips lingered above it. When she raised her head again, she
looked into his eyes. "I will be there, within your heart—and
here too," she said as she stretched herself upward to kiss his
forehead and then his temples. "In your heart and in your mind
forever."

"Alana," Rafe called, but again she would not let him speak.

"No more," she pleaded, her hands going to each side of his
face. "For the love I give you always, say no more before I
crumble and shame myself. Love me, Rafael, love me one last
time before the sun comes. Love me so that I may carry your
memory and love to my grave."

Rafe's eyes were misted by the emotions that filled him. He
did not speak; rather, he took her into his arms and covered her
delicate mouth with his. Gently, he did as she had commanded
him, and they joined together one final time, giving of each
other in a way that would never be forgotten by either of them,
for neither took, but both gave totally and unselfishly. Each was
giving the other the gift of their promise of a love that could
never be but that would always stay alive.

When they once again reached that special place that only
they two would ever know, they clung to each other, denying
that there would ever come a tomorrow.

But when the sky began to lighten, Alana wordlessly left the
bed. After she put on her nightdress, she gazed down at Rafe.

"Good-bye, my love."

After she left, Rafe sat back in the bed and accepted what
had happened with the knowledge that it was because Alana
was so strong that he loved her. He had known all along that
she would never leave Jason.

Rafe also knew, without any doubt, that despite the fact that she would marry Jason, every word she had spoken was the truth.

He knew, too, that there would never be another woman who could take his heart the way Alana had, and for as long as he lived, he would never allow himself to give up the hope that she would one day be his, completely.

9

"Now you hold still, chile'!" Lorelei ordered as she pulled back on the drawstring of the corset.

"Why bother?" Alana asked, looking in the long oval mirror. "I don't need this thing." It wasn't vanity, it was a simple truth. The corset did nothing to alter her already-slim midsection.

" 'Cause, Alana chile', dat fine and beautiful weddin' dress ain't gonna fit you without dis. De dress be made to ride on de corset, not on de skin." With that, Lorelei tugged once again, and at last Alana felt an answering pressure. But it was in the further uplifting of her breasts, not in the contracting of her midsection.

When Lorelei finished with the corset, she inspected Alana's face minutely. "I doesn't like the way you is lookin'," she said almost beneath her breath as she began to rub a rose petal on Alana's cheekbones.

While Lorelei worked, Alana listened to the low sea of voices that floated in through her open window, reminding her that in half an hour she would be walking along the aisle created by all two hundred of her guests.

Where has the time gone? she wondered. Ever since leaving Rafe's room yesterday morning, she had lost her perspective. Everything had rushed by, and although she had reacted normally, going about her day as if nothing were bothering her, she had felt herself floating above a dark abyss that was constantly threatening to open and swallow her. Her voice seemed to come from someone else; her movements seemed apart from her, and the smile that was on her face had become fixed without her feeling it.

She had greeted the guests warmly, even though part of her mind was in a constant state of mourning. She had been the perfect hostess and the perfect nervous bride. While she played her part, she had continued to oversee the preparations for the wedding.

Because of the number of early guests who would be spending the night, there was never a moment that Alana was alone, and although she had caught sights of Rafe throughout the previous day, he always had been far away from her. That had been the one thing that had allowed her to function normally.

With Lorelei now applying color to her face, the only thing remaining before the wedding was to put on the dress. A dark wave of doubt washed across her mind. Yet in the face of everything, Alana pulled her shoulders back and smiled at Lorelei.

"How is Jason?"

"Gabriel done dressed him, and when I saw him afore, he looked right handsome," Lorelei responded. Then she looked into Alana's eyes for a moment before she closed her own. "I's sorry chile'. May the Lord forgive me, but I's sorry fo' what you is about to—" The rest of Lorelei's words did not come; instead, tears did.

And those tears, so valuable to Alana because of the woman who shed them, became the one thing that gave her the strength to face what she must. Taking a deep breath, Alana held out her arms. It was almost a repeat of what had happened the other day between them, except that it was she who took Lorelei to her bosom. She held her old nurse tightly until Lorelei's breathing eased. When Lorelei drew back, Alana spoke.

"We both know that what I'm doing is right. And it is, Lorelei," she whispered fervently, "it has to be."

"Yes, Alana, chile', I knows dat—in my mind at least. But—"

"Then enough crying. Help me with the dress."

Rafe stared at his reflection in the mirror. He had been surprised at the prowess of the seamstress and at the way the hastily made suit complemented his physique.

The royal blue material fell in sleek lines from shoulder to boot, accenting his height. Beneath the jacket was a vest of the same hue and material. Beneath that was a white linen shirt with a high rolled collar and laced cuffs that reached to the thumb knuckle and not a hair's breadth further.

Rafe's jet and silver hair was combed back from his face. The gauntness that had been so apparent two weeks before was almost gone, and he was surprised at how much he looked like the paintings of his father that had graced his home in San Francisco.

Shaking his head, he tied the silken scarf into a knot and tucked it into the vest. The tips of the collar rolled over it, and the finished look was exactly right. Turning, he started toward the door.

He'd placed his emotions within a special area of his mind, closing the door upon them and locking away his secret of Alana where no one would ever learn of it. He was strong, just as Alana had stated. And because he was, he had no choice but to accept, this one time, what the fates had decreed. It was more than just his fate at stake, he knew, for if no one else would be hurt by his actions, he would have carried Alana off long ago.

"Steady," he cautioned himself. Rafe took several deep breaths and set the planes of his face into the same mask he had worn yesterday and last night.

When he was in full control of his emotions, he went to the door, opened it, and went down to the library so that he and Jason could go to the north lawn together.

Alana, with three young plantation girls carrying the train of her bridal gown, walked to where the narrow white carpet had been unrolled on the grass. As she did, she gazed at everything around her. To her right was the area that had been set up for the feasting and dancing that would follow the ceremony. Workers dashed back and forth as they finished placing all the accouterments on the tables.

At the far end of the area was a small raised platform with four empty chairs for the musicians, who would play their music for the rest of the day and well into the night.

Ahead of Alana were her guests. They stood in two groups

on each side of the narrow white aisle that ran for a hundred feet from the base of the flowered pulpit.

As she came closer to the white cotton runner, faces turned her way. Yet she held her head straight and looked only toward her destination and the three men who waited there. Rafe was by far the tallest, and the pastor was of medium height. Jason was seated in his wheeled chair but his head was held proudly; the sun sparkled from the brass buttons of his jacket.

By the time her feet touched the cotton runner, every head was turned toward her. Her veil did not hide the expressions of others from her, even though she knew it prevented them from seeing her very clearly.

All too soon, she was no longer able to think of anything except forcing herself toward her fate. Behind her, the three girls released the train and the material fell gracefully to the ground.

Alana walked down the aisle alone, much in the same way she had always walked her path in life.

Rafe's breath caught with his first sight of Alana. She stood straight, walking slowly toward him. The sun fell gently on her, illuminating the wedding gown with its pure light.

The gown itself was magnificent. The fabric started beneath her chin and flowed downward. The material hugged her shoulders and upper arms before billowing out at her elbows. The bodice covered her completely, arching over her breasts and then pulling sharply in to accent her small waist and flaring hips.

Then it billowed out again, as the many petticoats beneath it gave it a life of its own. The hem reached to the very tips of the neatly shorn grass, giving the appearance that Alana was floating just above the earth itself. The train flowed out behind her, tossed gently by the breeze.

Rafe's eyes tried to penetrate through the hazy veil to look at Alana's face. But in that he failed, and perhaps he was glad.

He looked briefly at Jason, trying to control his rage and jealousy toward the friend with whom he had been through so much. None of this was really Jason's fault. Indeed, Jason had claimed Alana before the war had even begun; this day had been set by fate long ago.

When Alana reached the pulpit, Rafe grasped the handles of Jason's wheeled chair and pushed it next to her. He noticed that Jason was alert and that he smiled kindly at Alana. Then Rafe stepped to Jason's side and, without realizing it, clasped his hands together so hard that his knuckles turned white.

Rafe looked neither left nor right; he concentrated on the pastor's words, waiting until the pastor turned to him and spoke.

"And who stands forward to witness this holiest of events?" the man asked.

Rafe tensed, his eyes locking first with Jason's and then with Alana's. Finally he looked at the pastor and spoke. "I stand forward," he said.

The pastor smiled, nodded his head, and turned to the bride and groom and began to speak again. But Rafe heard nothing save a drone in the air.

Before he realized it, the service was over and Alana was Jason's wife. Moving slowly, he bent to Jason and shook his hand. Then he looked at Alana and into the face that was no longer hidden by the veil.

He saw the moistness within her large blue eyes and the tense smile on her lips. Rafe did his best to smile. "Congratulations," he said in a full, if tight, voice.

A moment later a crowd of men surrounded Alana, and a crowd of women did the same to Jason. Rafe stood back, his mind numb. He was biding his time now. He had but one obligation left, and that was the promise he had made Jason to dance the first dance in his stead.

When the crowd began to break apart—most of the people headed to the refreshment area—Rafe tried to lose himself within them, but Jason called him back.

When he reached Jason's side, Alana was gone, spirited off by the women. He heard Jason's loud sigh, and within it the pain that was always present.

He wheeled the chair toward the open area and went to the table that was set for only two at the head of all the other tables.

"Are you all right?" he asked Jason.

"Fine," Jason nodded with a smile. "But I could do with a strong drink."

Rafe nodded his head. "I'll second that." Rafe looked around and waved a servant over.

"Bourbon?" he asked Jason.

"A deep one."

"Two," he told the man. A moment later the servant returned with the drinks.

"To survival," Jason said as he looked into Rafe's eyes.

"To your new life and marriage," Rafe replied pointedly.

Jason looked up at Rafe. "When are you leaving?" His voice held a tone of doubt that Rafe heard clearly.

"After the first dance."

"Then this is it, eh, old friend?"

"This is it, Jason."

"I know that you'll find the people who tried to destroy you," Jason said in a low voice.

"I will, Jason. No matter how long it takes, I will."

Before anything else could be said, a wave of noise reached the men at the tables as the women returned to the lawn.

At their fore, surrounded by a half dozen other women her own age, was Alana. The veil and train were gone. The sun bounced off her raven hair as the women escorted her to the area set aside for dance.

The musicians struck up a chord, and as the other women backed away, Alana looked at Rafe and Jason and waited. Slowly Rafe turned back to Jason and took his hand again.

"Thank you, Jason." Their eyes met again, and they stayed that way until Rafe finally released his grip. Then he turned back to Alana and walked the twenty feet it took to reach her.

The music continued, and he offered his hand to her. She accepted it and, as they began to move together, they flowed within the strains of the waltz.

They did not speak any words, but their eyes locked. This should have been their wedding; they should have been dancing their first dance as man and wife.

Halfway through the waltz, the other couples began to join them. Only when the dance was almost at its end did Rafe speak.

"If you ever need me, no matter what the reason, send for me, or come to me. I will always be there for you, as will my love."

As he spoke, Alana's eyes caressed his face. When he finished, Alana imperceptibly nodded her head as her hand tightened on his. The music ended. Rafe bowed, kissed the tender skin of her hand, and escorted her to the table where her husband awaited her.

After helping her to sit, Rafe turned and, without a backward glance, walked gracefully away.

He rode hard and fast and arrived in Charleston at four. After returning the horse to the livery stable, he paused to open the letter that Lorelei had handed him before he had ridden from Riverbend.

"Mister Rafe, Miss Alana asked me to give you dis. She say you ain't to open it till you be in Charleston."

Rafe had taken the letter and had felt the weight within it as he put it into his bag. "Thank you, Lorelei, for everything."

"You be welcome, Mister Rafe. And—"

Seeing the confusion on her face, Rafe had not pushed her; rather, he had waited patiently until she had marshaled her thoughts.

"I jus' wants to tell you thank you fo' makin' Miss Alana happy." With that, Lorelei had fled, leaving Rafe staring at the spot she had occupied.

Standing in the stable in Charleston, Rafe opened the envelope and peered within. The first thing he'd seen were three gold coins. Then he saw another object: a simple gold ring.

After taking them out, he'd unfolded the letter and read it slowly. When he'd finished, his eyes were moist, but he forced himself to reread every word.

> *Dearest Rafe,*
>
> *It is with a heavy heart that I must watch you leave me today. What we have shared is something given to very few, and it is something that I will cherish for the rest of my life.*
>
> *Our love is special, and it will live always within my heart and mind. I only wish that our lives could have taken a different path. But they have not, and so, my dearest love, I must say good-bye.*
>
> *Since you are reading this letter, you have already found*

the coins. Use them to take you home. Please, my love, please do that for me, if not for yourself.

About the ring. The band was my mother's and was left to me. It is something I value dearly, for it signified the deep love my mother had for my father. I give it to you so that you will always have it to remind you of my unending love for you.

And now I must close, lest I cry and blur the ink. I love you, Rafe; as God is my witness, I love you with every breath I take.

Farewell, my love.

Rafe folded the letter neatly and placed it in his jacket. Then, with the three gold coins—more than ample for his passage to California—in his pocket, he placed the wedding band on his small finger and went to the docks. There he inquired about ships bound for either California or New Orleans. He was told that no ships for California were in port, but that the *Angelina*, bound for New Orleans, was due to leave on the evening tide— in less than an hour. Moving quickly, he went to the dock offices and arranged passage on the *Angelina*. Rafe had no time to do anything other than be ferried to the boat.

As he was boarding the small boat that was to take him to the *Angelina*, he turned for a second and caught a sight that held him in thrall. Walking away from him on Bay Street's wooden sidewalk were two people. The man was of average height, and the woman was also. But what froze Rafe to the spot was the unusual color of the woman's hair. It was a silver, almost iridescent blond, and it made Rafe think of his sister. Before he could react, the couple turned a corner and disappeared.

"It can't be," he murmured aloud, knowing his sister could not be in Charleston. She would never leave San Fancisco and the family's business. And although Elizabeth's hair color was rare, he had once or twice before seen others with the same.

Rafe suddenly wondered if he was trying to replace his loss of Alana with a vision of Elizabeth. He shook his head slowly, and the small craft pulled away from the dock.

Once on board the *Angelina*, Rafe tossed his bag into his cabin and went topside to gaze at Charleston one last time.

The overall picture was of a city being rebuilt after a war that had almost destroyed it. New buildings had already gone up, replacing the burned-out shells of the structures that had once been the glory of the city.

Behind him, the piping of the bosun sounded and, as the bittersweet sounds died, the sails were unfurled. The ship shuddered when the first gusts of wind filled the sails, then started on her way toward New Orleans.

Rafe closed his eyes and let his memories of Alana go free now that he was no longer at Riverbend. When he opened his eyes again, the descending sun glinted from the golden band on his finger.

By the time the *Angelina* had reached deep water, quiet was settling in at Riverbend. The guests had finally departed, the last ones riding out long after dark had come. The plantation workers were still cleaning up and would continue to do so throughout tomorrow.

For the first time since his arrival, Jason was in the master bedroom on the second floor. Gabriel and Ben had carried him up the stairs and into the room.

After they had left, following Jason's tense instructions not to be disturbed until morning, he had undressed himself slowly and painfully, and then, without putting his nightshirt on, had levered himself into the bed.

When the clock struck midnight, he was leaning back on the bolsters of the big bed that had been unoccupied since Thomas Belfores's death. The room itself was large and contained two dressers and an armoire.

A second room led from the bedroom. That room had been Alana's mother's dressing room. Behind it had been her father's dressing room. Alana sat on the chair facing her mother's dressing table, brushing her long hair and trying to calm her nerves.

Earlier, Jason had told her that he expected to spend the night with his wife, and Alana had nodded her head in agreement. But when she learned that Jason planned on taking over the master bedroom, she had begun to grow nervous.

"Don't let it worry you. I plan on having a ramp built to replace one of the staircases. Until then, Gabriel and I shall manage the stairs."

He obviously didn't understand the source of her agitation. Without explaining, Alana acceded to his wishes as befitted a wife. But in the privacy of the dressing room, she began to feel the strain on her nerves.

Stop this foolishness, she ordered herself. *I have always loved Jason, and he has always been good to me.* Because she knew this was true, it helped to ease her heartache for what she could not have.

Thankfully, Alana had felt no pity for Jason. She did feel his hurt, his pain, and his loss, but she did not feel pity, only a tender love.

Alana took a deep, preparatory breath, put down the brush, and stood.

She had spent the early evening burying deeply within her mind all her memories of Rafe. She had forced her willpower to rise, and she had locked away the love that had been theirs. She knew she must not think of him now, especially tonight.

Alana realized that it was time to go to her husband and lie next to him, to hold and comfort him throughout the night.

Why am I so nervous? she wondered. She had no answer; she only felt that something was not quite right. There was about the night a sense of foreboding she had no reason to feel.

Pushing aside her nervousness, she went to the door and opened it. When she stepped into the bedroom, she saw Jason resting against a bolster, his upper chest bare.

Moving gracefully, Alana went to the sconces at the far side of the room and put the candles out. But when she started toward the two remaining ones, Jason's voice halted her.

"Not yet," he commanded.

Her body tensed. She looked at him. His face was pinched with pain, and her heart went out to him. "Your medication?"

"No. I want to remember our wedding night, Alana, don't you?" His voice was uncharacteristically hard.

She heard the mocking tones and went to the bed and sat next to him. Looking directly into his eyes, she did her best to smile as she put her hand over his.

"Don't torture yourself, Jason. We're together as we promised each other. Accept that, please."

Jason's eyes swept across her face. He freed his hand from beneath hers and turned his head to look at the curtained windows. "Every night for years, I dreamed of you and this night. I dreamed of holding you, kissing you, and making love to you."

"Jason—" Alana began, but he went on as if he hadn't heard her.

"When I was wounded, I still did not give up hope. But when the doctors told me that I had lost the use of everything below my waist, I wanted to die. I wanted to end my life. But I didn't. I was too damned weak!"

"No, Jason—"

"Yes. And so, instead of dying, I lived. And every day the pain reminds me of my cowardice. Every night that I lay upon that prison bed I thought of you and of what we would never have—the passions that your body promised me, and the beauty of your face. I dreamed of being with you, of lying with you, and of satisfying you. But that will never happen, will it?"

"Why are you doing this to yourself?" Alana asked, her voice choked with emotion.

"Because I'm here with you. Because of the cruelty of life itself that places you in my bed but will not allow me the pleasure of having you."

"But you do!" Alana stated in a louder voice than she'd intended. "You have me fully. I am yours and no other's. We are husband and wife. We are bound together forever." The very truth of her words was carried to him by the depth of her voice.

"And denied forever what it truly means to be husband and wife."

"There is more to a marriage than that, much more," Alana protested, willing herself to be strong and to keep the sudden onset of pity for him at bay.

"But every marriage must start with a consummation. What will ours be?" he asked, his voice once again mocking. His eyes had become glazed, and she saw his hands were now curled into fists.

"I don't understand," she whispered as a tendril of her earlier foreboding made itself felt.

"Undress, Alana," Jason ordered.

Alana stiffened. She stared at him without moving.

"Undress," he repeated. "Now!"

"Why, Jason? Why are you doing this?"

"It is my right as your *husband*. Do it!" This time the hard edge in his voice was like a slap to her face.

Reluctantly, Alana rose from the side of the bed and, with her eyes closed, opened the bodice of the nightdress and let it slip from her shoulders. When it was gathered at her feet, she stood deathly still.

From fear or chill or both she felt her nipples harden and contract; her skin from head to toe did the same.

"Turn and face me!" Keeping her eyes closed, she did as he commanded. "Look at me!"

Opening her eyes, Alana gasped. Jason's face was unrecognizable. His eyes were wide as they ran up and down her length. His mouth was half open; his hands were still clenched into fists.

"Walk for me, Alana. Walk around the room so that I may see in the flesh what I have dreamed about every night for the last years."

Alana, her face burning red with shame, did not speak as she obeyed his orders. She walked the length of the room, feeling his eyes on her with every step. Her breathing was shallow, her eyes downcast. She felt more than just naked; she felt totally exposed and helpless. She had never before known shame such as this, and she knew she would never forget this moment for as long as she lived.

"Enough. Come here!"

When she met his gaze, she saw that his eyes had turned into ash gray embers that terrified her as nothing else had ever done before. His eyes were unreadable, his face a blank. Only the heavy rise and fall of his chest told her of his state.

"Pull the cover down," he ordered.

Alana did not move. "Why, Jason? What do you want from me?" she asked in a low voice.

"Everything, as is my right as your husband. The doctors told me that I would never be a man again. But I have never tested the finality of their words. Now is the time."

"Jason, please."

He snapped angrily, "You married me today, Alana. You gave yourself over to me. I am your master, Alana, as surely as you are my wife. Now be a wife. Do your duty. Excite me, Alana; bring me back to life!"

Defeated and suddenly very much alone, Alana willed her arm and hand to move. Bending over him, conscious of the way her large breasts swayed before his face, she began to pull back the light cover. She did not look at him as she did.

When she felt his hand grasp her wrist, she stopped. "That's far enough for now. Excite me, Alana. Make love to me."

Their gazes locked, and protest flared from Alana's eyes, but Jason's angry, glinting eyes glared back at her, deflecting her anger as if it not exist.

His hand was still on her wrist, gripping it tightly. "Excite me, Alana. Do your wifely duty."

His other hand snaked out and caught her hair. He pulled her mouth to his and kissed her harshly. Alana did not respond, nor did she pull away. But as their lips touched, she knew that fighting him would do no good. He was her husband, come what may, and she had chosen him and had agreed to be his wife.

Her lips softened against his, and she tried to kiss him as would a wife, but even as she did, she felt her head being pulled back. Opening her eyes, she found him staring at her. "Kiss me like you mean it."

Ignoring the pain in her scalp, Alana brought her mouth to his. When their lips met, she kissed him deeply, moving her mouth against his, letting the tip of her tongue slide between his lips.

She held back a shudder of revulsion. Her breasts rubbed against his chest, but she felt no excitement filling them.

The hand gripping her wrist moved as Jason drew it to his flaccid length. Her fingers tensed, but he did not let her wrist loose.

The hand that was in her hair pulled her mouth from his once again, but instead of holding her and looking at her, he began to push her head downward as he moved her other hand on him.

The power in his arms was too much for her. The pain on her scalp sent sparks of light dancing before her eyes. She felt powerless to fight against his unrelenting demands.

Her face was suddenly buried in his chest, even as he continued to move her other hand along his still limp length. Nausea threatened to make her sick, but she fought it back, knowing that if she resisted him in any way he would use it against her for the rest of their lives. Finally, when she thought she could stand no more of this shame, tears of humiliation fell, and she surrendered her last will. It seemed as if something snapped within her mind at the outrage and horror she felt, and she was being drawn away from her physical body; her very essence had fled to a safe corner of her mind, protecting her from what was happening.

His hand pressed her harder, and Alana began to kiss the skin on his chest. As her lips worked on his skin, she felt his hand loosen in her hair. The pain in her scalp eased, although he did not fully release her.

A few moments later he pushed her head down further, and the narrow band of hair that ran in a downward line on his stomach was brushing upon her lips.

Above her, she heard his low groan, but still, her hand that held his length felt no response. Knowing that she would always hate herself for doing this, she began to work his length with her fingers.

She tried to pretend that she wanted him and that what they were doing was right, but the reality of what he was making her do would not permit even that simple lie.

He released her hand but not her head. Suddenly he pushed her down until her face was pressing against the hand that held him.

"Take me in your mouth!" he ordered. "Make me come alive!"

Alana closed her eyes. "I can't," she whispered.

His hand again tightened in her hair, twisting it cruelly. "You can," he stated. He twisted her hair further, and a lance of pain ripped through her head.

Then he pushed her. Once again, she knew the futility of resisting. Slowly she lifted his still-unresponsive member and, closing her eyes, did as he bid.

She heard his sharp intake of breath and felt his hand press her head down. Then she felt her head being moved about, controlled by his hand as he made her do what he wanted.

For endlessly long minutes he continued to control her, but finally, with a loud grunt of anger, he pulled her head away from him.

"Enough, damn you! Enough. We have just proven that I am indeed half a man. Not your warm lips, nor your hands, nor the sweet womanhood I have dreamed of is able to make me a man again. Don't look at me like that!" he shouted as her eyes had turned pitying on him. "Don't ever look at me like that."

Jason's face was scarlet with impotent rage as he pulled the cover over his nakedness. Then he twisted and looked at the night table beside the bed. "My medication. Give it to me!"

Alana, still naked, reached for the bottle and the spoon. When she brought them to him, he snatched the bottle from her hands and, with trembling fingers, opened it and drank the laudanum straight from the bottle.

When he finished, he handed her the bottle. After replacing it on the table, Alana picked up the discarded nightdress and started to put it on.

"No!" he ordered.

Alana turned to him, fear of having to once again repeat what they had just done reflected within her face.

"Lie next to me as you are. Hold me, Alana; I want to feel you beside me."

Alana again did as he commanded, and she held him to her until the drug eased the pain in his body and he fell asleep. His breathing was even and smooth when she slid her arms from around him and moved to the far side of the bed. Turning her back to him as the sounds of his breathing rose in the room, Alana cried quietly to herself for the final loss he had given her.

For on this night, he had truly taken from her the innocence that had remained within her heart. He had destroyed the gentle love for him that had always been a part of that innocence, and he had replaced it with the harsher realities of life and with the pity she had done her best never to feel toward him.

Book
II

Charleston, Riverbend Plantation,
and Abington Island
1866–67
San Francisco and Death Valley
1866–67
New York City
1867

10

August 1866

Alana stretched her cramped muscles. She had been sitting in the canopied carriage for four and a half hours and was finally nearing Charleston.

The late morning sun poured down its full might, and the driver could not go any faster for fear of killing the horse that already was sweating so profusely.

She had left at the first light of dawn so that the horse might be spared as much of the heat of day as possible—and because she had two very important errands in Charleston. She would need as much time as possible once she was there.

Although Alana hated to be out on the road in this heat, she had no choice. In a move born of desperation, and in the hope of salvaging her life, she had made several important decisions and needed to see them through.

She was on her way to Charleston to meet with Charles Ledoque and to somehow persuade him to look after the Landow Shipping Company for her. After that meeting, she would visit Dr. Lawrence to go over her final plans to do what was necessary for Jason.

Alana sighed and closed her eyes. She did her best to ignore the rivulets of perspiration that were already turning her dress dark. And as she concentrated, she examined the past ten months of her life.

A feeling of despair gripped her, but she pushed it aside and tried to look back over the long months logically, without letting emotions interfere with her mind.

After the first three months of marriage and of doing her best to make Riverbend return to its former might, she had found that matters were slipping further away from her than before. The hope that everything would become right again once Jason had returned had fallen from her almost as quickly as had her idea that they could live a normal and fulfilling life together. As the love she had once felt for him had turned into the worst kind of pity on their wedding night, so had departed the dreams she had always maintained.

Their relationship had disintegrated from the onset of their marriage as Jason retreated behind the pain-relieving stupors that his medication gave him. Shortly after the wedding, Dr. Lawrence had examined Jason again. He had given him even stronger pain-relieving drugs to help him; chief among them was a new form of opium that seemed to work the best.

But Alana had noticed that the drug seemed to take away Jason's ability to concentrate. By the time their first month together had ended, he had given over to her the full responsibility for running their affairs.

Another aspect of the medication was that his demands upon her had also diminished. The horrid scene of their wedding night had been repeated only twice more within the first three months. After that, Jason had never again shown any interest in her body.

She had wanted to depend on Jason in helping her to revive Riverbend, but he had proven himself incapable of sharing the benefits of his vast knowledge and business acumen. And so, by the beginning of the new year, Alana was even more deprived than she had been throughout the war, for she no longer had her dream of a happy future.

She and Jason had done no socializing, and whatever friendships she had maintained before his return home she'd been unable to keep up. During that same time of personal upheaval, she had met Charles Ledoque and had found him to be a charming, well-intentioned man who offered her both a platonic friendship and his help in managing the estate.

He had waited for several months after sending his original

letter before writing again and then calling upon Mr. and Mrs. Landow. When he'd arrived, he'd come prepared to handle all of Alana's objections and had brought a letter of introduction from Carlton Dupont, the Belfores family lawyer.

Alana had been ready to dismiss him as another greedy merchant reaping the benefits of war-devastated Charleston, but after meeting him and hearing his propositions, she had decided that he was a decent man.

Charles Ledoque was in his early forties, and Alana had been aware that he took good care of himself. His body was solid, and his slightly graying hair was well-kept. His features were pleasant, and his deep-set eyes were open and friendly.

After reading her lawyer's letter, which assured her that Charles Ledoque was an honorable businessman, she had explained about her husband's ailments in the most delicate terms. Then she had asked his advice about Jason's shipping company.

Ledoque had impressed her with his straightforward answers. He had made it a point to tell her that he would be glad to help with the shipping company, but because of the demands on him from his own company and his other business interests, he thought it best if Alana retained control of Landow Shipping.

What Ledoque offered instead were his docks, warehouses, and whatever help he could personally extend to her. He was willing, he told her, to have one of his managers keep track of her company and report everything to him, so that if problems arose, he would be able to advise her regarding them.

For his advice he had asked no fee. His only charges would be for dockage and warehousing. By the time he'd left, Alana felt confident that she had met someone who would be able to help her during her hard times. In one of Jason's rare lucid moments, she explained Ledoque's proposal to him.

Jason had accepted, but he had also shaken his head. "We still do not have an agent for the shipping business. Find an agent, Alana. Find someone who will look after the company, for you cannot do it."

"Why?" she'd asked angrily.

"Because you know nothing about shipping."

"I will learn."

"You're a woman, Alana; stop trying to be a man. Learn your limitations."

"As you have?" she had spat at him without thinking.

Instead of getting angry, Jason had smiled at her and stroked his useless legs.

That had been the last business conversation they ever had. From that point on, Alana had run Riverbend and the shipping business, relying more and more on Charles Ledoque's expertise.

Yet try as she had to resurrect Riverbend to its former might, the fates seemed to always challenge her. The first crops had not yielded what she had expected, and there had been no profits. The prices for rice were lower than at any other time in history.

Still, Alana had been certain that with time the fifteen thousand acres of cotton would become the most profitable part of the plantation. But they would take another two years to reach full fruition.

As spring approached and the land grew even more fertile, she still had had one path left that was not yet explored.

Until her mother's death, and even during the years her father had squandered the Belfores and Shockley fortunes, the horses that Riverbend had bred were always in demand. The last of the horses had been confiscated by the Federal troops near the war's end, but Alana had always kept excellent records and knew where all the stock had been sold. So in the spring she had sent out letter after letter in the hope that one or more of them would be answered and would offer her a chance to buy a stud that might still be alive.

In July, not three weeks ago, she had received her first reply. It was from a breeder in Maryland who had one original Riverbend stallion who had sired a promising colt.

The colt was three years old, and he would guarantee its fertility. He would have the horse delivered to her, along with a suitable mare, as soon as he received full payment.

The sum had staggered her beyond belief, but she knew she'd had no choice and had agreed to his terms. A week ago, on the eighth of August, she had sent the breeder a draft for one thousand dollars and instructions to deliver the horses in the second

week of September, when the heavy heat and humidity of
Charleston had abated.

And that, Alana thought as the carriage bounced in and out
of a rut, *is all I can do for now.* But Alana Belfores Landow was
not a woman who gave up. She was determined, no matter what
the odds, to make her life worthwhile, and that included shaking her husband out of his drug-induced lethargy to make him
face the world once again.

Alana had had enough of Jason's self-pity, and her own pity
had slowly turned into a desire to end the constant heartache
that Jason caused. The love that she had once held for him,
although never passionate, had been a large part of her vision of
Riverbend's future. But Jason's self-loathing and its terrible re-
sults were becoming impossible for her to bear.

Because of who she was, Alana would not allow Jason to
continue to destroy their lives. She could not escape him, but
she might be able to change him. It was her obligation to try to
help him and possibly, if she could, give him back the dignity he
had once worn so proudly. Perhaps then he would again become the Jason Landow that she had always known, and the
love she had held for him would return. She had decided that
she would do whatever was necessary to help Jason face life
once again—even if it meant devoting her every waking minute
to him.

"Oh, Rafe," she whispered aloud in the carriage. Her invol-
untary words shocked her. The blood raced to her face, and she
slowly shook her head. She had not let herself think of Rafe
often, and when she did, it had not helped her to face what she
must; rather, it had showed her that she had once had happiness that was forever gone.

Forcefully, she made herself think of something else, anything else, but the carriage started to rumble over cobblestones
and Alana realized they had arrived in Charleston at last. In
another ten minutes she would have her meeting with Charles
Ledoque, and she had to prepare herself for what she must ask
of him.

On her previous visits to Charles Ledoque, it had amazed
Alana to read the gilded letters on the entry doors of his offices.
The names of a half dozen shipping companies were proudly

displayed, along with an even longer list of warehousing and docking companies.

The offices themselves were in a large building that had once been the summer residence of a wealthy family. The building faced the East Battery, and Ledoque's private office afforded a view of the harbor and of Fort Sumter in the far distance.

But she was not there to see the view. She made herself concentrate on the man who had just entered. After greeting her, Ledoque sat behind his huge mahogany desk. Behind him, covering the entire wall, was a map of the world with colored lines of twill marking the trade routes his ships plied.

The office itself was decorated simply but elegantly. Nothing was out of place; the air smelled of tobacco, leather, and paper. Its very essence gave Alana a feeling of security.

"Although I must express my pleasure at your visit, I'm somewhat surprised," Ledoque said without hiding the open question in his eyes.

Alana took a deep breath and plunged ahead. "I have come to ask for a very large favor, Charles."

"My dear Mrs. Landow, you know you have but to ask," he responded magnanimously.

"It's not that simple, for I must impinge on your generosity once again." Alana paused for a moment. When she spoke again, her eyes held his and her hands lay clasped tightly in her lap. "You have already made it clear that you are too busy with your own business to be able to act as the agent for Landow Shipping. I know that the company is not large enough to bring you much profit as an agent, but because of personal problems, I find that I must ask you to do just that. Charles, will you please become the Landow agent? I will double the usual fee."

Ledoque shook his head slowly, his features showing great concern. "Let's not speak of money. What has happened to make you come here like this? Please, I consider myself more than just a business adviser. I believe I am your friend."

"You are, Charles, and I thank you for that friendship." Alana smiled hesitantly at him, and then, accepting his words completely, she forced herself to relax and tell him what she planned to do.

"I am taking Jason to Abington Island. His condition has not improved in the past months, and I find that the demands upon me at Riverbend have not allowed me to help my husband sufficiently. I now plan to spend as much time as necessary to help Jason recover. When we return to Riverbend, I fully expect Jason to take over our business affairs. But," she added when she saw a change flicker across Ledoque's face, "I need you to help me until we return."

When she finished, she let free a low sigh and waited for his response. Ledoque said nothing for several seconds, and Alana was afraid he was going to turn her down.

But finally he shifted in the chair and spoke. "Mrs. Landow —Alana, if I may?" He waited a moment until Alana graciously nodded her head. "Alana, I would be remiss in my duties both as a gentleman and as your business adviser if I turned away from your plea. No matter how busy I am, I will make time to see to your holdings as well as my own. Of course I will help you," he repeated gently.

"Thank you, Charles," Alana replied, releasing her long-held breath.

"Will Mr. Dupont be handling the accounts for Riverbend while you're gone?" he asked.

"No, I was hoping that you—"

"Say no more. It will be my pleasure to help you through this trying time. I'll have the proper papers drawn up right away."

"Won't our verbal agreement be sufficient?" Alana asked, knowing that any papers at all would take more time than she had. She'd planned everything down to the last minute and was prepared to leave for Abington Island the morning after tomorrow.

"It is to protect both of us, Alana," Ledoque told her. "I'm sure Mr. Dupont would insist on this also."

"I must return to Riverbend tonight. Papers will take too long."

"But mustn't you return to Charleston to go to the island?"

"No, Captain Bowers will take us directly from Riverbend to Abington. It's but a day's travel by boat."

"Have you eaten at all today?" Ledoque asked suddenly.

Alana shook her head. "I'm not hungry, and I must see Dr. Lawrence before returning home."

"Allow me to have some food prepared for you so that you

will not have to travel hungry. By the time you're finished eating, I'll have a simple agreement ready for you."

Again Alana smiled. "Thank you, Charles, for being so kind and understanding."

Ledoque stood and came around the desk. When he was before her, he reached out and took her hand. He held it firmly as he spoke. "It makes me happy to be of service to you. Wait here; I'll be right back."

True to his word, Ledoque returned within two minutes and seated himself on the leather wing chair next to hers. While they waited, he questioned her about several matters that they had discussed previously, and then he drew her out about her plans to start breeding horses again.

After ten minutes a servant came in, pushing a cart before him. Without orders, the man set the serving cart between Ledoque and Alana and efficiently served the meal.

When they finished and Alana had sipped the last of her wine, another knock sounded.

"Enter," Ledoque called.

A short man dressed in a high-collared suit entered with a sheaf of papers and handed them obsequiously to Ledoque. When he was gone, Ledoque stood. "Why don't you sit at my desk? It will be more comfortable for you there."

With that, he placed the sheaf of papers on the desk, and after Alana sat, he handed her a quill pen.

Alana stared at the papers and then at Ledoque. "So many— how is it possible to have them prepared so quickly?"

Ledoque smiled at her. "These were being prepared for another company that I represent. I had my clerk make certain changes so that the contracts are now in the name of Landow Shipping Company. The second papers are merely your power of attorney so that I may disperse funds for Riverbend when needed," he explained easily. "It is a standard agreement. In fact, Mr. Dupont himself drew up the original papers."

"I see," Alana replied. And because of the fact that he had shown himself worthy of her trust, she barely glanced over the forms. After signing each one where Ledoque pointed, she put the pen down.

"And now, Alana, go to Abington Island. Don't worry yourself about business matters, for they are in good hands until you return."

Alana looked at Ledoque. "I will not forget this kindness, Charles. Thank you very, very much."

Ledoque waved aside her thanks with a gesture of his hand and then took hers and brought it to his lips. "As I've already told you," he said, not yet releasing her hand, "it is my pleasure."

When Alana left the office, her thoughts were easier and her mind more settled. But if she had turned around as she left the office, she would have been shocked. Charles Ledoque's face no longer held the benevolent facade of seconds ago. Replacing his look of concern was a predatory grin that flashed darkly at her back, and his eyes, as they swept upward from her booted feet to the raven crown of her head, glowed with a hunger that permeated to the very core of their dangerous depths.

"It will not be easy, Alana," Dr. Lawrence stated.

"I understand that," she replied, her features set in fierce determination, "but you were the one who suggested that he be taken to someplace where he is not constantly surrounded by reminders of the time before the war."

"Be that as it may, I also suggested that Jason be admitted to a clinic, where he could be watched over carefully," the doctor replied.

"Even if Jason would allow that—which you know well enough he won't—I don't think I could. I am prepared to do whatever is necessary to help him regain his perspective on life."

"*If* he wants to," Dr. Lawrence added in a low voice.

"I think he does," Alana said honestly. "When he isn't overwhelmed by his drugs or feeling sorry for himself, I can see the man I used to know trying to break through."

Alana paused in an effort to control her emotions. When she succeeded, she continued, "I have to do this for myself as well as for him."

Dr. Lawrence nodded his head slowly. "All right, Alana, but as I said, it won't be easy. You will have to take him completely off the new drug and give him only laudanum. His body and his mind are very used to the stronger opiate. He will have a severe reaction to its loss. He may even become violent."

"I can take care of him."

Dr. Lawrence stared at her for a moment. "I think you can. But remember, he will be in a lot of pain. It won't be a pleasant sight."

"Dr. Lawrence," Alana said in a low voice, "the last ten months of my life have not been pleasant, either."

The doctor had nothing else to say and, turning from her, he reached into a cabinet and withdrew several dark bottles.

"This will see you through the first month. Take whatever opium he has left and bring only enough to keep him comfortable until you reach the island."

For the next fifteen minutes, Alana listened to everything Dr. Lawrence told her, and when he was finished with his instructions, she took her leave of him and returned to the waiting carriage.

Once inside, she leaned wearily back and closed her eyes. Knowing that she had done everything she could to prepare for what now lay ahead, Alana wondered if she could really endure it all. Give me the strength to see this through, she prayed silently as the rumble of wheels on the cobblestones echoed within the carriage.

In his East Battery Street office, Charles Ledoque sat back in his chair and exhaled a cloud of cigar smoke. He was very satisfied with his day's work and pleased that he had not used the extreme methods that he and James Allison had discussed.

The important contracts that Landow Shipping owned were now theirs, without the least bit of coercion. But, Ledoque thought as he drew on the thick cigar, there was still more that he needed to accomplish.

His goal was no longer just the acquisition of Landow Shipping and the transfer of the Montpelier contracts. No, what he had in mind was even more exciting and would be more rewarding.

When he had visited Riverbend the first time and had come face to face with Alana Landow, he had discovered a woman whose beauty had made him desire her so totally that he vowed he would one day possess her. From the moment his lips had touched her hand in greeting, his desire had roared to life. When he looked into the blueness of her eyes, when he heard the throaty quality of her voice, and when he took in the lushness of her swelling breasts, he could already feel himself being with her.

Yes, Ledoque promised himself, I will possess her so completely that I will be the only person or concern in her life!

11

At dusk, two days after Alana's meeting with Charles Ledoque, she and Jason arrived on Abington Island and moved into the only house on the small yet lovely strip of land three hundred yards off the Carolina coast. The island and the house had been made available to them by Alana's childhood friend, Annabelle Pomerance.

Although Jason had been protesting this move ever since Alana had told him of it, she had refused to bend to his will, and with the help of Gabriel, Lorelei, and two other workers, she had brought him to the island.

Alana had left Ben in charge of the plantation, with strict orders to report any problems to Charles Ledoque and to requisition any supplies through him. When Captain Bowers arrived, she knew there would be no turning back.

Leaving Riverbend just after sunrise, Alana had sensed that she was embarking on a new path in her life. She'd reached the point where she would either cave in completely, giving up on life in much the same way that Jason had, or she would take life by the bootstraps and make it work for her.

After they were settled into the house, and everyone except she, Jason, and Lorelei were on their way back to Riverbend, despondency fell over her. But she chased the feeling away and faced her task with determination.

She allowed Jason to have his opiate that night, but when he fell asleep, she took all the old bottles of medication and de-

stroyed them, replacing them with the ones of diminishing
strength that Dr. Lawrence had given her.

When Jason awoke the first morning, he called out for his
medication and Alana obediently poured his dosage. After taking it he looked at her strangely.

"That's laudanum," he stated.

"That is correct," Alana replied tersely.

"I want the other."

"No, Jason, there is no other."

Jason's face twisted with rage when he realized that Alana
was not backing down. "Take me back to Riverbend!" he demanded.

Alana shook her head. "No, Jason, not until you're ready."

They argued for a long time, but because the pain-dampening
effects of the laudanum did not work as well as those of the
opium, Jason grew too tired to continue.

Alana stayed near him throughout the first day, and by the
time night had fallen, she was exhausted. Lorelei had offered to
watch Jason for Alana so that she could sleep, but Alana would
not let her, knowing that it must be she who stayed at his side.

The night was long as Jason's body reacted to the absence of
the opiated medication and to the diminished doses of the laudanum; but the following day was even worse. His upper torso
thrashed about, his muscles and tendons knotting in pain, while
Alana, her face damp with tears, would not give in to his demands.

For five more days, Jason's reaction to the loss of his medication was a horrible sight to behold. He became delirious, alter-
nately begging for medicine and asking Alana to put him out of
his misery. But Alana did neither.

His eyes were unusually vacant, and at times his breathing
was frighteningly shallow. A strange form of cunning developed
within his fevered, pain-wracked mind; Alana realized it almost
too late.

At one point during the fifth night, Jason called out to Alana.
In the low light of a single candle, Alana had bent close to him
to hear his words. When she did, his arm snaked out and he
grabbed her around her head. His strength seemed to have
grown in proportion to his suffering, and as he dragged her

against his sweat-drenched body, Alana feared that he might crush her.

"Give me the medicine!" Jason demanded, his voice a coarse growl in her ear.

Alana, fighting to hold back any sign of fear, tried to pull away from his painful grip. "I can't," she protested.

"Do it!" he yelled.

"All right," she cried, her voice breaking convincingly. "Let me loose so I can reach it."

Alana did not believe he would release her, but, surprisingly, he did. As she jumped quickly away from him, she breathed a sigh of relief.

"In two more hours I will give you your laudanum," she told him from a safe distance, her chest rising and falling with the strain of her labored breathing.

"Bitch!" he screamed, the veins in his forehead bulging outward. "Merciless rotten bitch!"

Alana turned from him, tears flooding her eyes. But again she forced herself to hold on to the inner strength that was her only salvation, and when she felt herself under its steadying influence, she turned back to Jason.

But she did not speak, for once again Jason was no longer aware of his surroundings. His body quivered, and his arms shook. Alana knew that he would not harm her again tonight.

True to her word, two hours later Alana gave him a small dose of laudanum. But what she didn't tell him was that it would be the last dose of any medication that he would receive until his mind was finally clear.

And so, with Lorelei's unflagging devotion and support, she continued to live through the days and nights with hardly any sleep. Only her strong will kept her fighting for both herself and Jason.

The morning of the twelfth day found her dozing in the chair next to Jason's bed. It was after sunrise when something nagged at her senses, and she opened her eyes.

Looking around, she tried to find out what had disturbed her sleep, and only when she looked at Jason did she realize what it was.

His breathing was calm, and the muscles of his neck, arms, and shoulders were no longer knotted with his reaction to the loss of medication. When she looked at his face, she saw that his gray eyes were open and that he was gazing at her in a way she'd never expected to see again.

She rose hesitantly and started toward him. When she reached the side of the bed, she saw he was smiling. "Jason," she whispered.

"I feel like I've been through another war," he said in the husky croak that was all that remained of his voice.

"You have," she whispered.

"I—I can't remember the last time my mind was this clear."

"The pain?" Alana asked. Her own guilt at causing him so much suffering mingled with her happiness at seeing his eyes open and filled with intelligence.

"It's not too bad right now. Alana," he said earnestly, "I'm sorry for what I've done to you this past year."

Alana shook her head fiercely. "We will never discuss that, Jason. It's over." Then she wisely changed the subject. "Hungry?"

Jason shook his head. "Thirsty," he replied, "and tired. I feel as though I haven't slept in a month."

Alana bent down and brushed her lips across Jason's. When she stood, she could not hide the emotions that were on her face. "I'll get you some water," she told him.

"No, send Lorelei. You need some rest. Alana, I may have been half crazy—more than half crazy—but I was always aware that you were here. That's what helped me through it all. I—I just wanted you to know that."

Alana bobbed her head, afraid to trust her voice. When she turned to leave the bedroom, she found Lorelei already coming toward her with a tray. On it was a glass of water and bowl of broth. Then Alana knew that Lorelei had heard everything.

"You go and get yourself some fresh air, Alana chile'," she whispered. "Den some sleep. I be takin' care of Master Jason dis mornin'."

Alana smiled gratefully at her. "Thank you, Lorelei. I couldn't have done it without you."

"Don' be tryin' to give me any credit for makin' Master Jason whole agin'. You be de one, de only one who coulda done dat. It be your strength and your love dat do it, nothin' else, chile', nothin' else." With that, Lorelei went into the bedroom.

Outside, Alana breathed the warm salt air. Seagulls wheeled and cried high above her. The sun burned through the overcast sky to reach toward the earth for the first time in a week.

As Alana walked toward the white sandy beach, she was unaware of the tears that spilled from her eyes. All she knew was that Jason had survived and that a spark of hope was again alive within her breast, brought out by the way he had looked at her and by the way he had spoken.

When she had stood beside him, she'd glimpsed the Jason of her past, and in that moment she found herself once again seeing the future she had so painfully believed lost forever. And now, as Alana looked up at the sky and saw the wheeling gulls, her spirit soared with them. For the first time in almost a year, she was looking forward to the future.

"Are you sure, son?" asked the whiskered prospector, squinting up at Rafe Montgomery. The weathered lines of his face ran everywhere in a pattern of age-old wear from a life spent beneath the hot desert sun.

"I'm sure, Caleb," Rafe stated.

"Well, Rafe, I'll sure miss you, but I'm glad we found each other when we did."

Rafe nodded his head slowly, his mouth set in a tight line. "I owe you a lot, Caleb, more than I'll ever be able to repay."

"Shee-yit, son, you already repaid me. You believed in me," the old prospector said as he turned and gestured toward the side of the hill and the excavation site in its base. "I've been out here thirty-five years and I've never hit anything except a few panned-out veins. Tell you the truth, though I always dreamed about it, I never expected to strike the mother lode. Must be your joining up with me that changed my luck."

Rafe finally smiled. Twisting in the saddle, he glanced back at the three heavily loaded mules. Each carried a hundred and fifty pounds of pure gold ore—and that was but a scratch in the surface of Rafe and Caleb's mine.

"Just you make sure that them supplies and men are on their way, you hear?"

"I hear, Caleb. Don't you worry. I made sure about that last week. They'll be here in a few more days, mining supplies and all."

"Well then, son, I guess you best be getting on now, instead of us sitting around and jabbering like a couple of fools."

"I guess so," Rafe agreed. But he did not spur his horse forward; instead he spoke again. "Caleb, I'll be setting up the mining company office in San Francisco the way we agreed. It will be staffed with people I trust, who will run the business while I do what I have to. You just make sure that the ore is mined. In about three months, you take yourself the hell out of here and come to San Francisco. You understand that, old man?"

"I ain't that old that I don't understand, Rafe. Not yet anyhow," Caleb Magee stated proudly.

"If I'm not in San Francisco, I'll leave word where I can be reached."

"You do that, son. And Rafe—take care of yourself. Those people you told me about won't take kindly to your plans."

"I hope not," Rafe stated with another smile—but this smile held no warmth—only a promise of vengeance.

With a final wave of his hand, Rafe prodded his horse. As he started off, the three mules followed behind. Twenty minutes later, the mine was lost from sight as Rafe negotiated the slopes that led to lower ground, toward the civilization he had seen only twice in the past six months.

Settling back in the saddle, Rafe relaxed as he moved absently with the pace of the horse. He had a three-day ride to the mining town where he would deposit the gold and collect a bank draft that he estimated would total over two hundred thousand dollars.

With part of that he would establish the Magee and Montgomery Mining Company, and with the rest he would seek out the people who had destroyed everything that had once been his.

Feeling a dark cloud settle over him, Rafe thought back to when he'd first returned to San Francisco and had made his terrible and heartbreaking discoveries.

After the *Angelina* had docked in New Orleans, Rafe had purchased two stout geldings and started his westward trip to California. It had taken him six weeks, and the death of one horse in New Mexico, to reach San Francisco. When he had, he'd almost lost his will to live.

He'd ridden directly to his home, situated on a high hill that overlooked most of the city. When he'd stopped before the impressive stone gate, the sight that greeted his eyes had torn him apart.

Beyond the white stones of the fence, nothing remained of what had once been a large mansion except a few charred timbers. Opening the gate, Rafe had walked his horse onto the grounds and had stared at the destruction all around him.

Tears had flowed unashamedly down his cheeks at his loss. But the fear that his sister might have been caught in the fire galvanized his body into action.

He had mounted his horse and left the property, riding as fast as he could on the crowded cobblestone streets. Eight minutes later he was at the waterfront, moving toward the docks and the office building of the Montgomery Shipping Company.

But when he arrived, another devastating sight was before him. The sign of the Montgomery Shipping Company, which had hung for forty years, was gone; in its place was another sign that declared that the building held the offices of the Pacific Oriental Shipping Company and that its agents were Murdock and Caruthers, Importers.

Anger had rushed through him at this sight, but a small vestige of self-control had stopped him from charging into the building. He had realized then that the treachery that had befallen him during the war was connected to the building before him, and that knowledge had helped to stay his anger and lend caution to his mind.

Hating himself for not going inside, Rafe had turned his horse. At the waterfront he'd seen one of his old ships sitting at anchor in the bay. Squinting, he'd looked at the mainmast and seen that the Montgomery flag no longer resided in its rightful place.

Then he'd made himself stop looking and start thinking. He would have to find out what had happened to his sister and to their business; charging around blindly would do no good.

From the docks he'd ridden across town to Abraham Hampton's small house. Hampton had been Rafe's mentor and the former captain of the Montgomery Lines flagship; Rafe had asked Captain Hampton, who had retired, to work with Elizabeth during his absence and to help her whenever she needed assistance. Rafe had been sure that he would learn what had happened from Captain Hampton.

After tying his horse to the railing, he'd gone to the door and knocked. Several minutes later, the door had opened and Rafe had found himself staring into the surprised face of Abigail Hampton. When she'd looked at him, her eyes had widened and the blood had drained from her face.

"It can't be—you can't be—they said you were dead," she'd whispered.

Rafe had put his hands on her shoulders. "I'm very much alive, Abigail. Is the captain home?"

It had taken the older woman a few moments to collect herself, but when she'd realized that he was indeed Rafe Montgomery, she ushered him into the house. The captain was nowhere to be seen.

"What happened?" he asked bluntly after sitting down across from her in the small salon.

She'd shaken her head and had spoken in a low, fearful voice. "Abraham was *murdered* a year and a half ago," she'd said.

After Rafe had recovered from his shock and had offered his heartfelt condolences, he again had asked what had happened in his absence. "He was killed after those people took over your company. He told me the night he died that he was going to get to the bottom of it all. After he died, I went to the authorities and told them he had been killed. I even gave them what proof I had, but they said it was an accident, pure and simple."

"An accident?" Rafe had prodded, holding back his own thirst for information about Elizabeth and the company.

Abigail Hampton had looked at him moist-eyed. "They said he had drowned. That he was drunk and fell off the pier. Rafael, you know Abraham never drank, never."

Rafe had hissed involuntarily in surprise. He knew Abraham Hampton never drank. It had been the captain's belief that whiskey destroyed more ships than any storm. No officer that shipped out with him was ever permitted to drink, unless it was for medicinal purposes.

"Abigail, I know this will be hard, but you must tell me everything, every last detail."

And Abigail had. She'd spoken almost dispassionately, yet Rafe had seen the emotions pull at her face.

At the same time that Rafe was being tried as a Federal spy, his sister had been confronted by several men who told her that Rafe was being held a prisoner and would be hanged. They told her that the only way to prevent Rafe's death was to sign the papers that transferred the title and all possessions of the Montgomery Company to them.

So Elizabeth, forced by the specter of the death of her only brother, had signed away the company.

But that was not all. Two days after Elizabeth signed the papers, the Montgomery house had burned to the ground. No trace of Elizabeth had been found, and it was presumed that she had died in the fire.

Rafe, upon hearing this, had turned ashen, but Abigail Hampton had put her hand over his reassuringly. "She didn't die, Rafael. Abraham learned that. I'm positive that's why he was killed. You see, the day after she signed the papers, she'd told Abraham what had happened. She told him that when she had done everything they'd asked, and she'd demanded that they set you free, they had laughed at her. They told her you were already dead." Abigail had paused then for a breath and for control of the emotions that made her words so heavy.

"As soon as he'd learned of the fire, Abraham went to the house. He found Jamie, the caretaker, wandering aimlessly on the grounds, his face and head covered with blood. Jamie had seen four men break into the house that night. He said he was sure they were the ones who started the fire, because when they left the house, they were carrying Elizabeth between them.

"Jamie had run after them, and one of the men hit him on the head. The next thing he knew, it was daylight and the house was gone."

"Then she is alive," Rafe had whispered with hope.

Abigail had nodded her head. "But no one knows where."

"I'll find her," Rafe had promised. "And I'll find the men responsible for your husband's death, too."

"Be careful, Rafael," she had warned.

Then she'd asked him what had happened to him and why he had been away so long. After hearing his story, she had nodded her head thoughtfully. "How are you going to find Elizabeth?" she asked.

"I don't know yet."

"You have no money at all, do you?"

Again Rafe had said no.

Then Abigail had smiled for the first time. "I want to help you. Abraham left me secure, because Montgomery Shipping always treated him fairly."

Rafe's first reaction had been to refuse, but Abigail would not hear of it. "For my own peace of mind, please let me help."

Reluctantly, he had accepted.

With the money she loaned him, he had gone to the Pinkerton Agency and made arrangements for them to search for Elizabeth. But Rafe had known that his revenge would require more money than Abigail had. There was only one place to find that money—in the California gold fields that had once been so vast and profitable but that were now said to be played out.

After explaining to Abigail what he was going to do, Rafe had left San Francisco. He'd given Abigail's address to the Pinkerton Agency and had then told her that he would keep in contact with her.

In December of eighteen sixty-five, Rafe had ridden out of San Francisco, determined to regain his business and avenge the wrongs done to both himself and his sister.

Three weeks later he had ridden into a mining town at the edge of the old gold fields. He'd spent several days in the saloons talking to old prospectors and had found one man who seemed different from the others. Rafe's intuition had made him watch the man closely. The older man told no stories, and when the other prospectors had talked to him in jeering tones, he had ignored them.

Rafe had learned that most people thought Caleb Magee was crazy because he had spent the last ten years looking for a lost mine that was said to contain the mother lode from which the entire gold field had been spawned.

In a careful way, Rafe had listened to everything that had been said, and he listened, too, when Caleb spoke. He heard no bragging in the man's voice; rather, he'd sensed a deep certainty.

After five days of watching and listening, Rafe had approached Caleb Magee. He'd bought him a drink and let the older man talk for a while. When he'd seen that Caleb had said all he was going to, Rafe began to question him about the lost mine.

"It's there," Caleb said matter-of-factly.

"Then why haven't you found it?" Rafe had asked just as matter-of-factly.

"I don't know for sure, son," he'd replied to Rafe. "Maybe just bad luck."

"What makes you so certain you can ever find it?"

Caleb had stared at Rafe for a full minute before he replied, and when he finally had, he had not used his voice; rather, he pointed his index finger at his heart. A moment later, he'd backed up his gesture with words. "I feel it in here."

There had been something about the man that made Rafe trust him. It was a special feeling that told him the man was not crazy.

"Why aren't you out there now, looking for the mine?" he'd asked as he'd signaled the bartender for another round of drinks.

"It takes money, son, and I've plum run out of that."

Rafe had laughed at the man's honesty and had again felt drawn to Caleb. "There must be a lot of people who would take a chance on you for that kind of a find," he'd ventured.

"There are," Caleb had stated. "But I don't want their money, because once I find that lode, they'll sure as hell find a way to steal it from me. Besides, I'm getting too old to go out there by myself."

The next day Rafe had again approached the old prospector, and had looked directly into Caleb's eyes.

"I don't have a lot of money or a lot of time. I need to find a good strike, and I'm willing to work my butt off to do it," he had told Caleb flatly.

Caleb had studied him for several moments before he nodded his head. "I like you, son, and I like the fire I see in your eyes. How much do you have?"

When Rafe had told him, Caleb smiled. "That'll give us about two, maybe three months' worth of time. You got that much to spare?"

"When do we leave?" Rafe had asked.

"Tomorrow, after we buy the supplies and after we get over the hangover that we are about to acquire."

Rafe had laughed at that and had matched Caleb drink for drink until neither one of them could see more than three feet ahead.

But when the morning had come, along with the hangover that Caleb had promised, Rafe was standing in front of the supply store watching Caleb walk steadily toward him.

Two hours later they had ridden out of town. Three months later they had found their first thin vein of gold.

It had been a strange discovery, for when they'd reached a desolate section that was half mountain, half desert, Caleb seemed to come alive. He'd looked around, and then stared at Rafe. "I feel it, son, I feel it's near."

Rafe had not reacted in one way or another, but neither during the three long months had he given up his hope in Caleb, for he knew the old prospector was his only chance. Even so, when they had discovered a long-abandoned mine, its rotting timbers falling apart, Rafe had almost left.

"This is it!" Caleb had stated. Then both of them had ventured inside and had learned that it was nothing but a played-out shaft.

Rafe had wanted to give up, but Caleb would not. "This is the place, Rafe. Trust me, just trust me." For another day they had picked at the rocky surface of the hillside, and just when Rafe was starting to feel the hopelessness of his rash plan, he had heard Caleb's excited shouts.

A moment later he'd found himself staring at the starting traces of a small vein. "This is it, son! Look at the quartz. Look at the color of those flakes!"

From that point on they had worked like madmen; four days later they had mined ten feet into the hillside. As they'd dug, the vein had become denser. After another day's digging, neither man had any doubt that they had found a rich strike. What they hadn't known and would not find out for another month was that the vein itself would become as thick as Rafe's body and the color of it as pure as the color of the sun. They had indeed found the mother lode, not twelve feet from the sight of the original mine.

Taking just a little of their gold and making sure that it had a lot of impurities in it, Rafe had returned to the mining town and had exchanged the gold for four hundred dollars. He had bought three mules and loaded them with enough food and supplies to last a long while; then he'd filed a mining claim under the names of Magee and Montgomery. Finally he had gone to the general store and to the small postal desk at its rear. There he'd asked if there were any mail for him, and when he'd been handed a single letter, he'd gone outside and read it.

When he had finished reading it, he'd mounted his horse and started out of town, leading the mules behind him. But he'd seen nothing before him except the words that continued to swim in his mind.

Abigail had forwarded the Pinkerton's final report about Elizabeth. They had discovered, after two months of investigation, that a woman of Elizabeth's description had been seen in a small town in Nevada's booming silver strike territory, working in a bordello. But, the report had continued, when their agent went to that town, he discovered that a fire had destroyed an entire section of buildings, including the bordello in question. He had also learned that the woman he was searching for was reported to have died in the fire.

The agent hadn't stopped there, the report had shown, but had spent several days in the town, checking everywhere to verify his story and continuing to search for Elizabeth Montgomery in case she had escaped the fire. On the third day, the agent had found several witnesses who said they had seen her go up to her room just before the fire, and afterward no one had seen her again.

Seven bodies had been recovered when the ashes had cooled, and the Pinkerton agent was satisfied that one of those bodies had been Elizabeth Montgomery's.

By the time Rafe had put several miles between himself and the town, his grief had burst forth. Later, when he'd gained some control over himself, he'd sworn that no matter what might happen from this day on, the people responsible for his sister's shame and death would pay with their lives.

And then, for the first time since he had boarded the *Angelina*, he had brought out his carefully guarded memory of Alana and let it soothe his tormented soul. He had lost one of the two people he loved above all else, and the only thing that had kept him sane in that moment had been the knowledge that

Alana was alive and safe and that the love he felt for her was always alive in her heart, too.

Straightening in the saddle, Rafe looked up at the late afternoon sun. In two days he would be in town. The day after that he would take the first steps toward vengeance.

"Soon," he promised his sister's memory. "Soon."

12

Alana walked barefoot along the beach, enjoying the feel of the sand as it rose between her toes and luxuriating in the warm caress that the sun bestowed upon her face. The ocean breeze tugged at her simple cotton daydress, pressing it to her body and outlining her curves. Seagulls called out from the heights as they flew above Abington Island and the woman walking its beach.

Alana was happier now than she had been in a long time. For four glorious weeks after that special morning when Jason had awakened clear-eyed and level-headed, her life had taken on new meaning. Each passing day was better than the last, and now that their stay on the island was coming to an end, she almost wished that they could remain here forever.

Her old Jason had come back to her; if not in body, at least in mind. When he had regained his strength, he had refused to stay in bed and had let Alana and Lorelei help him into his wheeled chair at the start of each day.

Then he and Alana would sit on the veranda and spend their days talking, playing chess—which he loved and taught her—and then talking again until late at night.

At night she would lie in bed with him, no longer afraid of him and keeping to the far edge, but rather held within his arms, her head on his shoulder as they both slept peacefully through the night.

Jason had refused to take any more medication. Not once in

the past four weeks had he used the laudanum that sat on the bed table. Instead, he accepted his pain and through his own willpower defeated it. No gift that he could ever give her would be more valuable to Alana than the one he now gave—himself, whole of mind, healed of spirit.

After the first two weeks, and after finally making Jason understand that what had happened between them during the past year was not to be mentioned or thought of ever again, she and Jason had begun to talk of the shipping company and of Riverbend.

He had been amazed to know that Alana was having trouble maintaining Riverbend and the shipping company, for in his retreat within the drugs, he had never once given it any real thought. He had been wealthy before the war and had assumed he had stayed the same after. Alana had assured him that the money he had requested from England had been deposited into their account, but it had not been as much as he had expected. The war had cut deeply into the shipping company's reserves. The export of cotton was negligible and the importation of brandy, wine, and the other Montpelier goods had been sharply curtailed during the worst of the naval fighting. The costs of running Riverbend had also begun to eat heavily into their account.

This had not seemed to bother Jason, and he'd smiled disarmingly at her. "From what you've told me, Ledoque is a good businessman. With him as our new agent, I'm sure that the shipping company will be showing its usual profits soon. After all, our contracts with the Montpelier Company are enough to keep Riverbend and ourselves quite comfortable."

Since the time of that conversation, Jason had begun to give her small tidbits of advice, never once outrightly telling her she had done this thing or that wrong but suggesting in the patient way he'd always had that perhaps *they* should try to change this method or that crop.

By the end of their fifth week on the island, Alana had learned a great deal from Jason, and besides feeling a renewed and tender love for him, she knew that their life together would be smooth and comfortable from then on.

Alana stopped walking and turned to go back to the house. Within her, a glow of excitement was building. Tomorrow morning Captain Bowers would be picking them up for the return trip to Riverbend.

Happy with her thoughts of the future, Alana picked up her pace toward the house. She was no more than two hundred feet from her destination when an explosion shattered the peace of the day.

Seagulls screamed their outrage at the noise; several large dark birds who had been resting on the roof of the house took off in a startled flurry.

Then Alana saw Lorelei running out onto the veranda, and as she did, she realized that her own legs were pumping madly, propelling her toward the house. A dark shaft of fear sliced through Alana's mind, but she refused to acknowledge it. At the foot of the steps, Alana stopped. Looking up, she saw the terrible expression on Lorelei's face. Her heart began to race; her stomach twisted painfully. Her legs had suddenly turned to lead. Each step up took an eternity. But when she was on the veranda and gazing into Lorelei's tear-streaked face, she could no longer deny what her heart and mind told her.

When she started to go around Lorelei, her old nurse tried to stop her. Alana shrugged off the restraining hand and walked through the open door. Alana's breath caught painfully in her chest at the sight that greeted her eyes.

Jason was sprawled on the floor in front of his wheeled chair, a revolver still gripped in his hand.

She walked toward him. Her mind was spinning madly, unable to accept the vision that lay before her as she knelt down at Jason's side.

Willing herself not to give in to the beckoning darkness that sought to claim her, Alana forced back the bile that rose in her throat at the sight of the blood pooling on the floor beneath Jason's head. She did not hear her own low sob as she reached toward his lifeless form. Ignoring the blood that smeared her fingers, refusing to see the ugly wound on his temple, she lifted his head and brought her mouth to his.

When she drew her mouth from his unresponsive lips, she felt an unreasonable flare of anger at what he had done to himself. The happiness that had filled her so fully only moments before was now replaced by shock and mourning. She felt the deepest sorrow for the loss of a love that had ended before it could truly begin.

"Why, Jason?" she asked in a husky voice. "Why have you done this to us?"

Still holding him, Alana lifted her head and saw a sheet of paper gripped in his right hand. Carefully, her fingers trembling, she took the paper and looked at the neatly scripted words.

> *My Dearest Alana,*
>
> *I know that in the times to come, you will understand why I have done this. And when you do, I want you to realize that because of your devotion to me, I was able to find the strength to face my destiny.*
>
> *From the time I was wounded, I hid within a world I created, a world that separated me from everything else. The drugs I used were not just for my pain, but to keep me oblivious to life itself.*
>
> *When you brought me here, to Abington, and you forced me to face what I had become by making me come out of my drug-ridden world, I was able to think again and use my mind again for the first time in so very long.*
>
> *And because of this, your devotion and your unselfish giving of yourself to me, I have found the strength to do what I should have done three years ago.*
>
> *Do not blame yourself, for it is because of my love for you that I set you free in the only way I can. Live your life now, Alana, live it for both of us, and never look back at our past with regret.*
>
> *I thank you for these past weeks, for lying next to me each night, for allowing me to hold you close and give you what love I could. You are a beautiful and brave woman.*
>
> *Remember, Alana, that I have always loved you, no matter what pain I might have caused you, and wherever my soul goes, it shall carry that love with it.*
>
> *Good-bye, my dearest wife. Remember me with kindness and love.*

For endless minutes Alana stared at the paper, and then a low cry escaped her lips. Releasing the paper from her numbed fingers, Alana cradled his head on her lap, holding him close and rocking slowly back and forth.

She was unaware of Lorelei pulling her away from him and lifting her off the floor; all she knew was that she had lost Jason soon after finding him. Then the darkness that had been calling to her since she stepped inside the house overcame her, and she gratefully succumbed to it and sank into unconsciousness.

Alana stood on the veranda looking toward the drive. For the first time in the two and a half months since Jason's death, she was not wearing black. Her personal period of outward mourning was over and, she had told herself, it was time to be back at work.

Those first weeks after Jason's death had been the hardest for her. Harsh anger had combined with deep despondency, preventing her from doing anything other than lie in bed and stare unseeing at the ceiling.

Jason had found his way back from the pits of hell and had shown Alana once again the wonderful man he was. When he died, no matter what his note had said and no matter what he had believed, he had deserted her. She could not forgive him, and so could not accept his death or continue with her life.

But one day while she was lying in her bed, Alana had reread his note and had tried to see between the lines. As she did, she began to realize that perhaps it was she who was being selfish. He had shown her that he was capable of giving his love and of being her husband. But he could no longer live a life so filled with pain that he might be forced back into depending on drugs to survive.

With that revelation, Alana's ability to face the world had returned. But she had not been ready to begin running River-bend or take back the reins of the shipping company.

Instead of checking the plantation's accounts, or doing any of the hundred things she might, she would leave the house in the morning and go over to the horse-breeding pens that had been empty for so long. There she would gaze at the large roan stallion who had arrived on the day the breeder had promised. She would watch him for hours, taking in his majestic bearing and admiring the rippling muscles beneath his shiny coat.

She would watch him and find herself pinning her dreams on

his sleek back, knowing that within the year the first of a new breed would rise at Riverbend. Then she would go see the mare who was being kept apart from the stallion until she could be bred.

When they mated, she decided she would leave them together as much as possible until the female was near her foaling time. Alana wanted to add more mares, but she would not do so until she saw the first offspring of these two wondrous horses.

At noon Alana would go to the stable. She would spend the rest of the day riding in the fields, thinking about Jason and about Rafe. Alana did not believe she was sullying Jason's memory by her thoughts of Rafe, and those thoughts helped her regain her strength and purpose once again, for Rafe's image in her eyes was always one of strength and beauty.

Once she had reconciled herself to what had happened, the healing of her heart and mind began to speed along with the passing days until she could no longer sit back and do nothing. Then the day had finally come when she was ready to join the world and take control of her life once again.

That was why she was now standing on the veranda waiting for Charles Ledoque's arrival. But he was late, and Alana was filled with a restless energy that would not permit her to stand still for too long.

Turning, she called out for Lorelei. When Lorelei appeared, Alana told her to inform Mr. Ledoque that she would be at the breeding pens and would wait for him there.

Leaving the veranda, Alana walked the five hundred feet to the breeding area. When she got there, the stallion, now very used to her, came over and pushed his muzzle against her arm.

Smiling at him, she dipped her hand into the hidden pocket in her skirt, withdrawing a piece of carrot. She opened her hand and the stallion took it from her palm. After he chewed it, he lifted his head and whinnied to her. Then he trotted over to the mare, who had been let into the stallion's pen.

"Magnificent stud" came Ledoque's voice, startling her for an instant. Recovering quickly, she turned to smile warmly at him.

"Yes, he is," she replied.

"I'm sorry I am late, but I had a slight problem before I left Charleston this morning."

"Time isn't as important here as it is in Charleston," Alana responded with understanding. "Shall we go to the house?"

Ledoque gallantly offered her his arm. She accepted with a smile, but they did not speak until they reached the house and went into her study.

Lorelei had already set out a decanter of sherry. Ledoque poured the sherry into the two glasses, handed Alana one, and lifted the other.

"To a remarkable woman," he toasted.

Alana felt suddenly uncomfortable under his probing gaze. "I don't think I'm very remarkable."

"Take my word for it, Alana, you are. Very few women could have gone through what you have and come out the better for it."

Blushing at his words, Alana smiled her thanks to him as she sipped the sherry; however, she knew that if she were as remarkable as he said, she would not have been so helpless over the past months.

"You asked that I come to see you about business, did you not?" Charles said, graciously changing the subject.

"Yes," she responded as she put down her glass. "Charles, I find I must impose on you a little while longer."

"You will never be an imposition, Alana. And it is definitely no imposition to advise you on your business affairs."

"You are very kind," she said honestly, "and a good friend, too. Charles," she began after taking a breath, "I need you to continue as the agent for Landow Shipping. I do not feel confident yet to assume its control."

When she finished speaking, she saw Ledoque's features change, and she believed she saw a slight frown that he did not quite manage to hide. "What is it?" she asked.

Ledoque looked at her for several seconds, before he slowly shook his head. "If I had not received your letter, I would have been forced to come to you anyway. You see, Alana, Landow Shipping has suffered several setbacks in the past months. I have not sent word of them because of your own tragic loss, but I fear I must tell you now."

"But—" Alana looked at him questioningly.

"I'm sorry to be the bearer of more sad tidings, but it is a role I must accept. Two of your ships have been lost at sea. No trace of them has been found. A third was pirated off the coast of Jamaica. Because of that and the losses of their cargo, the Montpelier Company has invoked their cancellation clause and taken their contracts from Landow."

"No!" Alana gasped. "They wouldn't do that!"

"I'm sorry, my dear, but they have," he told her in a tone that made her accept his statement.

"What can I do?" she asked, doing her best to gather her thoughts and discover what her position was.

"I'm doing everything possible. I have shifted several of my own contracts to Landow, in order to help stop the losses, but even so, I'm afraid that your debts are getting out of hand."

"Debts?" Alana whispered with the shock of his words. "What debts? We had no debts."

"Alana, shipping has always been rife with problems; that's why the rewards are so great for those who succeed. After your first ship was lost, it became your contractual obligation to guarantee delivery of the next shipment. When the second ship was lost, Landow Shipping had to reimburse the Montpelier Company for the cargo, as was done for the pirated cargo of the third ship—and that ship has not yet been refitted for use because of the damages it sustained."

Ledoque paused, his face reflecting the position that Alana found herself in. "I used all the available funds to reimburse the shipper, but they were not sufficient. I loaned you some of my own capital, but I am limited at this time, and I was forced to make up the difference by going to the bank and borrowing money in your name."

Alana went white despite the control she was trying to maintain. Once again her world was collapsing around her.

"How deeply am I in your debt, Charles?" she asked in a barely audible whisper.

"That doesn't matter," he countered, "but my concern for you does. I will stand by you in this, Alana," he said, reaching out to take her hand.

She stared at her hand in his, then slowly looked into his eyes. For just an instant, she saw a flash of something she'd never seen before. A ripple of fear raced along her spine. Slowly, she withdrew her hand.

"How much am I in debt?" she repeated.

Ledoque stiffened slightly when she pulled her hand from his, but his face remained unreadable. "Forty thousand dollars. To me personally, only ten thousand. To the bank, thirty."

"Impossible!" she cried.

"I am truly sorry, Alana, but my figures are accurate."

Alana stood and walked gracefully across the room to gaze out the window. When she spoke, she did not look at Ledoque.

"I take it that you will no longer represent my company as its agent?" she asked.

"I would not abandon you now," he protested. "But it is my obligation to tell you of the problems you—we face."

"What would you suggest, Charles?"

"I believe that over a period of time, and by getting several good contracts, we can turn things around for Landow Shipping, but it will take more time than you have. There is another alternative, but it may not be enough."

"Yes?"

"I can try to find a purchaser for Landow, but we cannot ask too high a price. The company has no contracts, only debts."

"No!" Alana exclaimed immediately. "Landow Shipping has been in my husband's family for four generations. I will not sell it now."

"Then we must find some way to help you out of your trouble, Alana, for Riverbend was the security I was forced to put up to get the loans. The thirty thousand dollars represents a full mortgage on Riverbend."

Alana, still staring out the window, felt the blood drain from her face. A red swell of anger gripped her, and she fought against herself until she had her rage under control. Turning, she stared at Ledoque. When she spoke, her voice was as cold and hard as ice.

"By what right did you use Riverbend as collateral for that loan?" she demanded.

"By the right you gave me, Alana, by your power of attorney," he said in a level voice.

Alana shook her head sharply, unable to believe the words she was hearing. "That was only so that you could disburse expense funds."

"It is a full power of attorney, I assure you, and I had every legal right to do what I did. And, Alana, I did it for you.

However," Ledoque said as he rose and picked up a leather case that Lorelei had placed next to the chair, "I have brought the papers and the up-to-date accounts for you to review."

"Will they tell me anything that you haven't already?" she asked, her voice sounding harsh and unforgiving.

"No," he said.

"When is the bank note due?"

"In seven weeks."

Alana closed her eyes. When she opened them again to steady her suddenly wobbly legs, she saw Ledoque staring at her.

"I am truly sorry to have been the bearer of this news, but it was my duty. Think about what I've suggested, Alana, but don't take too long, please. Time is of the essence."

Alana nodded her head, her tongue refusing to work as he walked toward her. He took her hand again into his and raised it to his lips. As he did, a chill raced up her arm. When his lips touched her skin, she shivered involuntarily. Thankfully, he did not notice.

"I will see you soon," he said. And then he was gone.

Alana remained in the study for a long time after he left. When Lorelei came to tell her that dinner was ready, she found Alana seated at the desk going over the papers that Ledoque had left.

When Alana looked up, Lorelei saw that her face was creased with lines of worry. "Dere be someting wrong, chile'?"

Alana tried to smile, tried to say no, but the lie did not escape her lips. Instead, she nodded her head. "I may lose Riverbend," she whispered.

13

"I have only six weeks left. What can I do?" Alana asked as she stared at Carlton Dupont's lined face. Alana had known Carlton Dupont all her life, but today, for the first time, his white hair and tired eyes told her that he had long since passed his prime.

Alana had written him a letter the day after Charles Ledoque's visit, informing him of her precarious position, as well as sending him all the papers Ledoque had left with her.

In the following week she had tried to think of a way to remedy the situation and had been able to come up with only one idea—one she hadn't wanted to consider.

She'd also written a letter to Rafe, telling him of everything that had happened, including Jason's death, and asking for his advice on what could be done for the shipping company. Her hopes went along with the letter to San Francisco, but she knew that it would take too long for it to reach him and for him to reply. She did not have enough time.

"What can I do?" she asked Dupont again.

The lawyer shook his head. "Alana, I am extremely upset by what has happened. I feel that I have let you down."

Alana frowned. "Let me down?"

"Yes. As your father's friend and legal adviser, and then yours, I made a grave error. When Mr. Ledoque came to me to ask for a letter of introduction to you, I checked on his background with a colleague of mine, and with his bank as well. My

colleague gave him the highest of recommendations, and Mr.
Collingsworth at the bank did also. In fact, it was his words of
respect for Mr. Ledoque that gave me the confidence to write
my recommendation."

"But Charles has done all he could for me," Alana argued.
"What happened is not his fault." But her conviction suddenly
was not as firm as it had been. The memory of that brief
glimpse into his unguarded eyes rose within her mind. "What
kind of error did you make?"

"The worst kind. Like the old fool I am, I believed what I
was told. Alana"—Dupont paused again, gazing at her sadly—
"except for you, I no longer practice law. I have outlived all my
clients and my usefulness. This office is a sham. I keep it for my
pride."

Alana's heart went out to her father's friend, even in this time
of trouble. "No, Uncle Carlton, that's not true."

"Isn't it?" he asked in a self-accusatory tone. "Why would I
have let someone else guide you? Alana, when you sent me his
reports, I went over them very carefully. It was then that I
realized I had been duped. When I learned that the Montpelier
contracts had been lost, I was astonished. Those contracts were
irrevocable as long as any losses were repaid!"

"But—"

"But Ledoque, acting as the agent for Landow Shipping, approved the request to terminate the contracts."

"Why?" Alana gasped.

Dupont blinked. When he spoke again, he looked away from
her. "Because one of his own shipping companies was awarded
the new Montpelier contract. Ledoque's company is now the
exclusive shipper for Montpelier, and his import company is
their new American agent. Alana, Ledoque has gained a tre-
mendous amount of business, and you have lost all of yours."

"How is this possible?" Alana asked, her mind spinning with
Ledoque's unexpected and cruel treachery.

"He manipulated me, and he did the same to you. Yesterday
I spoke with another man who lost his business to Ledoque. He
told me that Ledoque owns Collingsworth's bank and has since
the end of the war. That was why Collingsworth had given me
such a glowing report about him. It seems that Charles
Ledoque controls almost all the warehouses, docks, and ship-

ping in Charleston and possibly in the entire South. Alana, this means that Ledoque owns the mortgage to Riverbend."

Dupont's words were too much for Alana's already-strained mind. She shook her head hopelessly while she tried to concentrate on what was happening. "But why is he doing this to me?"

"Greed, Alana. I have seen it all too often."

"You're saying that he has purposely set out to destroy me and that I have no recourse? I must lose everything?"

Dupont sighed, his kind face held in tight lines. "Legally, you have no recourse. Everything that he did was done according to the law." Then Dupont rose from behind his desk and came to Alana's side. He placed a gentle hand on her shoulder, and when she looked up at him, he continued to speak.

"After going over the reports, I spoke with a banker whom I trust, and I asked him for a loan to help you. He refused me, not because he didn't want to help but because he had already given out too many mortgages to help the old plantations recover. He lost the majority of his money when the plantations failed. He too is in the position of possibly losing his bank."

Although Alana heard the words and understood the enormity of what Dupont was telling her, her own problem would not let her pause to think about the banker.

"How will I get the money?" she asked, willing her voice to be steady.

"I don't know," Dupont replied. "I would give it to you myself, but I have not recovered from the losses I suffered in the war. I have only enough money to make ends meet. It's a hard time, Alana, a desperate time." He stopped himself, his hand tightening on Alana's shoulder.

"You will have to fight this devil Ledoque with his own methods. You must find one of the businessmen he has ruined and borrow the money from him. Use the shipping company to do this. Accept a partner who can fight Ledoque, for it's the only means left to you. Alana, I'm sorry I've failed you," he said as he took his hand from her.

Alana drew in a deep breath and stood. "I shall do whatever is necessary to save Riverbend, Uncle Carlton. But first I intend to face Charles Ledoque."

"Be careful," he cautioned.

"Why?" she asked. "What more can he do to me?" With that, Alana turned and walked regally out of the office.

Fifteen minutes later, Alana was ushered into Ledoque's private office by the same obsequious clerk she had met on her past visits. Once inside, she watched Ledoque rise and walk toward her.

"This is a wonderful surprise, my dear," he said with a smile.

But this time, Alana saw through the false warmth of the smile that had deceived her for so long. When he reached for her hand, she snatched it away.

"Why, Charles?"

"What's wrong?" he asked, his face showing concern.

Alana saw only the truth that lay beneath his mask. "You avaricious bastard! Why are you trying to destroy me?"

Ledoque noted the fierce set of her face and saw the fire blazing within the depths of her eyes; her soft lips were stretched into a thin, tight line. "Sooner or later you would have found out. I was hoping it would be later," he admitted in a calm, easy voice.

His tone, as well as the words themselves, shocked her. "You planned it all?"

"Not all. We have wanted the Montpelier contracts and Landow Shipping since the outset of the war. That was my prime motivation."

"Why Riverbend?"

This time Ledoque smiled. It was not a pretty sight, and Alana's breath hissed out in reaction to it. "You're not a stupid woman, Alana. Don't you know?"

Alana continued to stare at him, her mind whirling. Slowly she shook her head.

"For you, Alana, for you," he said truthfully. "Say the word, and Riverbend will be yours again."

"You've ruined my husband's company and are trying to take Riverbend from me because you *want* me?" Alana's words were hollow, filled with disbelief.

Ledoque caught Alana's shoulders and drew her to him. His eyes were bright. Within them she saw her fate burning darkly. "I have wanted you since I met you. I have watched you waste your life caring for a crippled shell of a man who did not deserve you. Alana, I can teach you what a real man is!" he declared, his voice husky with desire. Then he lowered his mouth to hers. Alana pulled back violently before his lips reached hers. She glared at him, revulsion on her face. His final words were the catalyst that jolted her mind into action, and suddenly her thoughts were crystal clear.

"A real man?" she asked, her voice dripping with sarcasm. "You consider yourself a real man?" She moved quickly, surprising Ledoque for only a second, but it was enough time to free herself from his hold. Stepping back, Alana's eyes riveted him with hatred.

"When my husband returned from the war, he was more a man than you could ever be!" With that, Alana spun and started for the door.

Before she reached it, Ledoque caught up to her, his hand clamping tightly on her arm. Their eyes locked in a silent, deadly duel, and then Ledoque smiled even as his grip tightened.

"I have remained a bachelor too long, Alana. And you will feel differently about me after we are married."

Refusing to acknowledge the chill that coursed through her body, Alana laughed in his face. "That will never happen!"

"Will it not?" he asked, his voice level against her rage. "Are you so willing to forfeit your home and everything you own?"

"You wouldn't dare."

"You have six weeks to make your decision. Either you marry me, or I will take Riverbend and Landow Shipping from you. Remember, Alana, I am offering you an honorable alternative. I could make you my mistress instead of my wife. But as my wife, you will provide my membership in Charleston's society."

A hatred so intense that she thought she would be sick built up within her. She stared at him but could not find the words to convey her wrath.

Ledoque, taking her silence as leave to continue, spoke again. "You are a beautiful woman, Alana, and I shall enjoy instructing you in how to please me."

"You're mad," Alana finally said as she tried to free herself from his hold.

"No, my dear, far from it." And then he pulled her roughly to him, his mouth hungrily seeking hers. Alana twisted her head from him; her free arm flashed upward. The strike of her palm against his cheek resounded loudly in the office.

Ledoque's head snapped back, his face twisting angrily. But when he spoke, his voice was so calm that it frightened Alana more than any shout could have.

"You have much to learn, my dear, and it will be my pleasure to teach you—for I shall not only have you but make you totally mine!"

"In hell!" Alana declared. She pulled her arm sharply back and felt his hand release her. Turning stiffly, Alana opened the door and marched out of his office. But before she could escape completely, she heard his mocking voice ring out.

"Six weeks, Alana. That is all."

Outside, Alana breathed in the clean scent of the salt air. Her mind was reeling, but with each step she became more furious and more determined to stop Ledoque completely.

On an unseasonably warm evening in mid-December, inside a brightly lit large house on Tadd Street—a house that had once been owned by an aristocratic South Carolinian family called Pomeroy—business thrived.

At the war's end, the Pomeroy house had been purchased through an agent, and three months later, to the shock of Charleston's high society, the occupants had moved in. The Pomeroy house soon became the most thriving bordello in the city.

The beautiful madam who ran the bordello had become as noteworthy as the Pomeroy house itself. Whenever she walked down the street, heads would turn and whispers would be carried on the air. Passersby would point to her unusual hair, and behind their hands they would whisper her name—Crystal Revanche.

On this December night, the infamous madam of the Pomeroy house was entertaining a customer herself. Although this was a rare occurrence, as she had ten women working for her, it was not unheard of. When a man wealthy enough or interesting enough to attract her attention requested her for the night, she could be obliging.

Tonight someone had indeed piqued her interest. He was a northern businessman, rather handsome in his own way, and extremely wealthy. It was not the first time he had sought Crystal's favors.

Her private apartment was decorated in bold shades of red wallcovering, accented by glowing brass oil lamps. A large brass bed dominated the room; its covering matched the heavy red drapes on the windows.

They ate a simple meal at a table of imported teak. The chairs they sat on were of a matching wood, with cushions that matched the draperies.

They finished their meal and the dishes were removed. Two bottles of the finest champagne had been placed next to the table in a silver bucket. Crystal herself opened the first bottle, and after pouring it, raised her glass in a silent gesture to the man. When they'd finished the entire bottle, Crystal, already knowing well what the man expected of her, slowly seduced him out of his clothing and into the bed she'd had built especially for herself.

An hour later, with the man temporarily sated, Crystal opened the second bottle of champagne and filled their glasses. After sipping some of the dry, bubbly drink, Crystal lay back on the bolster, her naked breasts gleaming with moisture.

Looking at the man lying next to her, she smiled and waited for him to talk. This was the fourth time he had availed himself of her favors, and Crystal knew that after he made love, he liked to boast of his business acumen. This was the prime reason why she allowed him to grace her bed and use her body.

Tonight he seemed reticent, so Crystal plied him with her own questions. Soon the man was once again bragging proudly of his latest acquisition. When he finished, he smiled and drew her near.

He kissed her, then caressed her breasts as if he owned her as he did his businesses. Crystal did not object. But the man did not yet pursue her body again; instead, he laughed aloud.

"Do you find my body amusing?" Crystal asked from beneath half-lowered eyelids, her lips forming a diminutive pout.

The man shook his head slowly. "No, I find you a wonderful and stimulating companion. I was just thinking how smart you are and how well you utilize your gifts in comparison to another woman I know who is trying to play a man's game."

"And you think that funny?" Crystal asked in a light voice.

"Women should not try to compete in businesses that they cannot handle," he said. "They should content themselves with feminine responsibilities."

"Am I not in business?" Crystal asked, purposely keeping her voice sultry.

"Exactly," the man declared, draining the champagne and holding the glass out to her.

After she refilled it, he smiled again. Then his eyes roamed her breasts, drinking in their fullness. His breathing deepened, and Crystal knew what would happen in a few moments. Still, there was time to learn more.

"Exactly?" She repeated his last word in an effort to get him to continue.

"Yes, you're in business, but it's a business suited to you. It is a woman's business. This other woman is trying to run her late husband's shipping company."

"Oh—but what is wrong with that?" Crystal asked innocently.

"Only one thing. The business is insolvent and riddled with debt. In trying to find a partner to salvage it, she shows how much a fool she is, and how little she knows. Especially," he added after he took a large drink of champagne, "since other interests are after the company. What she needs is a blind fool to back her, not a man with brains."

"I don't understand. Do you mean that there is somebody who is trying to buy her company and she won't sell it to him?"

"Not just somebody—but yes, that is just what I mean. Besides, I'm not stupid enough to waste my money on a doomed business and a virtuous widow." The moment he stopped speaking, he smiled lewdly at Crystal and spilled several drops of champagne onto her breast.

After putting down his glass, he bent and kissed the bubbling liquid from her skin. Knowing that any more questions would have to wait, Crystal put her glass down and wound her fingers into his hair as his mouth grew more demanding on her breasts.

Then Crystal Revanche blanked out her mind, chased every thought away, and willed her body to respond even as disgust with what she was doing welled up within her.

Two hours later, Crystal sat in the large tub, letting the hot water cleanse her body of the man who had left a half hour ago.

Leaning her head on the edge of the tub, Crystal closed her eyes and replayed a later conversation they had had.

"Who is this woman?" Crystal had asked after the man had satisfied himself again.

"Why are you so interested?"

"I am interested in many things. How else can I learn the likes and dislikes of men so that I may please them?"

The answer, as foolishly simplistic as it had been, seemed to satisfy the businessman, and he'd indulged her questions again. "Her name is Alana Landow," he'd told her.

Then, using all the skill she had, she learned that the Landow woman had come to him seeking a partner to help her save both her business and her home. As Crystal had already learned, she had been refused.

As the man spoke, Crystal began to feel the old pains and the anger that went with them. She had not let them surface; rather, she had stroked his chest and smiled inanely at him while he told her everything.

He spoke of a powerful man, part of a consortium that wanted to own the Landow Shipping Company. Crystal's customer had told her that this man had engineered Alana Landow's financial difficulties so that he could get control of her business.

As she had listened to the story, her mind had turned cold. Too many coincidental references had nagged at her. Finally, when the man had seemed to be talked out, she looked down at him, a seductive smile on her face.

"And who is this man who makes you so afraid?" she'd asked in a calculating tone that she knew would evoke the right response from him.

The man lying next to her had sat up, anger registering on his face. "I am afraid of no one."

"Yet you did not try to buy the company outright from the woman. I have heard you talk about taking an opportunity when it is offered. Surely, if she is about to lose her home, you could have made a good deal for yourself."

The man had shaken his head slowly. "That is why you are in this business and not in mine. Crystal, my dear, no one, unless they are as rich as Methusela himself, would go against Charles Ledoque and James Allison."

And with the names of the two men ringing in her ears, Crystal had found out just what she had wanted to know and what she had already half-expected to hear.

From that moment on, until the man had finally left, she had played the innocent, never once mentioning anything more about business.

Crystal opened her eyes and looked at the ceiling. Although the hot water eased some of her tension, it did not help to reduce the knot of hate that had arisen at the mention of Charles Ledoque.

"Poor woman," Crystal whispered as the memories of her own life paraded across her mind like an evil play that had been haunting her for four long and terrible years.

Hearing about Alana's troubles had opened up Crystal's old wounds, bringing back all the terrible times of the past. She remembered being forced to relinquish her family's business in order to save her brother's life. She remembered, too, the leering faces that had laughed at her after she'd signed away everything, telling her that her brother was already dead, hanged as a Federal spy by the Confederate Army.

Shame flooded Crystal. She tried to stop the flow of memories, but she was helpless to do so, and she finally allowed them to go free. As they did, she drew strength from them, reaffirming her resolve and determination.

The day after she had signed the papers and had learned of the duplicity of Caruthers and Murdock and of Rafael's death, she had gone to Abraham Hampton and told him everything. He'd advised her to stay in the house and keep all the doors locked until he had gone to the authorities and set matters to rights.

Crystal had done as he asked. But that night four men had broken into her home. They had attacked her, bound her, and then set fire to the house. The caretaker had discovered them leaving. To her horror, they had beat Jamie senseless and dragged his body into the bushes, leaving him for dead.

And then her nightmare had begun for real. The men had spirited her out of San Francisco that very night, and once they were away from civilization, the four had raped her mercilessly.

A week later, her mind on the verge of insanity, her body battered and bruised, her spirit almost broken, Crystal had found herself in a Nevada mining town, a prisoner in a brothel. She had learned that there was no escape. Yet Crystal had found a spark within the recesses of her mind and had clung to it desperately, knowing that somehow she had to survive and avenge her brother's death and everything that had been done to her.

In order to wreak her revenge, Crystal had made herself accept what was happening. She'd known that to accomplish what she'd set her mind to, she would need money—a lot of money.

So Elizabeth Montgomery had allowed herself to be turned into a whore. She took on the name they gave her, Crystal, and buried the one she had been given at birth. Although she was a prisoner of the bordello, she began to accumulate money from her customers. At the same time, she made a friend in the bordello—the cleaning boy, a mute former slave who was being treated far worse than she.

As horrible as her life had become, Crystal had seen how terrible Chaco's was. She had taken pity on the ill-treated black boy and helped him whenever she could. In return, Chaco would always stay near her, in case one of the bordello's customers decided to beat Crystal up—an occurrence that was not all that unusual.

Within three months, they had formed a bond of friendship that was soon unbreakable. And in that time Crystal had begun to teach Chaco a way to speak.

As part of her life as a wealthy and educated young woman in San Francisco, Crystal had been a volunteer teacher in the school for the deaf and mute, where she had taught young childred to use sign language. In Nevada, Crystal had put that experience to good use. Every day, while the bordello slept, she had taught Chaco how to communicate.

After one year, Crystal had put away enough money to escape. She had told Chaco of her intentions, and he had asked to be taken along. Her plan was simple: Crystal, with the judicious use of a gold piece, had convinced another of the whores to cover for her and use Crystal's room for the night so that she could make her escape.

As it had turned out, she needn't have bothered, for as she

and Chaco were climbing out of a back window, a fire had already started on the lower levels of the building.

In the confusion surrounding the fire, she and Chaco had made their escape. From Nevada, they had gone back to San Francisco, where Crystal knew she could not show herself. But once there, she had spent three weeks investigating the men who had taken over her business.

What she learned in that short amount of time had given her the base from which she would gain her revenge on all of the men involved—and especially on the faceless man who controlled all the others. Caruthers and Murdock had simply followed his orders. She did not learn that man's name, but she did discover another link: A man called Charles Ledoque, who lived in Charleston.

Four months later, Crystal and Chaco had arrived in Charleston, where she had purchased the old Pomeroy house and had set up her business. The money that had flowed into her accounts since then had been put to good use. Within a year, Crystal had learned all she could about Charles Ledoque. As her knowledge increased, she also discovered that Ledoque was but another step upward in the powerful consortium that included Caruthers and Murdock.

When Crystal had arrived in Charleston, she was no longer Elizabeth Montgomery. From the day she stepped into the house on Tadd Street, she had become Crystal Revanche—taking the French word for revenge as her new name.

Rising, Crystal stood and let the water cascade from her luxurious curves. After stepping out of the tub and drying herself, she sat at her dressing table and brushed out her silver-blond hair.

A rush of sadness struck her when she thought of the woman she had yet to meet, Alana Landow. She felt sorry for her because Crystal knew *exactly* what was happening to her.

"And I will help her, if she will let me," Crystal told the green eyes that stared so intensely back at her.

14

January 1867

Alana stared out the window of her hotel sitting room, peering into the gray, overcast day. Her hands were clasped together before her, the knuckles showing white. Her mind was adrift, her thoughts revolving around one single thing—the ten days remaining until Ledoque called in his notes.

For over five weeks, Alana had done everything in her power to find someone who would become her partner. But with each man she'd spoken to, she'd begun to realize more and more the impossibility of her situation.

She had met each businessman with high hopes and an open mind. But time after time, she had left with her hopes dashed. Either they did not want to do business with a woman or they did not want to risk their money on a shipping company that had no contracts and only liabilities.

And, increasingly, Alana thought about Rafe. She wondered what might have been, had she but listened to her heart and gone with him instead of bending to the obligation that had held her to Jason.

A persistent tap called her back to awareness. Smoothing her dress, Alana pulled back her shoulders and walked to the door. The man she had been waiting for, Robert Matthews, had arrived.

Please let him be the one to help me, she silently prayed as her hand hesitated near the large brass knob.

Carlton Dupont had told her of this northern businessman a week ago and had arranged a meeting in his office. When it ended, Matthews had promised Alana that he would give her his answer in a week. He was, she believed, her last hope.

Opening the door, she smiled at Matthews and invited him in. Robert Matthews was not overly tall, and his rotund body had a soft and pampered look. He had a round face partially covered by long sideburns and the chalky complexion of a man who spent too little time out of doors. Still, Alana cared little about his looks. Her only concern was for the help he might give her.

When they were seated across from each other, Matthews spoke. "I have given a great deal of consideration to your proposal."

When he paused, Alana felt herself nod her head as if that action would urge him on. But then she sensed something else in the way he was looking at her. Refusing to let her thoughts get out of hand, Alana waited patiently for him to continue. When he did, she breathed a sigh of relief.

"I must tell you that I am interested in the Landow Shipping Company. However, I cannot accept a forty-nine percent partnership in exchange for bailing your company out of its present financial situation."

Alana stared at him, sensing that he was not yet turning her down. But still she said nothing.

"When I came to Charleston after the war, I did so to increase my own businesses and to diversify into other fields. I can see the long-range possibilities of an investment in Landow Shipping—"

Get to the point! Alana screamed silently to herself.

"—and I would like to become your partner, Alana." When he said her name, the unmistakable intimacy underlying his voice was all too evident. "However, I will require a fifty-five percent share of the company."

"My terms are firm," Alana stated through suddenly clenched teeth. She and Carlton Dupont had gone over the figures enough times to know that forty-nine percent of Landow

Shipping was worth much more than what she was asking. The two remaining ships alone were worth more.

Matthews smiled. "I will relent. Fifty percent, and one other thing."

Alana could think of nothing else she had that he could want. "Yes?"

Matthews moved self-consciously in the chair. His chalky skin took on a pinkish hue. "I have been away from my wife for a long time," he said, each word coming just a little faster than the one before it. As he spoke, his eyes raked blatantly across the swell of her breasts. "I would expect a certain arrangement —a partnership in business as well as—"

"You are disgusting!" Alana spat as she stood to glare angrily down at him.

But Matthews only smiled wider at her outrage. "Do you think I haven't discovered why you're trying to find a partner? I'm your only choice, Alana."

"You, sir," Alana said in chilly tones, "are no choice at all. Leave—now!" Her last word was accented by the upward swing of her arm as she pointed one long, slim finger at the door.

She watched him, hatred pouring from her eyes as the man stood and went to the door. He looked at her once again and sadly shook his head. Then he was gone, and Alana was alone again.

Tears threatened to erupt, but she refused to yield to them. Staring at the closed door, Alana searched desperately within her for some last thread of hope; however, she discovered there was none.

"Oh, Rafe, if only you'd gotten my letter," she whispered. But even the mention of her love's name did not help her rise from her misery. She knew that Rafe would not approach her until she gave him the word, and she sensed that her letter had never arrived.

Slowly Alana sank back into the chair and stared out at the cold gray afternoon, trying to understand what had happened to the world she had once known, in which people helped each other in times of need and did not ask the impossible in payment. She wondered why there was no one, no single soul, who would come forth to help her. It seemed to Alana that this new world she lived in was populated only by those who wanted to use her, either for their profit or their pleasure.

She sat in the chair for a long time, thinking of all the radical changes that her life had gone through in the short span following the war. She was so lost in thought that she did not notice any passage of time, but slowly she became aware of a knocking at the door. Forcing herself to regain her composure, Alana went to the door. Opening it, she found herself face to face with a beautiful, delicately featured woman whose silver-blond hair sparkled jewellike in the low light of the hallway. The woman wore a high-bodiced blue chiffon dress with a collar that reached to just under her chin.

"Yes?"

"Mrs. Landow, may I speak with you please?" Crystal Revanche asked.

Puzzled, Alana motioned the woman in and then walked with her to the two chairs. After they were seated, Alana raised her eyebrows in question.

"My name is Crystal Revanche."

Alana stifled a gasp. She had recognized the name immediately and was shocked that the most notorious madam in Charleston was sitting across from her.

Suddenly Alana laughed. Her pent-up emotions broke free with her laughter. It took her a moment to control herself, and when she did, she found her laughter had brought tears to her eyes.

"Are you here to recruit me?" she asked in a bitter voice.

"Recruit you?" Crystal asked, puzzled.

"Yes. Everyone seems to want my body for their own purposes. At least you make no pretense about who you are and what you do."

Crystal's eyes widened. Then she too laughed. "No, Mrs. Landow, I am not here to offer you one of my beds. But I am here to help you," she stated.

"Help me?" Alana asked in surprise. "How?"

"I've heard of your problems, and I know you're looking for a business partner. I am in a position to be of service to you."

"But why? Are you planning on closing down your, ah— business?"

"Not at all. Mrs. Landow, I am offering you what you need. I will become your partner in the shipping business and pay off *all* your debts to Charles Ledoque. In return, I will need something from you."

"As usual," Alana said dryly. "Isn't the shipping company enough?"

Crystal rose from the chair and went to the window. She spoke as she looked out. "I have learned that in life there are many compromises. It is a lesson that perhaps you too must learn." Turning back to Alana, Crystal shrugged her shoulders. "You see, the good people of Charleston have recovered admirably from the war, or so it seems. They are beginning to reset order within the town; they are doing their best to close all the businesses that are not, as they say, in the best interests of their society.

"In other words," Crystal continued, "they're cleaning up Charleston, and the first thing to go will be businesses such as mine. Bordellos have outlived their usefulness now that most of the soldiers have left; Charleston's virtuous young women no longer have to fear their lusty advances."

Alana, listening intently to Crystal's words, was unable to understand what the woman was getting at. "But how will a partnership with me help you?"

"Before I explain that, there is something else I must say."

Alana found herself drawn into the intense yet warm green eyes of the woman while she waited for Crystal to continue.

Before she continued, Crystal returned to the chair. Sitting gracefully, she interlocked her fingers and placed her hands on her lap. She stared at her upturned palms for a moment before focusing on Alana's face.

"I was not always a whore, Mrs. Landow. In fact, my family was once quite wealthy. But—but certain things happened, and I am now as you know me. But I am not ashamed of what I do." Crystal paused to marshal her thoughts, knowing that she had almost said too much.

"Suffice it to say for now that I heard of your dilemma and that I despise Charles Ledoque. I am willing to be your partner and to help you make Landow Shipping into a profitable business. To do that, more money is needed than just the amount of your debts. In order to have that money available, I must stay in business."

Finally, Alana understood what Crystal Revanche was trying to say. She stiffened in spite of herself, and her eyes widened with the final revelation of Crystal's proposal. Before Alana could speak, Crystal slowly nodded.

"I see you understand. Riverbend is far enough away from Charleston so that the *good people* will not be overly upset. Yet it is close enough to Charleston to be convenient. Riverbend will be the way for me to stay in business, and the money that flows into its doors will be the means by which Landow Shipping will grow."

Alana knew that her jaw had dropped halfway to her chest, but she could not control her wildly spinning mind.

Crystal stood again, a shadowy smile on her face. "Now that I have truly shocked you, I will leave you to think over my offer. When are the notes due?"

"T-ten days," Alana whispered.

"I will contact you in a week. If you are in agreement—if you want to be your own woman and control your own life without someone else ruling over you—remember that I offer you the way. Good day, Mrs. Landow."

With that, Crystal Revanche turned and let herself out. In the hallway, she nodded her head to a figure in the shadow, and a tall black man stepped out of his concealment. With a rapid motion of her hand, she spoke to Chaco. The word she signed described simply what she felt—*perhaps.*

Inside her hotel room, Alana struggled with her stormy thoughts, wondering how she could even consider what Madame Revanche had asked.

Forcefully, Alana made herself stop floundering and think clearly. The ramifications of Crystal Revanche's offer were unending. Without any doubt, Alana would be labeled a whore. She would be looked down upon by everyone she had ever known. She would be dirtying the memory of her entire family, and of Jason's family as well.

Then she thought of the alternative: life with Charles Ledoque. It was a terrifying vision that filled her with the chill of death. *Would I be any less a whore with him?* she wondered.

More confused than ever, Alana did her best to push everything from her mind. Standing, she went into the bedroom and to the door that connected it with the servant's room. She knocked once and opened the door.

She smiled at Kitty and spoke with new determination. "It's time to pack and return to Riverbend," she told her.

Rafe paced angrily in the office of the Magee and Montgomery Mining Company. In the room with him were Abigail Hampton and Caleb Magee.

They had chosen this building to open their San Francisco offices because it was located near enough to the waterfront to be useful and far enough away not to attract any undue attention.

For three months, Rafe had been busy setting up the offices, hiring people he knew would be loyal and spending whatever free time he had investigating the company that had taken over Montgomery Shipping. But by the time Caleb had come to San Francisco from the desert mine, Rafe had found himself no closer to the answers he needed. And now, as he made plans to learn more, Caleb and Abigail both rose against him.

"Son, you can't just walk in there and ask them questions."

"I can't?" Rafe replied in a tense voice, his features stiff. "Watch me."

"Rafael, Caleb is right. They killed Abraham and as good as killed Elizabeth with their own hands. Do you think they won't do the same to you?" Abigail asked.

"Not if they don't get the chance."

"By marching yourself into that building, you're giving them that chance. Son, I didn't spend those long months riding the desert with you to see you get yourself killed now," Caleb said in a low voice. "The least you can do is to take some advice."

Rafe looked at the old prospector and then at Abigail. He saw the barely perceptible nod of her head and exhaled slowly as he sat on his chair.

"Go ahead," Rafe ordered Caleb.

"We're rich now, you and me and Abigail," Caleb began, smiling warmly at Abigail Hampton. The three of them each held an equal share in the mine and the mining company.

"And if I'm not mistaken," he continued in a level voice, "the reason you wanted to become rich was to avenge the people who took what was yours. You can't do that if you're dead.

Use the money. Damn it, son, we got plenty now. Use the money to lure them."

"Don't you think I've been trying to do just that? They won't rise to the bait," Rafe stated.

"Have you given them the right bait?" Caleb asked wisely.

"What is the right bait?" Rafe shot back.

"It sure in hell ain't what you've been trying, is it? Besides, we ain't got much time before I got to go back to the mine."

"You don't have to rush back. Tom McPherson can be trusted," Rafe said without any doubts. Tom McPherson had been the man in charge of the Montgomery Company's warehouses. He had lost his job when Elizabeth signed over the papers.

When Rafe had found McPherson, and the man had recovered from seeing Rafe's ghost, they'd talked for several hours. Rafe knew McPherson had had nothing to do with the company's loss, and he offered him the mining job, which he'd accepted immediately.

"I don't doubt McPherson," Caleb said, "I just don't like to be away from the mine for too long."

Rafe nodded his head. "All right, Caleb. What do you have in mind?"

"We have to make them trust us. And they can't know who you are. So," he began, "buy one or two small businesses, the type of business that would need a shipping company, and maybe an exporter." After pausing to fix Rafe with a knowledgeable stare, he continued to outline his idea. When he was finished, Rafe smiled, but Abigail looked apprehensive.

"It's very risky," she told both of them, but Rafe saw the special look that she favored Caleb with, and he found himself somewhat surprised.

"We'll be careful," Caleb promised her.

"Okay, Caleb, I'll try it your way for now. But it will take more time than I want to spend."

"Son, anything worth the while takes time. I waited thirty-five years to find that mine; I think you can wait a few months to find the people you're lookin' for."

"But I won't wait too long, Caleb." Rafe's words were both statement and warning, and his hardened eyes backed up his tone.

* * *

"Alana, chile', I sure hopes you knows what you're a-doin'," Lorelei said as she looked at Alana's strained features.

Alana shrugged her shoulders. Not a waking minute in the past week had been spent without thoughts of Crystal Revanche's offer. When she'd returned to Riverbend, she had told Lorelei about the strange turn of events.

Lorelei had said nothing, but Alana had seen the effect of her words on her housekeeper and friend. "I'm damned if I do and damned if I don't, aren't I, Lorelei?"

"I doesn't know about that, chile', I doesn't."

Alana drew her eyes from Lorelei and looked out again at the plantation. Today was the day she would have to give Crystal Revanche her answer, and she had yet to decide what that answer would be.

"If my mother were alive, she would never forgive me for turning Riverbend into a whorehouse."

"Chile', your mother ain't alive, and if'n she were, she would expect you to do what was right fo' you and fo' Riverbend, an' only dat!"

"But Lorelei, what *is* right?"

Lorelei looked away from Alana and took a deep breath. "Alana, dat answer be only in one place, chile', in your heart. Jus' like it was when Mister Rafe be staying here." When she finished speaking, Lorelei did not look at Alana.

"You knew all along, didn't you?" Alana whispered.

"Yes," Lorelei replied.

Alana had nothing to say. Thinking of Rafe made her wonder for the thousandth time if he had gotten her letter, but she was sure he had not. She knew, with the deep certainty of the love they had shared, that if he had, he would have come to her. "Is everything set out in the salon?" Alana asked.

"Yes'm," Lorelei replied.

Alana nodded absently while she looked toward the drive. Then she heard the sound of a horse and carriage. *She's here,* Alana thought, still fighting to make her decision. When the carriage, an exquisitely wrought English brougham, came into view, Alana went to the edge of the drive. After the brougham stopped, the tall, thin black driver left his seat and went to help Crystal Revanche out.

Once on the ground, Crystal smiled at Alana and looked around. "You have a magnificent home," she said.

"Thank you," Alana replied, feeling proud despite the strange circumstances. "Shall we go inside, or would you like to walk around a bit? I know it's been a long ride for you."

Crystal studied Alana's face. "I wouldn't want to be disappointed. Let's talk inside first."

Alana nodded her head and started to turn, but she stopped to look back at the driver, who still stood beside the carriage. Then she looked up at the veranda. "Lorelei, would you see to the driver?"

Lorelei came down the steps and spoke to the driver. The man did not respond or move to get up on the carriage again.

"He cannot speak, but he understands," Crystal told her. "Go with her, Chaco, I will be fine."

The moment Crystal spoke to him, Chaco nodded his head, made several motions with his hands, and then went up to the driver's seat. Lorelei joined him there and pointed out the direction.

"What was that he did?" Alana asked when the carriage drove away.

"He spoke to me. Chaco was one of the last of the illegal slaves brought into the country before the war. He was only ten at the time, and he never spoke. I taught him to speak with his hands. What he signed—said to me, was that he would stay nearby if I needed him."

"He is your servant?" Alana asked while she digested this interesting piece of information.

"In a manner of speaking, but you might say that he is more my friend than my servant." Crystal stared openly at Alana. "Does that shock you?"

This time Alana smiled. "Should it?"

Crystal shrugged her shoulders. "You were a slaveholder until after the war."

"No," Alana replied, "as a matter of fact, I had no slaves during the war. No human being should own another." Crystal's eyebrows arched, but she said nothing; instead, she followed Alana up the steps and into the house.

Five minutes later they were seated on the long settee in the salon. Lorelei poured tea and uncovered the small pastries that the cook had prepared for them.

When Crystal put down her cup, her eyes locked with Alana's. "Have you made your decision yet?"

Alana held the other woman's gaze for a long moment before she spoke. Her reply was simple. "Yes, I have."

15

Alana continued to hold Crystal's gaze as she spoke. "I had made no decision until just this moment. I've thought about everything you said to me in Charleston and agonized over whether I could do what you asked to Riverbend."

When Alana stopped speaking, Crystal let go of the breath she'd been holding. She studied the lines of tension accenting Alana's drawn features, and a heavy sense of loss overtook her. She had hoped that she and Alana could join forces to stop Ledoque and learn about the consortium. But beneath her hopes, she'd known that Alana Landow was still a southern aristocrat and not the type of woman who would go against her upbringing.

"I see," Crystal whispered.

Alana, realizing that Crystal had taken her words to be her answer, quickly shook her head. "No, I don't think you do. I have decided to accept your offer, Madame Revanche."

Crystal's surprise made her speechless. And in the few seconds that Crystal stared wide-eyed at Alana, her spirits rose.

However, she held back her elation for a moment longer because there was still more that had to be said. Exhaling slowly, Crystal began to speak. "You realize that you will be tarnishing your good name. That you will feel the ostracism that is part of being associated with whores. You will become alienated from all your friends."

"But I will not be a whore. I will be a businesswoman only!" Alana stated unequivocally.

"Nevertheless," Crystal stated, "your neighbors and the good people of Charleston will call you a whore."

"Aren't those good people the same ones who are standing idly by watching me lose everything? No, Madame Revanche, I don't care what they say. I know who and what I am. To accept Charles Ledoque's terms would make me a whore in fact, if not in name. We will be partners, Madame Revanche—or have you now changed your mind?"

"We will be partners," Crystal declared, and a smile of genuine warmth and liking for Alana wreathed her face.

Ledoque and James Allison sat across from each other in the darkened office. Allison, smoking a cigar as was his wont, slowly shook his head.

"Forget the woman. You did exactly what we set out to do. You converted the Montpelier contracts. The last two ships would have made a good addition, but we don't need them—we already have the other three."

"I won't give up in this. I want the woman, James, and I intend to have her, with or without her ships. Besides, she defied me and tried to make a fool out of me. I won't stand for that."

"Whatever, but don't let it interfere with our business," Allison warned.

"Have I ever let anything do that, James?" Ledoque asked with a nasty smile on his face.

"Not yet," Allison replied.

"What about the South African routes?" Ledoque inquired.

Allison blew out a stream of smoke. "That is going very well at present. My tooling company has been awarded a contract by Maklin-Parkins for mining equipment. They have also given our new company, Marquette Shipping, the exclusive trade rights for America. Yes, everything is going well. We have an office and warehousing in Cape Town, and I am negotiating with Parkins to form a new partnership with the consortium. Judging by his latest communication, he seems interested."

"Very good," Ledoque said approvingly.

"Yes, it is. And now, Charles, the figures for the last quarter?"

Ledoque reached to the stack of papers on the table and handed them to Allison. He knew that when Allison was finished, the consortium would be extremely pleased with the gains he had made in the past three months and with the almost-total control he was gaining in all the southern ports.

But as James Allison went over the figures, Ledoque's mind was busy with the question of Alana Landow. She would have to be taught a lesson, and so would the whore who had helped her to escape from him!

Four months after Alana handed Charles Ledoque a bank draft for the entire forty thousand dollars, she discovered that Crystal had become more than just a partner—she had become a friend.

Riverbend was now considered by all to be a bordello, and Alana herself was openly called a whore, but she had not once regretted doing what had been necessary.

It had taken a full month of whirlwind activity and hard work to organize the house and set it up so that it could function as a real home as well as a . . . business.

It seemed as if the old plantation house had been built with Crystal's plans already in mind. Everything on the main floor remained the same: The salon was now the place where the men awaited their ladies and were served refreshments; the library and study became the private offices of Alana and Crystal. Upstairs the master bedroom suite continued to be Alana's private domain. Her old bedroom suite became Crystal's. The five bedrooms down the hall were turned into shared living quarters for the ten girls Crystal brought with her. The five large two-room suites in the guest wing were restructured into ten bedrooms without any major work required.

The one very important item that the two women had decided on was that Riverbend the plantation would stay separate from Riverbend the bordello. Alana ran the plantation with the same determination and iron will with which Crystal ran her business, and by the time the second month of business ended, the money was, as Crystal predicted, flowing through the door.

The women had bought a riverboat and hired a captain to

bring customers to Riverbend via the Ashley. However, Alana still utilized Captain Bowers and his boat for plantation business whenever possible.

The partnership agreement had been drawn up by Carlton Dupont, and although he had voiced reservations about this new partnership, he had not condemned Alana as the others had.

The Landow Shipping business was looked after by Crystal, who, showing unexpected expertise, began to get small but lucrative contracts. It took Alana several weeks before she realized that invariably two days after Crystal "entertained" a man herself, a new commission would come to Landow Shipping.

Knowing that she had agreed to everything Crystal had set up, Alana kept her own counsel about what she saw and thought.

Slowly over the months Alana and Crystal's relationship began to change in little ways—the confiding of some small thing, the way one would look after the other, the opening of their minds to each other, and the caring that both women showed.

But the friendship that was building was cemented one early spring morning.

Alana was having a solitary breakfast when she heard the shouts of Jeremy, Ben's son, as he ran toward the house. Going out to the veranda she saw Jeremy's tear-streaked face and knew something terrible had happened.

"What is it?" she called as she raced down the steps.

"De horses," he said between shallow breaths.

"The mare? The foal?" Alana screamed. But Jeremy couldn't speak—all he could do was look at her with huge, tear-filled eyes.

Rather than try to get the answer from him, Alana had run to the stables where the stallion and the mare were kept.

The mare had been nearing her time to deliver, and anything could have happened. But when Alana got there, she discovered a truth more horrible than anything she had imagined. When she looked into the stallion's stall, her stomach twisted sickeningly.

Clamping her teeth together, she fought off nausea and made herself look at the mutilated horse. Then she climbed over the railing and walked to the mare's stall. When she got there, a wave of blind agony rushed through her. The mare was dead, too, horribly mutilated. The foal was still within the mother's womb.

Her scream reached out to shake the very foundations of her mind; rage and fury darkened her soul at this desecration of life.

She did not know how long she stood staring at the mare, her mind mired in hate. She might never have moved, but Crystal had taken her in her arms and pulled her away.

She heard Crystal shouting orders to the workers. Then she found herself sitting on the settee with Crystal and Lorelei both hovering above her.

A few moments later, she spoke. "Why?" she asked Crystal. "Who would do this?"

Crystal's face tightened; her eyes looked distant. "Don't you know?"

Alana started to say no but stopped herself when she saw something in Crystal's green eyes. "He wouldn't do that," she whispered.

Crystal said nothing; the hard set of her face was answer enough.

"Why? Why would Ledoque kill the horses?"

"Because he knew how much you valued them. Because he knew it would hurt you!"

She heard the truth in Crystal's words. "I will kill him!" Alana swore, her mind a black mass of rage.

"No, you shall not, Alana, but he will pay. As God is my witness, he will pay."

It was in that moment that Alana knew she and Crystal had truly become one in their quest to fight Charles Ledoque, and with that understanding, her heart opened fully to Crystal.

"We will make him pay!" Alana affirmed with the same vehemence as Crystal.

From then on, the two women spent each morning together. They concentrated on working out ways in which they could build their shipping business up to the point where they could start to hurt Ledoque and possibly even regain the Montpelier contracts.

In the early evenings, before most of the men arrived, Crystal and Alana would sit together over dinner and talk about themselves. At first they had spoken in generalities, but as their relationship grew, so did their trust in each other. Alana found herself confiding in Crystal perhaps because she had never had this close a friendship with another woman near her own age, although Crystal was four years her senior.

She often talked about Jason and the hopes she'd had for them. One night she even spoke to Crystal about the hard times at the beginning of her marriage.

"Was there no one else besides Jason?" Crystal had asked in a soft voice.

Alana had started to shake her head but stopped when she looked into the openness of Crystal's eyes. "Yes, there was," she whispered truthfully. "He was a wonderful man, and I still love him completely. But it was a love that could not be." She never once spoke Rafe's name.

"Because of your promise to Jason?"

"Because of my duty to Riverbend and my obligations to Jason."

"Your . . . other love sounds like a good man," Crystal said.

"A strong man also, for if he had not been, I would have gone with him rather than stay here and face the loss of life without him."

"It could be argued that he was a fool for letting you send him away."

After a brief surge of anger, Alana smiled slowly. "He was not a fool. And one day he shall return for me." Once the words left her lips, she realized that it was the first time she had voiced her secret dream aloud.

Alana saw more questions forming on Crystal's face, but she appreciated the way Crystal held herself back from voicing them.

"I hope so, Alana, I truly do," Crystal said.

A few moments later, Crystal spoke again. But when she asked her next question, her voice was hesitant. "Do you—I mean, after loving only one man, and then living for a year with another who could not make love to you, do you not find yourself wanting a man?"

Again Alana started to take offense at Crystal's words, but she sensed that there was more to the question than Crystal had asked.

Slowly she shook her head. "Only when I think of—" Alana stopped herself from mentioning Rafe's name. She would not do that, ever. It was hers alone to know and speak within her mind, until that day when he might again claim her love. "Only when I think of him. But I have never desired another man."

"I have never desired any man," Crystal stated suddenly.

Alana stared at her in surprise. "But you're—you are a—"

"Being a whore does not mean I hunger for a man's touch, Alana," Crystal said with a hard smile. "You know I was forced to become a whore."

"But you chose to stay one after you had escaped."

"What could I do? No man would love me after learning I was a whore."

"Need he have to learn?"

"I would have to tell him. I would not hide so harsh a secret from a man. It would be wrong. It would be a lie."

"There will be someone," Alana had said.

"I think not. You see, it takes all my willpower not to scream when a man touches me. I hate it, Alana—I hate it with every inch of my being."

"Then why?"

"How else could I make the money I do? How else could I have been able to help you? I have something that must be accomplished in my lifetime, and I will not stop until I have done it!"

Alana had nothing to say to that, but that admission had told her more about Crystal than anything else ever could have.

When they both stood, Alana to retire to her room for the night, Crystal to go to work, Alana went over to Crystal and suddenly, impulsively embraced her.

"Thank you, Crystal, for everything."

They held each other for several minutes, and when they parted, both women's eyes were misty.

A few nights after that, they were again sitting in the dining room, once more talking about their lives, when Crystal began to talk about her brother. Crystal found it too painful to mention her brother by name, and indeed she was reluctant to discuss him at all. She revealed only that her brother had been ordered to be killed by those who wanted to take over the family business.

Alana saw that Crystal held herself responsible for her brother's death and her losing the business.

In order to help Crystal with her sadness, Alana deftly changed the subject. "What about Chaco? I have never seen a black man so devoted to a white woman."

"I had been afraid that it might offend you," Crystal said after she'd gained control over her emotions.

"Why?" Alana asked, puzzled, remembering the conversation the first time Chaco and Crystal had come to Riverbend.

"Because he is always near me. It would not be the first time someone thought him to be my lover."

"No," Alana said with a curt shake of her head. "It is clear that he is devoted to you as a son to his mother or a brother to his sister."

"You are wiser than you let on," Crystal said. Then she told Alana the story of Chaco's life—of his being taken from Africa when he was a child and sold in the black market of the Caribbean islands and then brought to the South. When the war had started, his master had sold him to a slaver who had taken Chaco west. By the end of the war, he had been sold again, not really as a slave, but a fee was paid for his services to the bordello where Crystal worked. She explained how their friendship grew and of Chaco's devotion to her.

After hearing the story, Alana understood not only the relationship between Chaco and Crystal but also just how good a woman Crystal Revanche was.

And so, one pleasantly warm April day, with the sun pouring through the window, Alana was not surprised when Crystal threw open the door of her study.

"It is time," Crystal proclaimed.

"Time?" Alana asked with raised eyebrows.

"I spent all night going over the figures for Landow Shipping. Even with the small contracts we get from time to time, it is not enough. Unless we do something, we shall never be able to hurt Ledoque! We must find a European or Oriental contract."

"How?"

"Alana, in order to be successful, really successful, a shipping company must have either an office in a major port or an agent in that port." Crystal paused only long enough for her words to sink in to Alana's mind. "Before we can decide on either of those options, we must decide on whether we want to go after the European or the Oriental trade."

For the first time, Alana spoke. "European. The Oriental routes must be handled from the West Coast. That's too far from here."

"Agreed," Crystal stated. "Then we'll go after European shipping. Now," she said as she sat across from Alana, "do we hire an agent or open an office?"

Alana would never recover from Ledoque's treachery as an agent. "An agent will be too costly and too risky. How do we know who to trust?"

"Exactly. That's why we must open our own office out of Charleston."

"But—"

"Ledoque presently controls Charleston and the South. We can't fight him here. We must do it from afar and return to take him on when we are strong enough! We will have to use an agent at the beginning; however, it will not be the usual arrangement. We will secure an agent only for the first European contract. Even then, we will be using the agent only as a broker. After that we will handle all our own business affairs."

"Good," Alana said, still waiting for Crystal to explain everything.

"Our next problem is this: Who will go to New York and set up our office?"

Alana stared at Crystal, unsure of what she should say. There was only one clear thought in her mind. "I—I can't run a whorehouse," she whispered.

Crystal's laugh was light and musical. "I know that, Alana. But I can run a whorehouse and also manage your plantation while you're away."

"When?" Alana asked hesitantly.

"Not for a while. We have much to do. A few months at the earliest."

Leaving Riverbend was the last thing Alana wanted to do, but she let the memory of the pain Charles Ledoque had caused surface. "All right," she said in a strong voice.

She saw a figure by the open door but ignored it as Crystal outlined more of the details of what they would be doing. Alana was uneasy at the way the shadowy shape had moved past her study, but soon she was lost within Crystal's words as she gave Crystal her full attention.

Charles Ledoque stared at the beautiful young woman who stood before him in his private study at his residence. His eyes roamed over her as his tongue moistened his lips. Her dress was low cut and tight across her breasts, giving him an unrestricted view of deep cleavage.

"What news have you brought me?" he asked the young prostitute.

"News enough to earn my money," she said confidently.

"Let's hear it."

The woman smiled for a moment before she spoke. "Crystal and Alana are going to open an office in New York. They think that they can build enough of a business to be able to hurt you."

"Do they?" Ledoque asked absently as he continued to stare at the woman. "When will they take this, ah—bold step?"

"Crystal told Alana they would do it in a few months."

"Tell me everything they said, everything!" Ledoque demanded.

When the woman finished, Ledoque handed her several gold coins. But instead of leaving, she stayed and smiled brazenly at him. "You've paid for more than I gave you. Do you want something else?" she asked in invitation.

Ledoque's eyes turned hard. "Do you find me attractive?" he asked.

"Oh yes," she whispered in a husky, seductive voice.

"No, my dear, it's my money that attracts you, nothing else. And that is how I want it. Go back and be a whore. Keep your eyes and ears open. Report anything to me about the dealings of those two women, anything at all!"

The woman knew when to leave and did so, aware of the vast amount of money she could make by giving Ledoque only small pieces of information at a time.

When she was gone, Ledoque sat back, a satisfied smile on his face. "So you want to hurt me, do you, Alana? You'll never be able to do that, my sweet."

Suddenly Ledoque laughed. When his laughter died, his face

turned hard and his eyes darkened. In his mind he already had her and was taking his pleasure of her slowly, very, very slowly, almost as slowly as he had killed the stallion and the broodmare.

16

May 1967

A month after Alana and Crystal had decided the future of
Landow Shipping, Alana was in her office opening a letter that
had just arrived from Carlton Dupont. When she finished reading, her thoughts took off in a wild fancy of imagination and
hope. Forcing a modicum of restraint on herself, she left the
office to find Crystal. She didn't have far to go, as Crystal was
already at her own desk in the library.

Alana fairly danced in, released the letter, and watched it
float down onto Crystal's desk. "I think we just got very lucky,"
Alana stated.

After reading the letter, Crystal smiled broadly. "It does look
that way. I guess this means that you'll be going to new York
sooner than we had planned."

"But why? If this commission works out, surely we can still
run everything from here?"

Crystal shook her head emphatically. "Now it's even more
important that we open an office in New York."

Silence fell while they both thought about the change the
letter signified. The commission had been forwarded by Carlton
Dupont, whom the women had decided to keep on as the company's lawyer, despite his own protestations that he had failed
Alana once.

The commission was for Landow Shipping to deliver a con-

signment of goods to New York, where it would then pick up a
second consignment of equipment destined for Cape Hope,
South Africa. The return shipment would be materials ear-
marked for Charleston.

It was the largest contract they had been offered since becoming partners and one that they knew they could not turn down
—the profit from this one triangular commission would be too
high.

"This will be the start of our becoming a large shipping company," Crystal prophesied. "It's the chance we've been looking
for!"

"Then we'd best go to Charleston."

"Yes," Crystal agreed.

An hour later, Alana, Crystal, and Chaco were on the
riverboat, heading to Charleston. Lilith, Crystal's assistant, was
taking charge of Riverbend in their absence.

In Charleston they went directly to Dupont's office, where
they learned the details of the commission and of Carlton Dupont's doubts.

"I don't like it at all," Dupont stated after handing the
women the contract. "I've never heard of this company, and I
must object to their conditions."

Gazing at Dupont, Alana sensed a change in the older lawyer
—a positive change. Carlton Dupont seemed to have shed several years since she'd last seen him. He was more animated and
much more like the man she had always remembered—a dis-
penser of good sense.

"But it is a standard clause," Crystal stated after glancing at
the loss/reimbursement section.

"For a large shipping company, perhaps, one that can afford
the new maritime insurance—but not for you. If your ship is
lost, not even the sale of Riverbend will be sufficient to reimburse the company."

"Then we mustn't lose the shipment," Alana declared.

"Are there any other reasons for you to object to this contract?" Crystal asked Dupont in a level voice.

"A feeling I have. Whatever that may be worth."

"Is it possible that you're being overcautious because of
Ledoque?"

"Of course it is," Dupont said with an irritated shrug. "But even considering that, can Landow risk the loss of one of its two ships?"

Alana's mind was already made up as she looked at Crystal for support. "We know that it was Ledoque who cost us our ships, not the vagaries of the sea. Uncle Carlton, we may never get another chance like this."

"I still feel it my duty to advise against accepting this commission," the lawyer reaffirmed.

"Crystal?" Alana asked.

Crystal looked from Dupont to Alana. But when she spoke, her question was directed to Dupont. "I take it you investigated this agent?"

"I did. I telegraphed an inquiry to an attorney in New York whom I've known for a long time. Nathan Bennet is a man whom I trust implicitly. His reply was that Jonathan Martin is an independent agent of the highest repute."

"Why doesn't that satisfy you?" Crystal asked.

"I keep asking myself the same question," Dupont remarked. Leaning back in the chair, the lawyer ran his fingers through his thin white hair in a thoughtful gesture. "It does not satisfy me because I don't know the agent personally. He could be another of Ledoque's minions."

"He could be," Crystal agreed, "but if we think like that every time we're offered a commission, we'll never grow. Landow Shipping will be doomed to extinction. No, I agree with Alana, we must take the chance."

"Very well," Dupont said. "Sign this contract, and I shall pray that you are both right and I am wrong."

"So shall we," Alana added as she looked at her father's friend. Thanking Dupont for his advice and help, Alana asked him to make arrangements with the lawyer in New York to begin the process of setting up an office for Landow Shipping.

After leaving Dupont's office, the women went to Tadd Street and the house that served no longer as a bordello but rather as the city residence for Alana and Crystal. Once there, the women ate a light dinner that the housekeeper prepared for them.

They would return to Riverbend in the morning, but tonight, Crystal had declared, would be one of celebration and planning.

The two women talked well into the night as they made their

plans. When they finally went to sleep, they were unaware that Chaco, who had been close by, went downstairs to seat himself near the front door.

For Chaco had heard everything they had planned and knew that until Crystal had succeeded in defeating her enemy, he might strike at any time.

Chaco would never allow that to happen, never.

Rafe paced the confines of the office, looking more like a trapped lion than a rich businessman. His tall, powerful body was tense; the expensive shirt he wore did not hide the rippling muscles of his chest as he stalked angrily back and forth.

"No more!" Rafe stated. Stopping, he fixed Caleb Magee with a hard glare. "I listened to you. We did things your way. We did everything we could, but we learned nothing! Now I'm going to do it my way!"

Caleb did not immediately reply. When he did, he stared directly into Rafe's narrowed eyes. "Son, I can't help but agree with you." His admission made Rafe's tight features ease.

"No!" Abigail Hampton protested. "It's too dangerous. Give it a little more time."

Rafe shook his head in denial. "How much more time, Abigail? We've spent months trying to learn who is behind Caruthers and Murdock. Even after they accepted me as a businessman looking for a shipping company, they never gave the slightest hint about who is controlling them. I know damned well it wasn't they who took my business."

"How can you be so sure?" Abigail challenged, her wise eyes no longer looking old but strong and probing.

"They had one small office before the war. They were pariahs who lived off the leavings of others. They were nothing. But three months after I left, they owned my company. They had neither the brains nor the money to do that. Someone smart and powerful is behind them. That's who I want."

Abigail nodded her head. "But I still don't agree that the use of force will get you any more answers."

"We'll know in an hour, won't we?" Rafe said simply.

"I think I'd best go with you, son," Caleb said.

Rafe shook his head. "Not this time, Caleb." With that, Rafe picked up the jacket he had carelessly tossed onto a chair and left the office.

Behind him, Caleb looked at Abigail. "I don't think I should be staying here," he said.

"Neither do I, Caleb. Rafe's a good man. He's young and strong and hotheaded. But he's also being controlled by his hate. That's dangerous, Caleb, very dangerous. He could make a mistake because of that—a fatal mistake."

"I don't know, Abigail. Rafe's burning up inside. The only way it's going to stop is when he finds out who tried to destroy him. I think he can control his temper, at least until he finds out the name of his enemy. And I know he can damn well take care of himself. It's the unknown—the people he's going up against —that worries me."

"Then you'd best be going along, Caleb."

"Yeah, I guess so." Just before he left, he bent and took Abigail into his arms. His lips covered hers for a quick moment. When he drew his head back, he saw the sparkle in her eyes.

"Just make sure that both of you come back, Caleb Magee!"

"There ain't a thing that's going to stop me from doing that, Abigail," he promised.

When Caleb left the office, there was a special smile on his face, a smile that matched, to the very last detail, the one on Abigail Hampton's face. But he pushed all of that from his thoughts and followed Rafe through the back door of the office building that was just closing down for the day.

Rafe walked up the wooden stairs at exactly six o'clock, his every step catlike and quiet. He knew his destination, and he knew, too, that the office manager would be the last person to leave for the day. He had watched the building for two weeks and knew the routine.

Once he had realized that neither Caruthers or Murdock would let slip the name of the man, or men, behind them, he had dropped that line of questioning shortly after they'd sat down to discuss the shipping contract that had been Rafe's ploy to meet with them.

This week both men were out of town, and Rafe believed that of all the people in the company, the office manager, Reginald Harris, by the necessity of his position, would have to know all the details of the business. Rafe had two ideas in mind for when he talked to the man. The first was an outright bribe; the second —he preferred not to think of that yet.

Rafe stopped at the back door of the second-floor office. Putting his ear to the door, he listened intently for any sounds on the other side. His body hummed with tension and his blood raced through his veins, building a sharp edge to his anticipation.

When he was satisfied that no one except the office manager was in the room, he stepped back. Taking a deep preparatory breath, Rafe lunged forward, slamming his shoulder into the wood.

He ignored the jarring pain in his shoulder as the lock snapped. An instant later he was inside, facing the wide-eyed office manager, who had been halfway to the other door on his way out of the office.

"Who are you? What is the meaning of this?" the man demanded. "We keep no money here," he added quickly.

"Mr. Harris," Rafe began as he nonchalantly straightened his jacket, "I am here to make you an offer, not to rob you."

The office manager was backing away from what he assumed to be a madman. For the moment, Rafe let him think that.

"What kind of an offer does someone bring when they break into a private office?" A nervous tremor laced his words.

"An offer of five thousand dollars in exchange for certain information," Rafe stated in a flat, unemotional voice.

The man's eyes shifted skittishly. "What kind of information?"

"Caruthers and Murdock have a partner. I want to know who it is."

"Partner? Don't be ridiculous," Harris said. He had backed against his desk as he spoke, and when his words ended, he raced around to the other side.

"I'm being far from ridiculous, Mr. Harris. It's a fair offer." Watching the man carefully, Rafe did not miss the way his hand crept toward the desk drawer.

"I wouldn't do anything foolish," Rafe advised, his voice still flat and unemotional.

"Get out."

"You will not consider my offer?" Even as he spoke, Rafe's muscles tensed; his legs were ready to spring him forward.

"I'll tell you what I'll consider," Harris half shouted. Moving quickly, he opened the drawer.

Rafe launched himself at Harris as he lifted a short-barreled pistol. Time seemed to slow as Rafe's leg uncoiled, sending him arcing through the air toward Harris.

Rafe's hand locked onto Harris's wrist. The force of his lunge carried him all the way across the desk. His shoulder rammed into Harris's midsection, and he heard the man's loud grunt mix with the clatter of falling debris.

Then he and Harris were on the floor, Rafe struggling to disarm the man, Harris fighting to shoot Rafe. As they fought, Harris shouted loudly for help. But an instant later, Rafe knocked the gun from Harris's grip and was pulling the man to his feet.

Using Harris's lapels as levers, Rafe hauled Harris to his feet just as the door burst open and two dockworkers charged in.

"Get him!" Harris yelled, twisting vainly in Rafe's grip. The men advanced on him, and Rafe saw that both were large, burly men, used to lifting hundreds of pounds without thinking about it.

Moving quickly, Rafe shoved Harris at the worker on his left and dove toward the other. Before the bigger man could react, Rafe's fist met his unshaven chin. A bolt of pain shot along his arm, but his other hand was already in the man's stomach. He heard a startled grunt, and the man doubled over. His other hand struck upward once again.

A heartbeat later the dockworker sank unconscious to the floor. Turning to face the other two, Rafe saw that Harris had untangled himself from the second worker and that the bigger man was charging at him.

Rafe ducked a wildly thrown punch and, catlike, hit the man in the stomach. Unlike the first, this man didn't react to the blow, and Rafe knew he had a real fight on his hands.

Rafe ducked another roundhouse blow that, if it had landed, would have broken his jaw. Spinning, Rafe lashed out with his fist. The second it connected, he released his other hand.

But the instant he swung, he knew he was too late. Before his fist reached the man, an explosion of pain erupted in his chest. The dockworker had struck first and struck hard.

Recovering quickly, Rafe backed away from the dockworker. Out of the corner of his eye, he saw Harris rising from the floor, the short-barreled pistol in his hand.

"I have him covered," Harris declared.

The remaining dockworker looked at Harris for instructions.

Rafe watched them both, his chest rising and falling powerfully, his mind racing as he slowly reached for the pistol that was tucked into the waistband at the small of his back.

"Hurt him, Bailey. Make him remember his mistake," Harris ordered with a nasty smile on his lips.

The dockworker started forward but stopped when yet another voice was heard.

"You do that, Bailey, and your boss is a dead man," drawled Caleb Magee.

Rafe exhaled as the prospector stepped into the office, his long-barreled Colt pointed at Harris's head.

"Drop it, mister," Caleb ordered.

Harris did exactly as he was told, and the big dockworker backed away from Rafe.

"I thought I asked you not to come here," Rafe said to Caleb as he drew his own pistol from its hidden holster.

"Is that what you said?" Caleb replied innocently. "Glad you didn't need my help. Are you finished with them now?"

"Not by a long shot, old timer," Rafe replied. Going over to Harris, he stared unblinkingly at the man. Then he smiled; it wasn't a nice smile at all.

The office manager's eyes widened; his face turned ashen. "What are you going to do?"

"Are you the same man who just told Bailey to hurt me? To hurt me bad?"

"I made a mistake," Harris pleaded.

"Yes," Rafe agreed in the same flat voice he'd used earlier, "a couple of them."

Rafe cocked the pistol and lifted it. Still smiling, he placed the tip of the barrel near the center of Harris's forehead.

"Mr. Harris, you have exactly five seconds to tell me what I want to hear. If you don't, I kill you."

Behind Rafe, Harris saw Caleb Magee smile. His fright increased threefold. His raised hands shook visibly, and his legs did the same. His mouth was parched, and his heart threatened to explode with fear.

"I don't know," he pleaded weakly.

Rafe's nasty smile disappeared, his mouth thinned into a tight, narrow line. He began to count. "One. Two. Three. Four." On four, Rafe pressed the barrel firmly into Harris's skin.

"Al—Allison. James Allison," Harris shouted, his voice breaking with the name.

Startled, Rafe shook his head, unable to believe his ears. "James Allison of Allison Shipping?"

"Y-y-yes," Harris stammered.

Rafe looked at the dockworker. "Take care of your friend," he ordered. When the man moved toward his still-unconscious cohort, Rafe withdrew the gun from Harris's forehead, but he did not lower or uncock it.

"Why?" he asked, his eyes piercing in their intensity.

"I don't know the answer to that, mister. I'm only the office manager," Harris whined.

Instantly, Rafe pressed the barrel back on Harris's forehead. "You're not from here, Harris, you're from New York. I checked that out. That's why I came to you. You're the only man who knows everything about this company."

Rafe's words faded as a new connection struck him, one that he had not thought about before. "Allison himself put you here, didn't he? He doesn't trust your bosses."

Harris shook his head in denial, knowing that to admit such a thing might cost him even more. "I don't know what you're talking about."

"Yes, you do. Allison controls it all, doesn't he? *Doesn't he?*" Rafe shouted, pushing the barrel painfully against Harris's skin.

"Yes," the man finally admitted. "Caruthers and Murdock are a front for Allison's consortium."

The admission sent waves of anger charging through Rafe's mind, but he showed no emotion at all. Instead, he carefully stepped back and turned to Caleb. "I think we're finished now."

"It's about time, Rafe," Caleb said pointedly. Together, the two men backed to the doorway and raced down the stairs and into the street.

When they were two blocks away, they stopped. Rafe looked at Caleb, his eyes as hard as emeralds.

"I'm going to New York, Caleb."

In the office, Reginald Harris was still remembering looking into the barrel of Rafe's gun and thinking about the death he'd just narrowly escaped.

Then the name the old man had called the younger one registered in his mind. There was something familiar about that unusual name. Rafe? Where had he heard it before?

Suddenly, Harris knew. Rafe had to be Rafael Montgomery. Only Montgomery was supposed to be dead.

Without looking at the two men, Harris raced out of his office. He would have to send word to Allison and warn him of the resurrection of Rafael Montgomery. Perhaps, Harris thought, something good might come of today's disaster.

"If you worry about Riverbend, you will never be able to do your best for the shipping company," Crystal warned Alana.

Looking up at the night sky, Alana sighed softly. It was a beautiful, clear evening. A half-moon hung in the heavens above Riverbend, bestowing a gentle cast on the flowers and bushes in the garden.

Behind the women, sounds of laughter mixed with the low babble of voices as Crystal's women entertained their customers in the main house.

"I know what I must do, but it's not easy," Alana admitted.

"Of course it isn't, but it's necessary. Alana, we'll grow, and when we do, we'll have the power to fight Ledoque and the others!"

Alana smiled hesitantly at Crystal. "I can still be nervous, can't I? I've never been away from this part of the country. Crystal, I've—I've never even been on a large ship."

"You will love it. Tomorrow you'll learn about the wonder of the freedom and openness of the ocean. Don't be afraid of it, Alana. When you board the ship tomorrow, look toward the future, not at the past."

The scent of magnolia teased her nostrils; the call of the owl was comfortingly familiar. "Ben will handle the plantation. He's a good man and a good overseer," Alana said at last.

"I know," Crystal replied.

Alana had nothing else to say. Crystal, sensing that Alana wanted to be by herself for a little while, embraced her and returned to the house to look after business.

Alone, Alana breathed deeply of the night scents. A thousand thoughts raced in her mind. Memories of the past twenty months blurred her sight. She recalled the heavy passions that Rafe had brought out in her, and the powerful love he invoked settled around her.

She walked to the gazebo and sat on the divan where she and Rafe had shared their love, and she thought of the short time they'd had together. But before she let sadness overtake her, she left the gazebo.

Walking aimlessly through the garden, her memories of Jason and of their life together replayed themselves before her eyes. She relived the bad times and remembered those last, peaceful weeks.

The horror of Jason's death had been numbed by time, and the memories she had of him now were only of the gentle man that she had always known he was.

On the heels of her good memories, hatred and disgust for Charles Ledoque rose within her. Her rage at what he had done to the shipping business, to her, and to the two innocent horses made her head spin.

Alana stopped walking and looked around. She found herself standing in front of the four rosebushes, staring intently at them without really seeing them. The love she had for Rafe and the tender, sisterly feeling she'd always bestowed upon Jason stirred her heart. But it was the hatred she felt for Ledoque that gripped her and fed her determination.

"I will beat you!" she declared to the image of Ledoque that was floating before her eyes. "You will never destroy us! Never!"

And then, with the moonlight filtering over the rosebushes, Alana saw a sight that she had not seen in over five years. Months before it should, her mother's bush had given birth to one small bud.

Bending slowly, she knelt on the soft earth and carefully cupped the little bud between her palms. "At last," she whispered, ignoring the tears that fell from her eyes.

17

Alana stood on the dock, the strong noon sun pouring down upon her head. Her large-brimmed hat matched her blue traveling dress and accented her strong blue eyes.

The *Harmony*, the larger of the two clipper ships of the Landow Company, rested at anchor two hundred yards from where Alana stood, her holds filled to capacity for the short trip to New York harbor. The dock itself was just calming down after several hours of frenzied activity. All that remained was the loading of Alana's three trunks into the longboat. Above, sea gulls cried out in their never-ending quest for food.

Lorelei stood silently, having already said her tearful good-bye to Alana and having extracted a promise that when Alana was settled in New York, she would send for her.

Chaco waited three steps behind Crystal while the two young women spoke. His eyes were never still, and his body never relaxed.

"It will not be easy," Crystal said again, "but then, your life has not been one of ease. Be wary of everyone, trust only yourself and your instincts," she cautioned.

"I shall miss you," Alana said truthfully.

"And I shall miss you," Crystal replied. Emotion welled up strongly within her as she tried, but failed, to manage a smile. "But what we are doing is important."

"I know."

The first mate of the *Harmony* came up to them and fingered the bill on his cap. "We have to leave now, Mrs. Landow."

Alana opened her arms to Crystal. The two women embraced tightly, but as Alana started away, Crystal stopped her with a gentle touch.

Alana looked at her friend questioningly as Crystal called Chaco to them. "Chaco is going with you. He will protect you in New York." Alana's mouth formed a protest, but Crystal cut her off. "You do not know that place. You will need him," she stated.

Again Alana started to object, but Crystal waved her hand to stop her words. "Trust me, Alana. It is important. Without Chaco, anything might happen."

Alana gazed into her friend's eyes and saw concern within them. "All right," she said in a low voice.

Crystal nodded to Chaco, who turned and picked up a canvas bag. Without another word from Crystal, he went to the edge of the dock and waited for Alana.

With a soft sigh, Alana turned and walked toward the waiting longboat.

The first mate offered her his hand to help her down, but Chaco, after tossing his bag into the boat, reached Alana's side and handed her into the boat himself. Alana smiled at him.

When everyone was seated, and the longboat had started on its way to the *Harmony,* Alana gazed back at Crystal and Lorelei, who waved their final farewells. Alana refused to let her emotions surface, and as the faces of her friends grew smaller, she held her head proudly.

"What?" Ledoque screamed to the woman who stood before him. His rage sent shivers of fear skittering through the young prostitute's mind. "Why didn't you get to me sooner?" he demanded.

"I couldn't get away. Crystal only allowed me to come with them today because I told her I might be pregant and had to see the doctor."

"Damn it all! Are you sure?"

The woman nodded her head slowly as she repeated what she had said only minutes earlier. "Mrs. Landow is going to New

York on the *Harmony*. She is going there to set up the new office for her company."

"It was that meddling whore's idea, wasn't it?" The question was more a growl than words.

The young woman nodded her head again.

"Get out, damn you, get out!"

"My money?" she asked, her greed making her brave.

Ledoque almost refused her, but even in his frantic state he knew that he might still need her services. He reached into his pocket and withdrew a handful of coins, which he tossed disdainfully to her. As the coins clattered to the floor, Ledoque was already racing out of his office.

On East Bay Street, he paused to look out at the harbor. In the distance, its sails already unfurled, the *Harmony* was heading gracefully out to sea.

The sight of the clipper ship galvanized Ledoque into immediate action. Not caring that his usual dignified demeanor was notably absent, he raced toward one of his own docks, hoping that he would not be too late.

His perfect plan had been spoiled by Crystal Revanche. He had refined the details of the plan until he knew that nothing could possibly go wrong and that soon he would be able to claim Alana for himself.

Ledoque had believed his scheme to be foolproof. He had arranged, through indirect channels, for a reputable agent in New York to offer Alana and Crystal a commission that they could not turn down. The agent himself did not know that the original commission came from Ledoque; he believed it to be from the Marquette Shipping Company.

When the women had accepted the contract, Ledoque knew he had Alana within his grasp, for he had issued orders to his most trusted captain to capture the *Harmony* before it reached New York. The cargo would be transferred to his own ship, the *Harmony* sunk, and any survivors were to die so that no word of the piracy could be learned.

He had never expected Alana to be on that ship. "Damn!" he shouted as he reached the dock. Several workers turned to look at him, but the minute their eyes met his, they turned away.

Ledoque breathed a sigh of relief when he saw that the captain of his ship had not yet left the dock.

"Carson!" Ledoque shouted at the large man.

The captain turned in surprise. "Something wrong?" Carson asked, taking in Ledoque's strained features.

"A change of plans," Ledoque called. "I will be accompanying you on this voyage. We will leave on the evening tide."

"But—" Carson began. Ledoque, not wanting any witnesses to their words, quickly cut him off.

"Come with me," Ledoque commanded.

"Yes, sir," the captain said. He turned to his second mate, who was waiting in a longboat. "Have the ship made fast," he ordered.

As they walked down the dock, Ledoque told the captain that he would travel aboard the ship to New York. Once Alana Landow left the *Harmony* and the boat was loaded with its new cargo and bound for South Africa, the captain was to capture her. All hands were to be killed, for they still could not chance any witnesses. But instead of sinking the *Harmony,* they would change its name and sail it to Africa as one of the Marquette ships.

The captain smiled when Ledoque finished speaking, and Ledoque finally composed himself, sure that this time he would at last bring Alana Landow to her knees.

Eighteen days after he had gotten the vital information from Reginald Harris, Rafe had arrived in New York and had begun his own investigation into James Allison and his consortium. In the week that he spent investigating Allison, he had been able to learn only a little more. On this day, he was dressing to meet with the attorney who would lead him through the bureaucratic maze and help him to meet James Allison and his secretive consortium.

Rafe had figured out what the consortium appeared to be up to, but his main concern was to expose Allison as a thief and murderer and to avenge his sister's death. In order to do that, Rafe knew he had to infiltrate Allison's organization.

Rafe had let his beard grow during the trip; because of its denseness, the three-week growth was already turning into a well-defined look that masked his strong features. Although he had never met James Allison, he knew it was always possible that someone involved with Allison might recognize him as Rafael Montgomery.

Rafe's plan was amazingly simple. He would pose as a wealthy businessman looking for investments and power—the very things that James Allison would respect.

He had genuine letters of credit with him, under the assumed name Richard Sutcliff, that backed his story of being a wealthy businessman, for the essayers and engineers who had finally surveyed the mine that he and Caleb had discovered valued it in the millions. The bank that Rafe dealt with had no qualms about giving him unlimited letters of credit under whatever name he chose.

Rafe hoped that by the time his meeting with the attorney was over, he would have made enough of an impression on the man to gain his first entry into Allison's confidence.

Rafe finished fixing his collar, then adjusted his vest. A moment later he slipped into an excellently tailored jacket and left his hotel.

Outside, instead of riding, he slowly walked the fifteen blocks to the attorney's office. As he did, he replayed and refined the story he would tell the lawyer.

Alana stood near the bow of the *Harmony*, enjoying the warm caress of the sea breezes on her skin. The five-day voyage was nearing its end, and not once had she allowed herself to let her mind ponder unwarranted worries. She knew that she had to maintain firm control of her inner emotions as well as her surface gestures. She must always play the part of a confident and strong woman used to dealing with men and business matters.

To help her pass the time, she'd asked Chaco to teach her the signing language that Crystal and he used. Chaco had agreed, and although his face was always expressionless, she had sensed that her request had pleased him.

For the past four days they'd spent many hours together, Alana saying a word, Chaco slowly moving his hands in the silent translation of that word. And now, with New York drawing near, she was able to converse in short phrases with Chaco.

Each night Alana had taken dinner with Captain Sanders, who she knew had not only been Jason's friend, but was also the most valued captain of the Landow fleet. They would discuss business and the future as Alana saw it. After dinner, the captain would stroll with her on the deck, pointing out the various constellations that glittered in the sky.

When she went to sleep, Alana would hear Chaco laying out a sleeping mat at her door. On the first night she'd told him it was unnecessary, but he had refused to accept this. Each night as she lay in her bed, she knew that Chaco was sleeping at her door and would let no one enter without her permission. Although Alana had no fears on board the *Harmony,* Chaco's presence outside her door had been comforting in its own way. But once in New York and at the hotel, Chaco would have to sleep in the servant's room, not in the hallway.

"Mrs. Landow," came Captain Sander's voice from behind her. Alana turned to him. "We'll be docking in two hours. I'll have the first mate accompany you to the hotel."

"Thank you, Captain." When he left, Alana looked back at the coastline before going to her cabin to pack. Behind her, Chaco followed silently.

Three and a half hours after the *Harmony* docked, Alana was in her hotel suite, which comprised a sitting room, a necessary room, a bedroom, and a servant's room. It was more luxurious accommodations than Alana would have chosen, but Crystal had insisted on using the best hotel.

"The expense of the hotel is not all that important. You must keep up the image that we are wealthy women—it impresses people. You need only stay at the hotel until you've found suitable living quarters. Mr. Bennet will undoubtedly already be looking for your new residence."

After unpacking and making sure that Chaco was settled in, Alana went downstairs to the dining room. Chaco, as was his habit, stood off to the side of the entrance, watching her and anyone near her. When she finished eating, Alana ordered a meal sent up to the room for Chaco.

The combination of a day spent at sea and the rush of moving into her hotel room had tired Alana sufficiently to allow her to sleep undisturbed through the night. When she awoke, the sun was well up into the sky.

Her first day in New York passed in a whirlwind of activity that left her exhausted by evening. The next two days were the same. She met with the lawyer, inspected the sites he'd chosen for the Landow office, and looked over the three residences that were available and suitable for her. And when she was in the streets traveling in the hansom that her new attorney had put at her disposal, she stared in wonder at the great city of New York, a city that made Charleston look like a small town.

In between the business meetings, Alana spent several hours each day at the dock. It had taken two days to unload the *Harmony*'s cargo, and it would be another three days before the new cargo would be ready for loading. Because of the amount of the cargo, and because of the bulk of the mining equipment, it would take at least three more days after that before the *Harmony* would be ready to start its lengthy voyage to South Africa.

On the evening of the fifth day, the day before the *Harmony* was to take on its new cargo, Alana was leaving the hotel's dining room after having enjoyed a light dinner. Crossing the elegantly appointed lobby, its deep carpeting like a cushioning cloud beneath her tired feet, Alana moved toward the stairs. She had not been overly entranced by the hotel's use of that strange new invention, the mechanical elevator, and preferred to walk up the three flights of stairs. Halfway to the steps, she sensed eyes on her. Turning her head slightly, she saw a dark-haired, bearded man staring at her.

Within the recesses of her mind, a tantalizing sense of recognition stirred, but Alana knew no one with a beard. Not wanting to be caught staring at a strange man, Alana turned away. And so, as she reached the stairs, she did not see the bearded man's startled look nor hear his sharp intake of breath as he stared at her retreating back.

Rafe, feeling very pleased with himself at this day's business, had sauntered into the lobby of the hotel, his mind reviewing what he'd already accomplished. He was confident that in another week he would become a full-fledged member of the consortium.

Today he had spent the afternoon with James Allison and the lawyer. The men had hinted of their plans and of the power they would one day wield.

Rafe had sensed that Allison had already judged him and

approved him. All that was left was for him to meet and be accepted by the three other important men in the consortium. Rafe had learned that Caruthers and Murdock were considered to be only junior members and would not be present at any meetings.

When Rafe was twenty feet inside the lobby, he caught sight of a woman whose long raven hair reminded him of Alana's. But when she suddenly turned toward him, he paused in mid-step. In the half second he'd had to look at her face, his heart had almost stopped.

Impossible! he told himself. Yet he continued to look at Alana's unforgettable profile.

He started forward, but then stopped. *Why is she here?* he asked himself. Was it really Alana? Then he saw the tall, lanky black man who followed close behind her. He noticed the way the man's eyes watched everything. The moment Rafe had started toward her, the black man's face had gone tight. When he'd stopped, the man relaxed.

Before he could take action, he spotted a man across the lobby whom he'd met the other day. This man knew him not as Rafe Montgomery, but as Richard Sutcliff of San Francisco. If the woman was Alana and she called him by name, it might prove fatal.

Instead of following her, Rafe went to the front desk and asked the clerk if a Mrs. Landow was registered at the hotel.

"Why, yes, Mr. Sutcliff," the clerk replied cheerfully, "she's been staying with us for several days now."

Thinking quickly, Rafe nodded his head. "I've done a lot of business with her husband. I must pay my respects immediately. What room is she in?"

"Suite three seventeen," the clerk stated.

"Thank you." Rafe left the desk and went to the stairs, his mind reeling with the knowledge that Alana was here. And even though his blood pulsed through his body in the madding way he had not felt since that long-ago morning when Alana had left his bedroom, he wondered why she was here. *And Jason?* he asked himself.

* * *

Alana had not yet started to undress. Chaco was in his room, eating the meal that had been waiting for him when they'd returned a few moments before.

Alana poured a glass of water from a leaded crystal pitcher. She stared at the water, and as she did, she thought about the strange feeling she'd had when she'd seen the man in the lobby.

She realized that he had resembled Rafe. He was as tall as Rafe, and the silver in his dark hair had sparkled in the same way. His resemblance to Rafe was tantalizing.

"Oh, Rafe," she whispered. Abruptly, she cut off her thoughts. Raising the glass to her lips, Alana started to take a sip. Before she could, there was a knock at her door.

Putting the glass down, she went to the door. "Yes?"

"Mrs. Landow?" came the muffled voice.

"Yes?"

"I must speak with you."

Alana opened the door, and when she did, she found herself looking into the same bearded face she'd seen downstairs. Again, that familiar tickle teased her mind.

"Yes?" she repeated as the tall man stepped into the room without being invited.

"Hello, my love," he said in a low voice.

Her breath caught. When she looked into his eyes and saw her own feelings reflected within their brilliant green depths, she knew it really was Rafe.

Then he reached into his collar and withdrew a gold chain. Alana's eyes widened further when she saw her mother's thin golden wedding band hanging from it.

The world spun frighteningly around her. Her legs turned to rubber; her eyes blinked at the sight before her. She reached out to him, her fingers going to his face. She ignored the short hair on his cheeks as she traced his features.

"Rafe," she whispered. "Oh my God, Rafe, it is you. . . ."

Rafe reached out. His arms went around her, bringing her to him, holding her tightly as his mouth met hers. Then their lips touched for the first time in almost two years.

But even as they kissed deeply, Rafe saw from the corner of his eye a dark blur charge toward him. Before he could release

Alana and turn, a hand caught his hair and jerked his head back. The tip of a knife rested on his jugular vein.

"No! Chaco!" Alana shouted. "He is a friend."

Slowly the knife was withdrawn from Rafe's throat and his hair was released. Turning, Rafe gazed into the ebony eyes of the man that had been following Alana in the lobby.

The men stared silently at each other until Alana, her breasts rising and falling with a combination of fear and love, spoke to Chaco.

"This is Rafe Montgomery, Chaco. He is—" Alana paused then and squared her shoulders. "He is much, much more than a friend." Using her hands, she gave Chaco a private message.

To Rafe's surprise, Alana made several motions with her hands. The tension flowed out of the lanky black man's body, and Chaco favored Rafe with a nod of his head.

A quick flash of memory struck Rafe. He remembered how proud his sister had been when she'd learned the signing language and had started to teach children who could not speak with words. But he thrust that thought aside as he watched Chaco leave the room.

"Just who is he?" Rafe asked after the door closed behind Chaco.

"Chaco is my bodyguard," she said, using the term for the first time.

"I see," Rafe replied doubtfully. "What did you tell him?" he asked while his eyes feasted on Alana's beauty.

"That you are the man I love. Oh, Rafe, did you never receive my letter?"

Rafe's features tightened. He stepped closer to Alana. Looking deeply into her eyes, he lifted one hand and stroked the silkiness of her cheek.

"When I returned home, I found . . . everything had changed. My business and my home were gone. My sister, Elizabeth, had died. There was no place for your letter to be delivered. In fact, few people know I'm alive."

Alana closed her eyes to this news. "I'm so sorry," she began, but Rafe cut her off, unwilling to go into that now.

"What happened to you, Alana? Where is Jason?"

"He died last summer," she replied. Before he could ask any more questions, she pressed his hand tighter against her cheek.

"Later, Rafe," she whispered. "Oh, my love, we'll have time to talk later."

The boldness of her words and the hunger in her eyes spoke a thousand words to him, and Rafe knew her desire was more than reflected by his.

Alana rose upward on tiptoe. Their lips met, and fire blazed from their kiss. The kiss lasted a long, long time, and the endless months of separation were put aside as their love, too long denied, burst forth in a passionate rebirth that left them both too shaken to speak when their mouths reluctantly parted.

With her heart pounding and her stomach deliciously tight, Alana grasped Rafe's hand in hers. She took him through the sitting room and into the bedroom. Then, strangely, Alana became self-conscious. It had been so long since she'd seen him, since they had loved.

Rafe sensed Alana's hesitation, yet the desire and love that were so suddenly reborn would not let him hold back. He drew her to him, his arms going around her as he looked deeply into her eyes.

"We've been apart too long, Alana."

Alana closed her eyes for a moment. When she opened them, she slowly nodded her head. "Love me, Rafe. I need you to love me."

With their eyes feasting upon each other, they stepped apart and slowly undressed.

When she stood naked before him, her long hair spilling over one shoulder and reaching below one perfectly formed breast, she spoke. "How I have missed you, Rafael, with all my heart and soul."

"And I missed you no less," Rafe whispered gently, catching her to him. His lips were demanding; his hands held her willing prisoner against his bare flesh. Their breathing grew ragged, and when Rafe drew back, Alana's closed eyes snapped open.

A moment later she was in his strong arms and floating four feet above the floor. Her long raven hair trailed toward the carpet as he carried her to the bed and placed her in its center. Rafe joined her there, his lips devouring her mouth, her neck, luxuriating in the fullness of her breasts.

His lips were burning embers that scorched a pathway along her breasts. Her hands gripped his hair and pressed his face more tightly to her when he took a desire-stiffened nipple into the heated embrace of his mouth.

Her ecstasy was so intense that her low, throaty cries grew louder in the room. When she could take no more of his mouth on her breasts and nipples, she drew his head up to hers and met his mouth avidly.

Their tongues danced, and their skin glowed hotly upon each other. And when the passion and love that filled them could not be held back any longer, they joined together and became one.

With Rafe above her, holding her, filling her with himself, their eyes remained open and locked together. Alana's eyes misted, and Rafe's handsome face became a ghostly vision of shimmering beauty above her as tears of happiness spilled from her eyes. Yet even then, Alana would not close her eyes, for fear Rafe might be gone when she opened them again and she would find herself in nothing but a dream.

But he did not disappear; rather, he guided her along their journey to that very special place in the universe that they had created for themselves almost two years before. Once there, the very fabric of the world shattered with the exploding climax of their love.

Later, after their breathing returned to normal and they lay quietly, still under the influence of the magic that they had created, Alana gazed at him, her finger tracing the full curve of his lips. At last she spoke.

"I have dreamed of you so often, but I was afraid that my dreams would never come true," she said truthfully, not at all embarrassed by her admission to the man she loved so deeply.

"Never has a day passed when I did not think of you. I had hoped that you would find happiness, even as I hoped that one day we would be together again."

"And now we shall stay together!" Alana declared vehemently. "I will never, never lose you again."

"Yes," Rafe replied, his voice as determined as Alana's. Then he shifted and sat up, drawing Alana with him, his arm around her, her head resting on his chest.

He bent, pressing his lips to the top of her head and breathing in the special fragrance of her hair. When he took his mouth from her silky raven strands, he exhaled slowly. "Alana, talk to me. Tell me why you're here."

18

Alana closed her eyes. When she opened them, she saw the silhouetted shadows of their bodies flickering on the wall across from the bed, projected by the low cast of the brass oil lamps.

As she luxuriated within the heady scent that clung to Rafe's skin, she took a deep, preparatory breath. Without lifting her head from the comforting feel of his chest, she spoke.

She told Rafe everything that had happened between Jason and herself, sparing nothing. When she finished the first part of her story, she listened to the steady beat of Rafe's heart. Then she went on, detailing the troubles with the shipping company and the losses she'd suffered at Ledoque's hands. Finally, she told him about her new partnership with the notorious madam, Crystal Revanche, and outlined the way everything had been arranged at Riverbend. She did not explain all of Crystal's background, but simply noted that Crystal, too, had been nearly destroyed by Charles Ledoque, and wished to see him ruined.

After she had finished, she paused for a moment in thought. When she spoke again, her voice was low, her words distinct. "She saved my life, Rafe, and even if she is a whore, she's the only person who helped me. Does it bother you that I am in business with a—a prostitute?"

Only after she fell silent did she look up at Rafe. She saw the lines of tension around his eyes, but a moment later, she felt the reassuring pressure of his hand on her arm.

"Yes, for a moment," Rafe admitted truthfully. "But I was thousands of miles away and of no help to you. You did what was necessary. And you kept your integrity at a time when it would have been easier to give in. No, Alana, I'm not bothered by what you've done, only that I could not have been there to help. Besides," he said with a full smile, "this Crystal Revanche seems more angel than whore, at least from the way you describe her."

"At times she is," Alana agreed, her mind calmer now. Then Alana explained the reason she was in New York.

When she had completed her tale, she lowered her head and ran her mouth across Rafe's chest, enjoying the way his hair tickled her nose and the feel of his skin against her lips. Lifting her head again, she fixed him with an open and frank stare. "And now, my love, it is your turn."

Rafe spoke for almost an hour—dispassionately, as if it were someone else describing his life since he had left Alana. In unemotional words, Rafe detailed what he was doing in New York and how he planned to expose the man he was seeking. When he finished, the tight line of his lips softened and he smiled down at Alana.

"And so I am now Richard Sutcliff."

Alana, her eyes moist with emotion, reached up to him. "I'm sorry, Rafe, for what happened to you and your family. I can't help but wonder, my darling, why both of us have had so much sorrow and suffering."

Rafe shook his head slowly. "But it will soon be over."

"And then?" Alana asked.

"And then, Alana, I promise that we shall never be apart again."

Alana blinked back her tears and lifted her head. "I won't let you break that promise, Rafael Montgomery, even if I must chase you around the world itself."

"I left you once," he told her, his green eyes sparkling intensely. "It won't happen again. I'm not going anywhere without you, Alana," he stated as his mouth closed on hers and he showed her the truth of his feelings without the use of words.

"How will this turn of events affect us?" Ledoque asked when James Allison finished speaking.

Before answering, Allison looked at the dark-paneled walls and at the paintings that accented the elegance of the private room within the Wellington Club. Allison considered both the room and the club to be his own personal domain.

"It could be a minor bother if Montgomery tries to bring charges, but he has no proof. But," Allison said, his eyes narrowing into small slits, "before it comes to that, I hope that our people will find him and convince him of the error of his ways."

"Or silence him forever. How did he escape from that trap we'd prepared during the war?"

"I've no idea." Allison shifted irritably in his chair. "And what of your problem?" he asked, thinking of the delay in the delivery of the most important piece of mining equipment consigned to South Africa. "Will the delay alter your plans for the Landow woman?"

Although Allison didn't smile, his words carried a mocking tone. James Allison was no stranger to lust, but for him lust took the form of a thirst for power and control. The passion of a man for a woman was no stranger to him, but he had never met a woman whom he desired more than he desired power.

Ledoque's smile matched the sarcastic tone that Allison had used. "A few days will make no difference."

"I still think you're wasting your time on the woman—and your energy."

Lifting a large crystal snifter, Ledoque took a deep drink. "What of this new man who wants to join the consortium?" he asked, changing the subject deftly.

"Very rich. Very ambitious. He has a great deal of money, and I think his West Coast mining contacts will be useful. I have a meeting set in three days. You will meet Sutcliff then."

Ledoque nodded his head thoughtfully. Although Allison was the largest investor in the consortium and thereby controlled it, Ledoque's investment was not much less than Allison's. And while Ledoque didn't believe they needed anyone else, he did agree that entry into diversified areas was important if they were to gain complete control over the country's economy. Before Ledoque could pass judgment on this man's usefulness, he needed to meet him.

* * *

Rafe left Alana's room just as dawn lightened the sky over New York. After changing out of his wrinkled clothing, shaving, and dressing again, he returned to her room to escort her to the dining room.

They had a leisurely breakfast, and when it was over, Rafe walked Alana to the door and handed her up into the carriage that would start her on her daily rounds. Today was the first day of loading the cargo into the *Harmony*'s hold.

When Chaco stepped onto the carriage's rear foot ledge and the carriage started down the avenue, Rafe went back inside the hotel and arranged to have his baggage transferred to the suite next to Alana's. With that accomplished, he left the hotel to keep an appointment with a man who had been another victim of Allison's avarice. Rafe wanted to have every possible bit of information available to him when he walked into Allison's office in two days to meet the other members of the consortium.

When Alana arrived at the dock, she found Captain Sanders waiting for her in the agent's office, his face set in angry lines.

"What's wrong?" Alana asked immediately.

Sanders turned pointedly to the agent, who said, "There has been a delay on the delivery of one piece of equipment."

"How long a delay?" Alana asked, alarmed at this unexpected problem.

"A few days. A week at the most. The foundry notified us that they discovered a crack in the casting. This item is the single most important part of your cargo. Your ship cannot leave without it."

"But our contract calls for a specified departure date," Alana argued.

"And my crew cannot sit idly by for a week," Sanders added. "I'll damned well lose half of them!"

"I have already received the authority from the Marquette Company to change the dates specified on the contract and to reimburse you for any extra costs because of the delay," the agent told Alana. "As for your crew, Captain Sanders, I shall personally see to it that any man who deserts will be replaced. Does that satisfy you?"

The lines on Sanders's face eased as he accepted the agent's guarantee.

"Then I suggest you begin loading the other cargo today so you will be ready to leave the moment the last piece arrives."

Sanders glanced at Alana. She nodded imperceptibly.

After speaking with the agent for a few more minutes, Alana left the office and went to the dock where the *Harmony* was berthed.

She spent the morning on board talking with Sanders and watching the crew load the cargo, but no matter how hard she tried to concentrate on the work being done, all she could think of was Rafe and the coming of night.

Just before noon, Alana left the docks to go to her attorney's home, where she was expected for lunch.

After lunch, Mrs. Bennet would take Alana shopping for furniture for her new home—a small townhouse Alana had chosen yesterday, sandwiched between two much larger houses on upper Fifth Avenue—and she would also introduce her to the shopkeepers with whom she would be dealing.

And then, Alana thought, she would have dinner with Rafe and spend another wonderful night safe within his arms.

"Mr. Denton is here," the valet informed Ledoque. Ledoque motioned for the man to show Denton in, just as the clock struck midnight.

When Denton stood before Ledoque, his eyes averted, Ledoque spoke. "Well?"

"She had dinner with the same man who left her room early this morning. After eating, they both went up to her room. They were still together when I left. He has taken the suite that adjoins Mrs. Landow's."

"Who is he?" Ledoque hissed. Blind rage built within him, blurring his vision with a red hate for both the man and the woman. *How dare the bitch sleep with another man after refusing me,* he thought irrationally.

"He is registered as Mr. Richard Sutcliff, sir."

"Sutcliff?" Ledoque asked, taken aback.

"Yes, sir."

"Could it be the same man?" he wondered aloud.

"Sir?" asked Denton.

"Never mind," Ledoque ordered. "Return to the hotel. I want to know everything about this man—everything!"

"Yes, sir," Denton replied.

After the detective had gone, Ledoque lit a cigar with angry, shaking hands. "Bitch!" he shouted.

The night and the next day flew by so rapidly that Alana could not believe the time had passed. But when night came again, she greeted it happily, for she would soon be within Rafe's arms, and nothing else mattered.

They spent a lovely two hours in the elegant hotel dining room, and when they'd finished eating, they went up to their separate rooms.

Because his suite adjoined hers, Rafe did not have to venture out into the hallway to come into her rooms. Instead, he just passed through the connecting door and a short passageway that was also part of the servant's quarters.

Alana knew that Rafe had arranged this for her benefit, so that her reputation would not be tarnished. Yet Alana herself did not care about her reputation; in the past months she had learned the true value of that often-misused word.

Once inside her bedroom, with Chaco having dinner in his own room—Chaco, even with Rafe at Alana's side, would not let her go anywhere unless he was near—Alana undressed, put on a long, light robe, and then brushed her hair. As she did, she thought about the past two days and the wonderful feeling of having Rafe by her side.

Alana realized that her love for Rafe was growing stronger with each passing hour. Whenever Rafe would look at her, smile, or brush his fingers on her skin, she would begin to feel light-headed.

She could never have enough of him. Each time they made love, it was emotionally and physically overpowering, yet afterward she would find herself wanting him again, almost as soon as their breathing returned to normal.

The feel of his lips always lingered on her skin, and the hunger that was so much a part of her need for him continued to swell within her. They made love whenever they could, perhaps, she thought, because they were trying to make up for all the time they had been apart. But whatever the reason, Alana was almost happy.

Almost. Until Ledoque paid for what he had done, and Alana and Crystal were avenged, she would not be totally at peace. With these thoughts swirling in her mind, Alana put down the brush. As she turned from the mirror, she found Rafe gazing at her.

Her startled gasp was quickly forgotten when she took in his presence. He wore the same pants he'd had on at dinner, but the matching vest and jacket were gone, and his linen shirt was open, revealing the dark mat of hair on his chest.

She was used to Rafe's bearded face, but she could still picture his clean-shaven, strong features. Yet the beard served to highlight his eyes even more than before. Their emerald depths seemed to glow in contrast to the black frame of hair.

As she watched him, her breathing deepened and the familiar heat of her passion rose abruptly within her. Alana moistened her lips with the tip of her tongue and silently advanced toward him.

Rafe studied the intent way that Alana was looking at him and felt the onset of desire flare between them. As she walked toward him, he saw the rise and fall of her breasts, outlined by her robe, and saw, too, the white flashes of her thigh that came with each step.

And then she was in front of him, her deep blue gaze searching his face, her moist, soft lips open and inviting. Lowering his mouth to hers, Rafe tasted the sweetness that she offered him.

But when his arms went around her, he felt her hands come between them. Tantalizingly, she opened his shirt. Then her mouth left his and trailed downward, skimming over the surface of his beard until he felt the gentle seeking warmth of her lips at the base of his throat.

Alana did not stop there. Her hands pushed the linen shirt aside, and her mouth greedily roamed the width of his chest. Rafe stood perfectly still against the wild coursing of his blood. When her lips captured his nipple, his hands tightened on her shoulders.

With the heat of her mouth sending little explosions through his chest, Alana drew away. Her eyes once again locked with his as she slipped the shirt from his shoulders. As it floated to the floor, her hands went to the waistband of his pants.

A few moments later, Rafe was sitting on the side of the bed, his eyes watching Alana, who stood two feet away.

Untying the sash of her light robe, Alana shrugged her shoulders. Rafe watched the material slide along her skin, taking an eternity before it fell free. But when it finally did, he drank his fill of Alana's magnificent body.

Stepping close to him, she looked down into his eyes. The love and desire within them only added to the excitement she felt. Dreamlike, she reached out, her hands going to his shoulders and gently pushing him back onto the bed.

When he was lying down, she joined him, her body draped over his, accepting greedily the tightness of his muscles against her own and the blazing heat that seared her length.

Then her lips were moving passionately on his, her tongue darting into the warm cavern of his mouth to fleetingly touch his own.

Her hands wandered everywhere, caressing and stroking him until she felt the full length of his hardness press against her side. She moved sensuously over him, her mouth skipping across his chest, stopping to kiss and then nip gently at its soft, curly hair.

Following the narrowing line of hair until it thinned just below his waist, she ran her fingers through the denser hair at the base of his manhood.

Her lips were never still, and her hands followed suit. When her hand captured as much of his thickened length as she could, and its heat spread along her palm, she raised her lips from his lower belly to gaze in wonder at his rock-hard velvet staff.

It throbbed in her hand, and as it did, she realized that Rafe's own hands and fingers were caressing her inner thighs and exploring intimately within her moist womanhood. Pinpricks of maddening pleasure shot through her with his touch, and as they did, she lavished his length with a series of slow, torturous kisses.

Releasing him suddenly, she turned, her lips darting upward until they were once again on his. She rose above him, her legs parting, her knees pressing against his sides. And then she lowered herself onto him, accepting his full, thrusting length within her.

When their tight curly hair mingled together, Alana held her body absolutely still, forcing herself to wait until the undulating waves of pleasure lessened.

She bent lower over him, her hips circling. Her breasts were crushed to his chest; her mouth was buried at the meeting of his neck and shoulder.

Her body moved of its own volition, controlling both their movements as she lay atop him. She could feel the hair on his chest as it rubbed against her breasts and could feel the way her rigid nipples pressed into his skin.

Beneath Alana, Rafe accepted the pleasures she bestowed upon him, letting her lead them on this loving journey. He did not try to take command from her; rather, he gazed into her eyes, showing her his love and need.

Soon Alana began to move faster. She rose up slowly until she was again sitting astride him. Her head was flung back, moving in perfect rhythm with her body. The dark waves of her hair bounced back and forth, and Rafe could feel their delicious tickle when her raven hair occasionally brushed the top of his thighs.

But above all, Rafe's heart filled with love and pleasure as he watched her ride him, watched the way her breasts bobbed and her stomach muscles rippled. Alana's dampened satin skin glowed in the low light of the oil lamps. Rafe's eyes flickered across the twin peaks of her breasts, returning once again to her face as she carried them both upward into a shattering climax. Their breath exploded simultaneously, and Alana shouted out her love for him even as her body tensed upon his. A moment later, Alana, refusing to allow him to escape from within her, lowered her torso onto his and snuggled her face against his neck.

"The hell you say!" Ledoque roared.

Denton seemed to shrink back from Ledoque's rage. "I'm sorry, sir, but that's exactly what I overheard."

Ledoque shook his head slowly. It didn't seem possible. "You're sure she called him Rafael?"

"Yes, sir," Denton replied. "As I said, I was sitting at the table next to theirs. They—" Denton paused, knowing that his next words would elicit another angry response, but he knew they had to be said if he were to be paid. "They had just finished their main course, and Mrs. Landow reached across the table and took his hand in hers. 'Rafael Montgomery, I love you,' she said to him."

To Denton's surprise, Ledoque said nothing, so he decided to continue. "The man, Sutcliff, tensed up and looked around to see if anyone was watching them. He never noticed me."

"So." The single word was like the hiss of a snake. "Richard Sutcliff is not who he says he is. But how does he know Alana Landow?"

"I don't know. I heard many references about the war," Denton added. "They talked a lot about that."

"Very good, Denton," Ledoque said. "You and your man are not needed any longer."

Denton bowed his head obsequiously and left, glad that he had not had to bear the brunt of one of Ledoque's famous rages.

But in the study of the townhouse he always maintained in New York, Charles Ledoque's anger knew no bounds. When he finally gained control over his temper, he stood, left the room, and called for his carriage.

Fifteen minutes later, at exactly ten o'clock, he entered the Wellington Club. Inside, he joined Allison in his private room and told him what he'd discovered. Allison, his features impassive after hearing that Sutcliff and Montgomery were one and the same man, spoke in a level but deadly voice.

"By tomorrow morning, Rafael Montgomery will no longer exist." After uttering his lethal proclamation, he called for two more drinks and smiled coldly at Ledoque.

"Charles," Allison said a moment later, his tone thoughtful. "While you're, ah—satisfying yourself with the Landow woman, I would like you to learn what the connection is between her and Montgomery. It's too much of a coincidence." Allison let his words trail off, knowing that no more need be said.

Ledoque, his eyes dark and alive, ran his tongue across his large lips. "You can be certain I shall," he promised.

* * *

At eight thirty in the morning, Chaco stood just inside the door of his small room, situated off the passageway between Alana's suite and Rafe's. For Chaco's purpose, it was the perfect location.

The short hallway opened into the sitting room of each suite. Except for the servants' entrance, which was near the rear staircase of the hotel, the only other entry to the hotel suites was through either sitting room.

From the moment he had met Rafe, Chaco had detected something very familiar about the man. He had seen for himself the love Rafe had for Alana, and he was not concerned for her safety when Rafe was with her.

He also did his best to stay alert when they were together, for at that time, more than any other, Alana and Rafe were vulnerable. But while he thought about those things, the nagging sense of knowing Rafe stayed with him.

A few minutes later, Rafe emerged from Alana's bedroom and went toward his suite. Chaco started to back into his room, but Rafe called his name.

Chaco looked at Rafe and waited for him to speak.

"Has Alana told you what I am doing?" he asked.

Chaco shook his head no. From what he had heard of Alana and Rafe's conversations, he believed that Rafe's activities were similar to those of Alana and Crystal.

"I am in a very dangerous situation. And I may have put Alana in danger, too."

Chaco signed a question, but Rafe did not understand it. And strangely, Chaco saw a flash of sadness in the man's green eyes.

"I wish I had learned to sign," he told Chaco. "My sister used to teach children to speak that way. Chaco, no matter what, just watch over Alana."

Chaco nodded once, and Rafe went into his suite.

Chaco's mind worked furiously on what he had just learned. Because Chaco had spent his life listening to people and not speaking, he had unconsciously developed a special sense. The way a person spoke and the inflections the person used told him a multitude of things. What he'd heard in Rafe's voice, Chaco realized, was a familiar pattern—the same basic pattern of speech and intensity of words that Crystal Revanche used.

Before Chaco could pursue that thought, he heard the door-knob in Rafe's suite being turned. Moving quickly, he went to the connecting door and pulled it closed, leaving just enough space so that he could see what was happening. When the sitting room door opened, a small, wiry man slipped quietly inside. Chaco stood tensely as the man paused, motionless, to listen for any sounds.

He saw a long blade flash in the man's hand as he slowly went toward Rafe's bedroom doorway. The small man stopped at the doorway, listening to the sounds within the bedroom. Then he started into the room.

Chaco bent quickly. When he stood again, the knife that was always strapped to his calf was in his hand. Silently, as if stalking an animal, Chaco opened the door and went into Rafe's suite.

It was not Alana, Chaco's intuition told him, but Rafe that this man was after.

19

Rafe stood near the bed, upon which was neatly laid the suit for his meeting later today. Although his mind was filled with thoughts of Alana, he understood that he had to banish them and concentrate on today's business. The meeting with the consortium was scheduled for noon at the Wellington Club. Allison preferred to conduct almost all his business from there.

Rafe had to be extremely careful. The least slip with the members of the consortium could spell his doom. Every word and thought must be controlled until they accepted him and welcomed him into their company. Then he could learn all the details of their business schemes before exposing and destroying them.

Shaking his head, Rafe forced himself to start moving. After dressing and having a light breakfast, he and Alana were planning to look over Alana's new residence. Then Rafe would go to the meeting with Allison.

As he took off his shirt, a floorboard creaked behind him. The hairs on the back of his neck rose; he spun around quickly.

Before he could fully react, a small man charged at him, a knife in his right hand. Rafe's mind turned to ice even as he started to bring his arm up to deflect the blow. But with a terrible clarity, he knew he was too late.

The man's arm was high, the blade ready to strike. Just before the blade reached him, Chaco sped into the room and lunged at the smaller man. An instant before the blade met

Rafe's skin, Chaco hit the man from the side. Knocked off balance, the attacker reeled past Rafe; the flashing knife sliced the empty air inches from his shoulder.

Reacting instinctively, Rafe spun on the attacker, his hand locking onto the man's right wrist, twisting it painfully in an effort to force him to drop the blade.

A half second later, Chaco's knife was at the man's throat. The attacker, realizing he had been defeated, released his knife.

With his teeth clenched together, Rafe glared into the ferret-like face of his would-be assassin. Chaco stood at the man's side, his face expressionless as always, his knife pricking the first layer of skin on the attacker's neck.

Hearing a startled gasp from the doorway, Rafe turned to see Alana staring wide-eyed at him, her hand pressed to the base of her throat. "What—"

Rafe shook his head once. "I don't know—yet!" Turning back to his attacker, he stared at the man for several seconds. A single muscle in his cheek ticked with the rage that was growing stronger with every second that passed.

"Why?" he asked in a hoarse whisper.

The man shook his head stubbornly.

Rafe glanced at Chaco.

Chaco smiled. He pushed the knife tip a fraction deeper into the man's neck. A trickle of blood seeped from the broken skin. As it ran into his shirt, the attacker's small eyes shifted nervously.

"Why?" Rafe repeated the question in the same husky whisper, controlling his anger as he held the killer's eyes.

"I was paid to kill you," he admitted.

"Why?" Rafe repeated one more time.

Chaco tensed visibly, and the man looked alarmed.

"I don't know why. My job was to kill you," the man stated boldly.

Rafe glanced at Alana. Her face was ghostly white; her hand still rested at the base of her throat. He saw, too, the way her breasts rose and fell in the aftermath of fright.

A sheet of ice descended within his mind. "Who paid you to kill me?"

"A man." Even as the attacker spoke, Chaco pressed the

point into his neck again. "That's all I know!" the attacker shouted.

"No, that's all you're saying, not all you know," Rafe stated matter-of-factly. "I want to know who paid you."

Even with Chaco's knife tasting the man's blood, he managed to shake his head. "Kill me."

Rafe studied the man's face and sensed that the man was not being brave; rather, he was frightened. Obviously he preferred death to facing whoever had sent him. "You don't think we'll kill you, do you?"

The man's small eyes, still nervous, stared boldly at him. Although he didn't speak, Rafe read the reply on his face.

Rafe's features expressed only sorrow at the man's words. "You're leaving me no choice. After all," he said in a falsely sympathetic tone, "for all I know, you came here to murder me for some reason of your own. Without knowing that someone really did hire you, how can I be sure you won't try to kill me again?"

"Let me go," the man offered, "and I won't be back."

Rafe knew he was telling the truth by the fear on his face. Rafe also started to read something else in the assassin's eyes— the knowledge that he was not the type of man just to kill someone. But to learn who'd hired the man to kill him, Rafe would have to make the man more afraid of him than of anyone else. "Who paid you to kill me?" he asked in a quiet voice.

"I—I can't—" The man seemed to gain a modicum of control over his fear. He stood straighter and looked into Rafe's eyes. "You won't kill me," he stated confidently.

Rafe's full smile did not reach his suddenly rock-hard eyes. "Chaco, take him into the back hallway. Kill him!"

Without a backward glance at the man, Rafe walked to Alana, took her elbow firmly, and started them out of the room. He gave a quick shake of his head at Alana's forming protest. Before they had taken two steps, the man's frantic cry reached him. "Wait!"

Rafe's hand tightened on Alana's arm, but he continued to walk, ignoring the man's plea.

"Benjamin Corsell," the ferretlike assassin shouted in a high-pitched voice.

Spinning, Rafe riveted the man with an unyielding stare. "I

don't know anyone named Benjamin Corsell. Chaco," he commanded. "Take him—"

"Wait! I—I'm not supposed to know this," the man said rapidly, his eyes shifting between Chaco's knife and Rafe's face. "Corsell hired me to kill you. He did! But Corsell is—he's James Allison's bodyguard."

With Rafe's loud exhale, Chaco's arm relaxed, but his knife stayed near the man's neck.

Rafe came back into the bedroom and looked quickly around for something to use to tie up the man. The drapes on the large window were held back by thick drapery cords, and Rafe knew they would serve his purpose well. After pulling them free, he returned to his attacker and bound the man's wrists. As he worked, his rage continued to grow. He thought of his sister and of what Allison and the consortium had done to her. He pictured in his mind the ruined timbers of his once-magnificent home. The anger that had been so much a part of his life in the last years screamed to be set free.

Only when he had finished tying the man's wrists and had found some slight control over himself did he look at Alana. "Today," he said in a deadly calm voice, "James Allison will pay for all he's done to me."

Alana stared at Rafe and saw a stranger in the place of the man she loved. His eyes blazed with rage, and his muscles were knotted tightly. In that instant, she knew that she had to stop him. "What are you going to do?"

Rafe laughed; his lips formed a taut, pale line. "First I'm going to get dressed," he told her logically, "and then I'm going to pay Allison a visit."

"Rafe—" she whispered, but he had already turned to Chaco. "Take him into the sitting room. I'll be there in a few minutes."

As he dressed, Alana went to the bed and sat on its edge. She watched every movement he made, but when he went to the large dresser and picked up the pistol, checked its load, and slipped the pistol into his waistband, Alana's heart almost stopped. Her skin turned cold and damp with fear. When he put on his jacket and turned to her, she rose and went to him, her mind working frantically.

He held her securely, and his eyes softened momentarily when they caressed her face. "It's almost over."

"I'm frightened, Rafe," Alana whispered, voicing her fear aloud. "What are you going to do?"

"I'm going to face James Allison, but not as Richard Sutcliff."

"Rafe," she began, pulling free from his arms, "don't do it this way. Go to the—"

"Law?" Rafe asked, finishing her words for her. His eyes hardened again. "Oh, I plan to do just that, Alana, but not until I'm finished with him myself. I need to look him in the eye and let him see his future in mine."

"Is that why you're bringing a gun with you?" she challenged.

Rafe didn't answer and, by the set of his face, she knew he would not. "How do you know where he is? He could be anywhere. Rafe, wait until you can choose the time and place," she argued, trying to use logic to persuade him.

"I know exactly where he is," Rafe stated, his voice still calm.

Too calm, Alana realized. The full impact of his deadly rage struck her ominously, sending chills along her spine as she took account of this side of the man she loved. She knew that his anger was as much a part of him as was his strength and his ability to love, yet this insight did little to ease her fear.

When Rafe went into the sitting room, Alana was at his side. Chaco stood next to the paid killer, his knife still in his hand. Grabbing the man by his shirt, Rafe started them both toward the door.

"Rafe, please," Alana cried in vain.

Stopping, Rafe looked at Alana and saw the fear and love that covered her beautiful features. But his need for vengeance would not let him bend to her words. "I've spent a year and a half working for this. I won't stop now, Alana; it must be done."

Alana straightened her shoulders and met his blazing eyes with her own determined ones. "Then I'm going with you, Rafael Montgomery!" she stated, remembering all the months that he had been away from her.

Rafe held fast. "To the Wellington Club? It's not possible, Alana," he said, pausing for a moment as he looked at her. "I've already lost Elizabeth to this madman. I will not lose you!

Lock the doors when I've gone. Chaco, stay alert." He turned back to his prisoner and started off again.

"No!" Alana's single word had the effect of a gunshot. Rafe froze at the hardness the word carried to him. Turning slowly, he looked into the diamondlike depths of her eyes.

Alana's heart beat furiously, but she refused to back down. "I will not let you go there alone! If you won't take me, then you'll damned well take Chaco!"

Rafe held Alana's fiery glare. Suddenly he sensed how important Alana's words were for her and for them. Their love pulsed in the air between them, reminding him of all they had already gone through. The rage that had gripped him so mercilessly released its control over him, and he began to think rationally for the first time since the attacker had come at him. Slowly the knotted tendons in his neck relaxed. "All right."

"What is the Wellington Club?" Alana asked, her thoughts still racing like lightning, her fear of losing Rafe once again strengthening her resolve.

"Allison's private club. He conducts most of his business there."

"What are you going to do with him?" Alana pointed one slim finger at the assassin.

Rafe glanced at him, taking in the man's rough, baggy pants and stained shirt. "I guess we'll turn him over to the authorities."

"No!" the man shouted frantically. Rafe saw a new kind of fear settle on his features.

"You belong in jail," Rafe told him.

"No," the man pleaded, "you don't understand. They—they control the jails and the police. I'll be dead by tonight."

As Rafe digested this new information, another thought rose in his mind—a plan that would be even better than his original.

"What's your name?"

"Murphy. Mike Murphy."

"Do you have family?"

Murphy's ferretlike face hardened instantly. He didn't speak.

Tension sprang into the air as the two men stared at each other. "I can help you, Murphy, if you help me," Rafe said, his voice friendlier, believable.

"I got to think of my family. Do you think I'd be doing this if

I didn't have a family to feed? These are poor times, mister. Money's scarce for them that ain't got any."

"If you help me," Rafe said, "I have a job for you."

"If I help you, they'll kill me. What good will that be to my family?"

"Allison won't know where you'll be. I promise you that."

"Allison will know. Them people he owns will know."

"Sign a confession, and I'll have you on the first ship for California. You and your family. You'll work for me, and Allison will never find you."

Murphy's face showed both fear and hope. But Rafe saw the underlying distrust still on the man's features.

"No more threats, Murphy. Do as I ask, and I'll make sure you and your family are safe. Don't make me turn you over to the authorities."

"All I have to do is sign a confession?" he asked doubtfully.

"And testify at Allison's trial. But I'll make sure you're protected."

"What kinda job?"

"My partner will work that out. It'll be at our mining company. You'll make good money."

Murphy was silent for a moment. Then he nodded. "But if you go to Allison today, he'll know I talked."

"That's my problem, not yours," Rafe told him. "After you sign those papers, we'll get your family and put you up in a hotel where Allison will never think to look for you. You'll have money and passage west. Agreed?"

Murphy stared at Rafe and, after he read the truth in Rafe's eyes, he spoke. "Agreed."

Rafe untied Murphy's wrists. Chaco slipped his knife into its sheath. Both men sensed that they had nothing to fear from the man any longer, since a new future had just been offered to him.

From that point on, Rafe asked myriad questions, and Murphy became a fountain of information that startled Rafe. By the time he'd finished, Rafe knew that he had the means to get Allison and destroy him completely. Murphy had done many jobs for Allison's bodyguard, and Murphy's confession would be enough to send the bodyguard to the hangman's noose. Rafe was confident that when the time came, the bodyguard would talk in order to save his own neck.

Two and a half hours later, Rafe and Chaco left the hotel suite. Alana, now armed with Rafe's pistol, left with them, but when the four people were on the street, Alana and Mike Murphy took one carriage, while Rafe and Chaco took another.

Alana was going with Murphy to his flat to get his wife and son. From there they would return to the hotel to await Rafe.

Rafe, armed with an unbelievable amount of incriminating evidence and knowing just how little help the authorities would give him at this time, was determined to face Allison and make him know that his days were numbered.

More than just anger guided Rafe toward this meeting. Rafe needed to make Allison nervous enough to make a mistake, and to have Allison mad enough to take Rafe on personally. He was going to the Wellington Club to show Allison that hiring someone wasn't enough; Allison himself had to be the one to come after Rafe.

Today would be the day he laid the groundwork to bring Allison's empire tumbling to the ground. He was confident that Allison would do nothing to him in front of the other members of the club, and that he would be safe enough until tomorrow. By then, he would have the confession in the right hands and Alana in a safer place than the hotel.

Having met Allison at the Wellington Club twice already, Rafe knew its layout and knew that Allison would either be in his private room or at one of the large leather-cushioned booths that lined the side of the main room. He was early for his meeting, but was certain Allison would be there.

At exactly eleven thirty, Rafe, with Chaco wearing an appropriate servant's livery, walked up the five marble steps leading to the wide mahogany doors of the Wellington Club. The uniformed doorman who had just admitted two other men still held the door open, but they stared speculatively at Rafe. When Rafe nodded his head familiarly, the doorman smiled as if he recognized him.

His muscles vibrated tensely when he stepped inside and smelled the heavy odor of leather and tobacco mixed with wood oil. When the door closed, Rafe looked around, Murphy's description of Allison's bodyguard filling his mind.

The club was fairly crowded, which helped to ease some of

Rafe's tension. But it sprang fully back when he saw Benjamin Corsell standing near the archway that led into the main room.

"Watch him," Rafe whispered to Chaco, nodding his head at Corsell. When Chaco's eyes locked onto the bodyguard, Rafe knew the man was no longer a threat.

A moment later an elegantly uniformed man bowed his head to Rafe and waited.

"I'm Richard Sutcliff. Mr. Allison is expecting me," he told the room attendant. "Is he at his booth?"

"Of course, Mr. Sutcliff," the attendant said as he started to turn.

"That's all right, I'll find him myself." Before the attendant had a chance to object, Rafe started into the ornate room.

The large room was lit by four evenly spaced chandeliers, aided by brass oil lamps resting in niches on each wall. The oak floor gleamed beneath its many coats of varnish, and the furniture was of the finest quality. Cigar smoke lay thick in the air, cloudlike above the heads of the members of this exclusive club.

Rafe walked steadily toward the booths lining the far side of the room. He felt apart from everything, a spectator watching a staged drama unfold. But that ethereal feeling left him quickly when his eyes found Allison's booth and he spotted the man he had come three thousand miles to destroy. He noted that Allison was not alone. Three other men were with him, none of whom he recognized.

In that very moment, when he saw his enemy sitting so comfortably, another thought suddenly attacked him. A picture of Alana, staring at him with love and fear, cautioned him to hold back the anger that threatened to explode. His love for Alana made him think of the possible future for the first time that day.

When Rafe was ten feet from the booth, Allison looked up. Rafe stopped to smile at the man's startled reaction. Allison lifted a hand in a quick signal. A moment later footsteps approached Rafe from behind. They stopped before they reached him.

Rafe smiled wide at Allison's suddenly stiff face, secure in the knowledge that Chaco had cut off the bodyguard. Reaching into his pocket, he grasped the handle of the knife Murphy had attempted to use on him.

When he reached the booth, all four men stared openly at

him. Allison had recovered from his initial shock and glared darkly into Rafe's face. The man sitting next to Allison looked at Rafe with disdain. His dark eyes were narrowed into slits; his thick lips were drawn into a sneer.

Moving quickly, Rafe drew the knife from his pocket and lifted it high. Four pairs of eyes followed the blade, each man's reaction different from that of the man next to him. Allison's face drained of blood at the sight of the blade. Rafe swung his arm downward. The blade glinted in the light and flashed dangerously as it struck into the heart of the large teak table.

When it entered the thick wood, Rafe heard the startled gasps of the other club members, but he paid them no attention. He wanted them to witness what he was doing. He knew, too, that not a single member of this club would raise a hand or voice to interfere. It just wasn't done. And although they would all watch from the corners of their eyes, pretending that nothing out of the ordinary was happening, Rafe knew they would hear everything that he said, and they would remember it.

Releasing the blade, Rafe watched it quiver back and forth in the silence that now filled the main room of the Wellington Club.

"It didn't work, Allison. I'm still alive. I'm still in your way. Now you're going to pay for everything you've done to me and my family!" Rafe drew himself taller. His hatred and rage bored into Allison as he spoke in a voice loud enough for everyone in the room to hear.

Rapidly Rafe detailed Allison's crimes against his family, then went on to tell of the other things that Allison had done that Rafe had only learned of that day. Not once in the entire time did he take his eyes from Allison's. Staring into the pale, hate-filled face of his enemy, Rafe told Allison of the signed confession and statement that Mike Murphy had given him.

When he finished, he boldly met Allison's stony glare. Only when the color began to rush back into Allison's face did Rafe step back.

When he was five feet from the booth, he stopped again. "You're finished, Allison," he said with conviction. "You're through."

When he reached Chaco, who stood with his knife pressed into the bodyguard's side, he motioned to Chaco with his head, and in less than a minute they were in the carriage and driving away from the Wellington Club.

Slowly Rafe leaned back into the seat. The rage began to ebb from him, and a faint smile touched the corners of his mouth.

James Allison's hands shook with anger and humiliation. His eyes followed Rafe until the man was gone. Then Allison looked around the room. The members who had not already turned away from the spectacle did so then.

"Montgomery will pay for this," he swore. "No one talks to me like that. No one!"

The glass in Allison's hand shattered. He paid no attention to the whiskey that spilled onto his lap as he absently shook the pieces of glass from his skin. Allison knew that the damage Montgomery had done to his stature today would follow him for a while. But he was confident that it would eventually fade away, for his power was strong enough to make the other members not pursue what they had overheard.

No, Allison's anger and concern were centered on Montgomery's next step. Everything depended on that.

When he realized that his bodyguard was standing at the booth, he looked sneeringly up at the man. "You stupid fool," Allison spat at the hapless man. "I told you to take care of Montgomery. You failed! You didn't even have the sense to follow him now."

"I'll finish the job myself," Corsell promised.

Strangely, Allison laughed at Corsell's words. "We'll see about that." His voice was suddenly light, and the other men at the table watched Allison carefully. "Montgomery is a predictable man. He's the type who believes that everything is either black or white—right or wrong. That's what made it so easy to get rid of him the first time."

"Not so easy," Ledoque said. "He came back."

"I'll kill him, Mr. Allison," Corsell promised.

"No, you won't!" Allison ordered, his eyes not leaving Ledoque's. "He'll die, but not quickly, and not by our hands. What I have in mind for Rafael Montgomery will make a swift death his dearest wish. Corsell," he said, "bring me writing material." The men waited in silence. An attendant came to clean the glass and liquid from the table. After Corsell returned,

Allison spoke in a low voice that could not be heard beyond the booth. When he was finished, everyone at the booth, with the exception of Ledoque, smiled in approval.

"Charles? What seems to be bothering you?" Allison asked pointedly.

Ledoque met his challenge. "Only one thing."

"Yes?"

"I shall be the one to implement this plan."

Allison frowned. "It would be best if none of us are involved at that level."

"No one shall know of my involvement. And it suits my other purpose very well."

Allison, seeing the lust in Ledoque's eyes, shrugged his shoulders. "Very well, Charles, but have it finished by morning."

"It shall be," Ledoque promised. "Oh, it shall be."

While Ledoque thought over Allison's plan for Rafe, James Allison set pen to paper. When he was finished, he signaled Corsell to him.

"Go to the *Venture* and give this to Captain Clarke. Tell him that I want to see him early this evening."

"Yes, sir. And then?"

"Find this fool Murphy and make sure that he cannot ever speak again. After that, you're at Mr. Ledoque's service."

"You've done everything you could for now, Rafe. We just have to wait for Allison's next step," Alana whispered as she adjusted her hat and looked into the mirror. The five hours she had waited in the hotel room for his return had been among the longest of her life.

"*I* have to wait," he corrected her as he paced aimlessly in the room while Alana continued to apply the finishing touches to her outfit.

After he'd returned from the Wellington Club, he'd taken Murphy and his family to the docks, where he bought passage for them on a ship that was leaving in two days. He had arranged for the small family to stay aboard until the ship left and had paid the captain accordingly.

He'd given Murphy a letter for Caleb Magee and Abigail Hampton that detailed everything that had happened, and he had told them of his promise to Murphy.

When he'd left the ship, he had returned to the hotel room and had spent the afternoon with Alana, making plans for his next step in destroying Allison. He would begin tonight.

"I'm ready," Alana said as she moved toward Rafe.

Rafe paused in his pacing, feeling the familiar warmth spread within him when she reached him. He took her hand and brought it to his lips, his eyes devouring her beautiful face. "I love you, Alana, more than life itself."

Alana blinked back the quick rise of tears that his words brought out. Then, when he'd lowered her hand, she drew it free. "We'll be late," she reminded him, willing the rise of her unending desire for Rafe to ease.

"We'll never be late, Alana. Other people will always be early, remember that."

The serious tone of his voice caught her off guard, and only the sparkle in his eyes told her that he was joking. But beneath the merriment, she sensed that his words said much more. It said that they were special.

A few minutes later, Rafe and Alana were in the carriage. Chaco rode on the foothold behind them as they went across town to have dinner with Alana's attorney and his wife.

At midnight, they emerged from the townhouse. They had had a pleasant dinner and had told the attorney everything that had happened today and over the past few years. Nathan Bennet, very disturbed, had promised to check into the situation.

"Your most important concern should be having Allison charged with the crimes for which you have a confession," Bennet counseled. "At the same time bring a suit against Allison and his companies for the return of your rightful assets. I give you my word that I shall personally use my influence to help you."

"Thank you," Rafe had said.

Once in the carriage, and with the horse's hooves echoing on the cobblestone street, Alana leaned comfortably against Rafe.

"Alana," he queried in a soft, sweet tone.

"Ummm?" she responded, a feeling of contentment washing over her while her head rested on his shoulder.

"Will you marry me tomorrow?"

Alana raised her head. She stared at him, her eyes misting over. She was barely able to nod her head.

"Good. I was afraid I'd have to steal you away."

"You did," she whispered, "on September twenty-sixth, eighteen sixty-five. The day you walked up to Riverbend and into my life."

He drew up the arm that was around her shoulders until his hand cupped the back of her uptilted head. Then, very slowly, he brought her face toward his.

Just when their lips met, the carriage came to a jarring halt. Alana was thrown across the carriage and, as Rafe reached out to help her, the door flew open and a dark object flashed through the air.

A dull thud echoed. Alana watched in horror as Rafe slumped to the floor and three men rushed into the carriage.

20

Everything happened so fast that by the time Alana opened her mouth to scream, one man had a pistol pointed at Rafe's head, another was aimed at her, and the third had spoken. The carriage started up again.

"So this is the man for whom you would turn me down?" Ledoque asked. "Bitch!" he spat, his hand snaking out to strike her even as he spoke the word.

Alana's cheek exploded with pain. Orange flashes danced before her eyes. She fought wildly to hold on to her senses. As she tasted her own blood on the inside of her mouth, Ledoque roared at her again.

"Watch him! See how your lover dies!" Ledoque nodded to the man holding the gun at Rafe's head.

"No!" Alana shrieked, launching herself blindly at the gunman. Before she could reach him, the second man grabbed her by her hair and yanked her harshly back.

"You want him to live?" Ledoque asked, his face partially hidden by the dark shadows of the carriage's interior.

Alana nodded her head quickly. Blood pooled in her mouth, but she ignored the pain in her cheek and the hand holding her hair as she glared her hatred at Ledoque.

"Then you will be mine from now on, won't you?"

"Pig!" she cried, spitting a mouthful of blood at him.

Ledoque slowly wiped his face. "Shoot him."

"No!" Alana pleaded again.

Ledoque held out his hand. The gunman waited. "You are the price for his life. Will you pay it?"

Alana was frozen within this terrible moment of time. She stared at Ledoque, her mind reeling. Then she looked down at Rafe. Her heart thudded loudly when she realized that his eyes were open.

Galvanizing her mind into action, she glared at Ledoque. "You bastard!" she shouted, launching herself at him in an effort to draw attention away from Rafe.

But her ploy failed. The man next to her held her fast, and the other gunman pressed the barrel into the side of Rafe's neck when he tried to rise.

Ledoque laughed while she looked on helplessly. "I'm still waiting for your answer, my dear."

"No!" Rafe yelled suddenly, fighting to push himself up. Before he could, his captor whipped the pistol into the air and smashed the barrel into the side of his head. Blackness claimed him instantly.

In the confines of the carriage, Alana saw the flowing dark stain of blood spread across Rafe's face. "Answer me!" Ledoque demanded.

Her mind twisted painfully in an effort to understand how Rafe could be lying on the carriage floor and Ledoque sitting across from her. But she could not.

She spoke without taking her eyes from Rafe's unconscious form. Her voice sounded far away and foreign to her ears. "Whatever the price, I'll pay it. Do not kill him. But if you deceive me, you will pay."

Behind her blue eyes, a spark of defiance flared, but she quickly hid it before Ledoque saw it. *I will pay the price,* she repeated silently to herself, *but not so great a one as will you.*

Ledoque lifted his walking stick, the same dark smooth object that had struck Rafe the first time, and rapped on the carriage roof. A moment later the carriage stopped.

When the door opened, two more men looked in. Ledoque grabbed Alana and pushed her from the carriage into their waiting arms. Then, when he stood on the street next to Alana, he called to the driver. "Take him away."

Alana tried to twist free of her captors, but she could not. "What are you going to do with him?"

"He won't be killed. That's all you have to know." With that, the first carriage rolled away and a second came up to them.

Alana, held fast by the men, watched her carriage leave and saw that Chaco was nowhere in sight. Then she was roughly lifted and shoved into Ledoque's carriage. A moment later, Ledoque joined her. This time, there were only the two of them.

When the carriage started forward, Alana stared at Ledoque. "Where are we going?" she asked, making her mind function and willing herself not to give in to fear.

"You shall see. And Alana, I would advise against your trying to run away from me. Think of Montgomery before you do anything foolish."

Alana glared at him, but she knew she was helpless to do anything—yet.

Chaco had spent most of his life enduring pain, and he did not give in to it now. Images of Crystal and Alana raced through his mind. He knew he could not let them down. He had been hit from behind on the head, but even as his body had rolled to a stop on the cobblestones, his feet had been under him and he had been up and racing after the carriage. He hadn't had time to see whether the driver, lying in the gutter, was alive or dead—he couldn't take the chance of letting the carriage out of his sight.

Suddenly another carriage had fallen in behind Alana's. Ignoring the throbbing in his head and the sharp pain from where the skin on his legs had been cut and torn on the cobblestones, Chaco had continued to follow the carriages, never once letting them out of his sight.

When both carriages had come to a halt in the center of a dimly lit street, Chaco had slipped into a doorway to watch and to wait for an opportunity to help.

He had tensed when Alana was pushed out of her carriage, but he knew that he could not yet free her. He waited to see what would happen and to see what Rafe would do. All too soon, he realized his wait was in vain, for the carriage started off again with Rafe still inside.

As Alana and the men walked toward the second carriage, the light of the gas streetlamp illuminated their features. Chaco's breath caught when he recognized Ledoque. Only then did Chaco know that he could not follow the carriage with Rafe but must stay with Alana.

Ledoque and Alana disappeared inside the carriage, and the two other men took their protective positions, one in front with the driver, the other in the rear. When the carriage started off again, Chaco slipped out from his hiding place.

Rafe's carriage drew to a stop at the waterfront, where the streets were still alive with people. Sailors walked with their women, while others brawled over anything at all.

The docks and the waterfront were a beehive that was never still, and like a beehive, they functioned perfectly as long as no one bothered anyone else.

No one took notice when Rafe's limp body was carried along one dock; it didn't pay to look at things too closely on the waterfront. And even those sets of eyes that marked the progress of the unconscious form knew better than to interfere.

At the edge of the dock, a stout, uniformed man waited. When the two men who carried Rafe reached him, he silently motioned to two other men behind him. They took Rafe from the others and carried him across the planks that led to the deck of the four-masted *Venture*. A moment later, the sound of a body thumping onto a wood floor was followed by the sound of the closing of a hatch.

"You may tell Mr. Ledoque that his 'cargo' is in the hold," Captain Clarke said in an uncaring voice. Turning, he crossed the boarding ramp to his ship. When he stepped onto the deck, he ordered the ramp removed.

When that was done, the captain issued further instructions to the first mate and then went to his cabin to get some sleep, for this merchantman-class ship of the Allison Shipping Company would be leaving on the morning tide, not four hours from that moment.

Alana stood before the mirror in the large wallpapered bedroom, staring at everything, seeing nothing. She wore the same dress she had been in when Ledoque had captured her, but now it was a mass of wrinkled fabric that no longer outlined her smoothly curved body. Her mind was a maze of worry and concern for Rafe and not just a little fear for herself.

The sun had just gone down. A full day had passed since the carriage had been attacked and Rafe taken from her.

When Ledoque had taken her into the townhouse, his hand had held her arm in a painful viselike grip. He had not spoken until they'd reached the third floor and he'd put her in this room. "There's no way out of this house. The doors are barred. Don't even think of trying to escape. Remember, I can still have Montgomery killed."

Then he had left. The clicking of the door's lock had told her just how much a prisoner she really was.

Alana had made herself inspect her prison. She'd gone to each window to look for a means of escape; she had found nothing. The windows weren't sealed, but the ground was three stories below. There was only a straight drop between this building and its neighbor, twenty feet away.

Then she'd gone to the door and tried the knob. As she'd expected, the door had not budged. She'd crossed the room and opened the door on the far side. It opened into a large necessary room with no windows. But there was another door on the far side. When she'd tried that, she'd found it locked.

Afraid to use the bed lest Ledoque return and find her in it, Alana had spent a long, sleepless night sitting in the single chair in the bedroom, trying vainly to make herself believe that Rafe was all right and that she would find a way to escape.

Whenever her fear of the unknown rose to taunt her, she fought it back, thinking of Rafe's strength and her own. She thought of Crystal and what her friend had done to survive, and she realized that she could do no less. There was too much at stake. Too many lives depended on her ability to beat Ledoque.

She'd thought about Rafe's last words to her, and she'd realized that if Ledoque had not done this horrible thing, she and Rafe would have been married by now.

Anger had flared at that thought. Dark rage had suffused her mind, adding to the strength of purpose that was still growing within her.

The puzzle of Ledoque's surprising presence in New York and his kidnapping of her had worried at her mind for most of the night. To help keep her wits about her, she'd tried to figure out why he had done this. Had he been following her in his efforts to ruin herself and Crystal? Could Ledoque be one of the people Rafe was after? Was that really possible, or was she stretching credulity and coincidence to help make herself less fearful? These and other unanswerable questions had paraded through her mind during the long night.

Morning had found her still in the chair, thinking. The only thing she had been able to decide was that she would do whatever was necessary to please Ledoque. First she must learn Rafe's whereabouts; then she would find a means of escape.

Shortly after reaching this decision, she'd heard the lock on the door click. One of the men who had been with Ledoque the previous night had entered. He'd brought in a serving tray and had set it on the dressing table. Without a word, he'd left, locking the door behind him.

Although Alana hadn't been hungry, she'd known she must eat in order to keep up her strength. When she'd finished the meal, she'd finally lain down on the bed and, as her eyes had grown heavy, fallen asleep.

When she'd awakened, the sun was setting. Sorrowfully, Alana had gone to the window to watch the sun depart from the sky.

"I will find you, Rafe. As God is my witness, I will find you!"

After the sun had set, Alana had left the window.

How will I do it? she'd asked herself, shivering at the thought of Ledoque's hands on her body. Pushing that fear aside, she'd gone to the mirror to stare at her image in the darkened, blue-papered room.

Now Alana remembered the talks that she and Crystal had been so fond of and the admission Crystal had made about her lack of desire.

"I make my mind a blank. I do what is necessary to please my customer. He never suspects my feelings, for I never allow them to show. When it is over, I control myself and I control the man."

I must not think of anything when he touches me, Alana told herself. And while she tried to build her determination to see this through, she once again found herself waiting as the night grew darker and the world more silent.

She was suddenly afraid that she had once again lost Rafe and might never find him again. *No!* she commanded herself. *Don't think of that.* But she could not help her thoughts, any more than she could slow the frantic beating of her heart as the fear of the known—and the unknown—attacked her.

"Damn you, Ledoque, get it over with," she whispered. As if in response to her words, she heard the lock click for the first time since the man had brought her the morning tray.

Whirling at the sound, Alana's breath caught. The door opened slowly, and at first Alana saw nothing. Then a young woman wearing the uniform of a maid entered, pulling a tub on wheels that was filled with steaming water.

Once the maid was inside, the man whom Alana had seen that morning stood guarding the door. The maid lit the gas lamps, then handed Alana a lace and silk nightgown.

"After your bath," the maid said, "you are to put this on." With that, the woman left and the man relocked the door.

Alana stared at the hot water for several seconds before her trembling fingers went to the bodice of her dress.

Alana looked at her reflection in the mirror, trying not to see the way every inch of her body showed beneath the sheer material of the silk nightgown. The dark circles of her nipples were clearly visible, as was the darker triangular shading above the joining of her thighs.

The nightgown's bodice was low cut, exposing more than an ample amount of her breasts. Beneath the sheer fabric, the rest of their rounded fullness was only slightly less visible. From her breasts, the material hung smooth and straight to the floor. There was no need for the dress to hug her contours, not the way it showed her body beneath it.

Her cheeks flamed scarlet the longer she stared into the mirror. Reaching behind her, she parted her long hair and brought two evenly divided sections forward, covering her breasts. *At least,* she thought, *I shall have some modesty.*

A moment later the door opened and the maid entered. "Come with me," she said in a monotone without looking at Alana.

Alana did not reply as her heart sped up. Instead, she took a deep breath and followed the woman. They went directly to the stairs, and as they did, Alana looked around, impressing every detail in her mind for later use.

They reached the second floor, and the maid led her to a set

of double doors at the far end of the hallway. There, she opened
one and stepped back, motioning Alana forward at the same
time.

Alana walked into the large room and, when the door closed
behind her, stopped. The rich fabrics decorating the walls of
this magnificent room were accented by the high sheen of brass
lamps damped to a soft glow. A large painting of a man em-
bracing a woman hung on one wall. Across from it was a huge
four-poster bed. A chill crawled up her spine as she looked at
the bed.

Her eyes flicked to the right where a small table had been set
for two. On it were two tall candles shimmering in silver hold-
ers. Next to the table was a silver serving cart. Beside the cart a
bottle rested in a polished bucket.

Then a noise caught her attention. She turned just as
Ledoque entered from another doorway. Time froze as she
stared at him. His hair was brushed away from his face; his lips
were formed in a half smile. He wore a waist-length silk smoking jacket, and his legs were encased in thin silk pants.

Alana repressed a shudder at the sight.

"Good evening, my dear," Ledoque said. He walked toward
her, his eyes raking her avariciously from her head to her toes.
When he stopped, inches from her, he smiled openly. "You
must be hungry."

Taking her elbow, he led her to the table. After they were
seated, Ledoque lifted a silver bell and rang it. Not three seconds later, a serving woman entered the room. Without instructions she served Ledoque first, then Alana, and then departed as
the aroma of lamb rose to Alana's nostrils.

As if reading her mind, Ledoque said, "Madame Lynche,
who just served us dinner, has been in my employ for eighteen
years. She and her daughter, who brought you here after your
bath, are totally loyal to me, for reasons you would not understand. No, my dear, they will not help you."

Then Ledoque lifted the bottle of wine and filled both glasses.
He raised his glass into the air in a silent gesture to Alana, his
eyes sparkling. After one swallow, he spoke.

"I chose that particular negligee so that I could see all that I
want. Your modesty is unwarranted," he stated pointedly, his
eyes narrowing in warning.

Knowing that she must do whatever was necessary to please him until she learned about Rafe, Alana lifted the hair that covered her breasts and pushed it behind her.

"Much better," Ledoque commented as his eyes feasted on the dark circles of her nipples. "Eat."

Alana looked down at her plate and was nauseated. "I—I'm not hungry."

Ledoque shrugged. "Suit yourself."

She watched him devour his food and drink three more glasses of wine before he tossed his napkin onto the plate. Alana had but a half glass of wine herself.

Once again, Ledoque rang his silver bell. When the serving woman reappeared, she cleaned the table silently and pushed the serving cart from the room. While she was gone, Ledoque consumed another glass of wine.

A few minutes later the woman returned. This time, the cart held a silver teapot and a decanter of brandy. She left the cart at the side of the table and left.

"Pour me some brandy," Ledoque ordered.

Alana stood, did as he instructed, and handed him the glass. He took it, but at the same time his other hand caught her waist. He stared up at her, and then slowly lifted his hand until he was cupping her left breast. Alana closed her eyes and made herself stand perfectly still.

"You will learn to enjoy my touch," he stated. Then he took his hand away and sat back.

Alana returned to her seat in a dark haze. When she looked at him again, she saw his eyes were glazed; his face was somewhat flushed. From drink? she wondered.

"Do you not want some brandy?" he asked.

Alana shook her head.

"A shame, you know. This is the finest brandy in the world. The most expensive liquor that man has ever made. It comes from the Montpelier vineyards," he added.

Alana froze at the mention of the name.

"Yes, among the many other things that the Montpelier Company exports is this magnificent drink."

"You bastard," Alana spat, unable to hold back her anger as he threw in her face his thievery and deceit.

"Careful," Ledoque whispered, his face suddenly tight.

Within her mind, she heard Crystal's words of advice about dealing with men. She willed her anger away and made her expression change.

"Much better," he said.

"How do I know that after—after you have had me, you won't have Rafe killed?" she asked suddenly.

"You don't," Ledoque stated. "Except that I have given you my word. But Alana," he said, his voice thickening from a combination of drink and lust, "if you don't please me, I will see to it that he does die."

Taking a cigar from the serving cart, Ledoque clipped its end and lit it with a candle. He completed the ceremony by drawing deeply on the cigar. When he exhaled, there was a low but persistent tap on the door.

"Enter," Ledoque called.

The man who had been guarding Alana's door walked to the table. He did not look at Alana, only at Ledoque. Bending, he whispered into Ledoque's ear.

Ledoque stood. "A small matter, my dear, I shall be back shortly." With that, both men left the room, the lock clicking behind them.

Alana breathed a sigh of relief at her reprieve, but she knew it would end all too soon. Standing quickly, she went to the window. The moon was full, the sky clear.

She listened for any sounds from behind her, and when she was sure that no one was coming into the room, she opened the window and leaned out. Looking down, she saw a straight drop to the ground two floors below. She wondered if she could survive the jump.

"If I have to," she whispered.

Leaning farther out, she saw that a vine-covered trellis reached the bottom of the window. She smiled for the first time since her horror had begun.

Then she pulled her head quickly inside, for she saw a dark, furtive shadow emerge into the alleyway. Closing the window, Alana returned to her seat and took a sip of wine to calm her jangling nerves.

I must learn about Rafe first, she reminded herself. *No more outbursts.*

After what seemed to be half an hour, Ledoque returned to

the bedroom. As he walked toward her, she saw that his legs were somewhat unsteady.

"A minor matter," he told her unnecessarily. Then he stopped, his eyes raking across her breasts. "But now there is something very important to be done."

Alana's heart almost stopped. Her stomach churned.

"Stand," he commanded.

Alana stood.

"Undress!"

Fear surged, but she fought it down as she moved away from the table and toward the bed. She knew she must do this disgusting thing; it was the only way she could learn what he had done with Rafe.

At the side of the bed, Alana bent her arms and pulled the nightgown from her shoulders. She grasped the material of the dress and slid it down her arms. When her breasts sprang free, she heard Ledoque's breathing deepen. Pushing the silken gown from her hips, she stood still as it gathered about her ankles.

"I have waited a long time for this," Ladoque said victoriously as he started toward Alana, his hands already working on the belt of his smoking jacket.

21

Alana remembered nothing of what had happened between them, and she felt only a soreness between her thighs. But she smelled his fetid breath, and when she opened her eyes, she saw Ledoque next to her, his too-pale body touching hers.

Alana lay absolutely still while she tried to determine if he was asleep. The way his breath washed across her cheeks made her think he was.

Moving carefully, Alana slid away from him. When his skin no longer touched hers, she put her legs over the side of the bed and sat up. But when she tried to stand, her arm was imprisoned by his hand.

"Where are you going?" he asked. "I am not yet finished with you."

"To cleanse myself," she stated.

"Don't take too long."

Alana left the bed and went to the necessary room, where she found a pitcher of water, a ceramic bowl, and two linen towels. While she made her ablutions, she tried to think of a way to get the information from Ledoque. When she finished, she returned to the bedroom and to the bed.

Sitting down, she steeled herself to keep up her determination, and she took a deep breath before she spoke.

But Ledoque spoke first as his hand went to her breast and stroked it knowingly. "I told you that I would have you one day," he boasted.

Alana's skin crawled when his fingers wandered on her breast. Her self-control snapped, and a red sheet of hate fueled her words. "My body perhaps. Nothing else!" Pulling back from his hand, Alana left the bed.

Ledoque was at her side in an instant, his face twisted with anger. "Everything about you will be mine!" Gripping her upper arms, he shook her violently.

Alana refused to speak. She only stared at him.

He released her, shoving her backward as he glared at her. "Are you so vapid that you really think your shipping commission was good luck? Did you really believe that having a whore for a partner would bring you success against me?"

His words pierced, arrow swift, into her mind. They confirmed things she had not thought possible, and an icy chill ran through her veins.

"What are you talking about?" Alana asked, absently rubbing the places that he had grasped so cruelly moments before. Her fear of him was gone, replaced now by an even greater sense of foreboding.

"I planned it all!" he half-shouted as he advanced toward her. "It was my company that offered Landow the commission. Your company will not survive another month. Your ship will never reach Africa. When you fail to fulfill your contract, you will lose everything you possess."

"That's impossible! You're lying!" Alana cried, but she did not feel the certainty of her own defiant words.

"No, my dear, it is very possible," Ledoque stated confidently, his voice now under control. He stopped speaking until he reached Alana, and then, as he started to speak, he reached out and cupped her chin in his hand.

When Alana tried to pull away, his fingers clamped painfully on each side of her jaw, holding her prisoner and forcing her to face him.

Ledoque stared at her through narrowed eyes, his thick lips moist from spittle. "It was I who arranged for the agent to offer you the contract—the consortium's contract. When the *Harmony* reaches Cape Town, it will no longer be your ship; it will be mine. We'll give it a new name. Of course," he said, releasing her at last, "in a week, two at the most, word will reach New

York that the *Harmony* was lost in a freak storm, not a week out of port."

"Insanity!" Alana declared, ignoring the pain his fingers inflicted. "The *Harmony* won't sail for another five days!"

Ledoque shook his head knowingly. "The last piece of equipment arrived today. It's aboard now, and the *Harmony* leaves tomorrow to meet its fate." Ledoque smiled again as he savored the distraught look on Alana's features.

"There will be only one survivor of that unlucky voyage. He will report that all other hands were lost, as well as the cargo, when the ship sank. You see, my dear, one of my ships has already left to intercept the *Harmony* shortly after she leaves port. Then it will be my crew, flying the Marquette flag, who will bring the ship to Cape Town. Your crew will not survive their journey."

Ledoque smiled at the shock so plainly visible on Alana's face. "You realize, do you not, that you are responsible for all those men who will die when the *Harmony* is boarded?"

"You're mad!" Alana declared.

"Perhaps," Ledoque agreed with a shrug. "But look at what my madness has gained me." Again he reached out. This time his hand caught her long hair. He dragged her to him until his eyes were a half inch from hers.

"You could have saved Landow Shipping when I made you my offer. You could also have saved Riverbend. But you're going to lose everything. When word of the *Harmony*'s loss reaches port, the agent will call for full restitution of the cargo, as is stated in the contract."

"No!" Alana shouted, twisting from him.

"Yes," Ledoque replied in a calm, victorious voice. Then he released her. "As I said, Alana, you should have accepted my offer when I gave it. You would have been the wife of one of the most powerful men in the world."

Alana was shaking inside, but outwardly she forced herself to appear calm, despite her nakedness.

"I accept the offer now, Charles," she said, her mind working frantically to think of a way to save the men of the *Harmony*. Calculatingly, she moved close to him and pressed her breasts to his chest. She moistened her lips with a darting tongue; her fingernails ran lightly up and down his arms.

"Do you think I would marry a whore?" he asked, staring
hard into her eyes, ignoring what she was attempting to do.
"That is what you are, Alana. You and that Revanche woman.
No, I will keep you until I grow tired of you, and then I will
throw you into the street where a good whore belongs!"

Alana spun from him. "As you did with Rafe?" she asked.

Behind her, Ledoque laughed explosively. "Your lover will
never see another street."

Alana stiffened; her breath was trapped in her chest as his
words bored into her mind. Yet she did not turn back to him,
for fear he would see the hope in her eyes.

Then she felt Ledoque come up behind her. His chest
touched her back. His hands went around her waist and began
to stroke her stomach as he pressed her tighter against him. She
could feel him beginning to harden, and she could not repress
the shudder that rippled along her body.

"You see, my dear," Ledoque continued as if he were having
a pleasant conversation with one of his peers, "Montgomery
had made an enemy of the most powerful man in New York,
and perhaps the entire country. This man wants Montgomery
to live out his life as a lesson in stupidity and futility. Rafael
Montgomery is to live with the memory of what he will never
have or see again." Ledoque paused to kiss Alana's shoulder.
His lips were hot and wet against her skin; his hands rose upward, pushing her arms away as he grasped her breasts and
fondled them freely.

"Montgomery is on a ship that left port yesterday morning
bound for South Africa. When the ship docks, Montgomery
will be turned over to a—certain party, who will take him to the
Transvaal, where he will spend the rest of his life in bondage,
working in a diamond mine like a slave."

Ledoque's last word echoed ominously. Alana reacted ferociously. Spinning, she dislodged his hands; her own hand rose
and flashed toward him. The sound, when her hand met his
face, was loud and sharp. Then she launched herself at him, her
fingers curved and clawlike, her nails seeking his face.

Her left hand sank into his cheek. She pulled it sharply down.

Ledoque's roar of rage filled her ears. Before she could strike
him again, Ledoque attacked. Pain exploded in her stomach.
She doubled over, gasping for breath, but before the pain

started to diminish, she was caught from behind as Ledoque grasped her long hair.

Her head was snapped back, and she found herself staring into Ledoque's maddened face. "Bitch!" Ledoque spat. Jerking her painfully to her feet, his other hand grasped her throat.

"I could kill you easily," he stated, his hand tightening on her windpipe. "But not yet," he finished in a whisper.

Alana stared, not into his eyes, but at the three deep red furrows her nails had made in his cheek. "You'll have to kill me, or I'll kill you," she promised in a flat, deadly voice.

Pulling her head back, Alana tried to escape his grip. He reacted by tightening his hand on her throat and cutting off her breath. He held her like that until spots danced before her eyes and darkness seeped into her mind. Then he suddenly released her and pushed her back.

Gasping for air, Alana could not stop him from grabbing her and carrying her to the bed. She was trying to fight him, but the way he held her prevented any but the weakest of moves.

Suddenly she was on her feet again, facing him, for he had set her down at the side of the bed. Without letting herself think, she lashed out. He caught her wrist in his left hand; his right palm struck her cheek. The force of the blow sent her tumbling back onto the bed.

She lay still for a moment, feeling blood flow from her lower lip. Ignoring it, she stared hatefully up at him. Then her eyes widened, and her body turned cold.

Ledoque laughed again, even as his eyes shone with insanity and lust. Alana realized that their fight had only served to excite him and that he was grossly swollen with desire.

She almost cried out, but she stopped herself.

"Good," Ledoque said, "very good, Alana. Maybe now you'll show some life when I take you, instead of lying beneath me like a dead sow."

Alana shook her head fiercely.

"Oh yes, you will. Now I will teach you how to please a real man!"

When he put one knee on the bed, Alana kicked upward toward his face. Ledoque had been prepared and grabbed her ankle. Then he caught her other ankle and locked them to-

gether. An instant later he twisted both legs and turned Alana
onto her stomach.

She tried to squirm away, but his fingers twisted into her hair
and he jerked her head back. She cried out in pain.

Then his hot breath rushed across her ear, followed a moment later by his voice. "Keep fighting, Alana. I like a woman
who shows life." He lifted his body and then forced himself
between her legs, his chest pressing heavily onto her back.

She stiffened when she felt his hardness pressing into her, its
hot, blunt tip probing where it should never go.

She squirmed anew, shouting as she tried to dislodge him, but
the painful way he held her neck stopped any move she attempted. Then his other hand was under her, lifting her backward toward him. His fingers slid cruelly toward her womanhood, while his rigid pole continued to try to gain entry.

Her body stiffened with a fear such as she had never known.
Anger and humiliation fed her mind, but they did not give her
the strength to throw him off.

"No!" she screamed when he pushed harder against her.

Throughout the entire first night, the whole of the next day,
and the early hours of this night, Chaco had stayed near the
townhouse. He'd walked around it endlessly, waiting to see if he
could catch a glimpse of Alana. Early that morning, he'd seen
Ledoque leave, but not with Alana. Ledoque had returned just
after sunset, and Chaco had gone into the small alley that separated Ledoque's house from the one next to it.

The feeling of dread that had been with him since he'd recognized Ledoque stayed with him, and it had not given him a
moment's peace. Yet until he knew where Alana was being kept
in the house, he could do nothing.

Two hours after Ledoque returned, Chaco had glanced up at
the sound of a window being opened. He flattened against the
building when he saw someone lean out of the second-floor
window.

When he saw it was a woman, he left the shadows, trying to
see if it was Alana. He thought it might be, but the woman had
withdrawn her head quickly.

Then all he'd been able to do was wait.

Later, the back door had opened. A woman and man had

stepped outside for a moment. Again, Chaco fled to the protection of the shadows. But he stayed within listening distance.

"Poor girl, I've never seen him like this. Not in all the years we've been here," said the woman.

"He's getting crazier every day," the man agreed.

"How long do you think he'll keep her here?"

The man shrugged his shoulders. "Not long. I heard Corsell tell Mr. Ledoque that Mr. Allison expects him to go to Washington with him tomorrow night."

"What will he do with her?"

Before the man had answered, another woman had called the two people inside. Chaco knew that he must act soon.

Looking up, he saw that light still flickered in the window, and he decided he would wait until it went out. He had already inspected the latticework, and he thought it would support him.

It was well past midnight when Chaco's senses urged him to move. He had seen the lights in two other rooms go out, but the lights in the upper bedroom still illuminated the windows.

He heard voices, loud enough to be heard through the second-floor window. His muscles tensed when he recognized Alana's tones. Then he heard her scream, and his body went into action. Pulling his knife from its sheath, he clamped it between his teeth and started to climb the trellis.

More shouts, followed by the sound of flesh hitting flesh reached him. Two minutes later, his hands were on the window ledge; his feet were anchored in the trellis.

Levering himself up, he looked into the window and froze. He saw Ledoque strike Alana in the face, and he watched as her body tumbled onto the bed. His rage turned cold when Ledoque twisted her onto her stomach and grasped her hair. When Ledoque yanked her head back and put himself between her legs, Chaco's anger broke all his control. He opened the window slowly, not once allowing the wood to make any noise. As Alana screamed in defiance, Chaco pulled himself into the bedroom. Freeing the knife from his teeth, Chaco reversed the blade and threw it at Ledoque's back.

As Ledoque rolled off of her, Alana bolted from the bed. When she stood and saw Chaco, her eyes widened and her breath escaped in a loud sigh. She looked at Ledoque's body, and knew immediately that he was dead. Realizing that she was naked, Alana wrapped the bedspread around herself. "Thank you," she whispered, tears suddenly spilling from her eyes. She would find out the rest later.

Chaco's hands moved quickly: *We must go.*

Alana shook away the fog that was part of her mind. "I need my clothes." Alana looked at the door. "This way."

Chaco pulled his knife free from Ledoque's back. Then he stepped in front of Alana and went to the door. Opening it, he peered cautiously into the hallway. When he saw it was clear, he motioned to Alana.

In the hallway, Alana took the lead, bringing them to the third-floor bedroom where she had left her clothing. Chaco stood guard while Alana dressed. When she was finished, she touched Chaco's arm.

Once again, Chaco was the first into the hallway. Silently he led Alana down to the main floor, pausing by each doorway to listen before going on.

When they reached the front door, Alana opened it while Chaco stood with his back to her, watching in case one of the staff appeared from the back of the house. A half minute later, they were out the door and into the street.

Breathing a sigh of relief, Alana looked at Chaco. "We don't have much time," she said. And as they walked quickly toward the hotel, Alana told Chaco everything she had learned.

Alana closed the last trunk and went to the writing desk in her hotel room. She had succeeded in blanking out most of the shame she'd suffered at Ledoque's hands, and she now concentrated solely on her first objective: to save the crew of the *Harmony*.

She wrote a note to Captain Sanders, ordering him to wait at the dock until she arrived. She stressed the urgency of her request, stating that there was a dire emergency. Then she sent Chaco to the dock with the note.

While he was on the errand, she went into Rafe's rooms and collected his belongings. When she found the golden chain with her mother's band on it, emotion welled up strongly in her. Pushing those emotions aside for now, she took the band and put it on her right hand. Then she returned to the desk and started to write again.

Dipping the pen into the inkwell, Alana first wrote Nathan Bennet, detailing Rafe's abduction and telling him that she would be leaving on the *Harmony* in an effort to save Rafe. She put Mike Murphy's confession in the envelope so the lawyer would have it for safekeeping.

The second letter was to Crystal. In the most minute detail, she wrote Crystal of everything that had happened to her and of her discovery of Ledoque's plans. She wrote that she would accompany the *Harmony* and deliver the cargo. Once she arrived in Cape Town, she would not leave until she had found Rafe and freed him from whatever hell Ledoque and James Allison had sent him to. Having never explained to Crystal who her true love in fact was, Alana supplied some of the pertinent details about Rafe, and about the miracle of her finding him again. She finished the letter by telling Crystal that she was leaving all business matters in her hands.

As she sealed and addressed the envelope, Chaco came into the sitting room. Looking up at him, she spoke. "Captain Sanders will wait for me?"

Yes, Chaco signed.

"Good. I will arrange for my trunks to be taken down and for a carriage to take me to the dock. Chaco," she said, pausing for a moment, "I will never be able to thank you for tonight."

Chaco shook his head emphatically. Then his hands moved slowly so that Alana could read every word they spoke. *It was my fault you were taken. You were hurt because of me.*

"No, Chaco," Alana said as she stood and went to him. She grasped his hands between hers and looked directly into his eyes. "There was nothing you could have done to prevent them from taking me. They would have killed you. But I am here now because of you. That is what is important. And we will *never* discuss this again!" Alana stated.

Chaco held Alana's steady gaze for a moment before slowly nodding his head in understanding.

"Good," Alana said with a warm smile. "Chaco, when we go to the docks, I will arrange passage for you back to Charleston. You must see that Crystal gets this letter. It will tell her everything that's happened."

Chaco shook his head adamantly. Then his fingers flew in speech.

"Too fast," Alana said.

Chaco signed again, slowly. *Crystal say I must stay with you. Chaco stay!*

"You must go back to her."

No!

"Please, Chaco. I am going far away."

Chaco's face was expressionless, but Alana thought she saw a flash of amusement in his ebony eyes. His hands spoke again. *You will need me there. It is far away for you. It is home for me.*

"Home?" she whispered.

Chaco nodded his head. *I will help you find him. I promise this.* When Chaco finished signing those last words, he tapped his hand over his heart to emphasize he meant Rafe.

Alana could no longer argue with him. Rather than speak, she signed back to him, *Thank you.*

An hour and a half later, with the hotel clerk having promised to see the two letters posted, Alana's trunks were loaded into the same cabin on the *Harmony* that she had used on the voyage to New York. Alana herself went to see Captain Sanders to explain the imminent danger.

After she'd told Captain Sanders all of Ledoque's scheme, he'd called the first and second mates to him and ordered them to be prepared for the possibility of piracy and to have the cannons manned as soon as the *Harmony* left the harbor. Then he told the mates to check each of the new crewmen and find out who worked for Ledoque. After that, he'd given Alana his assurance that somehow they would reach their destination.

As the sun began to rise on the horizon, Alana went to stand at the bow of the *Harmony,* and soon New York Harbor was falling quickly behind.

She looked back at the city for one last time as it came to life under the dawn's light. When she turned away, she saw that three sailors had already uncovered one of the *Harmony*'s four cannons and were bringing out the stock of powder and shells.

"Perhaps we can outrun them," she whispered hopefully.

Book
III

South Africa
Cape Town, The Transvaal
1867–69

22

Rafe opened his eyes. A solitary beam of sunlight filtered down to where he lay on the earthen floor, trying to breathe the sweltering, humid air. His lips were cracked, his mouth dry, and his tongue swollen. He was weak, but he was also thankful that he was no longer in the hold of the ship.

Rafe blinked several times and forced his muscles into action. Sitting up, he looked around the darkened cavern of his new prison and wondered exactly where in the world he was.

Throughout the long ocean journey he'd been kept below. He had been allowed on deck exactly twice, but his brief respites outside had only made it harder to tolerate his fetid prison in the hold. No man on the ship spoke to him, and whatever he'd been able to overhear had given him no insight regarding his destination.

He'd not been fed or given water for the first three days of the trip. When his captors had finally shown themselves, they had been behind several guns. Resistance was hopeless. Weakened and outnumbered, he'd been unable to fight the men who had put manacles on his wrists and ankles.

Then they'd fed him and given him water. No one spoke to him, and he spoke to no one. After that he was fed two small meals a day and given water once a day—just enough nourishment to keep him alive.

Although he'd realized that they were trying to break his

spirit, he had not given up. Instead, he'd pictured Alana's beautiful face near his and felt her hands on him, her lips kissing his.

He had been forced to live like an animal; only rarely was the hold cleaned out. By the time they had arrived in whatever port it was, Rafe was only half conscious. He was barely able to move his arms and legs or open his eyes to see where he was.

But he'd been awake enough to smell the strange scents permeating the air. He'd been taken out of the hold on the second night and carried to this place—a warehouse, he was sure. Then he'd been dropped on the floor and left.

He didn't know how long he'd drifted between awareness and blackness, but when he opened his eyes again, he'd found himself staring up at the one thin line of light.

And as he had on the journey, he fueled his strength and resolve by thinking of Alana. Again he recalled the look that had been on her face when they had been attacked.

Rafe had seen, in those few moments before the man had knocked him out again, her look of abject terror. He had also seen the same man who had sneered so openly at him in the Wellington Club.

It had taken him awhile, but during the six long and lonely weeks in the ship's hold, he had come to the only conclusion possible: the man was Charles Ledoque, the same one who had tried to own Alana once before.

But Rafe never, in all the days of his capture, allowed himself to think of what might have happened to Alana. He made himself believe she'd escaped the madman's clutches, for to believe anything else would be to lose faith in himself.

There was a noise behind him, but he was too weak to turn. A moment later, footsteps approached his head, and a strangely accented voice spoke.

"Put him with the others. But give him food and water first. He won't survive the trip otherwise. Remember, he is to live!"

"Yes, sir, I'll take care of it," came another voice, this one pure cockney. Both men left, but ten minutes later the cockney returned and knelt at Rafe's side.

"You heard the boss. Listen ta me, mate. I'm going ta give ya some food an' water. Then I'm going ta load ya in the wagon. It's a long trip, mate, so try ta get yourself ready."

Rafe didn't argue. He drank all the water and ate all the food.

He felt some of his strength returning, but when he tried to
stand, he found his legs would not yet support him.

"Gave ya a rough time, didn't they?" the man asked as he
helped Rafe up and half-carried him to the door. When the
door was opened, Rafe closed his eyes against the brilliance of
the sun.

"Where am I?" he asked in a croaking voice. The man leaned
him against the side of the building while he closed the door.

"It ain't where ya are mate but where yer going. The Transvaal—ya be going ta work the mines."

Rafe's hand grasped the man's arm. "Where am I? What
country?"

The man shook his head sadly. "Cape Town, mate. Cape
Town, South Africa." Then the man started to bring him to a
wagon.

Rafe used the few seconds of rest to will strength into his
weakened limbs. He knew that, weak though he was, this might
be his only chance for escape. When the man reached out to
help him again, Rafe forced himself into action.

Lurching sideways, Rafe pretended to stumble. He moved
quickly, bringing his manacled arms up to strike the cockney
guard. But a sudden, unexpected pain burst in the back of his
head, and blackness took him before he hit the ground.

"Perhaps next time you'll listen when you're told that a man
is dangerous."

The cockney guard nodded his head silently to the man who
had originally given him his orders. Then, with the man's help,
he carried Rafe into the wagon, secured his manacles to the
long bar on the wagon's side, and closed the gate.

While the cockney guard climbed into the driver's seat and
started the horses, the other four prisoners in the wagon looked
at the unconscious man in sympathy.

Two hours later, Rafe groaned and tried to sit up. A wave of
dizziness washed over him. Then he felt hands helping him.
When he opened his eyes, he saw a man sitting next to him.

"You okay?" the man asked.

Rafe looked around in an effort to get his bearings. It was
dusk, and there was just enough light to see the somewhat barren land they were crossing. The earth seemed to have a pur-

plish hue, and there were great parched cracks wherever he looked.

The man who had helped him was about Rafe's own size and also had a beard. Across from them, three black men watched silently. All were chained to the side of the wagon.

"I think so," Rafe replied as he tried to organize his senses. "Where are we?"

"Two hours out of Cape Town, on the way to the Transvaal," the man answered.

Rafe moistened his lips as he readied another question; at the same time he realized the man was an American like himself. "Why?"

The man shook his head. "I guess that blow you got back there addled your brain. No one could be that dumb!" Getting no response from Rafe, he continued, "This is a prison wagon. We're being sent to the mines to work out our sentences."

"I'm not a criminal," Rafe whispered.

"I'm not either," the man said sarcastically, shaking his chains. "But if you're on this wagon, friend, that's just what you are, no matter what you think. I tried to smuggle diamonds out of the mine I worked for." The bearded man paused, his eyes suddenly far away. "But I didn't think I'd end up dying for them stones. What are you in for?"

Rafe looked into the other's eyes and exhaled slowly. "Stupidity."

Hearing an unusual commotion in the outer office, Edward Parkins left his desk and went to the door. When he opened it slightly to look out, he realized that this simple motion was either the gravest mistake of his life or the most fortuitous action he'd ever taken. As he watched the scene before him, he fell in love.

Looking out into the office, he watched a beautiful woman with a deeply tanned face and sparkling, jewel-like blue eyes that, like pale sapphires, blazed angrily at the clerk. Her voice grew louder and more deliberate.

The wealthiest and most powerful man in Cape Town stood transfixed by the sight of the woman. She wore a simple traveling dress that rose to the base of her throat; in no way did it hide the absolute perfection of her body. As she argued with the clerk, he became entranced with her lyrical accent, recognizing it as both American and deeply southern

Sensing that things had gone far enough, he stepped into the large, open office. When he did, several heads swung around. The clerks sitting at their desks watched him with smirks on their faces and pity in their eyes for the hapless woman.

"What seems to be the problem?" Parkins asked in a commanding voice. The woman and the clerk turned to look at him. From the corner of his eye, he saw a tall thin black man stiffen when he approached the woman.

"M-Mr. Par-Parkins," the clerk stammered. "Th-this woman insists that her sh-ship has a cargo to be delivered to us."

Edward Parkins looked at the woman, his eyebrows raised slightly. "And you are?" he asked.

"Alana Landow," she replied tersely. "And you?" she challenged.

Edward Parkins bowed his head to her in a polite gesture. "I am Edward Parkins, the owner of this company."

"I see. Then I have a manifest for you," she stated.

"There must be some mistake," he told her. He saw anger flash on her face. "However, if you would come into my office, I will try to get to the bottom of the problem."

"There is no mistake, and no problem!" Alana stated. But she let him usher her into his office. Before she entered, she turned to nod at the black man who had started following them. Chaco entered with them and went to the side wall, where he continued to watch.

After closing the office door, Parkins led Alana to a chair and returned to his desk. "Miss Landow," he began.

"Mrs. Landow," Alana corrected, studying him for the first time since he'd appeared in the outer office. He was a distinguished-looking man in his mid-forties, with a pleasant yet strong face, salt-and-pepper hair, and gentle brown eyes. He had, Alana sensed, an air of honesty about him. Yet she would not allow any of her senses to interfere with her goals.

"Mrs. Landow," he repeated, aware that she was appraising him closely, "would you please enlighten me about this—difficulty?"

"My ship is attempting to deliver a consignment of mining

equipment for which my company, Landow Shipping, was contracted," she told him.

"And our shipping is done through Marquette," he replied.

"So I've been informed," Alana declared. "For three days my captain and myself have been arguing with your warehouse manager and every clerk that we've been sent to."

Parkins shook his head slowly. "I still don't understand."

Alana took a deep breath, stood, and put several sheets of what appeared to be a signed agreement on the man's desk. When she stepped back, she did not return to her seat; rather, she paced the floor.

Before Parkins could look at the papers, Alana stopped in the middle of the floor to rivet him with a gaze that combined pure hatred with unrestrained fury. Edward Parkins had never seen that look in a woman's eyes before.

"My attorney will be notified of everything that has happened. I intend to bring charges against Marquette and the Maklin-Parkins company for fraud and piracy unless the terms of our contract with both your company and Marquette are honored to the letter!"

"Madame," Parkins said, his tone stiff and formal, "I have no idea what you're talking about, and unless you enlighten me, I shall have no choice but to consider you beautiful but somewhat insane."

Alana stiffened. She thrust her shoulders back; her eyes blazed. "Perhaps I am somewhat insane. Why else would I have crossed thousands of miles of ocean, involved in a running battle most of the way against another ship that was trying to pirate mine? My ship lost five men during the battles, and another seven were wounded—all to deliver *your* equipment."

Parkins stared at her, astonishment plainly written on his face. He held the papers Alana had put on the desk, but he was not looking at them; his eyes were for Alana only.

She pointed one slim finger at the papers. "Those are the manifests and our contract with the shipping agent, Jonathan Martin, in New York. If you will look them over, you will see that they are in order."

Ten minutes later, with Alana still pacing the floor, Edward Parkins looked up from his reading. "Everything is in order.

But I still don't understand. Our agreement with Marquette is exclusive. This is a violation of that agreement."

"That is not all that has been violated," Alana said bitterly.

Again Parkins shook his head. "Please, Mrs. Landow, I am more sorry than you could imagine for your troubles, but I know nothing of what has happened. My company has an exclusive contract with the Marquette Company for all American shipments. However, your allegations disturb me greatly, and the validity of these contracts cannot be denied."

"Then you will accept delivery and make payment?"

"Absolutely. But I also want to know why this has happened. I want to know everything!"

"The story isn't short," Alana said in a voice softer than she'd yet used that day.

"In that case, Mrs. Landow, please join me for dinner so that you can tell me your story. Seven thirty?"

Alana gazed at him, wondering whether she should accept his offer. She was by no means certain that he wasn't involved with Ledoque or the consortium.

"Please, I would consider it an honor."

A sudden, intuitive feeling told Alana she could trust him. For a change, she gave in to that feeling. "Seven thirty," she agreed.

Alana arrived at precisely seven thirty. When she stepped down from the carriage Edward Parkins had sent to her, she stared up at the stone facade of his huge home. It reminded her, in many ways, of Riverbend. The house's lines were simple yet elegant, and she felt comforted looking at it.

When she and Chaco reached the top step, the door opened and a butler, momentarily astonished by Chaco, ushered them in. He brought Alana to a well-appointed salon and informed her that Mr. Parkins would be with her directly. Chaco took up a position by the door, and the butler had no choice but to leave him alone.

While she waited, Alana looked around the attractively decorated room. The brocade furniture was both expensive and tasteful. Two magnificent landscapes hung on the hand-painted wallpaper.

It was, she thought, a very masculine room that gave ample

evidence of wealth. *And what of Parkins?* Alana asked herself for the tenth time since leaving his offices. He had seemed truly shocked by what she'd told him. He did not appear to be a part of Ledoque and Allison's schemes, although only time would tell her that for certain.

Alana believed she was becoming a better judge of people than she had been two years ago, and she sensed that Edward Parkins was a decent man, a man who might help her.

"Welcome to my home, Mrs. Landow," Parkins said when he entered the salon.

"Thank you," Alana replied. When he took her hand in his and raised it to his lips, she found it somewhat comforting.

"Would you care for a sherry before dinner?" he asked, motioning to the serving tray near the settee.

"I'm afraid it would go to my head. I haven't had a chance to eat since dawn," Alana said truthfully.

Parkins smiled. "In that case, there's no point in delaying." Taking her elbow lightly in his hand, he escorted her to the dining room.

Inside, Alana gazed at the room, once again feeling the masculine hand that had decorated it. The formal dining table was of red mahogany. Eight matching chairs surrounded it. A large but not ornate crystal chandelier hung over the center of the table. The dozen brightly glowing candles gave a soft illumination to the room.

Two places had been set at the table; Parkins guided her to one. On her left was a red mahogany sideboard; its glass doors revealed a magnificent set of porcelain china.

When she sat, she looked up at her host. "You have exquisite taste."

"Thank you, Mrs. Landow." Then he went to his seat, and they were served soup and wine. When they were alone, Parkins lifted his glass to Alana.

"To a very beautiful and unexpected guest."

Alana smiled at his compliment. She found herself warming toward the man, and she tentatively lowered her defenses. "Thank you," she replied after sipping the light white wine.

"I want you to know, Mrs. Landow, that after you left, I looked into your charges."

"And?" Alana asked with genuine interest.

"The Marquette Company agent said he had no knowledge of this strange commission of yours, but he did say that Charles Ledoque was a principal of Marquette. When I showed him the manifest and contract, he said that they appeared to be legal. He seemed as mystified as I."

"Is he an American?" Alana asked.

Parkins shook his head. "From England, as I am."

Alana tasted the soup and found it delicious. "I would like to speak with him myself."

"I shall arrange it," Parkins promised.

They finished their soup quietly, and when they were finished, a servant appeared and took away their plates.

In the ensuing silence, Alana took the opportunity to again study Edward Parkins. His handsomeness, she realized, had a lot to do with the calm maturity in his eyes. He was in excellent health and had kept himself very fit. The heavier gray at his temples gave him a warm and dignified appearance.

"Do you approve?" he asked suddenly.

Alana blushed. When she realized she was blushing, the red turned bright scarlet. "I—I'm sorry," she said.

"Don't be," he replied with an easy grin.

No sooner did he finish speaking than the servants appeared with the next course. Dinner consisted of rack of veal, with ample amounts of broccoli and carrots complementing the meat in both color and taste.

Another bottle of wine was opened, and the white wine, although barely touched, was taken away. "I do hope you're hungry," Parkins said.

Alana gazed openly at him again. "I'm starved," she replied honestly as she picked up her silver knife and fork.

Edward Parkins laughed at her statement. "Well then, I shall not bother you with useless conversation." Then he too picked up his utensils and began to eat. He maintained polite conversation with Alana, but never once made any inquiry that might make her uncomfortable.

An hour and a half later, they were in the salon. Alana sipped from a floral tea cup while her host drank coffee.

"I think that now is the time for me to hear your story, Mrs. Landow. I do hope it will explain why you are here without your husband."

Alana put the delicate porcelain cup down thoughtfully. "That is a part of the story," Alana said. At her words, Edward Parkins sat back in his chair and gave her his undivided attention.

Alana had prepared herself for this moment, and she knew that if he was as decent a man as she believed him to be, she must tell him everything. So as Alana spoke, she reached back into her memories and gave him the detailed story of her life. She faltered several times as she spoke, primarily when it was about Rafe or Jason. But Parkins never interrupted her. He just sat silently while she poured out her tale.

When she spoke of Ledoque's original treachery, her voice grew harsh with anger, but she regained control of herself, and spoke as calmly as possible.

She told him of the way Ledoque had tried to destroy the Landow Shipping Company and told him of Crystal's help, omitting the fact that Crystal was a madam. But when she spoke of what had happened in New York, her voice trembled.

Alana, ignoring the wavering of her voice, simplified her tale, saying only that Chaco, her bodyguard, had saved her life and ended Ledoque's.

She described the running sea battle between the *Harmony* and Ledoque's ship and told of their relief when they had lost the other ship in a storm three weeks after leaving New York.

Parkins saw her sorrow when she told of the deaths of the seamen, and he applauded the way she and two other sailors had nursed the wounded men until they reached Cape Town and were able to bring a doctor to them.

When she was finished, he said nothing. He handed her a linen handkerchief so that she could wipe her tearstained cheeks.

"And you are certain," he said at last, "that your fiancé was brought to Cape Town?"

"Yes, I'm certain it is exactly as Ledoque said."

"Then tomorrow we shall speak to the authorities and find your Rafe Montgomery."

Alana smiled gratefully at him then. "You are very kind, Mr. Parkins."

"Edward, please."

"Edward. I—I do not know how to thank you."

"By letting me be your friend. By letting me help you," he said honestly. Edward Parkins knew he was in love with Alana, but he was also a gentleman, and because he had learned of her love for another, a man who could not be there to stand up for himself, he would not take advantage of her.

"All right, Edward. And please—call me Alana."

At nine o'clock the next morning, Edward Parkins arrived at the dock to find Alana and Chaco waiting for him. He greeted her and was then introduced to Captain Sanders.

"Everything is arranged for the unloading?" he inquired.

"Yes," Captain Sanders replied with a happy smile.

"The injured men? Are they being well treated?" Edward asked.

Again Sanders nodded his head.

"The medical expenses are to be sent to my office."

"That's unnecessary. It is my responsibility," Alana replied.

"Not if you are going to carry my goods to America, it isn't," Edward stated flatly.

"What?" Alana asked, startled by his words.

"Marquette violated their agreement with my company. Therefore I have the right to cancel their contract. Will Landow Shipping be able to accept my commissions?"

For the next ten minutes, with Alana's mind working at lightning speed, she asked every pertinent question she could. When she had digested all the answers, she looked at Captain Sanders.

Sanders inclined his head a fraction of an inch, and Alana smiled. "We shall be happy to accept your offer, Edward."

"Excellent. Then as soon as the *Harmony* is unloaded, I shall have the next shipment for Charleston sent aboard. The contracts will be ready before you sail."

Emotions welled strongly at his kindness and at the fact that with his words the future of Landow Shipping had been not only salvaged but assured.

"And now I think it best we be on our way," he told Alana.

Alana nodded and started to leave the dock with him; Chaco trailed several feet behind. When they reached the carriage, Edward paused to look at the tall ex-slave.

"Basuto?" he asked Chaco.

Chaco held Edward's gaze for several silent seconds.

"He is mute," Alana informed him.

Edward did not look away from Chaco. "But he can hear?"

"Yes," she replied.

"Are you Basuto?"

Chaco slowly nodded his head.

"I thought as much. You were only a boy when you left, were you not?"

Alana spoke for him. "He was taken as a slave. He was sold on the black market before the war."

Edward sighed. "Do you remember much?"

Chaco nodded his head again.

"Then you know you must stay here for now."

Chaco lifted his hands and signed to Alana. *He is right. But I should stay with you.*

"I trust him," she told Chaco.

I trust no one.

"Wait here, please," she asked Chaco.

Chaco met her gaze. *I wait. Have him explain about my people.*

"I will," Alana promised. Then she turned to Edward. "Shall we go?"

Edward helped her into the open carriage. When he was seated next to Alana, he turned back to Chaco. "She will be safe with me," he said. A moment later, the carriage started off.

23

Alana's day with Edward Parkins went smoothly. First they spoke with the Marquette agent, who Alana realized knew nothing. Then, as she and Edward went to the various government offices, Alana learned a good deal about the English colony of Cape Town. She discovered that the colonial British bureaucracy was a hopeless maze that grew more confusing the longer one walked through it. Yet despite her inability to gain further word about Rafe's whereabouts, she persisted in keeping up her hopes.

And as the day wore on, Edward continued to be a staunch supporter, all the while giving her a history lesson of Cape Town and all of South Africa. But the most important thing he told her was his words of caution about Chaco.

He explained the taboos and restrictions of South Africa concerning the "colored," as the blacks were called. After he finished, Alana turned to him with a look of disgust on her face.

"Our nation fought a terrible war because of slavery. Is your system any better?"

Edward replied in a calm voice, "It is the way in which this country has developed. Prejudice is something that, once entrenched, cannot easily be rooted out."

"I will not have Chaco treated in that manner!"

"Nor do you have to," Edward said. "But be careful that someone does not harm him because of the way you treat him.

It is unusual, to say the least, for a white woman to have a black manservant."

"I care nothing for what others think," she stated bluntly.

"I'm just telling you how life is in South Africa. Chaco knows this, too. He is a Basuto." For the next twenty minutes, while they went from one government clerk to the next, he explained about the Basuto, the largest tribe in South Africa and the only one that had the British crown as protector.

When their day ended, Alana and Edward returned to his home, where they ate a light dinner. Afterward, they talked about what Alana's next step might be.

"Are you sure there are no more places where he might be listed?" Alana asked after a short silence.

Edward shook his head. His eyes searched her face, and he knew he must tell her the truth. "If Ledoque was telling the truth, then perhaps he had Rafe smuggled into a prison camp. It would be the simplest way. Once there, without having a name on the official roster, he could be worked to death with impunity. Alana," Edward added gently, "although it may have only been a week or two since his arrival, I cannot in good conscience offer you much hope of finding Mr. Montgomery. The interior is not a kind place to those who do not know it. And the new diamond mines are even crueler."

No longer able to be shocked by the callousness of the country, Alana just stared at Edward. "Then I shall go to each mine and look for him."

Edward shook his head sharply. "You can't. It's too dangerous."

"Do you think I care about danger after what I've been through?"

"Perhaps you don't, but I do." The moment his words were out, she saw him stiffen, and she realized that what he had just admitted had not been well thought out.

"Edward," she whispered, "you are very kind."

"No, Alana, but that doesn't matter. There is another alternative."

"Yes?" she asked hopefully.

"I own—my company owns several large mines. Seven, to be exact. I have a man whom I trust implicitly who will be leaving shortly on an inspection tour of the mines. I can have him check not only our mines but all the others in the vicinity."

"But that will take so long," she whispered.

"No longer than what you propose—*if* you were to make it past the first mine."

Her brows knit together in puzzlement.

Edward looked at the beautiful yet innocent expression on her face and knew he could never allow her to go to the mines. "There are not many women near the mines—some prostitutes and the occasional wife of an administrator. A woman alone . . ." Edward let his words trail off.

"I see," Alana responded. "Then there really is no choice?"

"My way will work," he said. "Your way might, but it's doubtful. If he is being held in a mine, do you think you could free him? Will your words carry any authority?"

Alana had no answer.

"Trust me, Alana. If he is at a mine, I will find out. When we know for certain, I can have him freed. I am a man of no small power in Cape Town," he told her.

Alana smiled hesitantly. She knew his words had not been spoken in boast; rather, they were a statement of truth.

"All right, Edward; we shall try it your way."

"It will be several months before we learn anything. It's not easy getting word from the interior. But the moment I hear something, I shall act upon it. If he's there, I shall free him and send him to you in America."

"No."

By now he should have known Alana was unpredictable, but her response caught Edward off guard. He stared at her.

"I am staying here until Rafe is found."

"Where will you stay? How will—"

"It doesn't matter how or where. All that matters is that I find Rafe."

Edward continued to stare at her. "Your love is strong, Alana; a wonderful thing to behold. I envy your Rafe Montgomery."

For another hour, Alana and Edward argued. Edward tried to convince Alana to return with her ship, while at the same time hoping selfishly that she would stay. If Rafe Montgomery were in a prison mine, he would not live very long. Most didn't.

Perhaps that was why, in the end, he gave in. He'd known since the moment she had stormed into his office that he was hopelessly in love with Alana and would accept just having her near, if nothing else.

Alana repeatedly refused to do anything other than stay in Cape Town and wait. When Edward unexpectedly offered to have her stay with him, she was more thankful and appreciative than shocked.

"What will your friends think?" she asked a moment later.

"What does that matter? We are not lovers. You shall have your own rooms, quite separate from mine."

"But I don't want to harm your social standing," she told him.

"And you shan't, Alana, for you are now a business associate from America, and as such there can be no impropriety. Stay. This house has been empty for too long."

Alana heard the warmth in his words and the offer of refuge he so gallantly proffered. "All right, Edward. When the *Harmony* leaves, I will accept your kind offer."

"Thank you," he said.

Ten days later, Alana stood on the deck of the *Harmony* and handed Captain Sanders a letter addressed to Crystal. He stared at her for several seconds before he spoke.

"I would be remiss in my obligations to you and to Landow Shipping if I allowed you to stay here, Mrs. Landow."

"Captain, I appreciate your concern, but I am staying in Cape Town. I have things that must be done before I return home. You know this well."

"It's too dangerous. You're not like the people of this country. You're an outsider. You don't know their ways. And what of your home, Mrs. Landow?"

His words brought out the memories she had held in abeyance. She thought of all the sacrifices she'd already made for Riverbend, and slowly she shook her head. "I have no home without *him,* Captain."

Sanders knew exactly what Alana meant, and he could not find it in his heart to argue any further.

"Make sure that Crystal gets this and the new contracts. With luck, I shall be ready to come home when you return."

Sanders took a deep breath. His weathered face broke into a smile. "Take care of yourself, Mrs. Landow."

"I shall, Captain. And, Captain, thank you for helping me."

Sanders nodded, then escorted Alana back to the dock, where Chaco, her trunks, and Edward Parkins waited. Turning again, she looked into Sanders's face. "A swift, safe voyage, Captain. I shall eagerly await your return."

"Yes, ma'am." Stepping back, he favored Alana with a bow. Without further words, Sanders returned to the deck of the *Harmony*. Orders soon rang out, and men swarmed the masts.

An hour later, the *Harmony* was no longer in sight, and Alana turned to Edward. "I'm ready to go now," she told him.

December 1867

Crystal looked out the large window and watched the falling snow. Although it was warm in the room, she shivered at the thought of going outside.

She hated New York, hated the weather, most of the people, and the very reason she was there. But she would stay until she either succeeded or was found out.

She had been in New York three months now, and in that time she had made more progress than she had in four years.

She was as close to James Allison as possible and had worked hard to get there. Again, Crystal shivered, but this time it was the thought of Allison that chilled her to the bone.

Four months ago, when she'd received Alana's letter, her world had been once more torn apart, and she had almost gone insane with anger and grief. She and Alana had indeed fallen into Ledoque's trap, and they had almost been destroyed. Yet there was hope. Alana must have reached South Africa, as Crystal had heard no word to the contrary.

And the brother she thought dead, had not been. How could that be? she asked herself, as she had every day since she'd read the letter. How could Rafe have been Alana's secret lover? How could she not have realized that? And why had she not learned of the fact that he was alive?

Realistically, Crystal accepted the truth that she was as much to blame as Alana for what had happened. She had never once mentioned her brother's name, or even her own true one. "How stupid," she berated herself. "How damned stupid I was!"

After reading Alana's letter, she had put together all the information she'd gathered and deduced that the powerful shipping baron, James Allison, was the mysterious leading figure behind the consortium.

When she'd read of her brother's abduction and Alana's decision to go to South Africa to find him, Crystal knew what she had to do.

She'd wanted to go to Cape Town and help Alana search for Rafe, but instead Crystal had gone to Carlton Dupont and explained the situation. Dupont himself had received a letter from Nathan Bennet in New York. Dupont had wanted to go to New York and join Bennet in destroying Allison, but Crystal had talked him out of it, knowing just how powerful Allison was. Instead, she'd convinced him to stay in Charleston and to look after Landow Shipping and Riverbend while she went to New York to take over where Rafe had left off.

After explaining her plan of attack against Allison, she'd returned to Riverbend and appointed Lilith Dupre, her second in command, to take her place as madam.

And so, a month after receiving Alana's letter, Crystal had said good-bye to Riverbend and had come to New York via the second Landow ship. She had arrived with a bank draft for fifty thousand dollars.

She had registered at the elegant and exclusive Parktown Hotel, then gone to the bank that Carlton Dupont had arranged to handle her account.

Finally, she'd gone to see Nathan Bennet, whom Dupont had already contacted. Bennet, who had been prepared to meet Crystal Revanche, had been startled when Crystal told him that she was Rafael Montgomery's sister. She had seen his face fill with doubt, but his skepticism fled upon her complete explanation.

When she'd begun to question him about what he'd learned of Allison, he'd stopped her with a shake of his head. "What you are planning could be very dangerous," Bennet had cautioned.

"No more dangerous than what Alana is doing. Obviously

we must fight them in the manner in which they have fought us," Crystal stated.

"I've uncovered a great deal about James Allison, Miss, ah— Revanche?"

"That is the only name I will use until Allison is taken care of," Crystal had replied to his unasked question.

"Very well," Bennet had said. Then he'd gone on to detail all he'd learned, which was quite a lot. He had determined, among other things, that James Allison's passion was power and money, not women. Allison did have his women friends, but, Bennet's informants had said, he had no one single woman that he cared for or kept. It was, Bennet had learned, one of Allison's more unyielding characteristics. He believed that power was his mistress, not a woman.

"Then we will have to change his mind, won't we?" Crystal had asked. Crystal knew there was always a weakness. She would have to find Allison's weakness.

"I still don't understand how meeting Allison, and possibly seducing him, can help your brother or Alana," Bennet had questioned honestly.

"It's the only way I *can* help them. If I'm successful, I will find out where Allison sent Rafe."

"But to risk yourself so—"

"Is nothing more than I've been doing. Mr. Bennet, are you going to help us?"

Their eyes met in challenge. "Of course. I have already arranged for you to be introduced to a man who is in Allison's social circle. But that's all I can do," he'd said.

"That will be enough," Crystal had declared confidently.

It had been. Five days later, she'd attended an elegant affair with the gentleman Bennet had arranged for her to meet.

The man had thought he was escorting the wealthy widow of a southwestern mining magnate. Crystal's reason for being in New York, she had shyly admitted, was to find someone she could trust to become her financial adviser. She had *sooo* much money, she had explained, and she wasn't quite sure she knew what to do with it.

The man, hearing her sweet sad voice, had promised to introduce her to people who could help. Crystal knew it was because he wanted her. He would not have her, however.

Her first priority had been to meet Allison and pique his interest in her. When she met him she would be able to determine what approach to use.

When she had come face to face with Allison, she had instantly known the kind of man he was. He was just as Bennet had described him; yet he wasn't. She had seen that women meant little to him, but all the same he did look at them with more than a passing interest. Crystal sensed that Allison would use a woman for his selfish pleasure—a pleasure devoid of real passion—and then move on. Power and money were his true lusts. She had seen it written on his face and heard it in his voice. She knew she must change that.

Three minutes after her escort introduced her to James Allison, explaining that Crystal was looking for a financial adviser, she had known what to do.

Smiling shyly at him, she spoke in a low voice. "My late husband, Robert, told me never to trust the advice of anyone who had less money than I. Are you wealthy, Mr. Allison?" she had asked. That had done the trick. By the end of the evening, she and Allison had made a tentative appointment for the following week.

Now Crystal sighed and turned from the window. She wondered how Alana was faring, and she hated that it took so long for correspondence to reach New York. She had sent a long letter to Alana explaining who she was and the reason why she had never mentioned Rafe or told Alana her true name. She had apologized, blaming herself for much of what had happened to them, and she told Alana that she was now trying to find out where Rafe was.

She had recently received Alana's latest letter, mentioning the new commission for Landow Shipping, and she had given her reply to Captain Rogers, who was taking the second Landow ship, the *Marabella,* to Cape Town while the *Harmony* was being refitted and readied for yet another shipment of equipment destined for Maklin-Parkins. Crystal hoped to discover Rafe's whereabouts before the *Harmony* left for Cape Town. *Soon,* Crystal told herself. After all, she had been James Allison's mistress for three weeks now.

Her plan had worked to perfection. It had been the lure of her money, not her sex, that had intrigued Allison. After sev-

eral long and lingering luncheon engagements, Crystal had begun to sense Allison's growing interest in her, an interest she
had fostered by refusing to flirt or make any suggestive moves
toward him.

Crystal knew that Allison would go only after that which
promised to elude him. So she had played him carefully along.
She had showed herself to be a desirable and rich woman who
resisted all his attempts at seduction while allowing him to
think that he would be able to advise her on money matters.

By the second week, she'd sensed his frustration. During the
third week of their business luncheons, Allison was talking less
about her money and more about his own money and power.

In the middle of the fourth week, she'd known she had
trapped him, for he'd taken to escorting her to a variety of
social functions and to dinner whenever he was not involved in
business meetings.

Then one night James Allison had presented her with a gift.
It was a magnificent diamond and sapphire necklace that radiated fire with every step she'd taken.

"James, I—I can't accept this," she had said in a husky
whisper while favoring him with a longing look.

"Of course you can," he'd countered confidently.

"No, I'm sorry." Taking the necklace off, she'd handed it
back to him. "I can't accept it from you."

"Why?" he'd demanded suddenly.

She had not explained; instead, she'd shaken her head at him.
"Please, James, can't we leave things as they are?"

Allison had been dumbfounded, and Crystal realized that no
woman had ever turned down so expensive a gift from him.
Although he had not accepted his defeat well, she'd seen him
control himself—except for the way his eyes had suddenly
flashed with desire. It had been the first time she had ever seen
so raw a look from him. That had been the first major break-
through for Crystal.

Two nights later, they had been in Crystal's hotel suite having dinner and discussing an investment that Allison had suggested. Tension was thick in the air, and Crystal had maneu-
vered herself in such a way that she'd innocently been able to
touch him freely, seemingly unaware of doing so.

She had leaned forward at strategic times to tease his eyes

with the fullness of her breasts or to favor him with lingering, smoky glances. And she had seen, when he'd thought her to be looking away, the hungry look on his face.

When the meal had ended, Allison had dismissed further business talk and boldly stated that Crystal was the first woman he had ever really wanted. It was an admission that she fully believed.

"Why me?" she asked. "There are others who are prettier. Why, James, with your money you could have anyone at all!"

"There are many women attracted to my money and my power," he told her. "I don't want them. I want you."

"I'm sorry, James," she had said, looking sad and downcast, "but I—it's been so short a time since Robert died. I—"

"Do you feel nothing for me?" Allison had asked.

Crystal's eyes had flickered sadly across his face. Then she'd turned from him. "I cannot let myself feel anything."

Allison had turned her to him. The instant he had, Crystal had known she was in control. It had taken her over a month, but she had done it!

"We are alike, you and I," he had told her. "I have never desired a woman before. Not the way I desire you."

"I want you, too, James," she'd admitted in a husky whisper. His eyes had flared with desire. "But we cannot—"

"We are above other people! We can do what we want. Crystal, I want you."

"Not yet. It is happening so quickly, James," she had pleaded as she'd pulled away from him. "I—I must think."

"I will call for you tomorrow," Allison had replied, eager to please her. "I want you to look over the papers I've drawn up. And afterward—"

Crystal had gazed at him, moistening her lips with her tongue. "Afterward?" she asked.

"It will be good for us, Crystal, very good." With that, Allison had left, and Crystal had known that when he called on her tomorrow, it would be the final test.

When Allison arrived the next day, he'd been all business, yet Crystal had felt a heated inner tension radiate from him. When it came time for Crystal to sign the papers, she had tensed up visibly.

"What's wrong?" he'd asked.

"James," she'd replied, staring directly into his eyes. "I think that what you have arranged is wonderful for me, but—"

"Is there something wrong with the papers?"

"No," she'd said, lowering her eyes and moistening her lips as if she were having a great deal of trouble. "It's just that—last night you said you desired me as no other."

"I do," he whispered in a husky voice. Reaching out, he'd taken her hand in his. "I still do."

"James, you are—" Crystal had paused dramatically, making a show of how difficult her words were to say. "You are the first man that I have felt . . . comfortable with since Robert died. I have never been a passionate woman. I don't know if I ever will be. Robert—Robert was a kind man, a gentle man, but in the last years of our marriage, he was more a father to me than a husband. I know so little of passion."

Allison had stared at her for several seconds before her words registered in his mind. And when they had, she had seen the shadowy smile he had almost, but not quite, hidden.

"I am not very experienced in those—" and Crystal had made herself blush to accent her innocence.

"That doesn't matter," Allison had said.

"There is something else," Crystal had whispered. "I—I want you, too, James. But if I sign these papers, I—we cannot."

"Why?" he'd asked, a look of frustration mixed with naked lust.

Crystal had made herself cry then. It was a silent crying that let tears fall shamelessly from her eyes. She said nothing, she only looked at him.

"Tell me," he'd commanded.

A long moment later, Crystal had spoken in a low voice. "I've told you that Robert died after a long illness. He was much older than I, and before he died, Ro—Robert made me promise that I would never let a man control my money if I were—involved with that man. He said that I would never know if it was the money the man loved or me."

Allison had stared at her in disbelief, and Crystal had feared she'd gone too far. But his next action had told her just how perfectly she had judged him.

Allison had lifted the financial agreement and torn it in half. "I will find someone else to handle your money."

Victorious, Crystal had still held herself back. She'd shaken her head slowly. "James, I—I'm afraid of being . . . looked down upon."

"Are you asking for marriage?" he'd asked, startled.

"No!" she'd exclaimed, just as startled. "I never want to marry again! I've already told you that. No, I just don't want to be gossiped about. I don't know if I could bear it."

Allison had smiled. "You won't be," he'd promised.

Then he had lifted her and took her into the bedroom of her hotel suite. After he had undressed her, she felt yet another victory at the look on his face when he saw her completely naked. Then he had joined her in the bed.

For the first time since she had been forced into the life of a whore, Crystal had not made her mind go blank. She'd known that she could not do that; she needed to have all her wits about her, for she must make Allison believe everything she had already told him.

She'd acted shy, holding herself back while he began to fondle her. In small ways, she'd reminded him that she was inexperienced and almost afraid of what was happening.

Allison, filled with a new desire that he had not felt before, had done his best to ease her tension and bring out the passion in her.

Willing away her revulsion, Crystal had made herself respond to Allison and, when he was firmly entrenched within her, she had begun to show him some passion.

She had made her face flicker with surprise and had widened her eyes to stare at him in wonder, even as she had spoken his name, and she had cried out about things she had never before felt.

Using every bit of knowledge she had ever learned, Crystal had made him think that he had unleashed a passion that had been lying dormant within her, just waiting for him to find the special key to free it. By morning, he had admitted that, until Crystal, he had never sought a woman.

She had shaken her head, stroked his cheek, smiled shyly at him, and laughed nervously. She told him that he must have had many women, because of his experience and wonderful ability.

Proudly, Allison had admitted that he'd had many women,

but he told her he had never desired any of them except for the quick release they had afforded.

"But you, Crystal, you have taught me why men act as foolishly as they do."

Acting insulted, she had pouted at him. "I make you act like a fool? How does that make me look, James?"

"No," he had explained hurriedly. "I meant only that I have never known such feelings as you bring out in me. Crystal, you must marry me," he had exclaimed unexpectedly.

Crystal had drawn away from him. "No, James. I shall not marry again."

"Do you not feel the same toward me as I do toward you?"

Crystal had not allowed her smile to show. Instead, she had taken his hand and placed in on her breast.

"Feel the way my heart beats, James, and never again ask that question. But know also that I will be no man's property again."

Crystal had seen that for possibly the first time in his life, the wealthy and powerful James Allison was at a loss.

"It doesn't mean I will not stay with you, James, or that I do not—love you."

Then Allison had smiled and Crystal had seen that the powerful man, reeling under the twin attack of desire and conquest, had known what to do next.

"I will find a house for us. One that no one knows of. We can be together there whenever we want."

For the next three weeks Crystal had lived with the man, attended all his functions, and while he had grown more and more infatuated with her, she had grown increasingly disgusted at his every touch. Yet she had learned a great deal with her seemingly innocent questions. She had also discovered that he was like a little boy with her and would boast of his great achievements whenever given the chance.

She had learned about the consortium, and she knew every member by name. She was with him when he'd gotten word that Maklin-Parkins had canceled their contract and given it to Alana.

She'd let him rage on and had even heard him shout Rafe's name, but she'd known it was the wrong time to probe her brother's fate.

Every day she had carefully written down all she'd discovered and sent the information to Nathan Bennet. Soon she would be able to bring down Allison's empire. But she would make no move until she had discovered Rafe's fate. And that, Crystal realized, might be harder than everything else, for each time she had tried to get him to speak of "how he took care of those who opposed him," he would suddenly change the subject. Crystal had no choice but to drop the topic immediately.

"Soon," she promised herself as she heard her door opening.

She smiled when James Allison stepped inside, his eyes bright with desire, a desire, Crystal had learned, that never flagged. Soon, she repeated silently as she chased away the knot of disgust that was once again forming in the pit of her stomach.

24

Alana sat at Edward's desk in the wood-paneled study, her hands trembling as she held the letter from Crystal. She wanted to open it and read it, yet at the same time she was afraid.

In the five months since she'd arrived in Cape Town, her life had changed drastically. In the beginning, after the *Harmony* had left, each day had been spent in search of information concerning Rafe.

No word of Rafe had come from the Maklin-Parkins representative who traveled to the company's mines and other properties, although detailed reports constantly arrived at the main office in Cape Town.

When she'd learned nothing further in the port city, she had insisted on going to the small settlements near Cape Town and then to the other ports that line South Africa's coast.

Edward had been more than patient with her and had accompanied her whenever possible. They had traveled overland, across sections of the interior's great plateau. They had gone to Port Elizabeth, to the Natal province, and to the port at Durban. Still they had learned nothing, but Alana had at least been busy trying.

They'd returned from their search by ship, passing through the Cape of Good Hope, and when they had arrived in Cape Town, Alana had realized that all she could do now was to wait and hope.

Late yesterday, the *Marabella* had docked. This morning,

Crystal's letter had been delivered. Edward had left it on the table for her.

"So kind," she'd whispered, thinking of Edward's unlimited patience and consideration. She had never met a man like Edward Parkins, who she had learned was a titled nobleman as well as one of the richest Englishmen in Cape Town.

Edward had never once made an advance to her, although, as Alana had discovered, he was in love with her. She'd seen it written clearly on his face, and she sensed it in his every gesture.

Edward had finally spoken of his feelings for her two weeks before. It had been at dinner, and Alana had sensed that he wanted to speak to her of more than just generalities. Aware of the warm look he'd favored her with, she had gently questioned him on his silence.

"I don't want to push myself on you," he said.

"In what way?"

"Surely, Alana, you must know by now that I have certain feelings for you."

Alana had dropped her eyes for a moment, but then she'd looked at him. "I have sensed that, yes. I am sorry, Edward. I like you very much, but I—"

"You love another. I know that, Alana, and I understand. If I did not—" He'd left the rest unsaid.

"Perhaps I should find myself different living quarters," she'd ventured in a low voice.

"No," he'd said quickly. "The fact that I love you does not mean you cannot stay here. I will never force myself upon you. I respect you too much for that. Let us remain friends, and please do not mention leaving again."

Alana's eyes had misted. "I've never known a man like you, Edward. I thank you for understanding."

After that evening, no mention was made of Edward's feelings again, and Alana continued to stay on in his house. Not once had she given up her hope of finding Rafe.

Sighing, Alana lifted the silver letter opener and neatly sliced the heavy envelope. She took out three sheets of paper and began to read. By the time she'd finished, tears had blurred many of the words, and she no longer saw the paper she held or the room she was in.

Her mind was in a state of shock, and she fought vainly to
recover her senses. It was all too much, she realized. All the
coincidences, all the strange happenings were interconnected;
they had been from the start, and she had never once recognized it.

Crystal was Rafe's sister. The reality of that knowledge was
like having the sun break through a storm-laden sky. Suddenly
Crystal's story of the loss of her family business came into her
mind, and when it did, Alana quickly saw what she had missed
before. She remembered, too, the way Rafe had spoken of his
sister Elizabeth.

"How could I not have known?" she asked herself. But she
realized that everything had been cloaked in mystery, and for
that very reason nothing had been clear until now.

She thought about Crystal's—Elizabeth's, she corrected herself—tale of becoming James Allison's mistress, and terror
struck her fiercely. She was afraid for Crystal, even though she
knew Crystal had devoted her life to destroying the man.

Alana did not know how long she sat at the desk, but when
she blinked her eyes, she saw Edward standing across from her.

Edward had formed the habit of returning home for lunch
ever since Alana moved into his home. And today, when he'd
reached the house and found that she was not on the porch
waiting for him, he had gone to look for her. When he saw her
tearstained face, he said nothing until she acknowledged his
presence. "What is it?" he asked, his voice filled with concern.

Alana couldn't speak; she simply handed him the letter. A
few minutes later, Edward put down the sheets of paper and
went around the desk.

He took her hand firmly in his. "She is as brave a woman as
you. Perhaps she'll find out where Rafe is."

Alana tried to smile, but she could not.

Chaco's long legs stretched out over the flat ground; his chest
rose and fell powerfully with each deep breath he took. He was
a mile from Cape Town, and the freedom of the open plateau
and the scents brought to him by the sea-bound breezes all
stirred his senses.

Every day for the last months, when he was not traveling

with Alana, he had come to the edge of town, removed all but his pants, and had run beneath the gentle sun.

Chaco's promise to Crystal and his devotion to Alana—as well as his lingering guilt over what had happened in New York —kept him in Cape Town, rather than returning to the interior and to the people from whom he had been stolen thirteen years before. He would not desert Crystal or Alana until Rafe Montgomery had been found and Alana no longer needed him. Only then would he return to his people and become the man he had been destined to be since birth.

Chaco slowed his pace and finally stopped. He looked down at the small tattoo, just below his left nipple, that had been put on him just after his birth. No one in Cape Town, white or black, had ever seen that mark. None would until Chaco returned to Basutoland to claim his rightful place.

Chaco, only nine at the time he had been kidnapped and then enslaved, was the grandson of Moshweshwe, the greatest king of the Basuto people. Moshweshwe had aligned his people with the British when the Boers started their great trek through Basutoland and had allowed the British to protect them from the Boers.

It was during that time that the last bands of white slavers roamed the plains looking for blacks to capture and sell far across the ocean. It had been Chaco's misfortune to have been out at that time practicing the hunt, as was his duty.

When he had been captured, they had tried to break his spirit, but he had not let that happen. Instead, he had taken refuge in silence, swearing to himself that he would not speak again until he had returned to Basutoland.

Now Chaco was almost home. And each day that he ran free, he began to use his long-neglected voice. At first he'd discovered that he could not speak at all, and he feared that his years of silence had become permanent. But when he ran, he tried to chant a tribal song. As the weeks passed, he started to make strange, almost strangling noises. Once he found he could make sounds, he forced himself to continue.

At the beginning, the pain was intense. The taste of blood always rose in the back of his throat. But that had not stopped him, and on this day, even as Alana read Crystal's letter, Chaco took a deep breath and let out a loud, piercing shout that echoed across the flatlands.

"I am ready!" he declared to himself.

A half hour later, he was in the black section of Cape Town. This too had become a daily habit for him. He stood silently wherever groups of his people gathered, listening to the rumors that were always rife within the community.

But this afternoon he sensed a difference in the atmosphere. Standing in the shade of a small building, Chaco watched a group of men whom he knew to be Zulus. A few moments after he'd arrived, an excited babble broke out. Chaco watched two emaciated men being half-carried between several others.

They looked fearfully around, and when they were certain there were no whites about, the other natives lowered the men to the ground.

Chaco pretended disinterest, but his ears were sharp. He discovered the two were escapees from a prison mine, and as he listened, he heard a tale of horror that made the memories of his slavery return fresh to his mind.

But this was even worse, he realized, as the men told of their desperate escape. They spoke, too, about a white man who was with them, a man who had been shot a half day after they had broken free.

Slowly, trying not to show any emotion, Chaco went over to the men. In the Basuto language, he asked about the prison and especially about the white man who had escaped with them. He realized he had broken his vow of silence, but the information meant more to him than his oath.

The escaped prisoner he spoke to looked up at Chaco and studied him silently. Then he responded to something he saw within Chaco's face. "He was a good man, a brave man. He said he was from a land called America."

"Describe him," Chaco commanded. In that instant the eyes of all the other people were upon him, and somehow they sensed that he was not just another man. The tone of his voice and his commanding stature told them that he was much more than he appeared to be.

The escaped prisoner gave Chaco a description of the man, telling of his full beard, light eyes, and dark hair. He told Chaco about the prison mine they had been in, deep within the Vaal, a mine that was worked by black political prisoners and white criminals. When he was finished, Chaco had no choice but to believe that the man who had died was Rafe Montgomery.

He left, trying to figure out how he could tell Alana what he had learned. He knew Alana was a strong woman and that she would survive this as she had the other difficulties in her life.

Yet Chaco understood how much his words would hurt her, and his anger at the way people used other people erupted dangerously.

"Dear God! How is it possible?" she asked, turning her back to Chaco after he had conveyed, in sign language, the information he had learned.

He had not spoken aloud because he did not want to shock Alana any further and also because he still believed in his vow. Until he returned to his people, he would resume his silence.

Alana turned back to him. "How can you be certain?"

Chaco signed his answer; the finality of his statement only added to Alana's grief.

"I shan't accept that. Not until I see his body and kiss his lips one last time!"

Then she fled the room. Alone in her bedroom, she allowed herself to cry out her grief and loss, even though her sorrow went against what she had told Chaco moments before.

When Edward returned at the end of the day, Alana greeted him dry-eyed. With Chaco present, she told him Chaco's story.

Edward stared at her and felt Alana's sorrow. "It seems hard to believe. Is he the type of man who would try to escape?"

"With every ounce of his strength."

"I am sorry," Edward whispered. "Where was this prison?" he asked Chaco.

Chaco began to sign, but he realized that his signing vocabulary was American and that he could not sign the African or Dutch names. Instead, he slowly spelled out the letters.

"Germiston mine," Alana translated.

"That makes no sense," Edward said, shaking his head slowly.

"Why?"

"It is a well-known prison mine. It is also a poor surface mine —the diamonds found there are of little value. It's used for colored political prisoners and for only the worst white offenders. It's regularly inspected. The officials would discover a man who was not properly sentenced. But I shall check on it, Alana, I promise you."

Alana said nothing as the spark of hope was again rekindled in her breast.

Chaco, looking at her now hopeful face, was not so certain. He was experienced in the ways of the white man, and he knew that those in control did things with impunity. Chaco believed Rafe was dead. But Chaco's face did not reflect the blame he placed upon himself for Rafe's death.

Two weeks later, Edward learned the story of the escape at Germiston prison camp and told it to Alana.

"I was wrong," he admitted. "The white man who escaped was not on the roster of prisoners. He was an American, and—" Edward paused when he saw the flash of pain cross Alana's features. He made himself go on, knowing that to soften his words would only add to her hurt.

"His description matched the one you gave me of Rafe Montgomery. He was tall with dark hair, and he was very clearly an American. It seems that only one American has been sentenced to serve in a mine, and that man is four hundred miles from Germiston. I am afraid, Alana, that it was indeed your fiancé who was killed."

Alana accepted his words stoically, but a moment later, her eyes flared. "Then I will claim his body and give him a decent burial."

Edward shook his head slowly. "That is impossible. He has been dead over a month. He—they never buried him. He was left in the bush. That is the way with escaped criminals."

Alana's eyes dulled. She stared at Edward, turned, and left the room. She went up to her bedroom, closed the door, and sat on her bed. No tears spilled from her eyes; rather, her mind brought out her memories of Rafe, and she willed herself to relive them, from the very first day they had met at Riverbend a lifetime ago.

She refused to accept Rafe's death, and she refused even to think of it as she retreated within her memories. And soon, she was safe within a world she created for herself. A world where she and Rafe lived and loved and were happily at peace.

Edward, knowing how grief-stricken Alana was, left her alone. But when the night passed and two more followed without her emerging from her room and with her refusing all food sent to her, he could no longer stand idly by.

He went to her on the third day and found her standing motionless, staring out the window, wearing a plain nightdress. Her tangled hair hung limply around her face. Her eyes were dry, red-rimmed, and vacant. Her face showed no emotion; her skin was as white as a ghost's.

Edward's heart grew heavy with compassion, but he ignored his pity as the knowledge of what must be done ruled his mind.

He took Alana's arm and spun her to him. Then he looked deeply into her eyes, hoping to find some semblance of the fire that had once dominated their gemlike blue depths.

"You can't do this to yourself, Alana," he began.

Alana's only answer was an attempt to turn away.

Refusing to allow that, Edward made her look at him. Suddenly his hand whipped up and cracked against her cheek.

Alana's eyes widened momentarily; then her face returned to a passive and unresponsive mask.

"Damn it, Alana," Edward shouted. "Cry! Let it free!" His hands tightened on her arms, squeezing painfully to make her aware of herself.

As she stared at him, the waves of her terrible grief and loss broke loose. Tears welled; great wrenching sobs bubbled from her mouth. Her low moans of grief filled the room, and Edward pulled her into the security of his arms.

She cried for a long, long time and was unaware when Edward walked them both to the bed and laid her down. He lay next to her, still holding her, still letting her cry against him until she fell into a deep dreamless sleep.

When she awoke the next morning, she remembered everything that had happened and felt gratitude toward Edward, mixed with the loss of the love she would never again know. But she was alive once more, and with that came a determination to know which people in South Africa had been responsible for Rafe's death. While Crystal gained her information about Allison in New York, she would do the same in South Africa. *I will have my revenge,* she vowed silently.

That morning, Alana drafted a long letter to Crystal telling her everything that had happened and promising that she would continue to seek revenge with every breath she took. The letter left three days later on the *Marabella,* which was making its return voyage to Charleston.

By late summer of 1868, Alana had come no closer to determining Allison's counterpart in South Africa, even after another two months of traveling across the country. What she had discovered instead was that her feelings toward Edward were changing.

Ever since that awful night when he'd forced her to release her grief, she had found herself growing more and more dependent on the security and help he offered.

Edward had also taken on the role of business adviser, and in the eight months since she'd left New York, Alana, with Edward's help, had begun to make Landow Shipping into a major force in the shipping industry.

By late summer, the Landow fleet had grown from two ships to five, three of which were used exclusively for the Maklin-Parkins shipping trade. The *Harmony* and the *Marabella* traveled the American route, while a third ferried between England and Cape Town. Landow Shipping was not only solvent, it was beginning to show profits, according to the latest communications Alana received from Carlton Dupont.

Alana knew that Edward was in love with her, and for several months she tried to love him in return. She never spoke of this to him; she just tried to find within her the emotion that she wanted to give him. But each time she willed herself to feel love for him, Rafe's image barred the way.

On one warm August night, as they sat on the porch of his house, Edward turned to her, his face lined with tension. "It has been almost eight months since you learned of Rafe's death, yet you still remain here. I can only hope it is because you are starting to feel something toward me."

Alana gazed at him, her mouth suddenly dry. Reaching out, she covered his hand with hers and started to speak, but before she could, he stopped her.

"There is much I must say. Let me, please."

Alana silently nodded.

"I have loved you since I met you. I have spoken of it only

once and never again because Rafael Montgomery was still alive. He no longer is, Alana, and I can no longer pretend to feel only friendship for you.

"My wife and son died fifteen years ago. Since then, I have not wanted to share my life with another until I met you. Now I cannot bear to think of life without you. I love you and I want to marry you," he said at last.

Alana gazed warmly at him, thinking of all he had done for her. "Edward," she began, slowly shaking her head.

Again, he would not let her continue. "I am twenty years older than you. I know you don't love me the way you did Rafe, nor would I ever think that I could take his place in your heart. But, Alana, your life must go on. You are too vital a woman to spend your life alone. You need a man to be with you—and I want to be that man."

Alana gazed at him for several seconds after he fell silent. She had listened intently to every word he'd spoken, and the memory of the past year spent with him—guided and protected by him—rose within her mind.

They shared a special relationship that was a strong and warm bond of friendship. And that bond told her more than his words could. In that moment she put Rafe's memory to peace.

"I will try, Edward. I will try to love you as you love me."

Edward did not reach out and draw her into his arms; it was not his way. Instead, he smiled gently at her. "That is all I will ever ask."

On September 17, 1868, Alana Belfores Landow became Alana Parkins, Duchess of Claymore, the wife of the wealthiest man in British-controlled South Africa. The small, private wedding Alana had insisted on was viewed by Cape Town's high society with more than a little suspicion.

Alana knew nothing of this, for Edward did not want to bother her with such mundane gossip. He was determined to make her happy, to protect her against all evils, and to show her that she could be happy and content with him.

It was on their wedding night that Alana understood that she had made the correct decision in marrying Edward Parkins.

In the dressing room of the master bedroom, Alana stared into the mirror. Her hands trembled slightly while she brushed her hair, and she had to put the brush down and clasp them together.

"How will I be able to do this?" she asked herself. Ever since she'd taken off her wedding gown, bathed, and put on the soft white nightgown, her nerves had been on edge.

She knew that once she entered Edward's bed, she must forever give up her dreams of Rafe. But Rafe had been her first love, and the only man who had ever made her body sing with passion, joy, and life. Although he was dead, forgetting him was still no easy thing to do. Discounting Ledoque's attack, no other man had ever made love to her.

How will I made Edward happy if I feel no passion for him? she wondered.

Alana pushed those thoughts aside, knowing that she must do the best she could, for Edward deserved no less. Nor would she resort to the tricks that Crystal had told her of, so that a man might believe he had stirred a woman's desire although the woman felt nothing at all.

No, she must be honest with herself and with Edward and trust that he would understand.

Alana picked up the brush and, with new determination, smoothed out her raven hair. Willing herself not to show just how frightened she was, she left the dressing room and entered the master suite. She crossed toward the hand-hewn bed, but before she reached it, she realized that Edward had not yet changed; rather, he was sitting on one of the two chairs near the window.

Stopping, she turned to study his face. "Is something wrong?" she asked in a low voice.

Edward stood and came over to her. He cupped her face tenderly in his hands. "No, you have made me very happy. But I do not know if it is wise for us to share this bed yet."

"I—I don't understand," Alana whispered.

"You have married me, but I don't know if you love me. I have waited a long time for this night, Alana; I can wait longer if necessary."

Tears welled in Alana's eyes, and a lump built in her throat. Blinking, she tried to forestall what his sweet words threatened to bring out. As she gazed into his soft brown eyes and kind, handsome face, a new feeling was born.

In that moment she realized that the love she had for Rafe would always remain sacred within her heart, but that there was room to love another. And as the sensation of this new love spread through her, she felt the certainty of conviction.

"I do love you, Edward, how could I not?" she asked truthfully. With her admission came the understanding that there was more than one type of love. She did not feel the wild and thrilling passion or the undying need that had always been a part of her love with Rafe, and she knew she would never feel that intensity again. But the gentle glow of her emotions told her that the love she had for Edward was a good love, a love that could only grow stronger with the passage of time.

"Please, Edward," she said as her hands covered his, "come to bed now."

When they were in the large bed, Edward turned to her and drew her to him. Just before their mouths met, she placed her finger to his lips. "I'm frightened, Edward," she whispered. "Help me."

Edward didn't speak; instead, he drew her closer to him. He did not caress her; he only held her tightly until the trembling in her body eased.

When he lifted her face to kiss her, he did so slowly, waiting patiently until he felt her acceptance of his kiss.

For long minutes, he kissed her. His passions never went out of control, although she felt his body grow warmer with each heartbeat. He did not rush her, and his hands were tender and strong as they caressed and stroked her body through the thin covering of the nightgown.

At last, he carefully removed her nightgown. When it was gone and her beautiful body bared to his eyes, he kissed her mouth. Then he trailed his lips along the side of her neck and lingered at the base of her throat for several seconds. When he felt the increased beat of her heart, he caressed and kissed her breasts in a slow yet hungry way.

Alana's mind became fogged. Desire mixed with fear to hold her prisoner. She could not move her arms to return his caresses, but at the same time, she did not want him to stop.

And as Edward continued in his slow pace, Alana realized that he was a sensitive lover who must have known her innermost thoughts. His hands were never still; yet never did they roam her body greedily. When he stroked her inner thighs, her muscles quivered in response to his feathery touch.

Soon his lips replaced his fingers, and the warmth of his mouth against the sensitive skin of her inner thighs was a wonderfully gentle sensation.

A short time later, Edward raised his head and looked into her eyes, seeking to reassure her with his words. "You will never have to be afraid of me, Alana."

Alana sighed. The warmth of his touch spread within her. And strangely, a new form of desire built. There was no loss of control, no frantic and merciless need driving her—just the tingling sensations of his hands and lips.

"I am not," she told him.

His mouth returned to her skin, lavishing her silken thighs with his lips and tongue. Then he began his upward journey, pausing at the juncture of her thighs to dip his tongue within her and taste her very essence.

Alana felt the spear of his tongue and let the pleasure he bestowed on her add to this new feeling of leisurely desire. The fear that had been holding her back vanished as Edward's mouth and body traveled upward. He kissed the tip of each breast as his experienced fingers began to work magically within her, moistening her for him, preparing the way.

As her breathing turned deeper, she raised her arms to him, and he came into them. He kissed her passionately, but he did not crush his mouth to hers. For the first time, Alana willingly opened her body to another man.

Edward rose above her. For a brief instant, Rafe's image wavered in her vision. And as it did, Alana willed it away. Then she looked at Edward, and as he positioned himself between her thighs, she reached between their bodies and captured him with her hands. When she felt his heated length in her palms, she caressed it, exploring it delicately before guiding him within her. And because it was she who brought him into her, Alana was able to banish the memory of Rafe's hands and mouth and give herself completely to Edward.

Edward proved himself to be a consummate lover: a gentle and thoughtful man who did not rush toward his own pleasure but guided Alana with him.

When they reached their climax, it was not one of pounding

hearts, roaring blood, and uncontrolled moans, but a lingering feeling of the gentle love that Edward had shown her she too possessed but had never before experienced.

Afterward, Alana fell dreamlessly asleep in Edward's arms. When she awoke in the morning, she was still in his arms and he was gazing down at her.

"Thank you, Alana, for making my life complete again."

Alana didn't speak. Instead, she lifted her mouth to his and kissed him. With the fresh memory of the way Edward had tenderly, thoughtfully, and unselfishly made love to her, Alana began to kiss him more passionately.

As she kissed him, her hands explored and learned his body as she had not done the previous night. She caressed his chest; her fingernails drew circles around his nipples. She traced the outline of his stomach and let her fingers play with the tight hair at the base of his manhood. When he grew hard, she followed her questing fingers with her lips and mouth, lavishing his torso with warm kisses until she reached his hardened length.

She caressed and kissed Edward's proud, straight shaft, returning to him all the pleasure and good he had given to her. When his member throbbed beneath her ministrations and his hands pressed into her skin in need, she turned. With her body covering his, she brought her mouth to his and accepted him within her.

She rode him gently, kissing him until she felt him become tense within her. A few moments after he released his heated flow, she again felt another of the same gentle climaxes he had given her last night.

Afterward, Alana again went into the security of Edward's arms, where she stayed for another hour before Edward kissed her and left the bed to dress. A few moments later, Alana did the same.

When she was dressed, she looked into the mirror and studied her face. Then, as it had the night before, Rafe's face floated within the glass. His emerald eyes gazed softly at her, but she saw no condemnation within their glow.

Although she knew the image was only in her mind, she realized that she was experiencing a lifting of the guilt she had felt in loving another man.

Turning from the mirror, she adjusted the bodice of her dress, took a deep breath, and started out from the dressing room. Determination to make Edward a good wife rose in her mind. And as it did, Alana put her past behind her, vowing that the rest of their life together would be happy and fulfilling.

March 1869

Crystal folded Alana's letter and put it into the left-hand drawer of her writing desk. "I'm glad you've found happiness," she whispered to Alana's image.

Her words came from her heart. Crystal had felt the same way after receiving Alana's letter in November, telling her of her marriage to Edward Parkins. The letter had also informed Crystal that Alana had been unable to learn anything new about Allison's people in South Africa. But Alana had insisted that her marriage to Edward would never stop her efforts, and Edward had been continuing to help her in the search. Only when she learned who had helped to kill Rafe would Alana put the past to rest.

At first the news of Alana's marriage had shocked Crystal, but after spending a lot of time in deep and introspective thought, she'd come to terms with it. Crystal had then sent Alana a letter expressing happiness at her good fortune, adding that Alana should feel no guilt or remorse because of her marriage. Crystal made it clear that she understood and approved of Alana's marriage to Edward Parkins, whom she knew was the new and guiding force behind Landow Shipping. She had also learned a great deal about Parkins through James Allison, who hated Edward Parkins for siding with Alana.

In the same letter that offered Alana best wishes for her marriage, Crystal had warned Alana that Allison wanted to destroy Edward. The voiding of the Marquette contract had set Allison's plans for expansion into South Africa back at least a year, and he was furious. Crystal knew Alana would take her warning to heart; Alana was all too aware of what Allison was capable of doing.

In subsequent letters to her friend, Crystal had expressed her belief that a marriage built on a foundation of kindness, such as Alana had described hers to be, must in fact become a very good one.

Alana's letters never stopped coming, and even as Alana told of her new life, she always included whatever information she had been able to garner about Allison's activities in South Africa. Even so, each letter had always ended the same way: "I have not yet discovered Allison's hidden people."

Like Alana, Crystal had written monthly to her friend, giving Alana the detailed information she obtained as Allison's mistress. She was sending Alana this information in case Allison found her out, for if he did, she knew she would not live long enough to escape him.

For her part, Crystal still had not learned who Allison controlled in South Africa, either. Although she had been forced to accept Rafe's death, she had controlled her rage, and had prevented herself from killing Allison with the knife she kept hidden in the bed table.

Crystal wanted her revenge. She wanted Allison to suffer. Until he did, she would not rest.

As Crystal was thinking of how sweet her revenge would one day be, James Allison burst into the bedroom. His face was mottled with rage; his eyes were hard and cruel.

"What is wrong, my darling?" Crystal asked as she went to him. A trace of the ever-present fear of discovery rumbled in her stomach.

"Those bastards!" he shouted. Crystal smelled whiskey on his breath. Allison, ignoring the way Crystal tried to embrace and calm him, pulled away and paced in the room.

"That Landow woman is trying to block me!"

"Block you, James? How? You're too powerful," Crystal stated, knowing that just a few words said properly were usually enough to get him speaking.

"They've added three more ships to Landow Shipping. They have eight now. Eight! She's undercutting the rates I offered the Tulbaugh Import Company for American shipments."

"Can you not underbid them as well?" Crystal asked innocently, seemingly unaware of how heavily Landow had cut their prices. But Crystal knew every move that Landow Shipping made, and she knew exactly what Allison was talking about.

"The other members of the consortium are giving me trouble over this. They've voted not to cut the prices further."

"But you control the consortium."

"I know," he said, somewhat mollified. "But it's also their money at stake. They will not stand for the high losses needed to break Landow. *Damn* that Ledoque for a lusting bastard!"

Crystal said nothing as he paced angrily about the room. Stopping suddenly, he stared at her. "I should never have trusted him to take care of her. He let that stupid woman stab him in the back and escape in time to warn her ship. I should have destroyed her the way I did her lover."

"Can't you do that now?" Crystal asked, her heart beating much too fast at Allison's mention of her brother.

Allison laughed bitterly. "It's too late. She's wound that damned fool Parkins around her finger and married him. She's too well protected now. Besides," he added in a lower voice, "I can't have a woman sent to a mine."

"I don't understand," Crystal said, coming closer to him. Subtly, she pressed herself against him, moistly kissing his neck and running her hand along his thigh. "You can do anything, my darling. What did you do to her lover?"

Allison looked into her idolizing eyes. His passion was stirring, and he knew that soon he would be unable to control himself. Even her lightest touch stoked his desires—never had he thought a woman could excite him so.

"I ended his life."

"You had him killed?" she whispered, pressing tighter against the growing bulge in his pants.

"No, he's paying the price for going against me!"

Crystal continued to stroke him, and she saw his face go tense with desire, but she said nothing. Then Allison reached around her to cup a breast and squeeze it tightly.

"He thought he could destroy me. But he couldn't. He came back from the dead, and I banished him to hell again."

Crystal gave a throaty moan, and pressed her hand tighter over the hardness beneath his clothing. "You're so exciting, James," she breathed in a low, husky voice. "So powerful, so manly."

Her words and actions were all part of the act she'd perfected for him. Allison reveled in power, and Crystal always made him feel that his power was so much a part of him that it drove her wild. When she seemed to become so uncontrolled, James Allison became proud and boastful.

Allison smiled down at her, his hand never still on her breast. His heavy breathing accented his words. "It was really quite simple," he boasted. "You see, a man in Cape Town, Johann Devreeling, had lost everything to the English. His hatred for them made him a perfect tool for me. I had Montgomery shipped to South Africa, where Devreeling arranged for him to work out the rest of his life in a diamond mine."

"Oh—" Then Crystal's hand paused tentatively in its movements as she widened her eyes. "But how can that be?"

"Criminals are hired out to mines instead of going to prison. It's cheaper and not wasteful. Montgomery is in one of those mines."

Crystal was afraid she might faint, but she reached deep down within her and steadied herself. "But surely someone will realize that he is not a criminal—or did you have him sentenced in South Africa?"

Allison laughed then. "No. I did something even better. He's serving his sentence under the name of a convicted criminal. The criminal was sent to another mine. No one will ever believe that Montgomery is who he says he is. And," he added proudly, "I receive regular reports on him so that I know he is alive and aware of why he's there."

"Oh, James," she whispered, "you're so clever." Then she rose on tiptoe and kissed him deeply. She put everything of herself into the kiss, for it was both a kiss of thanks and a kiss of death.

When Allison had spoken, every detail of Alana's letter concerning Rafe's death flashed through her mind. The man who had died escaping from his prison had had no name. He had not been listed on the mine roster. And Allison was still tracking Rafe. Like a brilliant explosion within her mind, one thought rang out clearly: Rafe was still alive!

Crystal made love to Allison in a frenzy of movement that made him believe that talking of his power of life and death over others had made Crystal more passionate than usual.

He had not understood the look in her wide-open eyes as she had devoured him. She had ridden him mercilessly, wringing every last ounce of strength within his body, and never once had her eyes closed. Never once had she made herself blank out her mind. She wanted to remember this night for as long as she lived.

When he left the next morning, he never knew how close to death he'd been. For it had taken every bit of her willpower not to plunge her hidden knife into his heart. During the long night, however, Crystal had realized that with Rafe alive, they would be able to destroy Allison—she would let him live to feel it.

After he was gone, Crystal wrote a note to Captain Sanders. The *Harmony* was due to leave for Cape Town on the evening tide, and she would be on board. Then Crystal packed. She filled four trunks, and after sending them to the dock, she wrote what she had learned and brought the letter to Nathan Bennet, instructing him to do nothing except observe Allison until she returned.

Next, Crystal laboriously wrote a letter to herself. She made sure that the handwriting did not look like her own, and when she was finished, she rubbed her eyes until they were bleary.

When she was ready, Crystal went to the Wellington Club and had Allison brought to her in the vestibule. When he saw her there, he did not see the desirable, sensual woman he had grown to know; rather, he saw a tearstained, distraught Crystal.

Taking her into a private room, he tried to find out what had happened since he'd left that morning, and slowly, in broken words, she'd told him.

"M-my brother," she cried. "I—I just received a letter. He was injured. I must go to him—he needs me."

"Go? Where? I will take you," he offered, strangely out of character for him.

Crystal shook her head. "England. He—he—oh, James," she

cried. "Please, I can't even talk about it. "I—please, my love, hold me a moment."

Handing Allison the letter, she buried her face in his chest and stayed there while he read it, not trusting herself to look him in the eye and tell the false tale.

When he had finished, she convinced Allison that she needed to see her brother, who had married into a titled, wealthy English family. He was, she explained between sobs, her only living relative. And in this, his time of torment, she must go to him.

She had drawn on her memory of Alana and explained that her brother had been injured in a hunting accident that had left him paralyzed.

"I will arrange passage immediately," Allison stated, acting the master and lover. "I will have one of my own ships readied for you."

Crystal drew back from him. "It will take too long, James. I've already seen to my passage. I leave on the late tide aboard the *Royal Dover.*"

"I shall take you there," he said.

Again Crystal shook her head. "Thank you, my dearest, but you are in a meeting. Just kiss me, my love, so that I may carry your touch with me until I return."

When they parted, Crystal's anger still fueled her. The tears that fell from her eyes were tears of rage, although Allison could not know that.

"I will return to you soon, my love, and then I shall repay you for everything."

"There is nothing to repay. All that I have done has been freely done. Just come back to me soon." For the first time in his life, James Allison meant what he said to a woman.

"As soon as I can," she promised.

Twenty minutes after leaving the Wellington Club, Crystal was on the bridge of the *Harmony.*

"Are you sure?" Captain Miles Sanders asked.

"I'm sure, Captain. My brother is still alive, and I'm going to get him out of that mine."

"This will be hard on Alana," Sanders commented.

Only then, did she realize what the news might mean to Alana.

"Oh, my God," she whispered.

As the months passed, Alana and Edward's life together cemented the bond that they had already formed. Alana became a familiar and welcome sight in the Maklin-Parkins offices as well as at her husband's properties in and out of Cape Town. Several times Edward took Alana on tour of his properties in the interior so that she became familiar with everything that he had built.

During her trips, Alana had begun to fall in love with the magnificent contrasts of South Africa: The Little and Great Karroos—part of the wide, high plateau that was the interior—were sparsely populated, parched land; the lush valleys of the Orange Free State, where the Boers had fled after the English gained dominance, was a bountiful land; and the Transvaal, with the purple pale that seemed to grow from the very earth itself, was hard and primitive.

As they'd traveled, Alana, with Edward's consent, continued to look for the people who were part of Allison's consortium. But no matter how hard she searched, she discovered nothing and no one that she could accuse.

Through all the time that had passed, Chaco had stayed with Alana and Edward. He was a loyal, devoted guard to Alana, and one whom Edward never doubted would protect his wife from any harm.

But on one sunny April day, Alana called Chaco into the study. She was aware that Chaco had been growing restless. She had seen the yearning, faraway look in his eyes.

When Chaco came into the study, Alana smiled at him. "We have been here for over a year and a half, Chaco. Why haven't you visited your home?"

Chaco raised his hands. *When I go to my home to my people, I shall not return.*

After she read his words, she looked deeply into his eyes. "You are my friend, Chaco. But you have been away from your people for too long."

You are safe with your husband, he signed. *But I must wait to learn if Crystal is safe also. She saved me and helped me when I needed it. I cannot leave this life until I know she is safe, too.*

Emotions welled within Alana. Only in this moment did she realize the depth of Chaco's devotion to Crystal. This knowledge made her aware, too, of the sacrifice he had been enduring since they'd arrived in Cape Town.

We must learn who is responsible for Rafe's death, he signed, his hands moving very slowly in emphasis to the words.

"Will we ever learn?" she whispered.

Yes! I must!

Alana's eyes locked with Chaco's, and she saw yet another emotion within their ebony depths. Intuitively, she realized that Chaco blamed himself for what had happened to Rafe.

"It was not your fault!"

I failed in my duty. I let those men capture you. Rafe died because of me.

"No! He died because of Ledoque and James Allison."

When you and Crystal and Rafe are avenged, I shall return to my home. With that, Chaco's face turned into an expressionless mask that forbade any further argument.

One evening after a particularly boring dinner party, Alana had not been able to contain her anger any longer at the way the other guests had spoken down to her. She and Edward lived quietly, disturbing no one, but the gossips insisted on circulating rumors about the American woman who had seduced Edward Parkins into marriage for his money.

"If it were not for you, dear Edward, I would have poured my champagne down Estelle Richmond's skinny chest!" Alana exclaimed once they were safely inside their carriage.

Surprisingly, Edward laughed. "Why didn't you? I would have loved to see her expression. That old dowager has been a thorn in my side since she arrived here with her pompous, emasculated husband."

Alana joined in his laughter for only a moment. "I would never do anything to shame you," she whispered. Then she leaned against him and tenderly kissed his cheek.

"I love you, Edward," she said.

Edward turned to her. "You have made me very happy, Alana, and I pray daily that I have done the same for you."

"You have, dearest one. You have shown me that life can be good and that I can look to the future without fear. We will have a long, wonderful life together," she stated.

When they arrived home, they went directly to their bedroom and, still feeling the warm glow that had suffused them in the carriage, they undressed and made slow, sweet love.

Later, as they lay within each other's arms in the bedroom, the light from the full moon filtering softly through the window, Edward turned to Alana.

"I only wish that one day you will carry my child," he said in an emotional voice.

Although this was the first time Edward had spoken of children, it was not a new thought for Alana. She had wondered why she had not become pregnant with Edward, just as she had been thankful she had not conceived the first time she had loved Rafe.

But as the months had passed, she had become increasingly worried that she might be barren. She had even visited Edward's doctor, making him promise not to tell Edward.

After his examination, the doctor had said he could detect no reason for her not to conceive. But, he'd added, experience had taught him that not every woman conceived easily. She should not worry about it, and one day she would carry her husband's children.

Alana now smiled up at Edward. "I too pray that I will one day carry your seed," she whispered. "It would make me so happy to be the mother of your son."

"Or daughter," Edward added. "Soon, I hope. I am not growing any younger."

Alana sat up then, and her hand traveled down his length. She stroked him with her fingers and felt him respond. "You don't seem to be growing, ah—older. In fact," she said in a husky voice, "you become stronger and younger each day."

Edward laughed again, then looked at her seriously. "You are a wonderful woman, Alana. You are a magnificent lover, an excellent wife, and possibly the best friend I have ever had. But I am not getting younger with each day. In three years, I will have lived a half century."

"And you shall live another half century," Alana declared,

"for I will make sure that when I am old, you are still holding me and loving me!"

Edward's smile was bittersweet. "Dear, sweet Alana, if I were to die tomorrow, I would do so happily, having known and loved you so completely."

"No more," Alana pleaded, tears rising to her eyes for no other reason than the talk of things she would never allow herself to think.

"No more," Edward agreed, seeing the distress on her face.

But his words did not ease her sudden fear of losing him. "Hold me, Edward. Love me," she pleaded.

Two days later, Alana accompanied Edward to the Maklin-Parkins warehouses for the company's annual inventory, a process in which Edward had made a habit of participating. Alana was with him because he enjoyed explaining to her the intricacies of his businesses as well as teaching her the way everything was done at Maklin-Parkins.

Three hours into the day, Alana and Edward were standing at the head of a long aisle. Four workers climbed over wooden crates stacked thirty feet into the air, calling out the contents of the crates to the clerks below.

Suddenly, one man slipped as the crate he was inspecting shifted. Shouting, he lost his balance and fell. Luckily, he didn't fall to the ground; rather, he ended up wedged between two large crates twenty feet up.

Before anyone else could act, Edward rushed to the ladder and climbed up to the injured man. Alana watched, her heart beating loudly in fear for both of them.

Edward worked the man's leg free. "Broken," he called down to the others. With his back on one crate and his legs braced on the other, Edward lifted the man and started to lay him on the top of the nearest crate. But as he moved, a loud crack sounded in the air.

Everyone looked up at the sound. The unstable crate had again shifted and was starting to topple. Too horrified to look away, Alana watched as Edward gathered his strength and pushed the injured man to safety.

But Edward himself was not able to move out of the path of

the falling crate in time. It struck him full in the chest, knocking him twenty feet to the ground.

Alana's scream tore through the warehouse. As the stunned workers stared, Alana raced to his crumpled form and drew him in her arms.

Holding him tightly to her chest, she saw that Edward's eyes were open. "I love you, Alana," he said in a barely audible voice. Then his eyes closed.

"No!" Alana screamed, piercingly. When the clerks tried to help her up, Alana refused to let anyone touch her or take Edward from her. A half hour later, Chaco picked up Edward's limp, broken body and took it and Alana home.

Five hundred miles inland, on the border between the Boers' Orange Free State and the Transvaal, was the Bristol mine—the most secret and dangerous diamond mine in South Africa.

This mine was not located in the purplish earth area where so many of the diamond fields lay. No, this special mine had been started following the advice of a new, young mining engineer who had come over from England two years before.

Instead of surface mining, which had been the only technique used until then, the engineer had set up a shaft mine, similar to those used for gold. After going down a hundred feet, he had discovered a higher quality of diamond than had previously been found. Three hundred feet deeper, they had found the diamond pipe—a vein of high-quality stones.

But because of the precarious nature of the mine shaft and the dangers inherent in this type of mining, workers had been almost impossible to get.

The owners had turned to the colonial judicial system and had offered monetary reimbursement for each prisoner sent to the mine to work out his sentence. Only one man in three survived a year. Only one man in five survived the second year. No one ever left the Bristol mine.

One of those who was into his second year was a tall man with black and silver hair and piercing green eyes that were never still. He rarely spoke after the first three months of his imprisonment, when he had tried in vain to explain that he was not who his papers said he was.

No one had listened to him, and Rafe Montgomery realized

that no one would. As far as they were concerned, he was Frank
Tremain, the American smuggler with whom he had ridden in
the prison wagon when he'd first been brought to the Bristol.

And so Rafe had stopped trying to convince anyone of his
true identity, and only thought about escape.

Four months after arriving in South Africa, he had attempted
his first escape. The guards had caught him almost immediately
and beat him senseless. It had taken two weeks for him to be
able to work again; a full month had passed before the pain had
gone.

While he was healing, he'd heard rumors of an escape at the
Germiston mine. Three men had reached freedom; two had not.
Of the two, one was said to have been an American. That was
how Rafe had learned of Frank Tremain's death.

From that point on, Rafe watched everyone around him as he
tried to think of a way to escape that would not end in death.
He noted that a shipment of diamonds had gone out three
weeks ago, and he learned that another was due to be sent out
in five weeks. He watched men die in mine explosions and in
cave-ins. Mishaps occurred weekly because of the shoddy mining methods employed hundreds of feet below the surface.

He had learned how to survive and to grow strong. He had
seen numerous escape attempts and had watched the men get
killed long before they could reach the freedom of the wild
country not a thousand feet from the mine shaft.

Rafe was also the last white prisoner left alive. The rest of the
workers were black, and most were innocent of any crime.
Greedy magistrates had found the defenseless natives guilty in
order to receive bonuses from the mining company.

But above all, Rafe kept himself strong and his spirit and
willpower alive, for he knew that one day he would escape, and
when he did, he would find Alana.

Eighteen months after he had arrived at the Bristol mine, he
had formed a plan of escape. It would be hard, but Rafe was
determined to get away from the Bristol mine alive. It was not
his hatred of Allison that kept Rafe going; rather, the memory
and vision of Alana had been his only reason for staying alive.

26

"Your Grace," said the butler, who had used Alana's title from the day she had married Edward.

Alana looked up in the darkened library. Her tired eyes held no hint of interest. "Yes?"

"You have a caller, madame," he informed her.

"I am not seeing anyone."

"Please, your Grace, I informed the woman of your wishes, but she is very insistent. She demands to see you. She is creating a scene."

Alana sighed. "Very well, Haines," she said. "Show her in."

When the butler left, Alana closed her eyes again. In the two weeks since Edward's death, she had locked herself in the house, hidden from the world, refusing to see any callers—not that there had been many. She had not even attended the reading of Edward's will, but had asked Matthew Conklin, Edward's attorney, to read the will to her in private.

When he had finished, she had stared at him in shock. Edward had left Alana most of his great fortune, all of his vast properties, and especially Maklin-Parkins. He had also given her one other thing. "But why?" she had asked.

"Edward loved you very much. When he rewrote his will shortly after your marriage, he wanted my assurance that I would not speak of it to you. Only upon his death were you to learn the contents of his will, for he feared you would make him change it."

"But what of his family in England?" Alana had asked. Edward had never spoken of them, and she had, for some reason, never asked.

"His brother died five years ago. He was Edward's only living relative."

"But isn't his request unusual?"

The lawyer had nodded his head. "But not without precedent. What it means," the attorney went on, "is that Edward did not want his family lands and titles bestowed upon a stranger. Nor did he want you to spend your life grieving over him. He wanted to assure himself that you would marry again and have a family. He wants any child you bear, whether his or another's, to be named heir to the title of Duke of Claymore. It is also the only way that you may keep your own title if you marry a man who is untitled or of lesser nobility than Edward."

"But if I do not remarry?" she'd asked.

"Upon your death, the title would revert to whomever His Majesty proclaims."

After Conklin had left, she had thought about Edward's will, his love for her, and his wishes. But she knew deep within her that she would not remarry, for she could never allow herself to be hurt like this again.

"Alana," came a familiar voice.

Alana's thoughts fled as she opened her eyes and looked at her visitor. A gasp escaped her lips, and when she stood, her legs trembled.

"Crystal!" she whispered. An instant later, she was in Crystal's arms. When she finally drew back, she searched her friend's face. "Why—what—?"

Crystal didn't smile at Alana's surprise. But she did take her friend's hands in hers. "I was so sorry to hear about Edward."

Alana nodded her head.

"But," Crystal said. Then she paused.

Alana stared at Crystal, waiting.

"Alana," Crystal began again, "Rafe is still alive."

Alana's mouth opened but no sound emerged. Her eyes widened, and a wave of dizziness swept through her. Her head spun; the room suddenly turned upside down, and she collapsed on the floor.

When she opened her eyes again, she was lying on the leather couch, her feet propped up by a large cushion. She saw that Crystal was shouting at her maid and the butler, demanding to know why Alana was in such frail condition.

"She wouldn't eat much, mum," Eleanor had replied in a frightened voice.

Haines, in his usual dignified manner, stated that he had been powerless to force Her Grace to eat properly.

"Go! Have the cook prepare some broth!" Crystal ordered. But before anyone left, Alana spoke.

"It's not their fault, Crystal. They tried to help me."

"But they didn't," she snapped. "Go!" The two servants left quickly. Turning to Alana, Crystal fixed her with a hard, green-eyed stare. "I need you healthy if we're to find Rafe."

Crystal's words brought out all of Alana's old memories, the ones she thought she had put to rest. Even the mention of his name was enough to make her heart soar and her hopes come alive again. Fighting off another wave of dizziness, Alana tried to believe Crystal's words.

"How can you be so certain he's alive? The report was quite clear about his death."

"Yes, it was," Crystal said, her mouth forming a tight smile. "However, the man who died was not Rafe. Rafe was sent to a mine under the dead man's name. Alana, he was not killed. Allison made that very clear to me. Rafe was to live and to suffer every single day."

Alana stood. She stared at Crystal and took a deep breath. "If he's alive, we will find him and set him free!" Alana exclaimed with determination that she had not felt since Edward's death.

As if to emphasize Alana's declaration, the library door opened and Chaco stepped in. He stared at Crystal for several long moments. Then an uncharacteristic joyous smile shaped his lips.

Midnight found Alana, Crystal, and Chaco in the study; the original trio that had been formed three years before was once again united.

Alana had told Crystal about Edward's tragic death, speaking of it for the first time. When she had finished, Crystal had

asked the question that had been on her mind since learning of
Edward's death.

"Could Allison have been behind Edward's accident? He
hated him terribly."

Alana had stared wide-eyed at Crystal, but Chaco had
shaken his head emphatically and then begun to sign.

He had explained that he had been spending his days at the
warehouses and docks in an effort to learn the answer to that
question. After two weeks of looking around and listening to all
conversations, he believed it had truly been an accident.

"Thank God," Alana had whispered. "I could not bear to
have been responsible for his death."

When Crystal's mind was eased of those thoughts, they had
tried to think of a way to find out at which mine Rafe was being
imprisoned. Although they knew the name of the man who had
sent Rafe there, they also knew the futility of trying to get the
man to confess. Alana and Crystal had decided they would look
for another way.

After dinner, they had gone into the study, where Alana had
looked through Edward's personal files. She had told Crystal
about the report Edward had received of the escape at the Germiston mine. She needed that report to learn the name under
which Rafe was listed.

At midnight, Alana discovered the report in a thin file box
with her name neatly scripted on it in Edward's precise handwriting.

Opening it, with Crystal peering over her shoulder, Alana
withdrew several tied bundles of papers. Only then, almost two
years after she had begun her search for Rafe, did Alana see the
voluminous amount of correspondence that Edward had received in her behalf.

Alana experienced a feeling of vertigo at the realization of
how much more Edward had done than she'd known. *He was so
good to me,* she said silently.

There were letters from all his supervisory people in the far-
flung reaches of the Maklin-Parkins empire. Mixed among
them, Alana found the report of Edward's touring mine supervisor, detailing the death of the unknown American. It also
named the American smuggler, Frank Tremain, but it did not
state at which mine he was serving his sentence.

"But we have the name," Crystal said hopefully. "Now we can find the mine—although that may still not be enough to free Rafe."

"If it *is* Rafe, then we will find a way."

After Chaco left them, Crystal and Alana continued to talk. Under Crystal's gentle probing, Alana spoke of her feelings and emotions for Edward. She told Crystal about their life together and of the wonderful and gentle love they had shared.

"If it is Rafe, what do I tell him? That while he has been suffering in prison because of me, I have been leading a life of ease and luxury?"

"Do you think he will condemn you for what you've done?" Crystal asked.

"I don't know. I thought him dead, but I never stopped loving him. Yet I shared another man's name and bed."

"He will have to accept and understand what happened," Crystal ventured, unsure herself of how her brother would react when he learned of Alana's marriage.

A moment later, Crystal laughed. "And what will happen when he learns his prim and proper sister is a whore? Poor Rafe," she whispered.

Perhaps it was the way the woman spoke, so secure in the knowledge that Rafe was still alive, that made them realize that no matter what they had done or been, just the fact that he lived was reward enough for now. The future would have to take care of itself.

They spent another few minutes deciding who to speak to tomorrow in the government offices, and then Alana reversed the roles they had been playing, gently questioning Crystal about what had happened to her in New York.

They finally went to bed shortly before three in the morning, and they were up again with the sun. By nine, they had entered the warrenlike complex of government offices and buildings that surrounded the governor's palace, which was the only truly official-looking government building, aside from the courts.

Going through the maze of government offices brought back the memories of those first months that Alana had spent searching for Rafe. She saw the same obnoxious clerks, bobbing their obsequious heads, who knew nothing about anything.

By eleven, Alana and Crystal had learned the name of the

mine where Frank Tremain had been sent. At eleven thirty, after being refused an audience with the head magistrate, and having learned that the governor was not expected back until that afternoon, Alana and Crystal had returned to Alana's house.

After eating a light lunch, Alana had the carriage return them to the colonial governor's palace. When they entered the anteroom of the governor's private office, they found themselves staring into the pinched features of the governor's chief clerk.

"May I help you?" the small man inquired airily.

"I would like to see the governor," Alana stated.

The man looked down at the large, leather-bound appointment book that rested in the center of his desk. "Do you have an appointment, madame?" he asked in a lofty voice. "If not, I'm afraid it will be impossible. The governor is a very busy man."

Alana smiled then. "Tell *acting* Governor White that the Duchess of Claymore wishes to speak to him immediately." The man's eyes widened, and an instant later he disappeared into the governor's office.

Crystal stared at Alana with both pride and amazement. "I never realized what a title could do," she said.

"Edward taught me," Alana replied.

The clerk reappeared a few moments later and asked the women to follow him. Once they were inside the large office, the acting governor dismissed the clerk and came from around his desk. He was in his late fifties, paunchy, with a large veined nose that indicated a life of too much drink. He carried about him an air of self-importance that Alana disliked, and it seemed to her that every time she saw him he appeared to be more entrenched in his temporary role. Yet Edward and the man had been friends, and she had never voiced her opinion of the acting governor aloud.

When he reached them, he took Alana's hand in his and brought it to his lips. "A pleasure, Lady Parkins," the governor said. Then he turned to Crystal and took her hand.

"Governor Samuel White, may I introduce Elizabeth Montgomery of San Francisco."

"A pleasure," the governor repeated.

After releasing Crystal's hand, he escorted the ladies to two large, ornate chairs, and sat himself on a third. "To what do I owe the pleasure of this unexpected visit?"

"Samuel," Alana began, using his name in a friendly way. "You were a good friend of Edward's, and I must impinge on that friendship now."

"By all means," White replied.

"Do you remember when my husband made certain efforts to locate a man we thought imprisoned improperly?"

The governor nodded his head. "About two years ago, wasn't it?"

"Yes. The man's name is Rafael Montgomery."

"Yes, quite," White said a little too curtly.

"We know where he is now," Alana stated, ignoring the governor's tone.

The governor sat straighter in the chair; his eyes locked on Alana's. "So now it all comes out, after Edward is safely in his grave."

Alana's blood raced angrily when she realized exactly what the governor had not said. Like the majority of the upper-class people in Cape Town, she saw that the governor also looked upon her as an interloper in their society.

Before Alana could reply, Crystal spoke. Her voice was calm and unemotional. "I am Rafael Montgomery's sister. And I have learned that my brother is in the Bristol mine. He is listed under the name of Frank Tremain, and I demand his immediate release."

"As do I!" Alana declared.

"And just who do you think you are?" the governor asked sarcastically.

Alana stared directly into his eyes. "The Duchess of Claymore."

"By marriage."

"Nevertheless, I am the duchess, and I have certain rights."

"Madame," the governor said in stiff formality, "duchess or not, you are in no position to demand anything." Fixing Alana with an accusatory stare, the governor continued to speak. "When you first claimed that your fiancé had been abducted, Edward brought your case to me. I personally conducted a thorough investigation because of my friendship for the duke—although I never believed for a moment that such a person existed." The governor paused, his eyes never leaving Alana's face.

"My colleagues and I believed that you had blinded Edward by your story of helplessness. When you managed to marry him, we knew we had been proven correct. After concluding my investigation, I was convinced that this Montgomery person had never been sentenced or sent to a mine and that your story was blatantly false."

Alana stared silently at the governor, unable to make her voice work in the wake of his accusations. Again, it was Crystal who spoke for her.

"Johann Devreeling is the man who arranged for my brother's incarceration. He switched papers and placed my brother in the Bristol mine under the name of Frank Tremain."

"Impossible!"

"He is there!" Alana declared in a loud, angry voice.

"What kind of a fool do you take me for, Madame Parkins? I am not as gullible as your late husband. If this man you now call Tremain has been sentenced, then it was because he deserved to be. If he is not using his own name, that simply means he is guilty. Or is this Tremain your lover, and now that you have gained both title and estate, you want him back?"

Alana tensed. "How dare you speak to me like that!" Her anger flowed too fast to stop. Stiffly, she rose to her feet. "You have made a terrible mistake, Governor White, one that will cost you dearly."

Alana turned to leave, but Crystal's hand stopped her. Crystal asked reasonably, "Will you not at least question this man Devreeling?"

"Johann Devreeling is a man above reproach. He is a trusted magistrate of the court, and I will not insult him in that manner."

"I see," Crystal whispered.

"I certainly hope so. Now you may leave."

Alana brushed off Crystal's restraining hand and stared bitterly at the governor. "My husband considered you his friend. He was mistaken, for you are far from that. He was mistaken also when he used his influence to help you gain your appointment to the acting governorship. But Edward taught me much, especially of the power that accompanies my family's nobility.

You shall regret both your words to me and your unwillingness to pursue this matter. I shall see to that, Governor White."

"Alana," Crystal whispered, trying to stop her heated flow of words.

Without taking her eyes from the governor, Alana continued to speak. "You are a sanctimonious, envious fool. If you try to interfere with our finding Mr. Montgomery, I will ruin you. Do you understand me?"

"Don't let your inheritance make you think you have the power your husband had," White said, his face livid at Alana's words.

"We shall see about that, shan't we? Good day, Governor." Turning regally, Alana left the office, never once allowing the man to see that her hands trembled with the black rage she felt.

In the carriage Crystal turned to Alana. "That may have been a mistake."

"I don't give a damn if it was or not. He had no right to talk to me like that, and as far as I'm concerned, he's as guilty as Devreeling!"

A heavy silence fell between them as the carriage drove toward her house. It continued until they were inside and seated on the leather couch in the library.

Then Alana sighed as she looked at Crystal. "I'm sorry I lost my temper. I shouldn't have. But he made me realize how much I've depended on Edward and not on myself."

Crystal wisely maintained her silence.

"That pompous jackass has made a big mistake. I will use everything I have to get Rafe free. Everything!"

"First we must make certain that it is Rafe at the Bristol mine," Crystal cautioned.

"It is," Alana vowed. "It has to be."

They talked for another hour, trying to think of ways to free Rafe without coming upon a workable plan. Then, as if she had been in a dark tunnel for too long, Alana saw the light at its end.

Her breath hissed out, and she closed her eyes in an effort to control her spinning thoughts. "Crystal, we've been fools."

"No, Alana, we've—"

"Yes, we have! We've been playing under the wrong rules, Crystal. We haven't yet let ourselves do things the way he does, because we care about people. Allison doesn't give a damn about anyone except himself and his wealth. It's time to do things his way. It's the only way to win."

Crystal played Alana's words within her head, and slowly came to the same conclusion. She had played Allison's game in New York, but since then she had been complacent by comparison. "How?"

Alana stood and paced the confines of the room. "Here is what we have to do. First, and most important, is to free Rafe. Then Devreeling must be forced to sign a confession, admitting his role. Only after those two things are accomplished can we go to the governor and present him with a *fait accompli*. The governor can do nothing against us then."

"Alana—" Crystal said, her voice holding an edge of doubt.

But Alana shook her head determinedly at Crystal's tone. "No! It was you who taught me how to survive. You're the strong one, Crystal. Don't change on me now."

Crystal shook her head. "It's not that. After what happened with the governor today, will he not mention our accusation to Devreeling?"

Alana's breath caught. "And I called *him* a fool! Of course he'll tell Devreeling what we said. And Devreeling will—"

"Will have Rafe removed so that there can be no evidence against him," Crystal finished for her.

"Then we have no time to lose!" Alana exclaimed, galvanizing her mind into action.

An hour later, Alana was in the offices of Maklin-Parkins, where she informed the head clerk that she was leaving immediately on an inspection of the company's mines along the border of the Orange Free State.

She asked for all the records of those mines, and then told him that no one was to know that she had left Cape Town.

When the clerk hesitated, she fixed him with the authoritative glare that Edward had used so often. "You served my husband loyally. I trust you'll do the same for me." Softening her tone somewhat, she added, "we are in this business together, Mr. Crawford."

The head clerk nodded his head silently. Then Alana issued instructions for him to have a supply wagon and the company coach readied for her by that evening.

When the head clerk started from the office, Alana stopped him. He looked at her in question, and she asked him to take a seat.

"Mr. Crawford, you've always worked closely with my husband. He believed you were indispensable to him in the running of Maklin-Parkins. I would like to feel the same. In my absence, you are in charge."

"Very well, Lady Parkins," Philip Crawford replied.

"And I must ask a favor of you, Mr. Crawford."

"If I can be of service."

"Between now and when I leave tonight, I need all the information you can find about the Bristol mine."

Crawford stared at her for a moment, his brows knitting together. "Have they made you any offers since—since your husband died?" Crawford asked suddenly.

"No."

"For a moment I thought—" Crawford paused.

"Thought what?" Alana prodded.

"They had approached your husband almost three years ago, seeking financing for their mine. After Mr. Parkins looked into the situation, he declined to invest. But I do believe," Crawford added thoughtfully, "that we kept all the information that was given us. I shall look for it."

"It would be a great help to me, Mr. Crawford. Please bring everything you can find to the house."

Crawford stood, but again Alana stopped him. "Why didn't Edward invest in the mine?" she asked.

"He didn't like the way they were planning to run the operation, nor did he like the idea of shaft mining the way their engineer proposed to do it."

"Shaft mining?" Alana questioned. "I thought all diamonds were surface mined."

"Most are. Several people have tried shaft mining, but most have been unsuccessful," Crawford informed her.

"But the Bristol?"

Crawford shrugged. "No one knows. Everything about the mine is secret. Perhaps there is something in the old file." With that, Crawford left, and Alana went to the docks to meet with Captain Sanders.

After explaining her plan to the captain, she told him what she needed him to do, and he willingly agreed.

Then she returned home to tell Crystal that all was in readiness. Two hours later, Philip Crawford arrived with the supply wagon, company coach, and the information Alana had requested. He told both women, and Chaco who stood behind them, about the original offer that the owners of the Bristol mine had made Edward. But the best information of all was a detailed sketch of the area and a layout of all the buildings as well as the proposed shaft mine itself.

When Crawford finished, Alana took the papers from him. "Thank you, Mr. Crawford. I don't know how long we'll be gone, but I'm sure that you will take care of everything in my absence."

Crawford stood, but before he left he spoke again. "Tim Foster, the supervisor of the Parkins Five, might know more about the current operation of the Bristol, which is only three miles from him. But I must caution you to be careful when dealing with the people at the Bristol. Your husband believed the men financing the mine to be somewhat unscrupulous."

"We shall be very careful, Mr. Crawford, and I thank you for your concern."

At midnight Alana and Crystal were inside the luxurious coach. Chaco was seated next to the driver. And while most of Cape Town slept, the two women, Chaco, the drivers, and two company guards rode out of town.

Unbeknownst to Alana, her carriage passed a small yet luxurious stone house wherein Johann Devreeling sat across from Harold Rankin, a British ex-colonial officer and the man who was currently in charge of security for the Bristol mine.

The two men had one thing in common: they both worked for James Allison, although no one knew it.

Devreeling had just finished explaining their problem and was waiting for Rankin's reply.

"I don't like it," Rankin stated.

"But you'll do it. Remember, if anyone learns about Montgomery, we're both finished." Exhaling loudly, Devreeling handed Rankin several legal documents. "These are the release and commutation papers for Frank Tremain. Make sure he does not reach Cape Town."

"He won't," Rankin stated. "I'll take him out of the mine with the next shipment. In ten days, Montgomery will never have existed."

27

Alana hugged herself against the chill in the night air, which was carried to them by the ever-present west wind. At her side Crystal did the same, while both women continued to stare at the dark mine in the distance. Only a few pinpoints of light from lanterns could be seen from their vantage point; the rest was pictured in their minds.

"It's time," Crystal whispered.

Alana nodded. Then the two women walked to the waiting carriage and motioned to the man who stood next to it.

Tim Foster, the supervisor of Parkins Five, went to the front of the carriage, grasped the horse's halter, and started him around. The women followed Foster on foot until they reached the curve on the mine's road that they knew would be hidden from the watchful eyes of the guards at the Bristol mine.

Crystal took two revolvers from her waistband and checked their loads. While she did that, Alana stepped close to Foster and said, "Thank you for your help. Now you must go."

"I'll stay," he stated.

Alana gave a sharp shake of her head. "You're a good man, Tim Foster, and that's why my husband hired you. But I'm in charge now, and I order you back to the mine."

Foster started to protest again, but Alana cut him off quickly. "Go, Tim, and if anyone ever asks, you had no knowledge of what Crystal or I were attempting to do."

"Lady Parkins—" Foster began.

"No more arguments, Tim. Go!"

Tim Foster knew that he had no choice. He knew also that if something went wrong with their plans, it must be looked upon as the work of the two women. If he were seen or caught, the consequences could be directed against Maklin-Parkins and their vast resources.

When he was gone, Alana went to Crystal. "I hope Chaco made it."

"He did," Crystal stated emphatically.

"Are you ready?" Alana asked.

"Be careful," Crystal cautioned. "Don't do anything crazy."

Alana laughed suddenly. "Crazy? Crystal, how much crazier can we be? But, Crystal, crazy or not, I won't come out without Rafe!"

"I know," Crystal whispered. "I know."

And as the first faint light of dawn began to paint the African plateau with color, Alana worked her way to the wooden barricade that was closest to the miners' barracks.

Obscured by the last vestiges of the night, Alana went to the fence and sat with her back near the already-weakened boards that would provide her entrance. As she waited for the signal, she thought about how her destiny had changed in the past years, leading her so far from home to this very spot in the South African interior.

After consulting with Tim Foster and memorizing the layout of the mine, Alana and Crystal had formed a daring but simple plan. Going through a fence near the barracks, Chaco would enter the mine at around three in the morning—a time when even the most alert guard would be drowsy. He would work his way through the barracks until he discovered Rafe. Then he would lead Rafe back to the opening in the fence, where Alana waited.

In the meantime Crystal would take a carriage and drive it toward the fortresslike entrance of the mine. The idea was for the carriage to hit and block the gate so that it would take some time for the Bristol's guards to get out to pursue Alana and Rafe.

The rigging of the carriage was jimmied so that at the right moment, a quick kick from Crystal's boot would free the horse.

Once Crystal was clear, she would mount the horse and ride to where Alana had set up the rendezvous.

Although it was dangerous, Crystal believed she would be able to jump free before the carriage collided with the gate. In any event Crystal would not allow Alana to dissuade her from taking this risk in order to free her brother.

Chaco had signed that he would find help for them. He had not explained what he would do, only that he would be back in time for the escape.

Except, Alana now thought as she looked around the dawn-lightened land, Chaco had not returned. Alana believed something had happened to prevent Chaco's return. She knew he would not willingly abandon them. She prayed that Chaco had gone directly into the mine without stopping to tell them he was back. If necessary, Alana would take Chaco's place, but she would not go in until the sun started to rise.

The sun finally rose, and with it Alana's apprehension increased. Unlike Crystal, who wore a traveling dress to add authenticity to her role and to confound the guards at the beginning, Alana wore pants, high boots, and a cotton shirt. Her hair was pulled tightly back, and her head was covered by a wide-brimmed man's hat.

Turning slightly, she looked at the section of fence that Chaco and Foster had loosened on Saturday night. She touched one board; it moved slightly in response.

It would take only seconds to pull the boards free and get inside. "And when I do," she whispered, "will I find you, Rafe?"

Inside the long, dark barracks were fifty narrow beds. The sounds of men sleeping—some moaning unknowingly in their sleep—filled the fetid, foul air.

Only one of the fifty was awake. He had awakened suddenly, sensing eyes upon him. It was not the first time that something like this had happened to Rafe. The lonely years of slavelike labor and the absence of women had turned many of the stronger workers into animals, lusting after anything they could get.

Rafe's hand moved slowly until his fingers curled around the small knife he had made out of a spoon. Then he froze. The man who stood above him was not making any move toward him. Rafe decided to wait and see what would happen.

His eyes, well adjusted to the darkness and aided by the faint light of the predawn sky, made out the shadowy form as the man leaned down. Rafe's arm tensed; he got ready to spring. But the man did not move as if he were attacking Rafe; instead, one hand touched Rafe's shoulder gently while his other hand went to his mouth, signaling Rafe to be silent.

In that incredible instant, Rafe recognized Chaco and bolted upright.

Chaco signed to Rafe, but realized he would not understand. Instead, he made motions for Rafe to dress.

Rafe smiled for the first time since he'd been taken from New York, and he left the bed. Less than two minutes later, he was dressed and ready. As silently as Chaco had entered the barracks—the fourth one he had entered in his search for Rafe—both men left.

Outside, leaning against the side of the building, out of the guards' sight, Rafe grasped Chaco's arm and asked in a quiet voice, "Is Alana here with you?"

Chaco nodded once and then led Rafe to the wall of another barracks, this one closer to the wall that surrounded the mine. The men moved quickly yet stealthily, avoiding the eyes of the guards in the tower. Rafe refused to allow his mind to wander as he concentrated on only one thing: escape.

When they reached the last building and faced the two hundred feet of open land between the building and the stockade wall, Rafe looked at Chaco.

Chaco held up his hand and then tapped his ear with his forefinger.

"Wait? Wait for a signal?" he asked.

Chaco nodded again.

Rafe exhaled and leaned against the building as the land was illuminated with the early light of the day. His heart was beating fast, powered by the adrenaline that pumped through his body and the hope that soon he would be free and with Alana. How she had managed this, he had no idea, but that was unimportant now. If he reached freedom, there would be time to learn how she had found him. If he didn't, it wouldn't matter.

Then, from the front of the mine near the large gates came

the thundering sound of wood ramming into wood. At the same instant Chaco pushed Rafe forward, and the two men sprinted for the fence.

As soon as Crystal had seen the leading edge of the sun crest the horizon, she had taken a deep breath and started the carriage forward. By the time she was a hundred yards from the gates, the sound of the speeding carriage was loud in the air.

She looked at the top of the gates and saw a half dozen guards staring down at her in confusion. She stood, balancing herself precariously, and shouted for help.

With fifty yards remaining between the carriage and the high gates, Crystal's heart thudded in fear. Her mouth was dry; her hands clenched the reins so tightly that her skin was sickly white.

At twenty yards, she saw the realization that the carriage would not stop dawning on the guards' faces. Shouts reached her, but she did not hear them in her fierce concentration.

At thirty feet the carriage was aimed at the center of the gates. And as the gates grew to the height of a mountain, Crystal used the toe of her boot to hit the rigging hook; the leather and wood parted from the carriage.

Unable even to take a breath, Crystal dove from the carriage, hitting the ground and rolling wildly to a stop as the sound of wood striking wood echoed loudly in the early morning stillness.

She sat motionless for a moment, her breath knocked from her lungs. Then she willed herself to move. Turning over, she saw that the carriage had struck exactly where she'd intended and had wedged itself into the double gate, effectively locking it until the carriage could be worked free.

Turning again, she saw that the horse had stopped fifty feet from her. She got to her feet, ran to the horse, and as the guards shouted out to her, used her knife to cut away the carriage rigging. Thirty seconds after reaching the horse, Crystal was mounted and galloping away.

Where are you, Chaco? Alana thought as she heard the echo of the collision between carriage and gate. She could not wait for him any longer. She worked the boards free from the fence and started inside, but before she could pull herself through the opening, she saw two men coming at her in a dead run. Chaco! And . . . could it be Rafe?

Gunfire erupted from the two nearest towers as the two men escaped through the fence. Bullets whistled over their heads, careening madly when they hit the rocky earth near them.

But the bullets meant nothing to Alana, whose eyes were frozen to Rafe's gaunt face, drinking in the familiar depths of his emerald green eyes. "Rafe," she whispered.

And then suddenly the air was filled with bone-tipped spears. Three dozen projectiles whistled overhead; the guards ducked for cover.

Astonished, Alana turned to see what appeared to be a full tribe of Africans standing on the rise behind them just as Rafe's whispered oath reached her ears. "Sweet Jesus!"

And then Chaco pushed Alana and Rafe, urging them onward. Neither wasted a moment to look back as they raced to freedom.

When the three reached the crest of the hill, Alana saw dozens of black warriors, some carrying rifles, others carrying spears. The warriors surged toward them, surrounding everyone.

Rafe's mind worked at lightning speed, but the events of the past hour had taken their toll on him. He stood in the center of a tribe of Basuto warriors; next to him was the woman for whom he had stayed alive.

A thousand questions rose in his mind, but he pushed them all aside as he looked at Alana again. "How did you find me?" he asked as he opened his arms to her.

Alana couldn't speak. Rafe looked terrible and smelled worse, but to her he was magnificent. She stared wordlessly up at him. Then, in the security of his arms, she lifted herself up on the balls of her feet and pressed her lips to his.

The feel of his mouth upon hers told her that everything would be all right again. When she ended the kiss, her tears fell, but she ignored them. She opened her mouth to speak, but then she saw Chaco signing to her urgently. *Go now. Talk later!*

Smiling, she took Rafe's hand in hers. "We must move quickly. A quarter mile from here is a carriage and—"

"And what?"

Alana smiled again as her eyes roamed his face. "You'll see," she whispered.

Crystal reined in the horse when she reached the hidden carriage. As she'd ridden, she'd heard gunfire coming from behind her. All she could do was pray that Chaco, Alana, and Rafe had made it away from the mine.

Dismounting, she pulled the horse's reins over its head and handed them to the driver. Then Crystal took a few steps in the direction of the mine. Her nerves were taut, but she knew that only time would calm them. She could do nothing else now but wait.

Ten minutes later, Crystal's mouth fell open in amazement. Before her unbelieving eyes came a large band of black warriors; at their head strode Chaco, Alana, and Rafe. Without further thought, Crystal started running toward them.

28

When Rafe saw the waiting coach, he breathed easier. He knew that a full platoon of guards would be out hunting for him very soon. No one had ever successfully escaped the Bristol.

Then, as he saw a figure running toward them, Rafe froze to the spot, his hand tightening ferociously on Alana's while he stared at a sight out of a dream.

"Elizabeth," he whispered. Confusion and shock were written on the gaunt lines of his face. He shook his head, and then he looked at Alana, whose smile told him that he was not hallucinating.

"She's dead," he insisted.

"No, Rafe, she's very much alive."

And then Crystal was in Rafe's arms, her hands digging into his back, her sobs echoing above the African plateau.

It took several minutes for Crystal to calm down. When she finally released her brother, she said, "We can't waste any more time. We have to go right away!"

Rafe, looking from Crystal to Alana, was still stunned. "How did you find me?"

"Later," Alana declared, pulling Rafe forward. "Soon we'll have all the time in the world. But not if the prison guards catch us."

Inside the carriage, Alana sat next to Rafe, and Crystal and Chaco sat opposite. They were jubilant as the carriage started out. Behind it, Basuto warriors followed at a half run, several of

them trailing long leafy branches that obliterated the tracks of
the wagon.

Rafe settled himself in the seat, drew in a deep breath, and
then looked at Alana. But before he could ask one of his thousand questions, Chaco spoke. At the sound of his voice, everyone in the carriage was struck speechless, an irony which did
not escape Chaco.

As the others stared, Chaco told them exactly who and what
he was. His much-abbreviated tale took a half hour to tell, and
when he finished, he turned to Crystal, who was the first to
speak.

"All these years," Crystal whispered incredulously.

"It was necessary for me," Chaco stated.

Crystal smiled, blinking back the tears that spilled from her
eyes. "I know Chaco, I'm—I'm just—" When words failed her,
Crystal used sign language to explain her feelings and to thank
him for his help, both here and ever since she had met him.

"We have shared so much of our lives, Crystal," Chaco said
in a low voice, "that it is very hard to think of leaving you. But
I must, for my father is growing old, and I will be the next
leader of the Basuto people."

"You will be a wise leader, one who will not be deceived by
the white men who are trying to own everything on this conti-
nent," said Alana, adding, "and you will be able to count on my
support, and that of Maklin-Parkins, too."

Chaco nodded gravely to Alana. "I thank you for myself and
my people. In the years to come, your help might make the
difference between the survival or the end of the Basuto people."

Rafe continued to gaze at the three players in this still-not-
quite-believable melodrama. Finally, he could hold himself
back no more and, turning to Alana, he spoke.

"I think it's time for my explanation. And," Rafe asked
dryly, "just why did the driver call you Lady Parkins?"

As they continued on their journey from the diamond fields
to Port Elizabeth, Chaco's warriors still followed behind. While
they traveled, Rafe learned first of his sister's life after he had
left San Francisco on his ill-starred voyage.

Crystal spoke slowly, explaining all that had happened in the past seven years. Three hours after she had begun, she was once again dry-eyed. She looked at her brother and waited for his angry response.

Rafe held Crystal's gaze for several minutes. All the old anger had risen with her story: the deep-rooted hatred for the men who had tried time and again to destroy his family. Added to his long-simmering fury was the new rage over what Crystal had been forced to go through. At first he had been devastated by the knowledge that his sister had become a whore, but that soon passed as he willed himself to think rationally. Finally, when he was able to speak, he did so in a level voice.

"You are here, Elizabeth, and alive. That is all that's important. You did what you had to do. That you did not die in the fire in Nevada is more important than what you did to survive after that. You not only survived, you prevailed. You enabled Alana to keep Riverbend and Landow Shipping, and because of you we are all here together today. You aren't a whore, Elizabeth, you're a lady."

Crystal went into his arms then and held her brother close.

A little while later, after Crystal returned to her seat, Rafe looked at Alana. "Talk to me, my love. Tell me everything."

Alana gazed at him as he took her hands. She tried to speak, but she could not. Taking a deep breath, Alana made herself tell him everything. She spared nothing, and every word she spoke was the truth.

When she finished, she tried to pull her hands free, but Rafe would not allow it. "I'm sorry, Rafe. If there had been a shred of hope that you were alive, I never would have married Edward."

Rafe shook his head and released her hands. He turned from her to look out at the land.

"In all the time I spent in that mine, I never once thought of you with another man."

Alana turned from him, unable to stop her tears. "Don't," she whispered.

Rafe said nothing; instead, he continued to stare at the land and the sky as he tried to digest all he'd been told.

They stopped several hours after nightfall to make camp. Rafe maintained his strange silence.

Two of Chaco's warriors brought game back for their meal;

neither Rafe nor Alana ate. They sat apart from each other, staring off into their own troubled worlds.

After the meal ended, Crystal, knowing that it would be the wrong time to speak to either Rafe or Alana, walked with Chaco and learned more of his past. They talked for an hour, and when they returned to the campfire, they found Rafe still staring vacantly at the fire. Alana was gone.

Chaco called out in his native tongue and was answered immediately. "She is walking nearby," he told Crystal. "One of my people is close to her."

Crystal went to Rafe and sat next to him at the fire. "Why can you forgive me and not Alana?" she asked.

Rafe didn't look at his sister; he just stared at the fire. Finally, he said sullenly, "You were forced into what you had to do; Alana married the man willingly."

Crystal did not look at her brother; rather, she stared into the orange flames. When she did speak, her voice was low, but her tone was intense.

"You were always a stubborn man, Rafe. Perhaps now is the time to bend a little. Alana followed you across the world. She spent months searching for you, fighting to get any word at all to you. When she heard the report of your death, she almost died herself. Edward Parkins saved her life because he loved her. He searched this entire country looking for you because he loved Alana. He never once tried to take advantage of Alana before or after the report of your death, because he respected not only Alana, but the love she had for you."

"I don't—"

Crystal would not let him continue. "When he asked her to marry him, Alana could not refuse after all the kindness he had shown her. And let me tell you something else, Rafael Montgomery! Edward Parkins was a kind and gentle man who not only gave everything unselfishly to Alana but also backed both of us in our fight against Allison.

"Alana never forgot, Rafe, not once. She spent enormous sums of money trying to find out who Allison's agents were in South Africa, for she wanted to expose them and have them sent to prison for killing you!"

"Stop!" Rafe roared, turning to face his sister.

"No!" Crystal shouted back. "You think about what I've told

you, Rafael, and you think hard! For I will not have any brother of mine treat a person I love the way you are treating Alana."

With that, Crystal left Rafe to try to come to terms with himself.

Alana wandered alone beneath the stars that covered the South African plateau. The scents carried upon the night breezes were vastly different from those with which she'd grown up. The night sounds were totally unfamiliar, too, yet she felt no fear of the night or of the land that was now a part of her.

But she did feel alienated from Rafe. Although she'd tried to prepare herself for this, it was worse than she had imagined it would be. She had hoped that he would understand, but she knew he had been through a great deal already and had never expected this.

Her love for him helped her to empathize with what he was undergoing. Even if he rejected her, the fact that he was alive and free was important to her, for she would always love him, come what may.

Clearing her mind, Alana turned and went back to the campsite. She saw that Rafe was gone, and Crystal was talking with Chaco. Silently she went to her blankets and lay down beneath the vast African sky. But as tired as she was from the long day and all the excitement, she could not sleep.

Rafe stayed away from the camp for the entire night, trying to sort out the thoughts that warred within him. But every time he tried to push Alana's marriage from his mind, the image of her with another man returned to attack him mercilessly.

When day chased night away, he gave up his fight and returned to camp. After eating a light meal in silence, they set out again. The two women went into the coach, while Rafe went up to the driver's seat with the driver.

At noon, when the coach stopped, Chaco came over to them. He smiled sadly at Crystal and Alana, then grasped Rafe's hand in his.

"I must leave you now," he told them. "My men have reported that the guards are a half day distant. We are at the border of my lands. The guards will not go into Basutoland;

they will believe that Rafe is hiding there. My warriors will
cover your tracks until tonight to assure your escape."

"Chaco," Alana said, walking to him and taking his hand in
hers, "thank you for everything. I shall never forget you."

"Nor I," Crystal stated as she joined Alana. But instead of
saying anything else, she used her hands to sign.

You are more than a friend to me. You are my brother also.

Chaco nodded his head. *As you are my sister. Find peace now,
make a life for yourself,* Chaco pleaded.

You know me too well, Crystal signed. *I have not yet taken my
vengeance.*

Strike swiftly, sister, before he learns too much.

I shall, Crystal promised. *Now return home and show your
people your greatness.*

Chaco nodded and stepped back. As the two women
watched, he gathered his people around him and walked
proudly away.

After they were gone, Crystal spoke. "Now we have to move
quickly. There is still more to be done."

"What else?" Rafe asked, unaware of all their plans.

"The man who arranged for you to become a prisoner must
be forced to sign a confession."

"Why bother? I'm free, and we can leave South Africa."

"But Alana can't leave so easily. Not now. And, Rafe, Alana
never made a secret about her attempts to find and free you. She
even approached the governor on your behalf. They'll know
that it was she who engineered your escape, and she will be
arrested unless we get a confession from Devreeling."

Rafe looked from Crystal to Alana. "Then we'd best get
moving." With those words he turned and went back to the
coach.

Alana watched him, longing to run after him, to grab him
and make him face her. Not once since yesterday afternoon had
he spoken directly to her, let alone touched her.

"Be patient," Crystal advised.

Alana stared unhappily at Rafe's back. Then she turned to
Crystal. "You can't go back to Allison now. It's too dangerous."

Crystal smiled. "Watch me."

* * *

Two days later they arrived at Port Elizabeth and rendez-voused with the *Harmony*. Alana smiled at the weathered face of Captain Miles Sanders.

"Are we ready to sail?" Alana asked immediately.

"Yes indeed," the captain replied.

They left the driver and coach at the Maklin-Parkins ware-house, and an hour later, Alana, Crystal, and Rafe stood on the deck of the *Harmony*, watching Port Elizabeth grow smaller behind them.

By nightfall Alana knew she was coming close to complete exhaustion, but she was afraid to go to her cabin. Last night, as she had slept in the moving coach, she'd had several horrible dreams—dreams of Rafe leaving her forever.

Rather than risk sleeping, Alana walked the port side of the deck, trying not to give in to the sadness that was only a thought away. She tried to think of what direction she should take with her life, but could think of none without Rafe.

Shivering, Alana turned from the railing, and as she did, she froze, for Rafe was standing not five feet away. His emerald eyes glistened from the light of the shipboard lanterns, and the strong features of his face were accented by shadows.

She realized that since they'd boarded he had shaved off his beard. His strong chin and sensually full mouth were once again revealed to her eager gaze.

Willing control over her wildly racing heart, she drew herself straighter. Smiling softly, she looked at his jet hair. "There is more silver than I remember," she said.

Rafe nodded his head. "Alana—"

"No," Alana said quickly. "Please, Rafe, leave me alone. I understand how you feel, and I accept it."

"Do you?" he asked, riveting her with his gaze.

"Yes," she whispered truthfully. "It hurts, Rafe, it hurts very badly, but I understand." With her eyes misting, she started away.

Before she could get very far, he caught up with her and took her arm. "Why, Alana?"

Alana didn't look at him, she just shook her head. "Because he was kind and good and helped me when no one else would. Because I realized that after your death, I could love another man—not the way I loved you, but with another kind of love. I will never deny that, nor will I be ashamed of loving him, as I was never ashamed of loving you."

"I'm not talking about Parkins," Rafe said in a low voice. His hand tightened on her arm when he spoke again. "I'm talking about you. Why are you being so damned understanding?"

Alana couldn't help smiling at Rafe's complaint, but one look at his face indicated he was serious. "Don't you know, Rafe?"

"No," he replied.

"Because I love you," she told him simply. Then she pulled her arm free and left the deck.

In her cabin, she continued to battle against her tears as she undressed and prepared for bed. When she damped the oil lamp and lay in the bunk, she tried to make believe she had not seen Rafe, or spoken to him on the deck, or felt his fingers on her arm.

A half hour later, Alana finally fell into an exhausted and dreamless sleep.

Rafe stayed on deck for hours after Alana had gone, his mind battling with his heart. He had almost come to terms with what had happened to Alana while he was imprisoned. But the one thing that still bothered him was Alana's behavior.

The fiery spark of life that had always been in her eyes was not there, and that bothered Rafe terribly. Yet he had glimpsed her passionate nature when she'd spoken just now of Edward Parkins.

Her voice had grown stronger, firmer, and after she'd left him, he had thought about what she said. Slowly the dawning comprehension that she had done only what she felt right had begun to grow in his mind as well as his heart.

The high-spirited woman he had fallen in love with five years before was on this ship with him now. And he was being a fool.

Rafe left the deck and went to Alana's cabin. Inside, he lit the oil lamp and studied her features as she slept. Emotions rushed madly through him, and he slowly sat on the side of the bunk.

Even in her sleep, Alana felt someone sit on the bunk and, rising through the myriad layers of sleep and fatigue that tried to imprison her, she opened her eyes.

"Rafe," she whispered. Sitting up, she blinked the sleep from her eyes. "Why are you here?"

"Because I love you, Alana."

"Do you, Rafe?" she asked, suddenly awake and alert. "Do you love me or the woman you fell in love with five years ago? I'm not that Alana any longer. I've changed. I've lived through too many things," she told him honestly. "I'm not the naïve woman that you found at Riverbend. I never will be again." She paused for a moment to look into his face.

"I've always loved you, Rafael, and I always will. There has never been another like you, and never will be. But I will not have my life questioned anymore. What I've done when I have been away from you is as much a part of my life as you have been and always will be."

"I know that, Alana."

"Do you?" she asked, sitting straighter. "Is that why you've barely spoken to me in the last three days? Is that the way you show your love and understanding? Or does your hurt masculine pride, the knowledge that another man has known my love, prevent you from loving me again?"

She glared at him, anger flashing on her face. Her eyes turned a dark sapphire as she fixed him with an unyielding stare.

"I never stopped loving you, Rafe. I learned a great deal from Jason and Edward about love, and about life itself. Love is something to be given to another—given, not taken by force. I will not force you to love me any longer, Rafe."

Rafe stood slowly and, towering high above her, looked down at her, his face a tense, angry mask. "Do you have anything else to say, or are you quite finished?" he asked in a stiff voice. "Because if you are, then perhaps I can get a word in edgewise."

Alana raised her eyebrows but said nothing.

"I came to tell you that I have come to terms with what you have done."

"What in the hell is that supposed to mean?" she asked sharply.

Rafe sighed. "You're not making this easy for me."

"Really? Forgive me, Rafe, but I don't find this situation easy. Everything I've done in the past two years has been in an effort to free you. And now that you are on this ship, rather than standing in some dark mine shaft, I'm being told that you've *come to terms* with what I've done! Well thank you so much for your understanding," she finished bitterly.

Rafe bent and glared down at her. "Damn it all, Alana! Listen to me and stop putting words in my mouth! I love you more than anything or anyone on the face of this earth."

Alana said nothing this time because she could not. All she could do was look at him and pray she would not faint.

But Rafe mistook her silence for more anger and stepped back. "I'm sorry, Alana. I won't bother you anymore."

He turned and went to the door. When his hand reached the knob, Alana moved; the sound of material whispered in the air. "Don't you dare walk out on me, Rafael Montgomery," she said from behind him.

Rafe whirled to stare at her in challenge. But his challenge fled as he took in Alana's naked body glistening in the light of the lantern. All of the old feelings of desire, admiration, and love were suddenly freed within him.

He returned to her and drew her into his arms. His eyes caressed her face even as his mouth descended, but before their lips met, he held himself back and spoke in a low voice. "The last time I held you, you promised to marry me the next day," he reminded her.

Alana said nothing; she simply smiled, raised her hand until it was at the back of his head, and pulled his mouth to hers.

As the well-remembered flames of their passion burst forth, Alana willed her mouth from his to look into the endless depths of his eyes. "Are you sure?" she whispered.

"Alana," he said, making her name sound like a warm caress, "I am more certain of my love for you than of anything else in creation."

"Can you wait until everything is settled before we marry?"

Rafe's eyes narrowed. "What do you mean by 'everything'?"

"Devreeling's confession. I want to be able to marry you and not fear that when I awaken the next morning you will be gone again," she said truthfully. "I could not bear it."

"I will not be gone, my love," he kissed her deeply and lifted her off her feet.

A moment later they were entwined on the narrow bunk. Alana held Rafe to her, and when he swiftly entered her, she cried out in welcome, knowing that they were finally together again and that nothing would ever again come between them.

29

At six thirty on the morning of May 7, 1869, Johann Devreeling sat in the small dayroom where he always ate breakfast. He was spreading jam on a thick slice of bread, and a steaming cup of coffee scented the room.

Devreeling was certain that everything was going according to plan. In another two days Rankin would rid the world of Rafael Montgomery. Tremain would supposedly be released, and the Parkins woman would not be able to substantiate her claim.

Devreeling smiled as he reached for the cup of coffee. Before he could pick it up, he heard the stifled scream of the cook, and a half dozen men broke into the room.

Devreeling stared wide-eyed at them, fear rising in the back of his throat. "What do you want?" he asked in a low voice, willing himself to appear strong in the face of this danger. "Do you know who I am?" he asked, louder.

"Most definitely," said a woman who stepped to the front of the intruders. Her silver-blond hair framed a beautiful face.

"Who are you?" Devreeling asked.

Crystal smiled. "Elizabeth Montgomery," she stated.

Devreeling's face drained of blood. He stared at her. "Wh-who?" he whispered.

Instead of replying, Elizabeth motioned the men forward. Moving quickly, the men of the *Harmony* caught Devreeling neatly between them, tied his hands behind him, and gagged him.

Less than a minute later, Devreeling was inside a Maklin-Parkins coach heading toward the waterfront. A half hour after that, he was sitting in a small cabin on the *Harmony* wondering what was going to happen to him. For the first time, he realized that there was a very good chance that he would die in this spot.

He stayed in the cabin throughout the long day, and only when night fell did two sailors come for him. They unbound him, took off his gag, and supporting him between them, took him to the master's cabin and pushed him roughly into a chair.

One lantern burned, but its light allowed him to see only within a small circle. Shadows danced at its periphery. He counted three faces, but he could not see them clearly.

Pain in his arms, from the returning circulation, attacked him. Before he could recover, a woman stepped into the light, and he recognized Alana Parkins.

"Magistrate Devreeling," Alana said in a level voice, "do you know who I am?"

"Of course! And you won't get away with this!" he bluffed.

Alana ignored his threat and continued to speak in a calm voice. "I would like a signed confession about your part in Rafael Montgomery's imprisonment."

"I don't know what you're talking about. I've never heard of a man named Montgomery."

"Then," Crystal said as she too stepped forward, "you shall go to your grave an innocent man."

"You can't kill me! I'm a magistrate of the court!"

"You're a minion of James Allison and a deceitful, ambitious man," Alana stated, slowly raising her revolver until it pointed directly at Devreeling's head.

"I swear I know nothing about Montgomery."

Alana cocked the hammer.

"Please," Devreeling whispered.

"Are you so afraid of Allison that you won't speak?" Crystal asked. "Because if you are, then you also know that if you fail him, he will do much worse than we could ever do."

"I—you won't kill me," Devreeling said suddenly. His voice

steadied, and he smiled at them. "You're not murderers," he
said confidently.

"No, they aren't," Rafe said as he too stepped into the light.
"But after living through two years in the shaft of the Bristol, I
could kill you easily."

Devreeling's jaw dropped. "You—you're dead."

Rafe walked very close to Devreeling and bent down until his
narrowed eyes were but inches from the man's face. "Am I,
now?" he hissed.

Devreeling's shoulders slumped and his features sagged. Soon
the knowledge that he was beaten appeared on his face. "Are
you going to kill me?" he asked, his hands trembling visibly.

"Give us a confession naming everyone who took part in
Rafe's abduction and imprisonment," Alana said authorita-
tively. "Everyone!"

"What's to stop you from killing me afterward?" Devreeling
asked again. Both naked hope and open fear showed in his eyes.

"Only your own belief that we're not like you and Allison,"
Rafe said in a low voice. "But if you don't sign the confession,
you can rest assured that you will die!"

Devreeling looked from Rafe's set face to Alana's furious
gaze to Crystal's flat stare. Slowly he nodded his head.

On the morning of May 8, without an appointment, Alana,
Rafe, and Crystal, pushing Johann Devreeling ahead of them,
burst into the governor's private office. Before the governor had
a chance to speak, Rafe put Devreeling's confession on the ornate brass and teak desk and spoke.

"My name, Governor White, is Rafael Montgomery. For the
past two years I have been illegally imprisoned at the Bristol
mine, on Johann Devreeling's orders."

The governor rose and stared at Rafe. "If you don't leave this
minute and present your case properly, I shall have you jailed."

"And I," Alana retorted, "shall see to it that all my wealth
and all the powers of the Maklin-Parkins company are used to
ruin you completely if you do not sit back down and listen to
what we have to say."

The acting governor stared silently at Alana, all the while
knowing that she did have the power to destroy him because of
what her husband had left her. Slowly he sat.

"This man," Rafe began again, "has signed a statement, confessing his part in the crimes committed against myself and . . . Lady Parkins. It details everything that happened and also states other crimes of which Devreeling is guilty."

The governor looked from Rafe to Devreeling, but Devreeling turned his face away. Then the governor lifted the confession and read it slowly in silence. When he was finished, he looked at Devreeling.

"Is this true, Johann?"

Devreeling closed his eyes and nodded his head.

"Why?" Samuel White asked.

Suddenly Devreeling's eyes snapped open; hatred blazed outward. "Why?" he asked. "Look around you. My family came to Cape Town a hundred and fifty years ago. We were wealthy, respected people. When the mighty British empire came, you took everything from us. We Dutch were forced to give up everything and move to the interior. My family lost its fortune, and what should have been mine was taken from me. Does it surprise you so very much that I should turn against you and all you represent?"

"We took nothing from you or your family, Johann. Your people chose to join the rest of the Boers in the interior. And your so-called vast wealth was nothing in comparison to what we brought. What your family lost was the will to compete against others. Your hate and anger should not be directed at us, but at your own people for not staying to maintain what they had created.

"Yet," the governor continued in a level voice, "you, Johann, chose to live with us and to become a part of us. In that you deceived us terribly, and you have made me ashamed that I appointed you to your position. I will see you tried and convicted for your crimes, Johann Devreeling."

Then the governor turned to Rafe. "Mr. Montgomery, I have wronged you in many ways, and I cannot even think of how to make amends for that. All I can do is ask you to accept my apology. And Lady Parkins, I must also ask for your forgiveness. I was wrong," he said honestly.

Alana's nostrils flared. "Wrong about what, Governor?" she baited him.

"Alana," Crystal whispered, but Alana was oblivious.

The governor met Alana's open stare with his own. Then he rose from behind his desk and stood to face her. "Edward was my friend, and I could never understand why he married you. He told me he loved you, and that you were a special woman. I tried to talk him out of this marriage, but he would not listen. 'When you get to know her, Samuel, you will understand why I love her,' he told me. But I never got to know you, until now."

Alana tried to comprehend what he was saying, but she was almost afraid to believe he was apologizing.

"I knew about your love for Mr. Montgomery because Edward told me everything about it. But after I made my investigation, I believed that you had concocted this outrageous story as part of a scheme to get Edward to marry you. I have ample evidence of the truth now, and can only admit that I was wrong and that Edward was correct."

"Thank you," Alana said.

"I will see to it that Johann's trial is brought about swiftly. I do hope that you will testify at that trial, Mr. Montgomery."

"Oh, I shall," Rafe said with a smile.

Two nights later, Rafe, Alana, and Crystal were in the Parkins house arguing fiercely.

"You will stay here!" Rafe shouted, his face red with anger as he confronted his sister.

"You're my brother, not my father!" Crystal spat back.

Alana sat silently, watching the war of wills between the two people she loved most. She wanted to say something to help, but she knew she could not.

"I won't have you going back into Allison's bed. No more!"

"I have to, Rafe. Don't you understand? I can finish him. I can bring down his empire."

"Or he can kill you."

"Perhaps, but it's a chance I must take."

"Then I will go with you," Rafe stated.

"Rafe! No!" Alana cried, speaking for the first time in a half hour. "You decided—we decided—you promised that we would stay together. We agreed to use all our financial resources to bring Allison down." She continued, "I don't like to put Crystal in danger, either. But we must attack him on both a professional and a personal level. He will soon know you're alive and out of the mine. He'll be waiting for you to come after him."

"But I won't let Elizabeth risk her life again," Rafe spat angrily. "She doesn't have to anymore."

Crystal took a deep breath and then took Rafe's hand in hers. "But I do, Rafael, I do. Please, I will be even more careful than I was before. I will run the Maklin-Parkins office in New York through our attorneys. No one will know I have anything to do with you and Alana. As Allison's mistress, I can learn his every move, and we can destroy him, Rafe, as he tried to destroy us."

"I don't care about Allison anymore, Elizabeth! I learned a great deal in that mine. I realized that I let Allison govern my life instead of living for myself. I'm not afraid of the man; I'm just ready to go on with my life. I want the same for you."

"When my time comes, Rafe, I will live my life also, but until that time I will live up to the name I gave myself—Revanche. I will have my revenge on James Allison."

With that, Crystal turned and walked regally out of the salon. A moment later, as her footsteps echoed from the stairway, Alana looked at Rafe.

"And where does this leave us?" she asked, her eyes flickering across his features. The gauntness was almost gone from his face now, replaced by a healthier glow.

"My life is with you," Rafe replied calmly, "whether here or in America. But that does not stop me from being afraid for Elizabeth."

Alana suddenly became terrified that Rafe would insist on accompanying his sister on her dangerous mission, leaving Alana alone—again. After all she had been through to be reunited with Rafe, this idea was enough to make her practically hysterical. Leaping from her seat, she cried, "I want you with me, Rafe. I want your children. I want a life that is peaceful and filled with love. I can't bear the idea of waking up and finding you gone. But I can't make you want to stay with me. If you want to chase all over the world, I won't keep you. Go with Crystal! But I'll be damned if I'll wait for you or look for you ever again." With a sharp intake of breath, Alana unclenched her fists and slowly dropped her arms to her side. "I think you understand how I feel now," she finished, her words choked with emotion.

Rafe nodded. "Absolutely. I only have one question."

"Ask it, then!"

"Do you like the name Rachel for a girl?"

Her stomach fluttered, and her heart melted again. "That was my mother's name," she whispered.

"I know. But if it's a boy, I want to name him after my father," Rafe told her, the corners of his mouth turning up in a smile for Alana.

Alana's heart almost burst with her love. "Oh, Rafe, I want your child, I want a lot of children."

"Then can we stop this pointless merry-go-round of words?"

"You really are staying," Alana said as the tears spilled from her eyes.

"I could never leave you again, my love."

And then he drew her into his arms and kissed her deeply, emphasizing just how true his words were. Before the kiss ended, Rafe had swept Alana from her feet and carried her to the staircase. With seemingly little effort, he climbed the stairs and went directly to the guest room.

Inside, he lowered Alana to her feet and gazed deeply into her eyes as he reached around her and began to undo her bodice. "Which should be first, a boy or a girl?"

With her eyes dancing merrily, and a smile now permanently affixed to her face, Alana said nothing; rather, her hands went to his shirt, and as he undressed her, she did the same for him.

Finally, when they were both naked, Alana spoke. "Either. Both. Whatever. But we will raise our children together, and watch them grow to become everything we want, and be proud of everything they achieve."

"Together, Alana—and when we are too old to make love, we will remember our lives and rejoice in our love."

Alana's lips twitched in silent mirth. She lowered her hand and slowly grasped his hardness. Stepping closer to him, she pressed her breasts upon his chest and felt the electric sharpness at the contact of her skin against his.

Within her hand, he grew even harder. "We will never be too old to make love, nor will we have to remember the past to rejoice in what we shall always have. And now, my husband to be, show me one of the wonderful ways in which you love me."

And Rafe showed her, and continued to show her, until the sun rose and flooded the room with its life, giving Alana the knowledge that, with the golden globe's arrival, Rafe was indeed still with her.

EPILOGUE

Three days later, Alana, Rafe, and Crystal stood on the forward deck of the *Harmony*. The ship, fully loaded with cargo, was resting at anchor. The entire crew lined the port and starboard railings. The captain, in formal dress and holding the leather-bound ship's Bible in his hand, stood before Rafe and Alana.

Alana wore a beautiful white gown that reached to the floor. Its bodice was a combination of silk and lace that clung to her breasts invitingly. Her long raven hair flowed freely down her back, and her face was hidden by a thin white veil.

Rafe stood next to her, dressed formally in royal blue. They presented a picture of perfection. His jet and silver hair was uncovered; the morning sun kissed it and made it sparkle.

Crystal stood next to Alana, wearing a blue traveling dress and a wide-brimmed hat. Tears flowed freely from her eyes as she watched her brother and her closest friend make their vows and become husband and wife.

The ship's crew was silent as they watched the wedding take place, and after Captain Sanders finished, they watched Rafe take a small gold band from his pocket and place it on Alana's finger. Then he drew her into his arms and kissed her deeply.

With the kiss, the crew roared out their approval, and then the bosun's pipes were sounded. Miles Sanders closed the Bible and offered Rafe his hand.

"Congratulations," he said with a serious smile.

"My thanks, Captain," Rafe replied, "for everything you've done for Alana."

Crystal embraced Alana, and both women cried tears of happiness. Yet Alana's tears were also blended with sadness, for Crystal was returning to America with the *Harmony*.

"I wish you would stay with us," Alana said, as she had been saying for the past two days.

"You know I can't. Rafe," she called, "make her stop."

Rafe came over to them and slipped his arm around Alana's waist. "Stop what?" he asked.

"She's trying to talk me out of going back."

"She's right. Elizabeth, you know I don't like what you're doing."

Crystal shook her head stubbornly. "He ruined me, Rafael. I will not be able to put my past to rest until I have ruined him in return." Turning to Alana, Crystal said, "Just make sure that my brother doesn't change his mind and go after Allison in person."

Alana looked up into Rafe's tightly set features, her eyes asking the silent question. As she held his gaze, Alana felt the security of Rafe's earlier promise. "He won't," Alana stated with the confidence of love.

A few minutes later, Rafe and Alana watched the *Harmony* sail out of Cape Town's harbor. They stood silently on the dock, their arms about each other's waists. And when the *Harmony* was but a speck in the distance, Rafe turned to Alana, his free hand cupping her chin and lifting her face to his.

"I miss her already," Alana whispered.

"I know, but we will be reunited soon," Rafe replied. Then he smiled gently. "And I am here. I love you, Alana."

"As I love you, Rafe."